FIRST MEETING

Creighton jumped out and came around the back of the buggy to assist her.

"Here you are, my girl." His voice suddenly was soft as he seized Laurie's waist and lifted her down beside him. She could feel the warmth of his body as he held her close for a moment before releasing her. For that moment she lost all remembrance of anything prior to that instant, a giddy, gay sensation as if the tightly closed blossom of her life had all at once begun to unfold.

"Thank you, Chace Creighton," she said.

"You say both my names as if they are inseparable." He retrieved her parcels from the carriage seat.

"I want to remember them—Chase Creighton," she teased.

"I'm flattered. Will you?" His free hand closed about her small waist, but he made no attempt to draw her to him again.

"I will indeed." She looked up into his face and wanted to feel his mouth on hers, wanted desperately for him to hold her near in those strong arms. It was another of her mistakes, to give her affections so quickly. She realized as she savored his nearness that this was a true man. Could he be the man whom her friends had said she would be sure to meet if she went to California?

MELLONA

KATHALYN KRAUSE

LEISURE BOOKS ❧ NEW YORK CITY

Dedicated to A. R.

A LEISURE BOOK

Published by

Dorchester Publishing Co., Inc.
6 East 39th Street
New York, NY 10016

Printed in the United States of America

Prologue
California, 19 September 1871

Ham Sewell hunched over the saddlehorn as the long-legged chestnut strained into full stride.

"Where the hell is he getting to?" Bert Hutchins asked as he watched from the elevated porch fronting Sewell's Hardware and Ranch Supply.

"Going down Mariposa Beach way." Pitt Sewell was a laconic man who tended to overvalue his position as storekeeper and postmaster for the coastal community of Forest Shores. Information could be wangled from him eventually, but one usually became frustrated before enlightened.

"Must have been mighty important, the way he took off." Hutchins wrestled a keg of roof nails into the back of his freight wagon and climbed back into the driver's seat. He was familiar with Pitt's ritual. "Come in on the stage, did it?" He picked up the reins and separated them, cosseting them in his rough hands.

Pitt Sewell paused long enough from inventorying the shipment spread on the plank porch to consider whether or not to answer. Putting the stub of pencil behind his ear, he leaned against the door jamb. "Did for a fact, Bert," he finally said.

"No way of telling what's important to folks like that, is there?" Bert ventured. "Letter, was it?"

Pitt's laugh, a bit too loud for the quiet street, caused heads suddenly to look toward them from the stage station two doors west. He wiped the wide grin from his face with a grimy hand. In a sobered voice

1

which barely hid the laughter, he replied, "Ask me, I'll tell you right out what them ladies holds most important. Come to think of it, the same could be said for the men down there, too." He winked an eye and smothered his urge to guffaw. "Ham there, he's had himself quite a time with a couple of them French ladies. Got paid some into the bargain, too, just to sweeten the pot—if you take my meaning." Pitt arched his right eyebrow toward a balding pate while the left one skewed simian-like over a squinted eye.

"You talking about the Jolais woman?" Bert asked, abandoning the question of the letter momentarily.

"No, no, not that one," Sewell answered with emphasis. "Funny though, you asking so quick about her." He sauntered over to the freight wagon and looked up at the squat horsetrader. "Hey, you ain't took a fancy to that one yourself, have you?" The look of anger that flashed briefly in Hutchins' sunburned face metamorphosed into a narrow-lipped smile so swiftly that the other man missed it completely.

"That sort's not for the likes of us, Pitt." Unconsciously he looked down at his thick arms and short, stocky legs. Flies had found a smudge of fresh manure on his boots and clustered about the sole. "She's a lady—born to it. Reckon any men she'd take a shine to wouldn't be no ordinary mortals like us." He took a long buckskin drover's whip from its socket on the dash. The turn of conversation did not suit him and he was eager to be on his way. Still, he wondered why young Ham had raced off to Mariposa Beach. "They ain't got the cholera down there, have they?"

"Cholera?" Walt Sewell joined them from inside the store.

"Why'd you ask that?" Pitt no longer grinned. Cholera close to Forest Shores would be no smiling matter.

"Way Ham took out, right after you got the mail off the stage, I figured it had to be medicine or money come in for 'em." Hutchins unfurled the whip, coiling the loaded tip on the seat beside him.

"Weren't no medicine," Pitt Sewell answered and shook his head. "No idea about money."

By now Walt was also curious about his nephew's mission to Mariposa Beach. "Then what the dickens was it?" he asked.

"Madame Jolais was expecting some letter from San Francisco. Real excited about it, she was. Asked Ham if he'd bring it down the minute it come in, so there he goes..." Pitt Sewell gestured with his thumb down the street toward the fast disappearing horse and rider.

From atop the ridge of low hills overlooking Mariposa Beach young Hamilton Sewell could see nothing of the notorious colony. Blue wood smoke hung low over pines which extended to within a few hundred yards of the ocean, but the cabins and lodge from which it rose were hidden by forest. The lean chestnut gelding was lathered from its race up the hills. Beyond the summit the way became easier where the slope resumed its gradual descent. Less fatiguing for both horse and rider would have been the graded wagon road through the Creighton property, but the hill trail gave quicker access to the little village. And, too, Madame Jolais had specifically requested speed. It was for her the nineteen-year-old risked the animal's and his own neck.

Even as the sound of hoofbeats ceased and before young Sewell hurriedly dismounted, a flash of gold outside the rambling lodge caught his eye. Madame Jolais rushed to meet him. The boy's heart hammered more from excitement than exertion.

"It came!" he yelled. He looped reins over a fence rail and swung fancy tooled leather cantanas from the saddlehorn. "Got it right here." With one hand he scooped off his hat and stood transfixed.

Mid-morning sunlight shimmered through the clearing, warmed to a glow the young woman's gown and pale golden skin. As she ran down the path toward him, skirts lifted high enough to disclose slim, booted feet and ankles, Ham let slip from his grasp the mail pouches.

"Where is it?" Her intense black eyes danced with anticipation. "Oh, give it to me quickly!" she pleaded as she drew close to the boy.

"Yes, ma'm. It's right here..." Ham lifted the cantanas to the fence rail. "I brought all the rest of the mail, too," he said, then dug into the bag, sorted through its contents and extracted a large envelope sealed with a blob of crimson wax.

"That's it! That's it!" Madame Jolais exclaimed as she inspected the imprinted return address. She broke the seal and unfolded a single sheet of stiff, cream-colored paper. As she bent over the letter, Ham Sewell stared down at the nape of her neck where dark, glistening hair parted and cascaded over her shoulders. Such was the warmth of her nearness and the delicately heady scent about her of roses and lilies and wild blossoms that the boy ached to touch her, press her to his body.

As she looked up into his face the gaiety of her smile, the sensuous curve of her lips against small, perfect teeth, were more than young Sewell could resist. Catching her in his arms, Ham bent to kiss her mouth. For sweet, long seconds he held her, giddy with his own daring.

"I'm...I'm...sorry. I shouldn't have done that," he stammered and released the woman, his arms suddenly leaden, his face burning scarlet. He turned from her and slumped against the fence. "I'm sorry."

Gently, Madame Jolais took one of his awkward hands in hers, pulled his fingers to her lips and kissed them. "Dear Ham, don't be ashamed." She put one finger under the boy's chin and coaxed his face around. His eyes met hers. "You must never be sorry for feeling things...like that." Slipping an arm about his waist she guided him up the pathway to her lodge. "I'm glad you like me well enough to want to kiss me." Her laughter was low and pleasant, carrying hint of neither reproval nor ridicule.

"Then you're not mad at me?" The boy was too embarrassed to look directly at her, but allowed himself to accompany her to the veranda.

"Of course not, my darling." She stepped onto the porch. "How could I be angry with you, of all people? Especially when you bring me such good news - and on such a beautiful day!" From a rustic bench beneath one of the windows she retrieved a voluminous fringed shawl, its myriad colored flowers embroidered on a molten-gold silk ground. As she flung it about her shoulders she said, "This is to be the most wonderful day ever!"

"Bring us some of that dry oak, Ham." Morgan Griffith slid the razor-sharp boning knife along the salmon's dorsal fin and with a few deft cuts flipped out a neat fillet.

"That ought to be enough for now." Adam Hinshaw wiped his eyes with the back of one hand as a whiff of smoke strayed from the improvised broiling rack. "Did anyone count how many people are here? Will we have plenty of everything to go 'round?" He tossed the last fillet on the rack, daubed it with herbed butter before sprinkling on salt and pepper. "Pansy, hand me another platter." Turning the potatoes with a long metal fork, Adam reached for the dish as his wife unpacked it from a deep wicker picnic basket.

"No need to worry," she said. "Some of the girls just brought down more bread. And there's johnnycake when that runs out." Pansy gave tin plates to picnickers who had just ridden down the lighthouse trail from town. "Just help yourselves to the salads and fixings. Adam will help you to the salmon and rock fish. And there are forks in a jar on the table," she directed them. The artists' community felt no need of an elaborate menu for their impromptu celebration. It offered instead, simple fare, with affection and congenial

5

freedom.

"Berthe! Over here!" Morgan Griffith waved a tin cup aloft and banged on it with the cooking fork he had taken from Hinshaw. "Adam, why don't you and Pansy go eat now while I watch the fires," he said. From the sawhorse and plank tables ran one of the girls with a pitcher of red San Esteban wine.

"Are you drinking beer or wine?" the girl asked as he looked into his empty cup.

"What have you there?" Griffith asked.

"Red wine."

He held out his cup and allowed her to fill it. "Ah, thank you, Berthe," the Welshman sighed. As she turned to go he stopped her. "Have you seen my cousin?"

"Down there, digging for clams. With Roy Wimbish and Lucia Orozco." The girl nodded her head in the direction of the beach. Even from such a distance they could see the radiant golden color of the young woman's gown and shawl. Morgan Griffith drank half the wine at a swallow. "She's so happy," Berthe said as she followed his glance.

"She is that," the man emphasized, but he did not smile as he watched the clam diggers.

Berthe studied his face, then said, "You've noticed—the same as we did." She came nearer and spoke quietly so only he could hear. "Something's wrong. She was thrilled by Mr. Retan's letter, that's true enough. But there's something else. Pansy and Adam saw it, too. It isn't anything we really know...we just sense it." She shrugged as if she could find no words to describe their misgivings.

"She said nothing to you? Nothing about being troubled?"

"Quite the opposite. She seemed very calm, almost as if she'd reached a difficult decision and was relieved it was settled." Berthe turned to watch the clammers.

On the far beach Madam Jolais shaded her eyes with her hand and looked landward, scanning the crowded picnic area.

6

"Yes, I quite agree. And she's hardly said a word to me all day. Except about the exhibition Retan arranged for us. And then, of course, about the picnic to celebrate." Griffith waved his hand to his cousin and automatically smiled, although she could not possibly read his face from so far away.

"It's as though she were expecting someone," Berthe said.

"No doubt you're right," Griffith replied.

"But who? All our own people are here. And everyone we invited is here." Berthe looked about at the gathering, mentally checking the faces one by one against the list of guests she and Madame Jolais had hastily compiled for their spur-of-the-moment beach party.

"Then whoever it is, must not have been on your list," Griffith said. He looked toward the beach beyond the fish rack. Young Ham Sewell and several young men from the colony were contending loudly for a leather football to the delight of billowy-skirted spectators. To Berthe, Morgan said, "Ask Ham to come see me for just a moment, will you? There's a dear..."

As she brought the young athlete to Griffith, the girl searched the crowd once again, trying to find some indication, some clue to Madame Jolais' behavior.

"Yes, sir, you wanted to see me?" Ham was somewhat intimidated by Griffith, as much by his relationship to Madam Jolais as by his wealth and fame as a portraitist.

"Ham, did Madame Jolais ask you to deliver an invitation to anyone not on the list Berthe gave you?" At the boy's hesitation and expression of doubt Griffith added, "You needn't answer if it would betray her confidence."

Stubbornly the youth eyed the Welshman. Berthe frowned at him and said, "Oh for heavens sakes, Ham! We're just worried about Madame Jolais. The least you can do is try to help us."

He considered a further moment, then replied, "I

guess it's all right—if you're worried." He looked toward the sand where the clam diggers were bent to their task. "No, there wasn't nobody else. Just them on the list. I rode by each place and hand delivered the notes, just like she told me." An anxious frown seemed out of place on his young face. "Something's wrong, ain't it?" he asked.

"We aren't sure, Ham. And we can't very well ask Madame. It's just that..." Once more Berthe groped for words.

The boy turned boldly to Griffith. "I'd do anything in this world for her, Mr. Griffith. Anything at all." It was said quietly; there was no question of his sincerity—it showed in his pale blue eyes.

"I know, Ham," Griffith replied. "So would we all." Sewell gazed toward the far beach where the bright shawl stood out against the sand like a lamp. They watched as Madame Jolais abandoned her shovel and bucket to Roy Wimbish and slowly walked back to the picnic area. Without further conversation, young Ham rejoined the ball game.

On the horizon to the west and north a burgeoning mass of clouds turned pink and orange in the fading light. A freshening wind sporadically whisked across the dunes, its sudden chill encouraging the revelers to gather closer to the fires. Madam Jolais, radiant in golden dress and Philippine shawl, paused by each cluster of guests, welcoming with kisses and embraces the newcomers, finding special words of banter for each person she passed.

Morgan Griffith failed to hide his puzzlement and concern. As she neared him he extended his hand. Taking it in hers she chided, "You're wearing your stern, fatherly look." She turned to the girl, Berthe, and teased, "What have you done? Morgan reserves this long face of his for only the gravest matters—it is his disapproval and consternation face. Come now, confess, what was your transgression?"

8

The girl laughed, relieved to hear Madame Jolais in such high humor. She picked up the wine pitcher and left the cousins alone, saying over her shoulder as she fled, "Once you confess, the fun's gone from the transgressing. No, no, I shall never tell!"

Griffith pulled his beautiful cousin to his side with one arm as he rotated potatoes on the rack over a glowing bed of oak coals. "Do you want to tell me about it, darling?"

"About what, Morgan?" She leaned against his shoulder, her hands enfolding his at her waist. The waning light intensified the pale glow of her flawless skin, exaggerated the blackness of her side-set eyes.

"I never pry into your affairs," Griffith began. "And I don't intend to now, but I have the feeling something is taking place that perhaps I should know about." He kissed the high forehead and looked squarely into her eyes, asking for an explanation. "You have been expecting someone all afternoon. Someone very important to you. I shall tend my own business, if that's what you prefer."

"We've always been so close—you and I." Her look did not waver. "But I'm not free to say anything right now. Not yet."

"Then you will tell me—eventually?" He smiled into her ecstatically happy face.

"Of course I shall, old silly!" She laid her dark head on his shoulder, the shoulder that had been her strength since they had been children together, exploring rocks and streams of Caernarvon.

"I'm worried about you," he whispered. "But I shan't press."

"Oh, Morgan, I've never been so happy in my life before. I didn't think..." Madame Jolais hugged her cousin impulsively.

"That you could fall in love so completely?" he ventured.

"Yes. That is it exactly." She looked up into his

9

face, her eyes misty with emotion. Pulling away from him she stood with her arms akimbo, head at an arrogant tilt. "You are sly, but I won't be tricked! In good time, I promise..."

"So be it. I shan't try again." They laughed easily, knowing there could never remain secrets between them for long.

"What time is it?" the woman asked.

Before Griffith could dig into his pocket for his watch, Adam Hinshaw answered, "Five-fifteen. Sun's going behind that cloud bank in a minute and it's going to get cold. Wind's already got a bite to it." Hinshaw passed a plate to Griffith for refilling from the fish rack.

"Pansy, you're freezing..." Madame Jolais loosened her golden shawl and draped it about the slender little woman.

"But I can't take your lovely shawl, dear," Pansy Hinshaw protested. "You'll soon be cold, too."

"I shall get another. I'm on my way up to my lodge right now. We're going to use up the last of my champagne. I've been saving it for a very special occasion, and this is it." Madame Jolais arranged the shawl across the woman's back with one end over each arm. "There—that is the way they wear it in Seville," she said as she patted Pansy's cold hands and started up the trail to the village.

"Why don't I send Ham or Roy up to fetch it?" Adam asked.

"No!" Madame Jolais answered almost too quickly. Hinshaw and Griffith looked at one another, startled at the note of dismay in her voice. "I shall bring it down in a few minutes," she insisted.

Her puzzled companions watched as she lifted her golden skirts and petticoats to make her way up the slope toward the lodge. She paused at the top of the last dune, waved gaily and called to them, "I shall be right back. We have so much to celebrate!"

The low sun burnished Madame Jolais' gown and pale skin, creating an aura that glowed against the somber forest shadows. She hesitated, looked back. Then as if putting into action some resolution, she gathered her skirts once more and set up the pathway. For a moment the gold of her dress flickered among the chaparral thickets along the trail.

In the next moment, behind grotesquely contorted cypress, Madame Jolais disappeared...forever.

Chapter 1

Until today, this very minute, Laurie Mathews had never really questioned her determination to remain in Forest Shores. The foreboding she had experienced when boarding the train at San Esteban four months ago had been pushed to the back of her consciousness. Why today did she once again sense a nameless impending danger, a danger which caused her to lift her head in fright at each small noise?

She had been unaware of its presence since arriving in the small vacation resort last August. Now with the approaching winter holiday season came the return of her presentiment.

"You may as well go on home before the storm gets here, Etta. No sense putting your eyes out in that light." It was already growing too dark to sew by the uncurtained workroom window. Laurie turned out the gas light in the front of her little apparel shop and stood by the young woman's side, marveling at the deftness of her fingers as she tacked peacock-blue silk tulle to an enormous, banded hat of black felt.

"I'm finished anyway. Now Mrs. Larcher can have it first thing Monday morning. She hoped I'd have it ready by then." The tiny seamstress snipped thread ends with gold stork-billed scissors and handed the hat to her employer. "I knew she wanted to outshine old lady Arvidson, so I promised she could have it."

"You probably shouldn't refer to her as 'old lady,' but I don't positively forbid it." The two young women grinned at each other. Laurie turned the hat about and inspected the work.

"It's lovely, Etta," she said. "You're such a wonder with a needle!" She placed it on a wooden blocking form and held up to it a variety of long hat pins, finally selecting several with light gray pearl heads.

"She already has pins for it. Or at least that's what she said." Etta Korby considered the effect, then nodded her approval. "Perfect! Very elegant, but not pretentious. She'll turn Mrs. Arvidson green."

"And I'll sell her the pins, too. Wait and see," Laurie vowed.

"You're smooth, you are." The seamstress began to tidy up the workroom and glanced out the window. "Guess that's why I'm back here and you're up front." She leaned closer to the glass. "We're in for a bad one tonight for sure. Look at those clouds over the water!" Across the broad crescent of Gutierrez Bay the entire sky had become deep slate color, the ocean an ominous black.

"You run along. I'll close the shop." Laurie knew Etta was worried about her daughter, six-year-old Fannie, who would soon be walking home from her grandmother's. "Better take my umbrella. I think you'll need it before you get very far."

"But what will you use if I do?" Etta asked.

"I'll catch the horsecar." Laurie handed a heavy black umbrella to the girl and emptied the trash basket into a metal drum in the alley outside. Etta donned a russet woolen shawl and pinned a small flat feathered hat atop her mass of dark upswept hair. Without checking the effect in a mirror she dashed for the front of the shop.

"Thanks, Laurie. See you Monday, bright and early." She looked out the front door and frowned. "No, it won't be bright. These spells usually go on for days. Do you want me to open up Monday?"

"No, no. It's easier for me. I'm on the streetcar route—you aren't. Now run along, or you'll get soaked." She shoved the girl out the front door and waved her on her way. "Goodnight!"

"Goodnight, Laurie!" Etta called back as she

13

almost ran going south on Birch Street. If she hurried she might catch up with her daughter before the deluge came.

Perhaps it was the rapid change of weather that had set Laurie's nerves on edge. She jumped in fright as wind slammed shut the rear door transom. No use trying to keep it open now that the wind had veered. Taking a brass-tipped pole she latched the transom, then locked the rear door. One block east the clock over City Hall struck four. She should stay open until six as usual, although there seemed little prospect of further business. She wandered about the small shop, straightened a display of silk artificial flowers, refolded a drawerful of lace-edged knitted underwear, evened up a row of boxed black hosiery. It was repetitious and useless, for it had been done several times during the afternoon and there had been no customers to disturb the neatness.

As the young woman stood alone behind the counter she was forced into retrospection. Still vivid in her memory was the hot mid-August day when she had first arrived in Forest Shores. The porter had seen to her luggage and had escorted her to an open coach. Already it was filled with noisy children and exasperated adults escaping the withering inland valley heat. Two weeks remained of summer vacation and it appeared as if half the children of San Esteban were on their way to spend them on the cool beaches of Forest Shores.

Soon the tracks had departed scorched, dusty ranchlands and the train chuffed along a series of switchbacks meandering up the eastern slope of the coastal range. From the summit where the engine crawled to a pause they could see the valley behind them shimmering in a mirage of early morning heat. Ahead tawny mountains disappeared into a white, rolling horizon of summer fog. As the train had ceased to labor and announced its descent with a shriek of metal, a drastic change in climate became apparent. Along with biting, acrid coal smoke from the engine had come damp, resinous forest smells carried upward by a gentle inshore breeze.

The train had plunged into the gloom of a shadowed cut between two densely wooded hills. Surrounded and overhung as it was by gigantic pines, the roadway seemed to follow a black and green tunnel. At first Laurie had welcomed the sudden coolness, but as they twisted deeper into the darkness of the forest she shivered.

Soon all but the nearest trees had been obliterated by swirling fog. At isolated crossings the whistle blasted and wailed its warning. Many of the windows had been pulled down against the chill. She shivered as she caught a glimpse of her reflection in the glass, a pale replica of herself superimposed upon a background of nebulous mist. Her imagination had distorted the image into one of a complete stranger—a young woman very like herself, but vastly different. For a fleeting instant she saw the molten-gold gown with its chevron bands and wide bows of deep brown velvet and the glittering gold coronet. And yet by the arrogant tilt of the head, the assertive thrust of the shoulders, it could not possibly be herself.

In that very instant of recognition and bewilderment the distortion had faded, and there it was—a reversed vision of herself, her neat ivory linen traveling suit with wide revers, flat-crowned straw boater with gay red ribbons, lace-necked guimpe neatly trimmed at the throat with a small cloissoné brooch of red and blue. She was not the sort to blush if caught inspecting herself in a mirror, but she turned from the glass and smiled at the ability of the dappled light of the forest to so warp a mere reflection.

During the four months after her arrival in Forest Shores, all memory of the golden apparition had been erased. Laurie had been far too busy to remember, much less care. She had begun a challenging, if not precisely exciting, new life for herself by deciding to buy the ladies' accessory shop on North Birch Street. Today, however, she realized she must reconsider the wisdom of her move.

The thought that one of her impetuous decisions

had this time probably ruined her life completely had occurred to her before, but in more optimistic moments had been rejected. Now as she stood alone in the shop after Etta had gone, she rued the seasonal progression.

Not that she hadn't expected winter to happen eventually in California, just as it had in Chicago. She had simply never thought about it. Spectacular fall days had been interrupted by coastal fog, but the temperature had remained balmy or brisk, never dropping to the marrow-seeking cold that had blown in off the Pacific about ten that particular morning.

Even in her small boutique, cold had crept in and chilled the corners. Ten feet away from the portable kerosene heater she had to pull her shawl about her for warmth, not just for bright decoration over the sensible, but smart, gray gown she reserved for working hours.

She gazed out the window at a passing buggy, its leather hood down and horse snorting displeasure at the wind in its nose. She had hoped it would be Mrs. Arvidson to pick up her order of silk gloves and embroidered silk lace mantilla for the fiesta next week. It was inconsiderate of women like Mrs. Arvidson to demand their latest whims shipped express from San Francisco and then fail to call for them when they arrived. Worse yet, at least for Laurie, was their utter unconcern about paying their bills within a reasonable time. They could afford to wait. Laurie could not.

Had it been the wrong decision? So many had been in her young life already. Had she made another wrong move, buying the Ribands and Roses?

It had seemed such a fine idea a few months ago, when the quaint seaside village was crowded with tourists. Then she could not keep enough stock on hand. Now most of the vacationers were gone, except for the usual week-enders, and they did not purchase the frivolous accessories she offered.

Receipts for the day did not make her feel any warmer. She tallied them and decided to take them home with her. Certainly there was no need to make a bank deposit. Across the glass of the front door she hung a flower-strewn, hand-painted 'Closed' sign and put the broom back in the storage closet. She would do the necessary cleaning Monday morning, before she reopened the shop. Right now she would do her shopping and hurry home before dark. She pulled a crocheted scarlet tam-o-shanter over her black hair and cocked it at a rakish angle across her high forehead. No need to ruin her new draped maline hat, for it was sure to rain before she could get home.

Hobart's Bakery was still open, its windows steamed, and the door, usually left open to entice customers from the sidewalk, had been shut against the rising wind. Dust swirled in grimy eddies, sweeping the concrete clean and stacking bits of trash and leaves in protected corners. Laurie hesitated, then went in, surprised that she was the only customer.

"Ah, Miss Mathews, you're wise to be getting home early. Looks like we're going to have a bad storm tonight." Elmer Hobart sidled behind the counter and waited expectantly. "Still have two apple turnovers. Or maybe a cherry tart?"

The display cases were almost depleted. He had been busy with ammonia and clean white rags, wiping down the glass and shelves. Laurie knew whatever she bought would be good, for Hobart's maintained quality despite competition from the large commercial bakery at San Esteban.

"The turnovers and a loaf of the seeded rye, please." Laurie found it hard to smile back at the rotund man, even though she was fond of him. Worry twisted the smile, and Elmer Hobart noticed.

"My boy's taking an order out to the Shell Box. Can he give you a lift home?" He rolled the white, waxed bakery paper out, tore it off neatly, wrapped and tied the parcel. "Won't be but a few minutes, if you'd like to go along. Save walking in this wind, and I think it's already starting to sprinkle." He attributed Laurie's expression of apprehension to the storm.

"That's very kind of you, Mr. Hobart, but I still have an errand or two before I go home. I'll try to catch

17

the horsecar. Thank you just the same." She counted change and handed it to him. Laurie was not too proud to accept the ride on the delivery wagon, but felt unequal to coping with Charlie Hobart's teasing banter.

"Charlie, you'd best get going," the baker said. "I'll finish up here. And don't you let that horse stand too long in this wind, hear?"

The tall, lanky boy unfolded from beneath the counter and took his mop and scrub pail to the back of the shop. "Yes, Dad. I'll get back just as soon as I can." He stuck his head though the doorway and took his coat from a rack at the end of the hallway. "Goodnight, Miss Mathews." His grin was all teeth under his sparse red moustache.

"Goodnight, Charlie." Laurie liked the boy, for he reminded her of another young man, one who had not returned from the war with Spain after the assault on San Juan Hill. As she began to remember, she forced herself to move, to talk. "Mr. Hobart, do you often get these cold winds along the coast here?" She picked up the bundle and tucked it under her cape.

"Oh, not too often. Maybe once or twice a winter. They last a few days—look for frost afterward. Clears the air real good and takes the rain farther inland. Mercy knows they need it over in the valley. Been terrible dry over there." Elmer Hobart still thought Laurie was worried about the approaching weather. "You'll be fine once you're home. That old Hinshaw place is sound as a nut. Wind won't ruffle a shingle on it."

"Yes, it is a fine old house, isn't it?" From the alley beside the bakery the bright green and gold delivery wagon turned and headed west on Main Avenue. She realized the baker wanted to visit a while, but she simply could not make conversation in her present state. She headed for the door.

"Goodnight, young lady, and don't you worry about the storm. You'll see how beautiful it is here when it's passed." Elmer Hobart opened the door for her and stood aside with a deep bow.

"Goodnight, Mr. Hobart," Laurie said and

managed a smile.

"Thank you, and come again." It was habitual with him, but it was part of his continuing success in Forest Shores.

Laurie shivered in the cold blast that burst into the overheated bakery, and clung tightly to the tasseled ties of her cape as the wind tried to peel it from her shoulders. The sky which had been ominously gray all day now made good its threat. Fine rain, driven almost horizontally, needled into her face as she crossed Main toward the butcher shop.

A buggy passed by, its acetylene lamps glowing in the premature dark. Another carriage, its side panels buttoned tightly in place, had been halted at the corner, but now traveled a few yards as Laurie stepped from the curb. It pulled over and once again stopped, this time in mid-block, a strange performance considering the worsening storm.

The commercial district had a desolate, deserted look about it, although most shops and stores would remain open for at least another hour. Everyone who could, had already sought shelter before the storm finally settled down to business. No dusk eased gloomy day into stormy night. Night was just suddenly there, wet and howling, only a shade darker than afternoon.

Hoyt Larcher, red and beefy as the sides of prime meat hanging in his cooler, was more garrulous than usual. Laurie smiled and nodded agreeably, even laughed softly at one of his jokes, but as she resumed her way home she could not recall a single word that had passed between them.

Outside the butcher shop Laurie stood in the biting wind for a few minutes waiting for the horsecar which customarily made the circuit of Main Avenue every half-hour. From the corner of her eye she observed the almost furtive movement of the halted carriage. The horse took a few steps and was checked by a sharp pull of the reins. The street was by now empty of traffic and the horsecar nowhere in sight. Deciding she could at least keep warmer if she began walking, the girl tighten-

19

ed the cape about her body and headed down the street. Amid the noise of the wind she heard the buggy wheels grate on the paving and the slow clop of the horse's restrained pace. No reassuring lights were visible in the area just beyond the gas street lamps of the business district. Due to the set-back of houses along Main, no lamplight carried far enough from them to illuminate the street.

"I'm being utterly foolish," Laurie told herself, but as she glanced uneasily toward the buggy, premonition became drymouthed fear. The carriage pulled to the curbside and stopped. She hastened her steps along the darkened sidewalk and without looking back could not be certain no one got out of the buggy to enter one of the nearby houses. Two blocks farther on she found herself almost running, her breath coming in short, painful gasps. It was too dark to be positive the vehicle was in the road, and over the wind impossible to hear.

Laurie gathered her skirts with her free hand and prepared to cross to the other side of Main. By that means she could perhaps elude the buggy if it really were following her. She stepped from the curb into a rapidly filling gutter. Pine needles, wet and slippery underfoot, claimed her attention as she made her way into the street.

Suddenly from out of the blackness hurtled the carriage, its horse driven to frenzy by a lashing whip. As it followed the slight downgrade, the carriage gained speed. By the time the girl had reached the middle of the street, it was upon her. Only a shadowy movement in the gloom warned her as the vehicle thundered murderously toward her.

Terrified, Laurie tried to reach the curb. The buggy bore down, yards away. It swerved toward her. There was no mistaking its intent. Running toward the opposite curb, she slipped in the treacherous debris. Her foot skidded and she felt herself lurching into the grassy parking, unable to break her fall.

Stunned, she was barely aware of the racing horse and the carriage wheels that passed only inches from her head. In that fraction of an instant she caught a glimpse of an ornate brass whipsocket affixed to the dash and a dark gloved hand wielding an ivory handled whip.

As the girl lay there, unable to move, a second buggy turned the nearby corner and drew up beside her. From the near side of the cab the driver leaped down and gently turned her over, his strong fingers holding her head out of the wet grass.

"You must have taken a nasty spill, Miss!" He smiled as she focused her eyes on him. In the spot of light from his phaeton's lamps she saw he was young with wide, heavy shoulders. "I don't want to lift you until we're sure no bones are broken."

She wriggled her arms and legs experimentally.

"Easy now!" he admonished.

"I'm all right, I guess." Laurie flexed her legs and rotated her ankles. It was apparent the man had not witnessed what had happened. Laurie could scarcely believe it herself. She considered the wisdom of telling him about the carriage, but it would sound too fantastic—who would have reason to run her down in such a fashion? "My foot just slipped right out from under...how awkward of me!" she said.

"Not at all! It's these blasted pine needles. They're a constant problem here. In the dry season they're a fire hazard—in the wet season they're worse than greased glass." He arranged her dripping skirts about her legs as she sat up. "Back's all right, too. That's good."

With little more effort than if he were retrieving a dropped newspaper he picked her up, astonished at how light she was. For a fraction of a moment longer than necessary he held her in his arms and looked down into her face. Her eyes, as black as the jet earrings she wore, gazed back into his from under their fringe of dark lashes. It would have been more modest, more ladylike, to glance away in feigned embarrassment, but Laurie was too forthright and honest to play such games with men. That had been one of her many mistakes.

"I'll drive you home, unless you'd like to see a doctor," he said.

21

"No, no. I'm fine, really," Laurie insisted.

"You're certain you aren't injured?" Laurie was surprised by the sound of genuine concern in the man's deep voice.

"I may have a bruise or two, but that's all," she replied.

"Good!" He handed her the dampened packages of bakery goods and lamb chops and settled her into the seat of the carriage, tucking a heavy woolen lap robe about her.

He knew who the girl was. He and every other man in Forest Shores with eyes in his head was aware of Laurie Mathews, who had bought the little shop on North Birch Street. Even young Charlie Hobart, the baker's red-headed boy, could not resist watching her as she made her way along the sidewalks with the wind folding her skirts and petticoats against her long, slim legs and affording them a glimpse of her patent-toed, high-heeled 'senorita' shoes. While their women inveighed against such outlandish modern costume, the men stared.

"Where to?" Her rescuer looked down at her as he picked up the reins of the driving harness. Even in the dim light he could see the top of her head was not burdened with the monstrous false hairpieces so many women affected. Instead, her hair was swept back from her temples in deep waves and caught in a twisted roll at the nape of her neck. Forest Shores had speculated that Miss Mathews must be of Spanish extraction when it first viewed her simple hair arrangement and mode of dress. Whatever she was, she was strikingly beautiful in her simplicity, a condition for which she could not be forgiven.

"I live at Mrs. Hinshaw's, at the corner of Shore Park," she answered.

"The old Hinshaw place?" He laughed as he clucked the horse into the road and slapped the reins gently over its chestnut rump.

"What makes you laugh? Is the Hinshaw place a joke?" she asked.

Instantly he saw she was offended. "Not a joke, no! It's just that when dear old Pansy Hinshaw decided to convert her house into 'apartments for ladies,' as she put it, everyone thought it would surely bring down catastrophe upon the neighborhood."

"And it hasn't?" Laurie knew she sounded peevish, but she suddenly felt peevish. She had almost been run down by a careening carriage, was wet through, beginning to ache miserably, hardly knew how she could manage to pay her rent, and now her rescuer chose to find her choice of living quarters amusing.

"So far, all is well," he said. "The ladies remain above reproach, although from what I hear, Miss Pickens, the school teacher, docs attend the Italian opera in San Francisco now and again." He turned to look squarely at his passenger. "Pansy Hinshaw was supposed to have lost the old place for back taxes, but she confounded the county and not only managed to hang on to it, but makes money, too. Perhaps to me that is the real joke of it."

"Then you believe it's all right for a woman to be in business and make money for herself?" This time she looked squarely at him.

"Absolutely, Miss Mathews. It seems a very sensible proposition. Men have no monopoly on business acumen."

"You know my name?" she asked in surprise.

"Of course," he replied. "In a small town, newcomers are always talked about. After the tourists go home for the season, Forest Shores finds subject matter in its residents."

"Yes, I know—it's called gossip!" She looked away from him into the darkness of the empty street. Somewhere in that darkness the lethal carriage had disappeared. But then perhaps it had merely been an accident. Perhaps she had only imagined it. Her mind was in a muddle as they drove in silence up the slope from downtown to the elevation the town's real estate dealers insisted on calling 'The Hill.' The gas street lamps were still not lighted in the residential areas and the dark

23

pines threshing overhead increased an impression of early night. The monotonous clop-clop of the sleek chestnut's hoofs on the concrete roadway was the only sound audible over a rising wind. Laurie felt as bleak as the scene about her, and her emotions were as buffeted as the swaying trees above them.

Ahead Laurie saw lights in Mrs. Hinshaw's part of the house and wondered if Thea and Olive were home yet. Tonight she needed company and hoped for an evening of sensible talk. They could always make sense from any situation, and usually came up with good advice and ideas. This particular night Laurie hoped they could be especially lucid.

The wind changed direction within a block of the house and rain slanted into the light phaeton, working its way beneath the leather canopy. The man reached across Laurie and muffled her to her chin with the robe. He was undecided whether to apologize for his unintended offense or resume a normal conversation. He did not know Laurie Mathews, only her name.

"I'm Chace Creighton," he said. She turned to look at him again. "I could almost be happy you took that spill if it weren't for your being hurt. I'm glad to have met you, Miss Mathews, although I might have wished for more pleasant circumstances for the meeting." It was an honest statement. He could see it pleased her.

She returned his smile with none of the coquetry that would have been understandable in such an introduction. Her lips parted over teeth as perfect as all else about her.

"Believe me, I should never do such a thing deliberately, not even to meet Teddy Roosevelt!" Her soft laughter was as appealing as her low-pitched voice. "I'm happy to meet you, too, Chace Creighton." Belatedly she realized she was being too open, too friendly—another of her continued mistakes, but she gave him her hand. He had taken off his glove, obviously in expectation of acknowledging her introduction. His hand was hard, his clasp firm, but not the sort at all

24

to go with his dapper soft-brimmed fedora and narrow-lapeled greatcoat. Rather it belonged to a man accustomed to using his hands in rough, productive work.

"You admire President Roosevelt?" He sounded a bit surprised.

"Doesn't everyone?" She did not dare to discuss her mishap, nor did she want to get into politics with a stranger. The truth about the carriage would sound like a fantastic fabrication to avoid embarrassment over her own awkwardness. And politics in Forest Shores was a matter of much heat and vituperation. In her few months' residence she had learned to be diplomatic, if not exactly evasive, on the subject.

"That's not a straight answer. I expect better from you." This time there was a serious note behind his comment.

"Why? You've just met me! You know nothing about me," she exclaimed.

"My dear Miss Mathews, I expect any girl with enough self-determination and courage to leave home, friends, and security behind to come here and go into her own business—well, I expect her to have perception and convictions. And the will to express what she believes." Chace Creighton surprised even himself in his comment, certainly a comment much too familiar for a stranger. "I'm sorry. I had no right to say that."

Laurie turned sideways to look closely into his face. It was large-featured and rugged, with a chin which in other men would be too prominent, and a forehead too wide and high for handsomeness. His mouth was not the straight, cruel slit of so many of his breed, but full-lipped and delicately defined, a promise of sensuality.

"Are we friends, then?" she asked.

"Of course we are!"

"Then, yes, I admire him. I may not always agree with his political stands, but we don't have to agree with everything if a man is getting on with his job. He had a good record of cleaning out corruption in New York, no matter who got in his way. That counts for something in this world." She was sorry they had reached the corner

25

of Shore Park Drive, but perhaps it was best this way—she would not unguardedly speak her mind and thus alienate a portion of Forest Shores. But somehow she felt with Chace Creighton she might be able to do just that and it would remain with him, not to be repeated as gossip about the new woman in town.

He tightened the left hand rein just enough to coax the chestnut into the driveway and up the slight incline beside the house. Laurie approved the way he handled the horse as if it were a fragile, sentient being worth gentle consideration. His hands were large and capable of great strength, but she felt they had shown cruelty to neither human being nor creature. He wrapped the reins about the upright whipstock which was set in its socket. The horse snuffled in irritation as rain ran down its face and into its nostrils. Laurie would not keep them out in the weather longer than necessary, and unwrapped the heavy robe. Creighton jumped out and came around the back of the buggy to assist her.

"Here you are, my girl." His voice suddenly was soft as he seized her waist and lifted her down beside him. She could feel the warmth of his body as he held her close for a moment before releasing her. For that moment she lost all remembrance of anything prior to that instant, a giddy, gay sensation as if the tightly closed blossom of her life had all at once begun to unfold.

"Thank you, Chace Creighton," she said.

"You say both my names as if they are inseparable." He retrieved her two soggy parcels from the carriage seat.

"I want to remember them—Chace Creighton," she teased.

"I'm flattered. Will you?" His free hand closed about her small waist, but he made no attempt to draw her to him again.

"I will indeed." She looked up into his face and wanted to feel his mouth on hers, wanted desperately for him to hold her near in those strong arms. It was another of her mistakes, to give her affections so quickly. But this was no slender red-headed youth in drab

26

uniform about to embark for Cuba. She realized as she savored his nearness that this was a true man. Could he be the man whom her friends had said she would be sure to meet if she went to California?

"I'll see you in." He took her elbow and guided her up the flight of shallow steps to the veranda which encircled the front of the house. A small white glass lamp was burning in the vestibule on a dolphin-footed center table covered with an ornate lace runner. He opened the unlocked front door and waited for her to enter, then stepped back onto the veranda.

"Thank you. You've been very kind. I'm greatly indebted," Laurie said.

"Not at all. A service I render to all beautiful young ladies. But if you think so, will you repay me by coming to the fiesta next week with me?" he asked.

"But I hardly know you!" Laurie said it aloud and was aware it really was so, but in her heart she felt she already knew him well. She wanted to shout and clap her hands and dance, but followed what etiquette decreed.

"Why not go to dinner with me tomorrow evening? Get acquainted, and then say you'll go to the fiesta with me." He noticed her hesitancy, but also the sparkle in her eyes, a sparkle that was not there before and was not a product of the pale glow from the hall lamp. "I'm single, and not spoken for—I believe that is the proper phrase—if that's what you're wondering. And it should in no way compromise you. Tongues will wag, of course, but that's just normal exercise for Forest Shores." He waited a moment more, then turned to go. "I'll call for you at seven," he said. "Goodnight."

"Chace Creighton, I haven't said I'd go," she protested.

"Please don't say my names like that. Just one will do fine."

"Chace..." Laurie began.

"I'll call for you at seven," he stated flatly.

"All right!" She tried to sound exasperated, but it did not come through; she was delighted, and delight

27

came through. Another of her many failings. "Till tomorrow. Goodnight."

"Goodnight, Miss Mathews." He replaced the soft brown fedora on his head and crossed the veranda before she closed the door. His back was broad, with massive shoulders which attested to their share of hard work. Even the expensively tailored greatcoat could not conceal his powerful build. She liked the way he walked, not swaggering as most young men she had known, but a solid, determined tread with the grace of a large, muscular animal.

Laurie closed the door and leaned against it. She knew she was smiling. She had to be, for her heart was beating a new and exciting rhythm. In the mirror as she passed the center table she caught a glimpse of herself and recoiled. Her scarlet tam-o-shanter was skewed at an unflattering angle, her wet hair plastered unbecomingly to her head, and she had a wide smudge of mud across her nose and forehead. Pine needles, affixed with tiny drops of resin, clung to her ruined cape. She squinted at her reflection and began to hum softly.

Chapter 2

Bright yellow and white, like a monstrous, overdecorated lemon cake, the old Hinshaw place occupied several lots at the corner of West Main and Shore Park Drive. With gardens and hedges and a scattering of out-buildings which gave it the appearance of a small village, the house had stood for over a third of a century and would stand for several more if the Civic Club had its way. They had made repeated offers to elderly Mrs. Hinshaw to take it over as their headquarters. They, of course, were no more successful than others of some twenty years past, for Mrs.Hinshaw retained her magnificent home against all comers, and reigned in her own quiet little kingdom.

At the beginning, it had been merely another canvas and slat summer cabin, along with hundreds of others, where vacationers could escape searing inland summers in peace and coolness among pines and rocky beaches. In time the other cabins gave way to more substantial dwellings, while wily Adam Hinshaw bought up lots adjoining his, removed the flimsy tents, and put up a baroque wooden mansion, with guest house and stables.

The present Mrs. Hinshaw, after falling heir to the huge, rambling place when her husband died leaving her short of funds, had taken what seemed to her a logical course: she had called in carpenters and announced in the newspaper she was ready to let out small apartments. Only ladies of good character, she was quick to add. Quite past their prime, both woman and house showed the passage of time, not ungracefully, but rather as if they both accepted the inevitability of becoming a bit shabby and refused to fight it by artifice. Both remained neat, tidy, and quite respectable.

Whatever whim of Mrs. Hinshaw's decided her to paint the enormous bulk bright yellow remained a mystery to the entire town, and especially to the Civic Club. That Sewell's Hardware and Ranch Supply had a quantity of yellow paint left on their hands from bankruptcy stock purchased over in the valley was the whim that decided the color, but who needed to know? Walt Sewell was not only a good businessman, but a compassionate one, as long as he profited somewhere. The bankrupt's misfortune was Mrs. Hinshaw's gain—and Sewell's, too.

Laurie Mathews had first seen the Hinshaw place on a brilliant summer afternoon, with late sunshine lighting up the confectioner's icing that frosted the roof line, corners, window frames and railings. Cinerarias embroidered a varigated purple and blue border under protruding bay windows and glowed in shaded areas of the lawns and garden that entirely surrounded the structure.

It had been so miserably hot in the hotel at San Esteban that she eagerly accepted the suggestion of a week by the sea. Twice each day the local train made a round trip to Forest Shores and back, the combination of freight and passenger cars not incongruous for the rapidly growing coastal area. The trip of thirty-seven miles made it possible for the more affluent businessmen of San Esteban to live in pine-shrouded Forest Shores and commute to their offices and shops. To encourage regular fares, the railroad stocked the parlor car with the finest liquors and imported cigars; to retain its monopoly of the rail system along the coast it subsidized freight and express until dependency was established, and then kept rates reasonable. Greater things were planned for the area, and the railroad intended to be part of them.

Laurie had taken the early train from San Esteban, arriving in Forest Shores long before the morning fog had burned away. As she made arrangements for her modest room at the Blue Roof Lodge she viewed the dismal shoreline with misgivings.

"Would you like to go right up to your room, or perhaps have a stroll along the promenade?" The elderly clerk perceived her reluctance to follow the bellboy. To anyone fleeing the searing heat of San Esteban the drizzly overcast would be welcome relief. For two decades he had watched the Lodge's guests rush to the cool promenade before even inspecting their assigned rooms.

"I'll have to find my coat before I can go out. I had no idea it would be so cold over here on the coast. Yes, I'll go upstairs first. thank you." She had left the glassed-in north wall with its sweeping command of shoreline and trailed the boy who struggled with the luggage ahead of her.

Once in her room, she unpacked her meager belongings and shook out the modish Monte Carlo jacket of black English broadcloth and silk braid trim, wrinkled from weeks at the bottom of her small trunk. It was suitable for Chicago and would be useful in Forest Shores. The last time she had worn it was in Chicago, at the C. B. and Q. railway station. It had been a raw, blustery April morning with the wind whistling off Lake Michigan. She had insisted no one come see her off. Had anyone come, she knew she would not summon the courage to turn her back and leave.

Laurie had counted her fare, thirty-three dollars to San Francisco, six dollars for Pullman tourist sleeping car. She then set her head resolutely to the west, and followed the porter to the waiting train. In the portmanteau which she carried were her entire savings and the largesse from Sergeant Lawrence Bowen's life insurance policy. They were to be married upon his return from Cuba, but an official letter from Washington had informed her their plans were never to be fulfilled. Sergeant Bowen had fallen at San Juan Hill. Later came the draft for the insurance, pitiful payment for dreams shattered by war.

The young woman had tried to pick up the pieces of her life after that, but the pieces refused to fit together anymore. For several years she had tried, until that dreary winter day when she had considered the open, unlighted gas jet as the way out of her puzzle. Even as she considered, she rejected the idea, resolved to break away from all that was old and familiar, and go to California and begin anew.

"It's so lovely out there, Laurie. Flowers and fruit in winter! Think of it! And all those men out there just waiting for sweethearts and wives! Why, they say the men outnumber women at least six to one!" She knew they were trying to encourage her to live again. She could not say when the decision had been reached, but once made, she proved resolute in carrying it out. She had taken the train to San Francisco, stayed a month, then journeyed south to San Esteban where it was sunnier and less urban. It was true, one could live quite nicely in California for around ten dollars a week, and she found herself enjoying life once again, with sightseeing to vast apricot and peach groves, wineries and produce fields, and Chautauqua entertainments. She had never once regretted her trip west.

At the Blue Roof Lodge, Laurie had tossed the jacket over her shoulders and latched the door behind her. She had not bothered to change from her ivory linen summer suit or straw boater and cared not a whit if the jacket were a chic accompaniment or not. The girl wanted to walk in the soft drizzle along the rocky bluff that edged a frothing, turbulent sea. In the local newspaper which was thoughtfully provided in each room, the tide tables were printed on the front page, testifying to the importance of the ocean's presence at Forest Shores. Soon it would be high tide, and Laurie would be there to see it, perhaps to draw from its violent strength a replenishment for her own.

Luncheon had been lonely. The headwaiter had seated her at his best window where she might see the cliffs for miles both east and west. Seals and otters cavorted about the outcroppings of dark rock which punctuated the narrow beach. Gulls wheeled in endless circles, their white wings contrasting against a pewter sky. Solicitous and gracious, the waiter had sensed her desolation. Laurie had toyed with the asparagus vinaigrette and red, ripe, sliced tomatoes. Excellent mocha-java remained untasted until cold.

Suddenly, as if a stage curtain had been hoisted, the fog had disappeared. Sunlight burst through the tattered bits and pieces of mist until it shone unhindered. Crimson and salmon and stark white shimmered in beds and borders of geraniums and marguerites which delineated the promenade along the bluff. Far to the west sparkled blue-purple veronica and bright yellow echeveria; to the east spread carpets of crystalline iceplants in rose and cerise. Backing it all, interspersed with multi-storied shore homes, were black-green pines, their ancient rounded tops spreading protective canopies over the town. If Laurie Mathews had been seeking a sign, she had seen one at last.

Precisely at three o'clock the Lodge's tallyho, a cumbersome, top-heavy carriage, had pulled in front of the main entrance with a blast of brass horns and crunching of white gravel beneath the hoofs of four dapple Percherons. Guests had been encouraged to take the leisurely drive along the shore before having tea or early dinner. It was said to be a stimulant to even the most flagging appetite. Laurie had joined enthusiastic tourists aboard a bright blue and gold carriage that jolted down Shore Park Drive and continued west to Calabasas Point Lighthouse. The sunshine had been deceptively hot, but the wind brisk as it blew landward off Gutierrez Bay. By the time they had visited the lighthouse and re-boarded the tallyho they were grateful for the guide's advice to bring along a warm wrap.

Late afternoon had begun to deepen lavender shadows under the pines before they had left the crazy spiderweb of trails which meandered through the government preserve and began their return trip along West Main Avenue.

And there it sat—the old Hinshaw place, all yellow with dainty white Victorian gingerbread trim, and Spanish moss draped silvery-green from enormous dark pines framing it. In the window of the glass enclosed veranda a sign had read 'Apartments to Let—Ladies Only.'

At first it had been only an amusing supposition.

"Suppose I stay on here in Forest Shores? I could get a small apartment in that adorable old place on Main Avenue. Perhaps I might be able to get a job or even a shop of my own."

It had been something which grew the more Laurie thought about it, until at last one day it was an accomplished fact. She had moved her few belongings to Mrs. Hinshaw's, and with almost the last of her money had purchased the Ribands and Roses Shoppe. She loved the damp, crisp air and the invigorating breeze that breathed incessantly over the town, clearing it of wood smoke and smells of civilization. And she loved her new home.

Geraniums on each side of the walk leaned at odd angles. Their blooms, shattered by the wind, lay on the lawn like gaudy bits of stained glass. The old yellow house dominated the entire neighborhood, looming high and wide across its several lots, an imposing sight even though past its prime. Laurie had built up genuine affection for it, and for Pansy Hinshaw and Forest Shores.

Sunday morning Laurie Mathews awakened to a dark, pouring day. Wind slashed rain against the south windows and rattled the panes in their sashes. She pulled the quilted comforter up around her ears and tried not to hear the howling outside. No use trying to sleep. She rubbed her nose with the back of her hand and yawned. As she remembered her dinner engagement for that night she curled up and closed her eyes. What exactly did he look like, this Chace Creighton? Olive Pickens said last night that he was a member of one of the elite local families, the ones who practically owned and ran the entire county to suit themselves. It should have intimidated Laurie, but it had not. She recalled his gentle hands, the way he managed the horse with a mere touch. She realized with surprise that she had no idea what color his eyes were.

"Why in the world did old Mrs. Hinshaw believe that a house in California didn't need a heating system other than fireplaces? Why couldn't she have installed gas or even steam heat?" Laurie slid from the warmth of the covers and groped her way into the gold plush robe from the foot of the bed. Soft velvet slippers were a comfort on the cold floor as she padded to the fireplace and poked the remains of last night's logs. Dead. Useless to try to start it again until the ashes were taken out. Instead, she found a match in the black wrought-iron holder on the mantel and lighted the coal oil heater, turning the wick up until the flame was orange, then down to a steady bright blue.

From the single faucet over the tiny sink she drew just enough water for coffee and put a blue and white enameled coffee pot atop the three-burner oil cooking stove and lighted it. By the time she finished dressing, it would be ready. Since Thea and Olive had accepted her offer of apple turnovers with their evening of talk last night, the seeded rye bread would have to do for her breakfast. There were two eggs and a piece of cheese in the ice box, and a jar of peach and cherry conserve in the cupboard.

Sensible talk with the girls had convinced her the episode of the carriage was innocent. The driver had

35

probably been drunk. And horses do become headstrong at times and run away with buggies. She told Thea and Olive only that she had fallen on the pine needles. It took little effort today to put the carriage from her thoughts.

This morning Laurie felt like eating. Since yesterday afternoon her world had changed. Even the dismal day beyond the windows could have no effect on her. She had met Chace Creighton!

What was it Thea Harris had said? Laurie tried to recall every word of their long conversation last night.

"Of course you should stay here and keep on with the shop! So what if you do go broke, Laurie? At least you will have tried. If you owe no one, you will at least salvage your good name from it. You'll be able to get a job somewhere." Thea had still smelled of the drug store in her cotton waist and worsted skirt. There was always a faint odor of chemicals and dried materia medica about her—valerian and hydrastis—and this despite the fact that she sold and dispensed most of the cosmetics and perfumed soaps and colognes at Jepsen's Pharmacy.

"Besides, we don't want you to deprive us of the pleasure of seeing Chace Creighton ourselves! If you decide you aren't interested, just head him our way!" Olive, at a ripe twenty-eight, was already considered a spinster. Few gentlemen had contemplated losing their heads about her when she was younger, but as she passed twenty-five and none of the eligible bachelors evinced concern in changing her single condition, the town's sage heads nodded and relegated her to eternal spinsterhood. She stirred tea leaves into a brown earthenware pot and placed a knitted cosy over it.

"Speak only for yourself, Olive! I wouldn't want anything to do with the Creightons!" Thea shuddered elaborately, but instantly regretted her remark. Her speech was frequently a bit ahead of her thought, but blushing was far behind her after clerking at Knut Jepsen's pharmacy for eight years.

36

"Why? Whatever in the world is wrong with the Creightons? I've heard about them ever since I came to town. And they're always mentioned in the society pages of the San Francisco papers, sometimes even pictures. What's the matter with them?" Laurie stabbed red coals in the grate with a heavy brass poker and tossed on another split pine log sending a shower of glowing sparks up the chimney. She set the damper to full draft until the log could ignite.

"I should keep my opinions to myself." Thea handed round a pink tin of bon-bons, her contribution to the evening's entertainment. "What I hear at the pharmacy I should keep to myself and not pass on. At least that's what Knut Jepsen keeps trying to tell me. But then, I didn't have to learn about the Creightons at the store."

"Oh, come on, Thea! We know you're going to tell us sooner or later. Don't make us coax." Olive placed the tea pot on a marble-topped mahogany table before the maroon baize settee. "You may as well trot out everything you've heard or we'll worm it out of you, bit by bit, and that might take all night."

Thea laughed, a deep, throaty, genuine laugh of humor, not embarrassment. "You're right. I'm a dreadful gossip—and I love it!"

"That's sinful, Thea." Olive hissed in shocked whispers, then burst out laughing with the other two girls. "Let's hear it all!"

"Pour me some tea first," Thea demanded and held out her cup while Olive filled it with steaming yellow brew. "Ummm! Smells marvelous. You say Mr. Chew gave you this tea?"

"Yes, poor little man. He finally brought his boy to school yesterday and enrolled him. The school board is absolutely adamant about making Sand Town send its children through at least the eighth grade. Mr. Chew was so humble and afraid. It must have been terrible in China for them to be so frightened of such a simple thing as bringing their little ones to school." Olive smiled as she remembered Mr. Chew's bashful presentation. "He said gifts to teachers are customary in their tradition. And you know, I'm going to see to it personally that his boy succeeds. He's such a beautiful child, so obedient—a real treasure."

"Didn't his wife come, too?" Laurie asked.

"No. I suppose that's not part of their tradition," Olive replied. "Not yet anyhow. I told him she'd be welcome to visit any time. Who knows? Perhaps she will one of these days. I've never met any Chinese ladies before."

"Have any of the Italians sent their youngsters yet?" Thea wondered.

"No, but they will, I'm sure," Olive said. "I think once they realize the unified school will be able to give them a much better education than that one-room shack down on the beach, they'll send them. After all, they want the best for their kiddies just as the rest of us do."

"But it was pretty high-handed to shut it down without even consulting their wishes. Maybe they'd prefer their one-room schoolhouse nearby than have to send the children over a mile and a half away. That's an awfully long walk for little legs, especially in bad weather." Laurie had read the paper and heard her customers discussing the school board's ultimatum.

"Yes, but dear girl, that's the way things are done in Gutierrez County!" Thea sounded annoyed. "That's the style of our elected hierarchy! Do as they want or rather as Creighton Development wants, and then ask 'by your leave.'"

Laurie waited for Thea to resume. She could see that something had hit the surface with the girl's last remark. Taking her tea she sat in front of the fireplace where the heat could bake out the soreness resulting from her fall. The fierce warmth proved comforting to her wrenched muscles.

"Just remember, the Creightons wanted to build the new school. That will do for a start as to what's wrong with them. They agitated and connived under the banner of better education, but always on the basis that they'd sell the land and build the school," Thea began. "Three board members all of a sudden turn up on the tax rolls as owners of prime lots in the Mariposa Beach tract—which just happens to be a Creighton project, too.

"As I say, that's the way business is done around these parts," Thea continued. "Long ago old Zedekiah Creighton wanted the railroad to put down a line into Forest Shores so he could sell off the lots and develop the area into a regular town."

"How did he manage that?" Laurie interrupted.

"He had cronies at the Capitol who brought in men from the railroad. Gave them huge holdings of their own on condition they saw to it the rails came to Forest Shores. That gave them the same opportunities to profit from its growth. Eventually most of the original landowners were squeezed out."

"When was that?" Laurie asked.

"About thirty years ago. No, closer to forty years now," Thea said. "Zedekiah came out here during the Civil War. Had something to do with keeping Gutierrez County in line with the Union and making sure a group of secessionists who had settled along the coast here didn't stir up trouble. California had a lot of copperheads - southern sympathizers, you know. Many of the Mexicans nursed a grudge against the federal government. They felt it was federal troops under Fremont who helped rob them of their land and sever them from their own lawful government. Not that they agreed with slavery—far from it—but many would never have wept to see the South triumph." Thea sipped the fragrant tea for a few moments as if to gather her thoughts rather than blurt them out at random.

"If he was sent to do the job, then it was honorable, wasn't it?" Laurie asked.

"Not when you conspire to cheat people of their land by pressure and intimidation! And that's what Zedekiah Creighton did. With the proper authority in one area of operation, he assumed the same in other areas where he had no right. Due to the terrible drought in the mid-eighteen-sixties many ranchers lost their livestock or had to sell at starvation prices. Creighton forced loans on some of the ranchers over in the valley and along the coast here. And, too, during the war, business suffered if you couldn't secure government contracts for what you had to sell—cattle, meat, hides, lumber, salt fish, grain. If you had no contract, you might as well shoot your cattle and let your produce rot on the ground. To get contracts, you paid Creighton!" Thea became incensed just speaking of what had happened.

"Oh, not that it would show on any records," she continued. "He was too slick for that. But pay you did, or do only local business, and local business wasn't enough to sustain most of the ranchers and farmers who stood on principle and refused to pay Creighton. He persuaded the railroad to demand cash for transporting their products. To get cash they had to get loans. They were forced to take out loans from Zedekiah Creighton!"

Thea's voice dropped to a low, quiet monotone, as if she had no wish to add inflection on her indictment. She looked into her cup and extended it to Olive for more tea.

"What a terrible thing to do! How did you learn so much about it? It was long before your time," Laurie said.

"Not all that long, really. But tell me, Laurie, where do you think I get my coloring—this straight black hair and brown eyes—this dark skin? Why do I go all the way over to San Esteban to church?" Thea did not wait for an answer. "My mother's people were the Orozcos. They were original recipients of a provisional concession, which became a land grant in the eighteen-twenties. They held at that time the entire Mariposa Ranch. Their concession originally came directly from Spain, dating from the late seventeen-hundreds."

"And Mr. Creighton took their land away from them?" Laurie was shocked.

"Yes, that is right," Thea answered.

"Oh, Thea, I'm so sorry. I had no idea." Laurie touched her friend's arm, a gesture of both apology and sympathy.

"Of course you hadn't, Laurie. I never speak of it any more than I have to. It does no good. My grandparents and parents died of all-consuming hate and anger. As they declined and died, the Creightons flourished. I don't say I could learn to love the name of Creighton, but I don't retain hatred anymore. If I did, it would eat me alive and serve no purpose."

"But didn't anybody try to stop him?" Olive wanted to know.

"Sure they did! Many of them tested him in court—and lost. Everybody lost to Zedekiah. He saw to it that his friends and business associates were appointed to proper posts in government to assure him of getting his way. His way was always profitable to them, too. Judges, commissioners, administrators, supervisors, aldermen. No one had proof enough to convict him, and even if the contestant were not Spanish or Mexican, the courts weren't really intersted in justice. After all, the more settlers who came, the more profits for the railroads and developers. And breaking up the large holdings meant more settlers, more business, more profits—for the right people." Thea's smile was cynical.

"I'm almost sorry I told Chace I'd go with him to dinner tomorrow. If only I'd known all this before, maybe I wouldn't have agreed so quickly." Laurie wondered if she had blundered again. Her dark eyes were troubled.

"Don't be so silly, girl! From all I've heard about him, your Chace Creighton isn't much like the rest of his tribe." Olive put down her cup on the marble-topped table and sat back into the settee. "It seems he had some pretty violent quarrels with his father and

41

brothers about building the new school. Mr. Larcher said Chace wouldn't tolerate inferior materials being substituted for those specified in the contracts. Seems two of the foremen on the job belong to the Masons and they got to talking about it at one of their meetings. Some of the men were all for trying to take the old man to court, but Hoyt Larcher convinced them to go straight to Chace with their complaints.''

"What happened?'' Laurie shifted as the heat became too much. She leaned against the arm of the Turkish leather chair in which Thea sat.

"A real family brawl, according to Mr. Larcher and Knut Jepsen. I overheard them talking about it at the pharmacy,'' Thea said as she forked a corner off the apple turnover and tasted it. "Say, that's good. That's Madge Hobart's, not Elmer's. I can always tell the difference who makes them. She uses more nutmeg and cinnamon.''

Laurie was on the point of asking for a taste, but decided it would not be very hospitable seeing that the turnovers were her treat. She had purchased only the two, for she had no appetite at the time. As unobtrusively as she could, she buttered a piece of rye bread and ate it between sips of tea.

"Do you think it's all right if I go with him? I don't want to commit a social *faux pas*. Should I go?'' Laurie was not at all sure that she would abide by their advice should they say 'no.'

"Why not? But if you meet the brothers or the old man, stay clear of them. Of course, people like us are never destined to meet their mother, but just in case be forewarned about her, too.'' Olive relished vicarious participation in town society even if it meant merely discussing it. "They say she can't keep maids more than a few months at a time. Nothing ever suits her. Old man Creighton once had an agency in Boston ship out some immigrant Irish girls to try to please her.''

"Did they?'' Laurie asked.

"Certainly not! Nothing can please her majesty!

They ran off and married ranchmen. One eloped with a commercial traveler from San Francisco. Didn't stay their year out, any of them," Olive replied.

"I'm duly warned! I gather she's unpleasant," Laurie said. "So far she hasn't turned up at my shop. Guess she must consider local commodities too plebian for her tastes. But if she comes, I'll take care." Laurie curled her nose in disapproval of the woman who ruled Forest Shores society, and indeed all Gutierrez County, with the proverbial velvet-clad iron hand. "I shall be on my guard. Maybe I'll even refuse to do business with her. If she's any worse than Mrs. Arvidson, especially about paying her bills, I couldn't afford to do business with her."

Thea laughed at mention of the other woman's name. "Why Knut Jepsen caters to that horrid woman I'll never know. Only the very best for her, but don't remind her she's supposed to pay for what she gets. Do you know she ordered a case—mind you, a whole case—of Violettes Celestes soap, six bottles of cologne, powder and sachet last month and hasn't paid for them yet? Raised such a fuss about our not carrying a full line of that, or of Aglaia, then lets us wait for our money as if it were her divine right. That woman actually uses Aromatic Schiedam Schnapps by the case, too. Says she suffers from internal problems—sure must suffer a lot, the way she uses it up! And makes it known, in loud tones and considerable emphasis, she does not touch whiskey." Thea's distaste was evident.

"Well, I'm not dining with either Mrs. Creighton or Mrs. Arvidson, thank goodness." Laurie had smiled to think she would instead be with Chace.

It had been close to midnight when the girls finished talking. The wind had not abated and still moaned from the northwest accompanied by continuous cold rain. Laurie had hung her wet garments on hangers from an improvised line strung across the room from a window latch to the oak clothes rack on the wall near the door. Along with the smell of damp woolen a pungent, resinous scent lingered in the room from smoke which had puffed back down the chimney with errant gusts.

Learning about Chace's family had not changed her first impression of him at all. Even Thea had spoken well of him, and she had reason enough not to. Laurie had buried her head between pillow and fluffy quilted comforter in the monstrous mahogany bed. From where she lay she could see the French windows which opened out onto the shallow balcony to the south. Moving ever so slightly, the lace curtains demonstrated the ability of the wind to penetrate closed doors.

For a terrifying instant she recalled the hurtling carriage and her headlong fall to escape its murderous wheels. The chilling remembrance caused her momentarily to stare with fear at the fluttering curtains.

She watched for a few minutes, listened to the wild music of the storm, then closed her eyes and slept, happy that tomorrow was so near.

Laurie had trouble recalling everything that was said last night. Words and phrases of womanish gossip about people whom she scarcely knew had faded upon first hearing, but still echoing in her mind were those concerning Chace Creighton.

The tiny oil heater warmed a corner of the room. She stood with her back to it as she surveyed the drenched lawn and gardens below from the French windows. Blue smoke curled from the chimney of Roy Wimbish's cottage, which loomed through slanting rain beyond the white picket fence that separated house and outbuildings. He might bring in another load of wood before he departed for church. If so, he would want to remove the cold ashes, too. She hastened to shovel them into the galvanized ash pail.

Heavy boots pounding up the stairs gave fair warning to the ladies that he was coming. Laurie rushed to open the door before he had to knock, an operation made awkward for him with an armload of split logs.

He had removed his oilskin slicker and hat in the summer kitchen before coming in the house, but his face and beard were dripping wet.

"Come in, Roy." She went to the tiny kitchen and took down two cups.

"Morning, Miss Laurie. I seen your lamp on up here last night till late, so I figured you'd need more wood to see you through the day. I guessed you'd be about out." He dumped the chunks of wood onto the hearth and stacked them one by one in the brick storage receptacle beside the fireplace. "Got plenty of kindling left, I see. I'll take your ashes down when I go and bring the bucket back up later."

"May I pour you some coffee?" the girl asked. "Just made it fresh."

"No, thanks. I'll be on my way to services directly I get my clothes changed. Very kind of you, I'm sure." Behind his heavy, grizzled moustache and whiskers his smile was almost invisible, but his ears moved upward a fraction of an inch and the lines about his eyes wrinkled to show it was there. He looked at her with tenderness in his old face, as if he were seeing in her something remembered from a long ago past. She had sensed it upon first meeting him when he helped move her from the Lodge to Mrs. Hinshaw's.

"I'm just having some. Come, sit down for a minute. I want to hear how you made out over at Hutchins stables about the wood." He had taken pride in telling Mrs. Hinshaw that he was able to obtain their fire wood almost for merely the cutting and hauling.

"Can't stay but a minute, mind." He perched on the straight-backed chair by the tiny dining table across from the girl and took the cup in his gnarled hands.

"Go on, tell me how you made out with Bert Hutchins," Laurie urged.

"He finally come 'round to letting me take out all the wood I want, just so's I don't fell no live trees. I pay him the hire of a team to haul it out, and that's right fair, I'd say." His satisfaction with his accomplishment was obvious, as well it should be, for Bert Hutchins ran his livery stable with profit in mind, not charity. Not even his lifelong friend, Roy Wimbish, could get him to donate anything if he could sell it. The fact that he might have to pay for clearing his property of fallen timber if Roy did not help by taking it for nothing was enough to induce him to consent. That it benefited old Mrs. Hinshaw might have had something to do with his decision, but Bert Hutchins would have refused to admit it. He had earned his reputation as a shrewd horse trader and a man with a hard eye to cash profits. He wanted no one to think he was about to change.

"From the looks of his place there must be a lot of dead trees to cut up. Quite a few carloads, don't you think?" Laurie chose to give Roy an opportunity to brag.

She poured him more coffee and sat listening to his explanation of the agreement. The man seemed at ease with her, unlike his stiff reticence with other ladies of the house. When the clock above the mantel struck eight-thirty he excused himself and left. As he paused at the open door and looked back at Laurie, the flicker of a soft, wistful memory returned to his sun-browned face.

When he had clumped back downstairs Laurie shut the door and stood looking out the balcony windows once more. In a few minutes Roy had donned his slicker and flat, oiled-felt rain hat and recrossed the lawn to his own cottage.

Roy Wimbish had never married. For decades he had been general handyman at the old Hinshaw place and had lived in the small house at the rear ever since it was built. Laurie had heard that he was not too bright, but was honest and thoroughly trustworthy, as devoted to his elderly employer as he had been to her husband. He had been Adam Hinshaw's man-of-all-chores and had continued as such for Adam's widow.

As Laurie watched him in the downpour, she resolved to ask Mrs. Hinshaw more about Roy. Who was it that she reminded him of every time he saw her? It was not her imagination, for she had surprised the expression on his face many times. There was no lechery or lust in his attitude, no repugnant leering. Laurie was fully aware of that look, especially since coming to Forest Shores. There was a sadness in Roy's expression. Had he loved a girl long ago, a girl with dark eyes and pale, golden skin?

Someday she must ask Pansy Hinshaw about Roy.

Chapter 3

Toward late afternoon the wind and rain slackened, with a cold drizzle replacing the vicious, slashing squalls of the previous twenty-four hours. Laurie had spent most of the afternoon pressing and trying on the few dresses in her wardrobe. Dinner with Chace Creighton was an event not to be attended in her plain gray business gown.

Although there were several restaurants in Forest Shores, only the Blue Roof Lodge, with its baroque ornamental dining room facing the sea, was considered a proper place for Sunday night dinner or late supper. Railroad tycoons and wealthy land speculators had found its cuisine equal to the best San Francisco had to offer, and many maintained year-round apartments within the vast hotel. Their glittering ladies provided still further ornament to an already exquisite decor. Jewels, delicate laces, and satins reflected candlelight from heavy silver candelabra which had seen service a century earlier in baronial mansions of the Continent.

"Thea, do you think this would be all right?" Laurie pinned an ecru lace fichu across her breast and stood back to view the effect. The rich gold of the gown was relieved by flounces of ecru lace caught up with bows around the hem.

"You really should wear a hip form," Thea said and patted the girl's behind. "I know you personally don't care for that style, but it would make that gown look much better. The hem dips a bit in the back, you know."

"But I don't want to wear corsets and padding! I

won't wear it!" Laurie turned and craned her neck to see the back of her dress in the tilted mirror above the dresser. "It isn't honest, all that wire and whalebone. And just why, for goodness sakes, does a woman have to look like a pouter pigeon? Women should look natural, not like deformed freaks of nature!" She said it with some heat and obvious conviction. Thea laughed and took a tuck in the lace with a pin.

"We'll just take it up a tiny bit, then," Thea said. She spoke around the pins in her mouth and inserted them one at a time in the flounce. "Who knows, you may set a new fashion all by yourself." She pinned, shook the ruffle, then stepped back. "Yes, that does it. Now it's even all the way around."

"Will we have time to fix it?" Laurie asked a bit anxiously.

"Relax! You still have hours yet." Thea threaded a needle with silk mending floss and waited for Laurie to step out of the gown. "You just finish pressing the petticoat and that fichu while I do this. Then all you have to do is put a rose behind your ear and you're ready."

"Oh, I want so much for everything to be exactly right!" Laurie sighed. "And I'll be bad advertising for my own shop if I show up as a hen-sparrow."

"You a hen-sparrow? You couldn't be a sparrow if you tried, girl! Especially not in this gold color." Thea laughed outright and sat back on the small settee. "An oriole, maybe, but a hen-sparrow? Never!"

"Do you really like it? It's several years old now." Laurie stepped out of the dress and held it up to her face, critically inspecting the effect against her skin. "It's always been my favorite color, this peculiar shade of gold. I think it's much more flattering than blue or rose. And I simply can't wear greens."

"Believe me, it's perfect for you. If Chace Creighton doesn't appreciate you in this, then he has to be blind." Thea began to shorten the ecru lace flounce with infinitesimal stitches.

"It just has to be right," Laurie said quietly.

"I know, dear." Thea looked up from the settee.

"It will be. He'll love you in it, I know." Although she would not under any circumstances want to go out to dinner with a Creighton, to go with any other eligible young man would be pleasant. But Thea Harris was not considered eligible herself, and so remained unsought, uncourted. She was an Orozco, and an alliance with an Orozco in Gutierrez County was tantamount to treason. If she were not invited to the Blue Roof Lodge, she could at least relish someone else going.

By four o'clock the garments were ready and carefully hung in the tall walnut wardrobe. The two girls joined Mrs. Hinshaw and the other women tenants downstairs for tea promptly at four-thirty, a Sunday afternoon custom of Pansy's household. Talk consisted of the usual busy trivia that made up daily lives of single females in all small towns, but in her impatience Laurie heard little. Promptly at six, again by custom, the ladies thanked their hostess and returned to their own quarters. Olive sighed as she reached the second floor hall.

"How I envy you. I've never yet been to dinner at the Blue Roof Lodge. Last year at the end of our summer school session we teachers treated ourselves to luncheon there, but that's not quite the same."

"I didn't eat dinner there either." Laurie held the door open for Thea and Olive to come into her room. "When I was staying there I went uptown to the White Front Cafe at night. That was much more within my means."

As they admired the gold gown, Pansy Hinshaw tapped at the door. In her arms was folded a long, stiff wrap of a deep, clear blue. "Since it's still so miserable outside I thought you might need a waterproof to go over your gown." She held out the voluminous cape, her old eyes betraying anticipation. "It's only been worn a few times. It will save your dress material from getting water spotted."

"It's beautiful, Mrs. Hinshaw. Thank you." Laurie took the wrap and spread it on the bed. "That will be lovely with the gold." She turned and gave the

50

elderly woman a hug. "I wondered how I could keep dry. I don't even own a waterproof. Thank you." She guided Pansy by the elbow to the large Turkish leather chair near the fireplace.

"It's a bit old-fashioned, but they don't really go out of style. I mean, waterproofs aren't the sort of thing the Paris designers are interested in." The old woman was pleased to be part of the excitement. Laurie smelled sauterne on Pansy's breath and knew that she had fortified herself before coming upstairs. In her quaint, bustle-backed black Sunday silk she looked like an elfin doll from fifty years before, ludicrously out of place in the second year of the twentieth century.

When the small clock chimed six-thirty the girls prepared Laurie for her evening, quite as if it were their own. At the sound of heavy steps on the stair landing below they looked at one another in surprise.

"Roy, dear, is that you?" Pansy Hinshaw stuck her head around the door and looked down the darkened stairs.

"Yes, ma'am, Mrs. Hinshaw." His voice had enough lilt in it to cause her eyes to widen. "I promised Miss Laurie some yellow roses. I had 'em drying a bit by the fire to make 'em open up." He lumbered up the steps and hesitated until he was certain it was proper for him to proceed.

"But, Roy, we don't have yellow roses." She looked puzzled.

"I know, ma'am, but I knowed where some was." He grinned and Pansy realized where he had obtained them.

"You can come on in, Roy. We're decent." Thea wanted him to present the flowers himself. She had seen him leave his cottage around two o'clock, head south through the trees across the street as if making for the Creighton place, then return much later clutching the roses upside down to protect them from the rain. Roy and Eusebio Villareal, gardener and stableman for the Creightons, had grown up together in San Esteban.

Laurie turned to face Roy as he entered the room.

51

In the lamp light that emphasized the gold of her skin and gown, the girl appeared radiant. Her dark hair, pulled back in soft waves from her temples and twisted into a loose chignon at the nape of her neck, formed a shining black frame about her oval face. For long moments Roy Wimbish stared at her, his lips parted and jaw slack behind its bushy beard. The soft, gentle expression she has observed in his face once more returned. Whether the trace of moisture that glistened in his eyes was from the rain or not was hard to say. He stood almost as if shocked at the sight of her.

"They're lovely, Roy." Laurie felt she must break the spell she had created and reached to take the roses from him. She held them to her nose and sniffed. "And so fragrant! Here, Olive, just smell them!" She held the flowers out to the young teacher sitting on the small sofa.

Roy turned to go. "Thank you, Roy. When anybody mentions them, I shall tell them you gave the roses to me. It was very kind of you, although I'm not at all sure you should have." Their eyes met over the yellow petals as she held the flowers to her nose again.

Roy's face pulled back into a wide grin and he nodded. "That's as may be, Miss Laurie."

She pinned them where the fichu crossed, the yellow petals enhanced by the beauty of her pale golden skin. He bobbed his head in approval and stepped backwards out the door, and with no further words pounded his way down the stairs. Laurie stood watching him disappear into the dimness of the first floor landing.

"Poor Roy." Pansy Hinshaw sighed as they heard the door to the summer kitchen slam shut behind him. "Well, girls, I shall leave you to your final primping." She rose to go. "Do have a wonderful time. You look so beautiful, child. You'll be a spot of sunshine in that dining room tonight. I'd like to see the heads turn when you go in on the arm of Mr. Chace Creighton. Goodnight, Laurie. Enjoy yourself."

"Thank you. And thank you for the waterproof.

I'll be most careful with it, I promise.'' Her heart ached for the old woman as she slowly descended the stairs, gripping the railing at each step without looking back. From the scent of camphor and cedar chips on the wrap, she knew it had not been used for a long time.

Sunday night dinner and late supper were traditions among the more affluent members of Forest Shores society. Weekend tourists and vacationers relinquished the spacious restaurant to the natives by Sunday evening, and the natives, as if in relief at the exodus, flocked to one of two places: Guido Ferranti's Shell Box Cafe in Sand Town, or the Blue Roof Lodge on Shore Park Drive. Both overlooked the sea, with glassed-in porches affording spectacular views of the shoreline; both featured seafood fresh from the waters of Gutierrez Bay and the best meats and produce the surrounding ranches had to offer. The difference between the two places was far from subtle, however, not merely in price alone, but in atmosphere, feeling, and elegance. Not that those who patronized one establishment refused to go to the other, for the food was faultless at both. Such things as fine Belgian carpeting as opposed to sawdust on the floors, delicate English porcelain and heavy earthenware separated them as effectively as did Point Piedras and La Gaviota Creek.

That Chace Creighton had chosen one over the other merely meant he felt his guest would enjoy seeing the assemblage of townsfolk who would be attending an evening musical in the grand ballroom. His mother had arranged the entertainment, inducing Rudolfo Ingres, the flambouyant operatic tenor, to travel from San Francisco for the night. Expense did not matter to her so long as the event served to enhance prestige and respect for the Creighton family name.

"I won't be at your soiree, Mother. I've told you so often it seems useless to repeat, but I don't like your gatherings.'' Chace had spoken reasonably to start with, but now he raised his voice to emphasize his refusal. "I don't like the people you invite and most of all, I don't like your tenors."

"It does seem the least you could do is please your father and me occasionally." Sybil Creighton's petulance was icy.

"Weeks ago when you planned this I told you I had no intention of going. If you've invited Aura Lee Striker for me, it's up to you to make apologies to her. I have another engagement and I intend to keep it." His chin jutted forward over the high Haldon collar more from obstinacy than discomfort. His hazel eyes glinted with a hint of anger that lay behind them.

Sybil rose and stalked to the two-story-high windows that looked toward Mariposa Beach. She studied Chace's reflection in the glass and realized that to argue with him was futile. Even as a small child the signals had been clear: the jaw thrust outward, teeth clenched, head cocked defiantly to one side. Surely his attitude sprang from some violent Highlander ancestor on his father's side, and not from her own aristocratic lineage which she could trace back several hundred years. That constant inbreeding had weakened the line was of no importance in her view of cultured behavior. "You defy me—humiliate me—to have dinner with that. . .that. . . shop girl!"

"Yes, Mother, with that shop girl!" Chace shouted. "She's one hell of a lot better than that simpering pale blue creature you keep pushing at me. My God! Doesn't she know there are more colors in the spectrum than that washed-out blue she affects all the time?"

"I will not have you abuse Aura Lee, Chace. She is not one of those cheap little opportunists you seem to prefer." Instantly Sybil regretted her remark. Chace spun on his heel and left her alone in the austere, cathedral-like room.

How unlike her other two sons he was. Beneath his disregard for her system of judgments and values was contempt for herself and all that she represented. At times Sybil Creighton felt Chace's calm hatred as a tangible thing. A nameless fear crept over her as she would glimpse golden fire in his deep-set eyes. Where there should have been love, only antagonism and hostility appeared. Chace refused to fit into the molds she had chosen for her sons. Now as she stared out the window past storm-tortured pines to the seething ocean beyond Mariposa Beach she again felt a cold clutch of dread.

"You taking the brougham, Chace?" Duncan had just poured a tumbler half full of rye whiskey. His brother shook his head when offered the decanter. Duncan followed him from the living room to the outer hall.

"No, I don't want Eusebio out in this weather. He's too old to be running around in this cold and wind. I'm taking the phaeton myself." Chace took his hat and gloves from the brass and mahogany stand in the entry. A log blazing in the hall fireplace did nothing to dispel the damp chill.

"That's what he gets paid for." Duncan swallowed half the contents of his glass and grimaced as the rye coursed hotly down his throat. "Father should turn him out and get someone younger who can earn his keep."

"To suit you?" Chace held Duncan in some affection, but loathed his utter disregard for others. The fact that he was frequently too drunk to get himself home without assistance was the major factor in his endeavors to have the old Mexican set aside. A younger man might manage to get him home without begging help from strangers. Duncan Creighton sober was a docile coward, but drunk he became unmanageable until felled by stupor.

"It would suit me, yes." The younger man placed his drink on the mantel and held his hands to the fire. Chace sensed this was not meant to be the end of their conversation and paused before opening the door. "Look, I'm sorry about this afternoon," Duncan said. "I had no right to score you off like that." He continued to face the fire, too chagrined to look at his brother.

"Are you apologizing?" Chace was not as indulgent with Duncan as his parents were.

"Yes, I am. It's hard for me to admit I'm wrong,

55

but I have to—to you. I could blame it on this rotten weather or on Catalina's wretched cooking, but I won't." He turned around and appealed to Chace. "I don't know why I do anything anymore, and you're the last person in this filthy world I should quarrel with. Forgive me?" He was more like a child than a man of twenty-four.

"On one condition..." Chace drew on his gloves and adjusted the angle of his fedora's narrow brim.

"And that is?" Duncan sounded like an eager boy seeking his schoolmaster's blessing.

"You go back to the university and try to make something of your life. You haven't done too well so far," Chace said.

"Not you, too?" The question was almost a wail.

"There's a lot of work to be done in Forest Shores—in California, for that matter," Chace continued. "And you can't tell me you're going to enjoy your style of living forever. Sooner or later it will begin to pall. Then what's left?"

Duncan laughed, the sound of it hollow and much too loud in the slate-floored entry. "Who's been telling tales on me this time?"

"I paid off Guido Ferranti yesterday."

"I made quite a mess of his back room, didn't I? Damn! I am sorry. He's been decent to me—both he and Teresa. What gets into me, Chace?" Duncan ran long white fingers through his unruly sandy hair and turned away from his brother to stare into the fire.

"I really don't know, but I do know you'd better get yourself in hand or you're going to get shipped back to Boston," Chace said.

"Father say so?" Duncan was alarmed.

Chace waited a moment before he answered. "No, Mother."

"Good God! She wouldn't!" The younger brother passed a moist palm over his flushed face.

"She is quite positive. Father has nothing to say about it. That was their agreement when he bailed you out last time."

56

"You won't tell them about Guido's, will you?" Anxiety grayed Duncan's thin face despite the ruddy glow of the fire.

"No. But it might not be me who finds out next time," Chace replied. "My advice is that you re-apply to Stanford."

"It's that bad?" Duncan asked.

"It is." As Chace opened the right half of the huge hand-carved arched door a sharp blast of air flung rain across the gray slate floor. "And if you're going to ask to borrow money again, forget it. Rosa Cantu can do without you for one evening. Besides, you won't have to spend any money tonight—just go applaud Mother's French tenor and hold Aura Lee Striker's fat little hand." The truth of his sarcasm caused Duncan to wince. "Goodnight."

Old Eusebio had raised the leather hood, checked the lamps, and brought the phaeton around to the front entrance. Arthritis made his movements slow and painful as he got down from the high seat into the graveled driveway.

"I gave you Tildy. She don't get excited in the rain." Eusebio caressed the little sorrel mare who nuzzled affectionately into his shoulder. "Long as she's got nice work to do, she don't care about the weather." He stroked her forehead, holding her bit in his hand until Chace climbed into the seat and took the reins. "If I'm 'sleep when you get back, you wake me and I rub her down good."

"Thanks, Eusebio. I won't be too late," Chace promised.

"You have good time, Mr. Chace." The old man released the bit and Tildy leaned into her driving harness and picked her way down the drive to Shore Park.

Both sides of the lane remained in darkness since the acetylene lamps illuminated only a small area on the right side of the road. Chace Creighton took a deep breath of the wet air and smiled to himself. Aura Lee Striker, indeed! In his imagination he saw her standing beside Laurie Mathews—pale plue satin and drab blond hair beside jet eyes, black hair, and gay tam-o-shanter cocked at an audacious slant. Even with her dirty face, Laurie had woven her spell about him to such an extent that he had thought of little else since last evening.

He coaxed the sorrel mare around the corner of West Main and into the narrow concrete driveway of the Hinshaw place. It seemed every window of the old home was lighted in welcome, certainly the front door opened even before his carriage had halted beneath the pillared portico.

Pansy Hinshaw, her black Sunday silk rustling in the wind, held the door ajar and beamed at him as he came from the walk up onto the veranda.

"Here's your young man, Laurie," she called upstairs and made no attempt at dignity or restraint. Approval was in her face and voice. "Please come in, Chace, dear."

"Mrs. Hinshaw, you look lovely as ever." He bent over and kissed her cheek. "I hear Roy made a pretty sharp deal with Bert Hutchins about clearing all that dead wood in the pasture. Joe Arvidson tried the same thing, but Old Bert turned him down flat. Seems Roy's turning out to be quite a businessman."

Small gossip of the neighborhood had always been Pansy's favorite topic of conversation, even when Chace had come to sit in her high-ceilinged white kitchen to drink whipped chocolate and eat gingerbread as a small boy. Duncan and Archibald had never returned after adolescence, but Chace had remained both champion and friend.

At the sound of steps, they turned to the stairs. Laurie hesitated a moment on the last tread. Twenty-four hours had not reduced his stature one bit, nor had her memory changed a single feature of his face. Strong jaw, deep-set eyes under heavy arched brows, the beautiful mouth that curved into a smile at the sight of her, all were the same as she remembered.

For the instant she waited, Chace was stunned. The muddy smudge was gone, and there were no stray pine needles clinging to the golden silk gown; no skewed tam-o-shanter hid the glossy jet hair. It was as though he were seeing her for the first time.

There were words of greeting, words of farewell as Pansy beamed, delighted as if she had made the match herself. Neither Laurie nor Chace were aware of the words, only of their hearts beating a trifle faster and a gladness that could ignore cold wind and chilling rain which swept under the leather hood and into the phaeton. Forgotten as a vague bad dream was the episode of the previous evening. Laurie was aware only of Chace's closeness and that she wanted to stay by his side forever.

Having converted to electricity for their more spectacular lighting, the Blue Roof Lodge management distrusted the swaying, fragile lines which connected them to the power station in San Esteban and retained auxilliary lamps and candelabra for cases of emergency. At five o'clock the wind had finally severed the lines, leaving the Lodge in gloom. One by one, the oil lamps were lighted and distributed throughout the hotel. High tea was taken on the glassed-in terrace in semi-dark to the accompaniment of pounding waves and soughing wind. A string trio competed for attention, each player increasing his volume as necessary to compensate for the distraction. By six, early diners began to fill the luxurious dining room, almost as if in defiance of the weather. The string trio became a quintet and shifted to a slightly raised dais in the center of the room, each musician intent on maintaining a hauteur in keeping with the renowned Lodge.

From outside, even in the sporadic rain, twinkling, warm candelight enhanced the baroque building as electricity never could. From both Center Street and Shore Park Drive the dining room was visible, a mecca for those who could afford its hospitality.

Chace handed the little mare to the attendant with a silver coin to see she was properly cared for until he needed her again. He rejoined Laurie on the flat marble steps leading to the cavernous reception room which faced Dumbarton Avenue. The doorman, his resplendent uniform concealed under a black slicker, opened the door for them and touched his cap.

"Evening, Mr. Chace." His smile was genuine when he saw who it was.

"Good evening, Blanchard. Bad night for business?"

"No, sir, not so's anybody'd notice. We've got the usual crowd and then some. Bunch of folks over from San Esteban, I hear tell, come to the musical." Although against the rules of the Lodge to indulge in talk with guests, Len Blanchard defied them long enough to greet Chace after he had swung open the ornate carriage-entrance door to admit them.

"Do you know everybody by name?" Laurie asked as soon as the door shut behind them. She admired a man who could greet even the menial help by their names.

"Until he was hurt in an accident on one of Father's projects over in the valley he was the best cabinet-maker we ever had. He's a fine man. Never asked for a handout, but God knows he could have used one."

"Poor man!" She looked back over her shoulder at the elderly man standing in the drafty entrance. Her quick sympathy brought a smile to the face of her companion. He felt like embracing her on the spot, but instead removed her blue cape and handed it to the girl in the cloak room just inside the door.

Despite a lack of electric power, or perhaps because of it, the Lodge interior assumed the rich glow of an antique court painting. With no indiscreet overhead brilliance, each woman became more beautiful; lines in aging faces disappeared; young ones became exquisite.

Chace looked at Laurie in disbelief as she walked beside him behind the head-waiter. Candlelight so enhanced the gold silk and emphasized the pale ivory-gold of her skin that she seemed to be walking in an aura of her own. The lace fichu enfolded her shoulders and formed a deep decolette in which nestled Roy's yellow roses. In front of her right ear one perfect bloom spread its petals across a black gypsy curl which slanted into the hollow of her cheek. As she moved her head the faceted jet earrings caught the candlelight, their flash dull compared to her black eyes.

Her body reminded Chace of the graceful Spanish dancers who entertained at the annual fiesta, but there was something more than grace in her movement. It was an assured, easy stride devoid of the inhibited, mincing gait most young women thought more ladylike. Nor was there false padding beneath her gown. The high firm breasts and slim hips were unfettered by laces and whalebone. This was to be his woman: natural, free, exciting.

As they entered the dining room, people at tables near the door looked up, nudged one another, forks forgotten in mid-air. By the time the 'Reserved' sign was removed from their table by an immense open fireplace, most of the eyes were riveted upon them. More than a few heads met behind fans as whispered opinions were exchanged. As a scion of the Creightons, Chace was accustomed to such attention, but he was furious that it should now include Laurie Mathews.

"May I recommend the sand-dabs, Mr. Creighton? And the tenderloin of pork is especially good tonight. Or perhaps bay Shrimp Creole?" The waiter hovered solicitously nearby as they studied the menus, his eyes in turn studying the lovely young woman. He had seen her somewhere recently. One doesn't forget such beauty. Ah! Yes! She had the ladies' shop on Birch Street. What a tidbit of gossip to repeat to his wife that night. He refolded the linen napkin on his arm and glanced about. Such a pity Zedekiah and Sybil Creighton were dining with their guests in the main ballroom. It would be worth a day's pay to see their faces.

The fireplace had been stoked with huge oak logs which burned slowly with a fragrant smoke that drifted back in through the ventilation louvers above the windows. Dinner at the Lodge was a leisurely affair, with impeccable service and attention to the minutest detail.

China and silver appeared and were removed so smoothly as to go unnoticed.

"Shall I serve the coffee, sir?" the waiter asked.

"Yes, please." Chace smiled at Laurie across the table. On the dais the string quintet played a Viennese waltz medley, violin and cello alternating in the refrains. They were not listenting to Strauss, however, but to an inner music their two hearts were making. For them there might have been no one else in the entire hotel.

"Happy?" Chace's low voice asked above the waltz.

"Oh, yes!" Laurie breathed. "It's so beautiful here at night. I had no idea it could be so pretty, especially with candlelight.

"Your being here makes it beautiful for me." He reached across the table and covered her hand with his, the light pressure he gave it telling her more than his words. His eyes said he loved her, but no one but Laurie could see their message.

He had always known it would be like this. He would someday see and meet one certain woman and would instantly know it was right to love her. Laurie with her wet skirts and muddy smudges had been a funny, touching girl, but Laurie in a golden gown and yellow roses was the one woman for whom he had been biding his time. It had angered his parents that he would not consider wealthy Amos Striker's granddaughter and thus pave the way to a closer relationship with the Striker railroad empire. Poor Aura Lee, such a plain mouse compared to the dark beauty who sat across from him. Aura Lee would have to look elsewhere for a husband.

The waiter brought a silver coffee service, placed fragile demi-tasse cups on the table, and poured with a flourish. As was customary at the Lodge, the bill would be presented only upon their leaving, thereby enabling guests to linger as long as they chose without feeling they must pay and decamp. Young Creighton and his lady lingered over their coffee until well past ten o'clock, when Chace signaled for his bill. Diners had come and gone and were replaced by others, but none missed the handsome couple sitting at the far end of the room near the fireplace.

"That's old Zed Creighton's boy, isn't it?"

"Who's he with? That certainly is not the Striker girl."

"Bless me if I know. But she's some looker, ain't she?"

"A bit too exotic, if you ask me." Behind their hands the women added, "Doesn't know the first thing about style—just look at that dress!"

But as the girl rose to leave and their men's eyes bent to follow her every movement, they were forced to wonder if it were they who knew nothing of style. Her simplicity, with no high, jeweled dog-collar to distract attention from her face, made most of the women inspect their own toilettes with sudden concern.

The reception hall which ran the width of the first floor was beginning to fill with guests from the grand ballroom. Stifled in the close atmosphere of the mezzanine location, and cramped from sitting throughout the interminable serving, they were taking exercise and air while the hotel staff cleared the dinner service and prepared the room for Rudolfo Ingres' concert. A grand piano, tuned especially for the occasion, had been installed on the musicians' stage and backed by a decorative Oriental screen of extensive dimensions. What quality the screen would lend to the accoustics was debatable, but Sybil Creighton had insisted it be used, regardless of the likelihood of its distorting Ingres' more torrid passages.

As the fashionable invited guests paraded through the hotel, Sybil Creighton led Zedekiah down the carpeted stairs, since they were unable to use the more prosaic but convenient elevator due to the power failure. From where she stood on the first step down, she could view the milling crowd below. With a gasp she urged her husband faster down the steps.

"What the devil's got into you, woman? I can only go so fast with this gouty foot, so don't keep pushing me, damn it!'' Zedekiah was irascible during his wife's social evenings, and the brandy he had consumed following dinner—contrary to his physician's warnings—had loosened his hold on his temper.

"How could he bring that woman here? How could he humiliate me in front of the Strikers?'' Sybil Creighton whispered.

"Who the hell do you mean?'' Zedekiah reached the foot of the stairs and leaned on the fern-crowned newel post. His bulk dictated that he move slowly; his gout necessitated that he move carefully.

"Your son, Chace!'' she spat.

"Careful, woman!'' The old man had turned surly with the brandy. "Every colt's got a dam!'' He cast her a venomous look and started toward the cigar counter by the door of the dining room.

Suddenly he stiffened and grasped his wife's arm, his fingers vise-like on her flesh.

"Zedekiah! What's the matter?'' she asked angrily.

He pointed with one finger, color draining from his leathered face. His entire frame began to tremble as if he were a rag doll shaken by a terrier. Sybil tried to hold him by his massive shoulders, but he slipped from her arms, his knees buckling beneath him.

"Oh, my God!'' Sybil's voice rang above the babble of after-dinner conversation. "Somebody help me!''

"Father!'' Chace ran from the doorway and eased his father to the floor. Quickly he tore off the old man's tie and removed the ruby stud to open the collar and shirt.

"Doc Eichner's upstairs,'' someone said. There was a shiftint of the crush to make way as one of the men dashed to the mezzanine.

"Ask Duncan and Archibald to come down here,'' Sybil ordered.

"Lie still, Father,'' Chace said. "Don't try to talk.'' The old man's mouth was moving in a spasmodic attempt to speak. "Bring me a pillow off one of those couches," his son commanded. As soon as it was tossed to him, he placed it beneath Zedekiah's head.

Doctor Eichner sped down the stairs, the crowd yielding a path for him to the stricken man's side. He was in black evening clothes, and at the sight of Zedekiah began issuing orders quietly. A bell-boy ran to the stable entrance to fetch the medical bag from the doctor's buggy.

"Please stand away, folks! You won't help him any by pressing in like this." He motioned them back with a wave of his arms. He bent beside Chace and briefly examined the old man, smiling reassurance to eyes which could not meet his own. "A little too much excitement, Mr. Creighton?" He kept up a murmur of encouragement, but whispered to Chace to telephone for the hospital ambulance to be brought to the hotel immediately.

Archibald Creighton elbowed his corpulent body roughly through the fringes of the crowd to his mother's side. He glanced at his father, turned to Sybil. "What's happened?"

"I don't know. He was perfectly well until we came down here. Probably too much brandy." Composure had replaced Sybil's panic. She looked about, scanning the faces of those staring down from the mezzanine balcony. "Where's your brother?"

"He just dashed out to get the ambulance," Archibald said.

"Not Chace! I mean Duncan! Where is he?" Sybil asked.

"Last time I saw him he'd abandoned Aura Lee and was back of that screen on the bandstand, getting drunk with that singer of yours," Archibald sniggered. "Seems Duncan located a weakness in Ingress: American bourbon, straight."

"Hasn't he one shred of decency?" Sybil's face was set with fury as she turned to her oldest son. "Get him down here immediately! How must it look to all these people if he refuses to attend his own father?'' She shoved him into action. ''I don't care how you do it, but bring him down here!''

''Yes, Mother.'' Archibald looked down at his father with no sign of compassion. A complete stranger would have elicited more concern on his part. He turned and strode up the wide staircase.

Chace returned and knelt by Zedekiah. ''You'll be all right, Father. A little too much to eat, Doc Eichner says. He wants you to stay overnight at the hospital, just to be on the safe side.'' He took his father's hands in his own and smiled down at him. ''You'll be fine.'' He tried to catch his mother's attention, but her cold disdain repulsed him. He looked back into his father's convulsed face.

With an effort summoning his last reserve of strength, Zedekiah raised his right arm and pointed toward the dining room, his mouth working to form words, but unable to respond to his bidding.

Shocked and bewildered, Laurie had remained on the top step of the restaurant entry which was elevated from the level of the main hall. Near her on the cashier's desk stood a tall silver candelabra, its dozen tapers casting their glow upon her. As a slight current of air disturbed the flames, the gold of the gown shimmered and shadows flickered across the planes of her face, subtly altering the girl's appearance. One slender hand was upraised to her breast, the other clasped a tiny black-beaded reticule. Even as she hesitated, frozen to the spot, she became aware of the turning of heads toward her, eyes searching for the apparition to which Zedekiah Creighton pointed.

Suddenly the old man attempted to raise himself on one elbow, still pointing toward the restaurant doorway.

''Yes, Father, what is it?'' Chace held his father's head in his arms and glanced in the direction he indicated. There standing on the steps above the whispering guests was Laurie, golden gown and yellow roses radiant in the candleglow.

In a voice coming from his own personal hell that sent a chill of horror through his wife, Zedekiah shouted:

"Mellona!"

Chapter 4

Etta Korby leaned over the counter and considered the peacock-blue tulle against the woman's steel-gray hair. She nodded approval and twirled her finger for the woman to turn around. "Let's see the back of it. Oh, yes, that's exactly right for you, Mrs. Larcher."

"I wasn't too sure about the color, but Laurie said it wasn't too strong for my complexion." The woman was tall and heavy in the solid, large-boned build of her pioneer stock. She was not pretty in the usual sense of even, delicate features, but handsome, with a ruddy face and blue eyes which contained undisguised merriment and good nature. She had the sort of disposition which bound friends to her closer by far than would have mere beauty alone. The peculiar blue shade that swathed the crown of the dramatic chapeau brought out the clear blue of her wide-set eyes. She toyed with the gray pearl hat pins that transfixed the huge hat.

"If you decide you can't use the pins, just bring them back." Laurie caught a stray wisp of the woman's hair, twisted it into place and secured it with a heavy tortoise shell hairpin. "I insist you wear them for your Civic Club luncheon today. You can tell us how the voting goes next time you're by. All right?"

"When you put it that way, how can I refuse?" Ethel Larcher was undecided about purchasing the pins after buying the extravagant hat. She took the hand mirror and once again inspected the effect. "No, Hoyt bought himself one of those fancy Masonic rings, and I'll just take these. Tit for tat, you know." Laurie and Etta exchanged amused looks and laughed.

68

"They're real pearls, and a very good price at just three dollars." Laurie refused to pressure her customers, but she was a good saleswoman and knew what was most becoming to them. "You wear them today, regardless. I don't want you to take them unless you're sure."

"No, I've made up my mind!" Mrs. Larcher opened her handbag, withdrew an old-fashioned leather farmer's purse, and took out several bills. "I want to pay you my bill and order some of that new silkateen underwear. I've always worn cotton and wool or silk and wool, but at my time of life the wool is just too warm, even in winter, if you know what I mean." She chuckled and fanned herself with the hand mirror.

"Of course I understand. I'll send the order in today and you should have them a week from Wednesday. Will that be soon enough?" There was nothing Laurie could do to speed up delivery of merchandise from San Francisco, but she felt it necessary to ask all the same.

"Sure, that will be fine. And how much did you say that fancy new long-hip corset was? Erect-Form, I think you called it." Ethel Larcher looked in the full length mirror at her ample figure and sighed. "I have to admit I need one. If I were as nice and slim as you two girls, I'd never wrestle my way into one of the things."

"Number 711, I believe it was..." Laurie consulted the catalog on the lingerie counter. "Yes, 711. It's two dollars."

"Well, you just order it for me and I'll either send Hoyt over for it or stop by myself."

"Thank you, Mrs. Larcher." Laurie took the money, gave silver change, and wrote out a receipt in her accounts book. "Please let us know how the election comes out."

"I will, Laurie. Thank you, Etta. You did a lovely job on the hat. Goodbye, girls." She beamed delight with her purchases and left the boutique.

When she was beyond earshot, Etta turned to Laurie. "She took the pins, too! You said she would."

"She deserves them. And she's looked at them

69

every time she's been in. Mr. Larcher is very generous with her that way." She did not need to add that his butcher shop was prosperous enough to afford his wife her little luxuries.

"I don't blame him. She's a wonderful person," Etta said. "I hope she wins over Mrs. Arvidson today. That Civic Club bunch needs women like Ethel Larcher to give the others a good kick in the rear now and then."

"She really did look lovely. That tulle is the perfect accent for her kersey coat. I'll bet she wins." Laurie closed the drawer where she kept records of her charge accounts and walked to the front window. "I hope it doesn't begin to rain again."

"Funny she didn't mention anything about what happened last night," Etta mused.

"Maybe she didn't feel it was any of her business. She's not much to gossip, you know." Laurie folded her arms and looked across the street where Emmet Lauder was hanging an 'Open for Business' sign in his tailoring shop window.

"I'll wager it's all over Forest Shores by now." Etta paused as she returned to the workroom at the back of the shop. "We really don't need a daily paper here. What do you suppose it meant? I mean the old man obviously thought he saw something. Must have scared him half to death."

"I guess it did," Laurie agreed. "When Chace came by this morning to tell me how his father was he said the stroke had completely paralyzed him. After Mr. Creighton shouted that one word, that was all. He hasn't been able to say anything since, and can't move a muscle."

"Then he can't even write to tell them what he meant?" Etta asked.

"No. Chace says it left him as if he's frightened out of his mind. His eyes roll about his head as if he were in terror."

"And none of them have any idea what it was all about?"

"None." Laurie's reply brought Etta back to face her.

"You can't fool me completely, Laurie. What's the matter? Aren't you telling me the truth?"

"Oh, Etta, it is the truth..."

"Come on, I'm your friend," the tiny seamstress coaxed. "What else?"

"Chace's mother swears it was all my doing!" Laurie sat down on the high stool behind the counter and buried her face in her hands.

"But you had nothing to do with it! You'd never even seen him before! How can she think you're involved?" Etta was furious.

"I don't know. I just don't know!"

"Oh, Laurie, I'm so sorry. It's so unfair! There's something more, isn't there?" Etta could see her employer was terribly upset.

"His mother has forbidden him to see me again, to have anything to do with me!" Laurie burst into tears and rocked on the stool in despair. "Why did this awful thing have to happen? Why?"

Etta Korby ran to Laurie's side and put her arms around her as she would have had it been her own little Fannie weeping. She led Laurie to the back of the store and sat her down on a chair beneath the alley window. "Chace is a big boy, honey. He doesn't have to stop seeing you if he doesn't want to. You know that, don't you?"

"But you don't understand," Laurie protested.

"What don't I understand? You like him—he likes you. And he makes no bones about not getting tangled up with any of those silly society belles his mother is always trying to marry him off to." Etta sat down beside Laurie and took her hands in her own. "Look at me and tell me the rest."

Laurie waited a minute until she felt more in control, then slowly replied, "Mrs. Creighton and Chace had a terrible row last night about me."

"Whatever for?" Etta asked.

"She had invited some girl for Chace to take to that

71

dinner party concert at the Lodge. Chace told her weeks ago he wasn't going, but he says she is so used to having her own way in everything that she thought she'd win this time, too. He flatly refused to go last night, and she had found out—probably through Duncan, the youngest of the boys—that Chace was taking me to dinner. She took it as sheer defiance of her wishes. Then, when his father had a stroke, she insisted it was because he'd seen Chace and me together, as if we were conspiring to humiliate both his mother and the girl Chace was supposed to be with. She blames me for Mr. Creighton's collapse!''

"That's ridiculous!" Etta got up and paced the small room, her face contorted in anger. "She has no right to say such a thing. That old fool has been working hard on a stroke for years—it's a wonder somebody didn't give him one long ago with the business end of a wood ax!" She turned to Laurie and asked, "Chace isn't going to listen to her, is he?"

"He says not, but his mother seems to have the driving hand in the family," Laurie answered. "I feel badly enough about the poor old man having a stroke and being paralyzed like that without being blamed for it myself.''

Etta stared out the window into the alleyway where a delivery wagon for the grocery at the end of the block was jockeying into position at the unloading platform behind the store. Her voice was low as she began, "Don't waste your sympathy on him, Laurie. He is absolutely contemptible, unconscionable. I'm truly surprised he's managed to live this long. If he dies, there are many of us who will celebrate. And his wife is, if anything, worse than he. At least Zedekiah is bold and does his own dirty work, but Sybil Creighton is underhanded and subtle. She uses her friends—like Mrs. Arvidson—even for trivialities.

"Like in the Civic Club election today—the Creightons, for some reason of their own, want to have control of the Club. Probably something Archibald's promoting. So Sybil pushed her friend, Mrs. Arvidson for the presidency. That's why I hope Ethel Larcher wins.

"Don't underestimate Sybil Ceighton. She's vicious. And she's determined to have her way or else. You don't realize yet how powerful a hold such people have in a place like this." She turned and grasped Laurie's shoulders and looked squarely at her. "If your Chace asks you to marry him, do it right away. Don't wait for anything—not if he's the man for you. Don't give his mother the opportunity to wreck things between you."

Laurie put down the teacup and brushed ravelings from her gray business dress. The shop door had opened and closed, and in the angled glass which allowed anyone in the workroom to see who entered the front of the shop she discerned Mrs. Arvidson. Her great maroon melton cloth coat filled the tilted mirror with an imperious summons.

"Yes, Mrs. Arvidson. May I help you?" Laurie forced herself to sound delightful with the woman's presence. And in her hope that she might pay her outstanding balance she was, indeed, glad to see her.

"You have my glove order from San Francisco? And the mantilla?" She sounded as if she would welcome a negative answer.

It was difficult for either Etta or Laurie to picture Mrs. Arvidson wearing the delicate black lace head-covering, but the fiesta brought many incongruous Yankees attired in colorful Spanish or Mexican costumes.

"Yes, they came in by express several days ago," Laurie said.

"I should have thought you'd notify me." It was useless to remind her she had sent a postcard to inform her of their arrival.

"Would you like to take them with you, or shall I have them delivered to your home?" Laurie fished below the counter and brought out the gloves and ethereal wisp of silk lace.

73

"Now that I'm here, I'll take them with me." The woman strolled about the shop fingering the silk flowers and shawl fabrics, her ferret eyes darting nervously, searching for anything unusual and unique with which she might adorn herself for the coming festival. "You heard of last night's tragedy, of course?"

"You mean Mr. Creighton?" Laurie doubted there could have been more than one tragedy the previous night which would be of enough interest to Mrs. Arvidson that she would mention it to a mere shop girl.

"Yes." Cunning crept into her expression, none too flattering in her wide, heavy face. "Terrible thing. Simply terrible. Such a blow to the entire community. And dear Sybil..." she lingered over the phrase so Laurie would not miss the implication of her association with the wealthy Creightons, "...dear Sybil is beside herself with grief."

Then why had she not been at her husband's side, consoling the old man, instead of the son he so thoroughly detested playing the role of comforter? Laurie longed to ask the question, but kept her face averted and said nothing.

"I asked Sybil if we should continue with the plans for the fiesta this weekend, thinking it only proper we cancel them. After all, Mr. Creighton *is* the fiesta!" Mrs. Arvidson wanted there to be no doubt that she was on intimate terms with the family. Laurie found it amusing to think of Zedekiah as a fiesta—perhaps a day of atonement or penance, but not a fiesta surely. "But she, brave woman that she is, insists we carry on."

"How splendid of her, especially at a time like this," Laurie said.

"Of course it is our one gala occasion of the year. People attend from San Francisco, even from Santa Barbara and Los Angeles." Holding a mirror which enabled her to observe Laurie inconspicuously, Mrs. Arvidson continued, "I don't suppose you will be going. Most newcomers aren't too interested in our fund raising events."

"Oh, but I am. I'm quite looking forward to it,"

74

Laurie replied.

The look of reproval on her customer's face told Laurie she should not have divulged the fact. She had made another of her many mistakes.

"How very nice." The eyes narrowed and lips pursed in speculation. Laurie was certain the woman had come to the shop only to garner what information she could and then repeat it to Sybil Creighton.

When the woman had gone Etta Korby ran from the workroom and hugged Laurie. "I saw it all! How wonderful! Oh, the look on that smug face of hers!" She danced around the boutique in a jaunty two-step of glee. "You so deflated her she'll have to stop by the bicycle shop for a pump-up!" Delight shone in Etta's eyes. "And did you notice she was wearing a plain cloth coat—no furs or diadems today? She really wants to win that election! I'm glad she didn't buy that coat in here. And that flowered hat! Ethel Larcher will win. I just know she will when they compare those two."

"It was one of my better *faux pas*. I should never have said I was going," Laurie said. "No telling what she'll make of it now. And she'll run straight to Sybil Creighton with it."

"Yes, you should have told her. And I notice she didn't pay her bill or pay for the gloves and mantilla. Honestly!" Etta's disgust was as evident as had been her joy. "What are you going to wear? It's just got to be better than what she is going to show up in. Imagine her in a mantilla and flowered shawl!"

"I haven't any idea what to wear. Chace just asked me Saturday night and I didn't take him seriously. Then last night he said he was taking me and I said I'd go, and this is only Monday." She sat on the stool behind the counter. "Oh, Etta, what shall I do? What am I to wear? I hadn't thought about it at all. Maybe I'd better not go."

"You go! Even if you have to go in regular everyday clothes! You've got to. Old Lady Arvidson..." Laurie shot a look of disapproval at Etta, but she continued, "...and Sybil Creighton shouldn't be allowed to run everything their own way. You'll go and dazzle the daylights out of 'em!''

Pansy Hinshaw stepped to the door of the kitchen and glanced into the dining room, satisfying herself that none of her ladies were near. Before opening the cooler door she also made sure Roy Wimbish was not on the threshold of the porch. The slatted, shelved box squeaked up from its cool, tin-lined cavity below ground. She must ask Roy to grease the pulley and gears. The old woman fastened the chain on a small iron hook, reached into the cage and pushed aside the butter dish and pail of cream. Behind a joint of cold roast lamb were several tall bottles. Taking one and placing it on the white-tiled counter, she smiled.

Adam would surely understand, she told herself as she cranked down the cage and shut the door. And since Guido Ferranti charged so little for the sauterne, Pansy did not feel she was being too extravagant. It came to him in huge barrels, so he could afford to charge less. He had told her so. The transaction had been a ritual with them for a good many years, ever since he opened the Shell Box Cafe in Sand Town. Mrs. Hinshaw saw nothing unusual in the fact that she was the only customer Guido would accommodate in such fashion. She sent her bottles to him for filling, and back they would come, filled and stoppered. It never occurred to her that wine was never bottled in such a way, nor that Roy Wimbish delivered a cord of wood to Guido now and then to make up the difference.

It was a great comfort, the pale sauterne. She twisted out the corkscrew and before returning it to the drawer poured a fragile lead crystal wine goblet full to the brim.

To Pansy it was worth pretending that no one was aware of her predilection for sauterne. She thus maintained pride and dignity, and still enjoyed the relaxing, warm glow that followed a glass or two of Guido's wine. Sipping slowly, she felt more placid as she contemplated the dark, dripping grove of giant pines across

76

Shore Park Drive to the west.

Even on a sunny day, when the Drive was busy with tradesmen and carriages, the aspect was far more formidable than inviting. These several hundred acres of virgin forest marked the eastern boundaries of Mariposa Ranch. A mile beyond the corner where her home stood, a white graveled road cut through the trees for yet another mile to where Zedekiah Creighton's massive, out-of-place mansion reared its gables three stories high, but still was dwarfed by the surrounding pine forest.

Since coming to California in 1849 during the gold rush, Pansy had felt ill at ease with the dark, brooding woods of the Pacific Coast which were so unlike the lovely hardwood forests of her more civilized New England. Adam Hinshaw had not been interested in the mad rush to the mines, but had established himself as a builder of solid, practical homes to house the survivors and victors. When in 1850 California had been admitted to the Union, he was busy earning for himself the reputation of master-craftsman and dependable builder.

The ensuing years had not lessened Pansy's fears of the gloomy, primeval acres toward which she must look from her kitchen and dining room. She had accepted them as part of living in still-strange Forest Shores, but held them in no affection.

"If only Adam were here to tell me what to do!" Pansy sighed aloud.

She poured at bit more sauterne into the goblet and crossed through the dining room to the music room with its high ceiling and bayed alcove for the piano. She ran one finger along the keys, struck a few chords and stood looking at the forest from the west window.

Pansy found she could talk to her husband and ask his advice if she put thoughts of everything else from her mind. Not that she ever really heard his answer, but if she closed her eyes she could still see his laughing face, his eyes twinkling with his jokes and pranks. She refused to remember how he looked when Zedekiah Creighton had brought him home the day of the accident. Zedekiah had wept and held Adam in his arms until he had drawn his last breath. Long ago she had stopped asking Zedekiah Creighton for advice and turned instead to her Adam. Somehow the answers came, and they were always right for Pansy, as with her turning their lovely home into an apartment house for ladies.

"Laurie's in love with Chace," she said aloud. "I can tell, Adam. It's just like when we were young together. Only Sybil will do something. I know she will. She's set on having her way with all her men-folk, even if she ruins them. Just look at what she's done to little Duncan already."

Picking up the hem of her skirts she slid onto the swivel-topped piano stool and arranged several selections of sheet music on the elaborate cherrywood rack above the keyboard. With a trill and flourish she began the introduction to 'Clorinda,' a spritely new march two-step. Tossing boughs outside the window caught her eye once more. She stopped in the middle of the melody and stood near the glass of the west window.

"Adam, something dreadful is going to happen and I can't stop it. I think it's already beginning, and I don't know what to do."

Laurie came up the steps and onto the veranda. Mrs. Hinshaw was playing the piano in the music room, her parlor door open to the stairs. Laurie glanced toward the open door, but called no greeting to the elderly woman for fear it would disturb her.

She walked quickly up the steps, pushed open her own door and placed her parcels on the table. In a moment she had lighted the oil lamp and sat down to remove her wet boots.

The lamp shed meager light over the large room. Corners remained black splotches, as if the gloom of the storm had begun to creep into the house and fill up around the edges. Laurie unwound the heavy knitted shawl and draped it over the back of the chair. She was cold and wondered if there would be any hot water left for her to take a tub bath before she prepared dinner.

The room was cold, but she filled the tea kettle and put it on to boil before she lighted the kerosene heater. For some minutes she stood before the heat, turning about until she felt warmth penetrating her chilled flesh.

After making a cup of tea she pulled the shades down and undressed before the blue flame of the oil burner, dropping everything into a heap on the floor. From the miniature cupboard beneath the two-burner kitchen stove she took the bottle of sherry she had been hoarding for a special occasion. Into her empty tea cup she poured the amber fluid and held it to her nose, sniffing the sweet, nutty bouquet. She warmed her plush robe before the heater, then wrapped herself in it, grateful for its warmth. She tasted the sherry from the cup and sat down.

From the hall below came the sound of the front door and Thea's loud greeting to Mrs. Hinshaw. Laurie felt a flood of relief at the sound of her cheerful voice. She waited until she heard footsteps coming up the broad stairs, then opened the door as Thea reached the landing.

"Hello!" Thea's face had the ruddy glow of her walk home from the drug store. "You're home a bit early, aren't you?"

"Etta closed the shop for me tonight. She had to wait to pick up Fannie anyhow." Laurie was not good at hiding her emotions.

"Hey, what's the matter?" Thea stood just inside the door, her dripping clothes plastered close to her lean frame. "You have another bad day at the shop?" She knew her friend well enough to recognize the signs.

"No, not really. . ." Laurie replied.

"Why not come over to my room and I'll fix us something to eat?" Thea held out a meat package. "I brought some round steak and if I hammer it hard enough, it won't be too tough." She saw the sherry bottle on the sink by the stove. "Or do you want to be alone?"

"Goodness, no! Not alone!" Laurie laughed as she realized her face must be downcast and somber indeed to worry Thea. "Tell you what: let's get Olive and pool our stuff and eat in here. That way I can get your ideas about the fiesta."

"Sure! Sounds great!" Thea dropped her meat onto the table and turned to go. "I've got to get out of these wet things before I get pneumonia, but I'll be right back. Is Olive home yet?"

"I think so, but I haven't heard her rattling any pans yet so I know she hasn't begun her dinner. I'll go ask her." Already Laurie felt better. Worry shared, she knew, was lighter.

Thea read the signs all too well. The Ribands and Roses was not proving as profitable as the previous owner had claimed it would be. Laurie had invested every cent she had in the shop, but since the summer rush, receipts kept dwindling at an alarming rate. Knut Jepsen had told Thea the gossip about Zedekiah Creighton's stroke the night before, that Sybil had blamed it on Laurie's rendezvous with Chase. With both worries on her mind, Laurie had good reason to be downcast. Thea thrust her feet into ugly felt slippers which cuddled her toes in high-cuffed comfort, then pulled her robe over her petticoat and camisole. Chances were that it would be another long evening for the girls.

"Then you still think it's best to wait and see what happens this winter? Give it until summer at least, or until the money runs out, whichever comes first?" Laurie buttered the heel of her loaf of rye bread and nibbled at it.

"Absolutely! It isn't as if you couldn't recoup your losses. If you were fifty years old, I'd say to heck with it," Thea said. "Cut your losses now, and get out if that were the case. But after all, you can always go to San Esteban or somewhere and get work. You're only twenty-three. If you fail, you fail honorably. But it wouldn't be insurmountable. Besides, you may be able to turn the shop around and get it going again. Christmas will be a big retail season."

"I guess that's what I wanted to hear." Laurie dunked her crust in the coffee. "I'd almost made up my mind to stick it out after our conference last Saturday night, but with what's happened now, I wondered if I should just quit and avoid a lot of unpleasantness."

"It's depressing, but don't let it get you down. Remember, if they weren't gossiping about you, it would be someone else." Olive stirred sugar into her second cup of coffee. "Even the principal at school had heard about Mr. Creighton."

Thea sprawled before the fireplace which was just beginning to blaze. The pine chunks snapped as flame exploded tiny pockets of resin within the fiber and sent showers of bright sparks to bounce off the mesh curtain. "And you've got to give the town a chance, too. Mrs. Larcher, Mrs. Hobart, they're already good customers. And lots of girls from Mariposa Beach. . ."

"You are going to the fiesta, aren't you? You aren't going to back out of it now, are you?" Olive had been delighted to hear of Mrs. Arvidson's deflation. "I have to be there, and Thea's promised to help at our booth. We want to see you go just to shame them all."

"But what am I to wear? You said you two are just wearing nurses' pinafores and caps, but I haven't a thing that I can make look Spanish. And I certainly can't afford to rent a costume."

"If we weren't selling chicken and sandwiches for the Well Baby Clinic we'd have to come up with costumes, too." Olive took her drink and went to the leather chair by the fire. "On my pay I couldn't afford. . ." She stopped in mid-sentence as a hesitant knock sounded at the door, bringing Thea to a sitting position.

"Come in. It's open." Laurie was too comfortable to get up and go to the door. Besides, none of the tenants were so formal that one had to meet them at the door with deliberate protocol.

"I just came up to see if you might still be interested in those old crates and trunks up in the attic, Laurie." Mrs. Hinshaw was apparently well into the bottle of sauterne she kept open on the kitchen counter. It was evident that she had been in the throes of making an important decision. "I had Roy tidy up the attic in case you might want to take a look at them." She was so pitifully hopeful Laurie had no heart to refuse her.

"That would be lovely, Mrs. Hinshaw. Yes, I'd like to have a peek at the things." Laurie pulled her overstuffed chair from under the window and placed it before the fireplace opposite the Turkish leather. "Here, sit down and have a glass of sherry. And thank you for the firewood. This is certainly the weather for it."

"Is this from that old dead limb out back? The one Roy was going to cut up?" Thea moved so the heat from the fire would reach the elderly woman.

"Yes, he finally got around to cutting and stacking it between showers today," Mrs. Hinshaw said. "He kept a tarpaulin over it so it wouldn't get wet." She sat primly upright, her back hardly resting against the chair. After all, these were tenants who paid for privacy, and she did not want to intrude. She insisted upon respecting that privacy. What most of the ladies regarded as her delicacy was, in fact, timidity. She had been raised a lady, and even after decades of taking paying guests into her home was still unsure of herself in their presence. "I think a nice open fire is a comfort in such weather. Mr. Hinshaw insisted each bedroom have a nice big fireplace when he built the house." She said it with pride, as if his decision were laudable and worthy of comment even now.

"He must have been a fine builder, Mrs. Hinshaw." Thea knew the old woman liked to hear her dead husband praised.

"He was indeed. But, my dears, I know I've told you all about Adam many times before." She smiled at her frail memory. "Mustn't bore you young things with past history. We must all look to the present and future." She squared her thin shoulders and sat more upright than ever. "Now, Laurie, since you mentioned wanting to buy up antique silks, old lace, beads—that

82

sort of thing—for your shop, I've made up my mind about all that collection in the attic."

"Are you sure now, Mrs. Hinshaw? I don't want you to give up anything that might have value for you, or that you might regret not keeping." Laurie's eyes sparkled with anticipation, but she wanted to make certain the old lady would not be sorry later.

"Why, child, I'm getting much too old to hang onto all that much longer. After all," she continued with a touch of archness, "I'm sixty-six, and not getting younger."

"I had no idea!" Thea lied so beautifully that the woman fairly glowed, although both knew they were playing a game. Thea was aware Pansy was well past seventy.

"If you're sure. . ." Laurie began.

"Oh, yes. Definitely," Pansy Hinshaw insisted. "Some of those boxes and trunks haven't been touched in over thirty years. Not since a while after Adam and I moved here. If I haven't looked at them, much less used anything in them, why on earth should I want to keep them?" She tasted her sherry and smiled as the wine warmed her throat. It was not an expensive sherry, but it was good. Its higher alcoholic content, she knew, was apt to make her a bit tiddly.

Tonight, however, Pansy did not mind getting tiddly, for she was doing something quite daring: she was determined to let Laurie Mathews have the old things in the attic. She adored her girls, with their young good looks and honest, quiet ways, so unlike a few of the tenants she had had to ask to leave over the years. Laurie needed antique and quaint items for her shop and she was welcome to them. Pansy hoped it would serve an altogether different purpose also, but she rationalized that it would help clear old things from the house preparatory to selling it. She had to admit to herself that the time was coming soon when she must think seriously about selling to the Civic Club. Property values were escalating and taxes increasing yearly. Yes, it was fitting that she should begin with the attic.

"I don't have much cash right now, but I can go to the bank tomorrow. . ." Laurie began.

Pansy held up her hand to stop the girl. "You can pay me whenever you want to. I'm not even certain there will be much you can use. My goodness, I trust you! And you're the one who's taking the chance."

"Thank you," Laurie said. "I'll go to the bank tomorrow though; I don't like owing anybody. It's a bad way to do business."

The elderly woman sank back into the chair. Now she had sold some of Adam's trunks, but perhaps he would understand it was the only way. "All right, if you insist," Pansy agreed. Roy, she knew, could use the money tomorrow, for she had promised him a few dollars extra for cleaning the attic.

"Good, that's settled then!" Thea was fond of the old lady and cognizant of the wounded pride which had agreed to accept money for hoarded mementos. "I'm anxious to see what's packed away up there. Can we go up tonight?"

"Yes, I had Roy put out clean newspapers on the floor and a stool to set your lamp on," Pansy replied. "I know Laurie wants to have a lot of pretty things ready for Christmas gifts before the year-end tourists come. That's the biggest time of the year here, after the summer season, of course."

She placed her glass on the marble-topped table after finishing the last sip. "Two trunks are old things of mine, from a good many years ago, from before Mr. Hinshaw's. . .passing."

It was difficult for her to say, but easier than admitting that she could not afford to store away clothing after he died. Indeed, she was still wearing and using garments that were out of date decades before, each one worn and remodeled until it could in good conscience be discarded. Not that she had not wanted to utilize some of the fine silks and linens packed in the attic, but she could not bear to go through the remnants of younger, happier years. Thirty years later her grief was still too near the surface to chance rummaging in the attic.

"And the crates have odds and ends, books, photos, nothing valuable, just little sentimental trinkets I couldn't bear to part with. There simply wasn't room for it all when I began to take in renters." Pansy fished in her apron pocket and handed Laurie a small filigreed brass key two inches long. "This is for the enormous camel-back trunk, the one bound in brass and fancy nail heads. Adam made me promise I'd not go through it as long as he lived, and I never did."

Her old eyes had a far-away expression which was not from sherry or sauterne. She shrugged as if physically shaking off a memory. "Now you run along and have fun. I do so hope you'll find something nice you can use. Roy says when you want anything brought down just let him know and he'll handle it for you. He thinks with our skirts it isn't safe to be trying to carry things up and down those attic steps. And we must humor him, mustn't we?"

"That's very kind of him, but I think we can manage," Laurie said. She knew the steps were more difficult for Roy at his age than he would like to admit. "Thank you again."

Thea unfolded herself from before the fire and rose as Mrs. Hinshaw went to the door. "If Laurie needs any help I'll run over and get Roy. I promise."

"If you can't use any of it, I won't hold you to our bargain." Pansy felt happily giddy and grasped the stair rail firmly before she carefully took the first step down. "Let me know how you do with it."

"I shall." Laurie held the key in the palm of her hand, but waited until she was certain the woman was safely down the steps and had disappeared into her own quarters on the west side of the house.

"Poor old thing!" Thea said. "That cost her a lot—deciding to get rid of part of her past." She was not the sort of girl to give way to sentimentality, but there was an ache in her heart for the old woman. Thea had seen the dissolution of her own family treasures as poverty forced their sale, one by one, until with the last silver heirloom, her mother had lost her will to live.

"I know. Isn't it sad?" Olive said. They waited until they heard the downstairs parlor door close, then took the lamp and a candle by which to make their way along the second floor hall and up the attic stairs.

The old house boasted woodwork of finest redwood and stair treads of heavy oak slabs with brass lips. Wainscoating extended a yard high, even up the stairwell to the attic. At the top of the steps a thick, paneled door of solid redwood swung inward, opening into a huge, fully finished storage room. Diamond-paned windows were tucked into triangles beneath the sharp-angled gables, and several massive brick chimneys lofted through from floors below. There was little of the mustiness of most such places in the Hinshaw attic, for periodically it was cleaned and aired, with its walls getting a coat of whitewash every six years or so. Roy Wimbish, not too keen of intellect, but a conscientious worker, took his jobs seriously.

"This sure doesn't look like most attics. See how clean it is." Thea was amazed as Laurie shone the lamp about. Neatly arranged along one wall were several pieces of leather-strapped luggage of varying sizes, a collection of wooden storage crates, and one huge camel-back trunk. These were set aside from the tenants' belongings which were stored only temporarily, and placed at the far end.

"These must be the ones, here by the chimney." Olive led the way, with the candle making her shadow a grotesque specter.

"Aren't you excited?" Thea could hardly wait for Laurie to unlock the trunk and delve into it. "Why on earth would her husband forbid her to look inside it? A bit like Pandora's box? Maybe she'd find something she wouldn't like."

"Remember he didn't exactly forbid her. Pretty sly, wasn't he? Getting Pansy to promise she wouldn't open it, but not forbidding it forever. He must have known how the feminine mind works." Olive placed her candle on a set-off of the chimney.

"All I can say is she had a lot more will power than

I'd have," Thea laughed.

"I guess she loved him enough to keep her promise, even after he died," Laurie said.

"Or she knew—or guessed—what must be in it and didn't want to have anything to do with it. That would make sense." Olive looked askance at the massive chest.

Although she had been joking moments before about its contents, Laurie shivered as she looked at the impressive humped trunk. Intuition now caused her to fear what might lie within. She inspected the ornate brass lock. With a physical effort Laurie dismissed the feeling, attributing it to too much worry and morbid imagination. "Be that as it may, let's leave it till last," she said. "Mrs. Hinshaw says there's material and lace in these others, and we don't know what's in this one. My curiosity can wait."

"How can you?" Thea was dismayed; her own inquisitiveness could not be so easily contained.

"I need a lot of holiday merchandise and the silk and lace will make a lot of dog-collars and jabots! That's what I need most. Etta Korby agreed to work at home on gift items as soon as I round up a batch of unusual materials to work with." Laurie tugged at a wooden crate top, surprised at the weight. "I should have begun this a long time ago, but I kept thinking business would pick up and I'd have enough money to order ready-made things." She placed the lid against the wall.

Inside, the box had been lined with thick cardboard which was tacked to the sides, making a serviceable, fairly tight packing case. On top were several thicknesses of newspaper, and an old muslin sheet tucked in to protect the contents.

"Look at the dates on the papers—1873!" Thea placed the fragile papers on top of one of the trunks and rummaged in the neatly folded clothing. "Oh, look at this!" The hat she held up was of pale gray faille trimmed with rose satin and fluffy pink ostrich feathers, some of which had deteriorated to thin spines. "It's darling—and look at this one. . ."

For an hour they pored over garments and pieces of material, holding up to themselves dainty, tight-bodiced, full-skirted creations with ruffled and gathered trimming. There were a few modish dinner gowns with low necklines and dropped shoulders. In a separate box were pairs of delicate slippers dyed to match what must have been party finery.

"Laurie, this may be silver." Olive held up a small bundle and laid aside the linen hand towel that wrapped it. Unfolding the tissue paper, she displayed a beaded and tassled handbag. The silver clasp and frame were blackened with age, but the tiny rhinestones set into the metal sparkled in the yellow light.

"I'd bet that's worth what you agreed to pay Mrs. Hinshaw. Is it real silver?" Thea took the bag close to the lamp, then handed it to Laurie.

"I can't tell for sure, but it looks like it. The mark will be inside somewhere." Laurie snapped it open to reveal a moiré lining of silver-gray. "In this light I can't read the mark. I'll have to look at it downstairs with a magnifying lens. I simply can't read such fine print."

"It's hardly been used." Thea thought it sad that Pansy had not worn it out by use, but of course her years with Adam had been spent in what amounted to a frontier village. Neither San Esteban nor Forest Shores would have afforded many opportunities to wear her lovely gowns and carry the dainty reticule.

"You struck a good bargain, girl." Thea was thinking in dollars and cents. Laurie needed odd and out-of-the-ordinary accessories for her boutique, and if the rest of the stored belongings proved as nice as the first few crates, she would have a storeful by the busy holiday weekend. Beaded and metallic braid collars and cuffs alone would pay half a month's rent on the shop. San Francisco vacationers haunted the unique shops of Forest Shores for the quaint and unusual. Laurie felt if she had good holiday business and could continue on until next summer her worries would be over.

Thea Harris shivered. Wind was buffeting the old

house and howling about its gingerbread ornaments. The brick flue beside the trunks and crates moaned as down-drafts passed through its red tile chimney pots. "Why don't we take all this downstairs where it's warmer?" she asked.

"I'd appreciate that," Laurie said. "Just put it anywhere in my room. I'll sort it out later. You might bring up my laundry basket for the little things. You know where I keep it, don't you?"

"Yes, I'll bring it up right away." Thea loaded her arms while Olive bundled smaller items into an old muslin sheet so she would have one free hand to hold the candle.

"I'll put another piece of wood on the fire, providing it hasn't burned out already. You know how fast that pine goes. Anything you want me to bring back up?" Olive tested the strength of the time-yellowed sheet, then took the candlestick from the brick off-set.

"No, but perhaps you could tell Mrs. Hinshaw that I'm getting my money's worth." She grinned as they looked wistfully at the unopened trunk. "Never fear, we'll get around to that one, too. Mind your step going down!"

When they were gone, the sound of the storm seemed to increase. Forest Shores, sitting on a slender peninsula which jutted northwest to form the southern shore of Gutierrez Bay, caught the full brunt of storms. Weathered, gnarled pine and beach cypress twisted landward in resignation to the fierce blasts. Wild, turbulent and dangerous, the coast was strewn with knife-sharp upthrusts of rock, its very inhospitableness to marine traffic making it all the more attractive to resident and tourist alike. Only homes as solidly built as the old Hinshaw place could withstand many decades of such onslaught.

Laurie looked up in alarm as an unusually vehement burst of wind shook the old house, pried at the roof and high triangular windows, and shrieked in frustration about eaves and tall chimneys. She shivered and turned her attention to the trunk. She fitted the filagreed key into the lock and threw back the humped lid. Newspapers were spread across the contents and tucked haphazardly down over bulkier objects resting near the top. She noted their dates: September 15, 1871. It had been over thirty years since someone had placed them there and slammed shut the lid. No one in all that time had opened the trunk, not even in curiosity. Why?

A cotton flannel sheet blanket covered the contents below the papers, its corners discolored with time and smelling vaguely musty. Laurie lifted the blanket. Beneath it shimmered rich gold silk, its luster and sheen undimmed by three decades. As she lifted the material an odor was noticeable, not the mustiness of storage, nor of camphor crystals and cedar chips, but a faint, elusive perfume. She held the silk to her nose and breathed its fragrance, then shook the garment loose and inspected it closely near the lamp.

The dress was long and flowing, of an intermingled gold and yellow as if the colors were washed across each other, blending and rippling in wide banks. Sleeves were wide and deep-set, with seams and edges piped in rich brown velvet cord. Striking chevron bands of brown velvet were bowed at their angles. It appeared to be more costume than ordinary dress, with hem falling to the floor in whispering folds, and a train, stiffened with a protective linen lining, cascading in tiers of ruffles. She laid the magnificent gown aside, taking great care to see it remained on the clean papers spread by the chimney, then returned to the trunk.

There were thin, silk-bound illustrated volumes of French and English poetry: Wilde, Browning, Hugo, Gautier. A toilet set made from satin-glass of the same peculiar shade of gold was packed in a flat box, the pieces wrapped in lace-trimmed undergarments. From the powder bowl sifted talcum dust, still faintly scented with lilac and violet.

In the silver-backed comb and brush were several strands of long, wavy dark hair. The satin-glass hair receiver contained combings, the color still as luxuriant black as the day they were placed there. A small, heavy, stoppered bottle had candle wax dripped about its edges. Inside was an amber-brown fluid stain. She held it to her nose. It smelled of lush blooming flowers—the same scent as the gown.

In another box was a jumble of photographs and tintypes, most of them turned dark with the years, and a handful of letters, some tied with ribbons, as if a woman's hand had fixed the dainty bows to signify their sentimental importance. There were other plainer dresses, but of the same luminous shade of gold, and petticoats, stockings, camisoles, and warm woolen undervests. At the bottom, as if hurriedly folded and tossed into the trunk with no thought of its being used again, was a full-length, deep brown and black banded cloak of heavy velvet with silk cord ties at the throat. Cedar chips between sheets of paper still retained their resinous scent, but the cape smelled of roses and lilies, and sweet wild broom.

At the sound of steps on the attic stairs she turned her attention once more to the collected pile atop the crate, but her eyes were drawn to the shimmering gold silk.

"I'm going to bed. I'll have to leave you to your treasures, Laurie. I have to be one step ahead of my seven-year-olds and I need my sleep." Olive whispered in consideration of the others ladies who had long since retired.

"All right, thank you for helping," Laurie said.

"It was fun!" Thea fingered a piece of scarlet silk.

"I want you both to pick out something nice for yourselves. If you have the time, maybe tomorrow," Laurie said.

"Fine. I had my eye on that piece of tan lace with the satin cording," Olive said hopefully.

"It's yours!" Laurie started toward the bed to locate the lace.

"No, don't try to find it now. It's much too late," Olive protested. "Goodnight."

Thea rubbed her eyes and yawned. She should be in

bed, too, for it was almost midnight. Jepsen's Pharmacy opened at seven. "I'll come over and see if I can help with any of the stuff, but I warn you, I'm simply awful with a needle." She stretched, and went to the door. "Goodnight, Laurie."

When they had tip-toed out, Laurie closed her door softly. Alone now, she returned to inspecting her hoard. Etta Korby would have a busy two weeks, but between them they would have a number of attractive and unusual items to present to their customers in time for the holiday party season.

Always her glance returned to the gold dress. She had barely looked at the letters in the trunk, feeling it somehow ill-mannered even after thirty years to read another person's correspondence. She had not bothered to bring down either letters or photographs, and intended asking Mrs. Hinshaw what she wished done with them. They were, after all, private.

"I could wear that dress to the fiesta," she mused. "If it fits me, I can air it out and press it. I have a few black mantillas still in stock, and Thea said her cousin would lend me one of her high combs." She tried to picture how her costume would look, for the idea of using the gold silk suddenly seemed exciting.

She cleared her bed of the accumulated pile of material and trimmings, and turned back the puffy comforter. Before she donned her batiste nightgown she held the silk dress up to her. She wa not at all sure that it was only the cold surface of the material that caused her skin to prickle into gooseflesh. She flung the garment to the floor as if it had been a live thing.

In the mirror over the dresser she could see her image as only a darkened silhouette. She moved the lamp to a stand beside the full length mirror recessed into one door of the large walnut wardrobe. Overcoming her fear, she picked up the golden gown. Once more she held the silk dress up to her. She was not at all sure that it in every seam and ruffle.

She seemed to know every feature of the gown. As if to refresh her memory, she stepped into it and pulled

92

it up about her body, then fastened the front closing of small, fabric-covered buttons and corded loops.

Turning about so lamplight fell fully across the gown, she was amazed at the precise fit of the tiny waist and high bust. Had it been sewn expressly for her, it could not have fit more perfectly. Like a small girl in her first party dress she turned and gestured, testing the fit of the sleeves and shoulder line. As she moved, a piece of paper fluttered to the floor from an inseam pocket of the skirt. Unnoticed, the paper lay beneath her foot.

She smiled at herself in the mirror and made her decision. "This is what I'll wear to the fiesta!"

It did fit well, and with proper accessories would be unusual enough to pass for a Spanish costume. Her thoughts raced ahead as she pictured herself on Chace's arm, listening to strolling musicians and perhaps pirouetting in one of the quaint, old-fashioned dances.

Her eye caught the flicker of white beneath the long train, and bending to pick it up, just for the merest instant, she saw from the corner of her eye a glimmer of movement in the mirror—movement other than her own. Automatically rejecting it as a fantasy of the light in the faulty old mirror, she retrieved the slip of paper.

Strange, spidery handwriting, the type taught decades ago, covered the stiff, parchment-like stationery, while at the top was a small ornamental embossed heading of black and red.

"What in the world?" Laurie held it to the lamp light. The ink was faded to brown and the edges aged a faint, mottled buff. She had trouble deciphering the flourishes:

'Dear Madam:

Mr. Renan has instructed me to inform you of his acceptance of seventy canvasses from your group presentation. He has taken the liberty, feeling there would be no objection on the part of your artists, of allowing certain of the gallery's patrons to view these works prior to the formal opening of the exhibit. By today's post he is sending several

*drafts covering sales of various paintings. He
will send them in your care knowing you will
distribute them personally to the members of
your group. Please be informed that the salon
will present the exhibition from October first
through mid-November, terms and rates as
agreed upon.*

     Best person regards,
     Burton Lynch.'

Written in a different hand at a slant across the bottom of the sheet was an illegible inscription in French and the bold signature, 'Etienne Renan' and the date, 17 September 1871.

Laurie held the printed heading to the light and attempted to read its extremely fine print. "Where are those tiny gold-wire spectacles Olive found tucked away in the trunk?" Laurie rummaged through the contents of the old muslin sheet before the fireplace. A glint of gold sparkled between several pieces of Venetian lace.

She polished the small lenses with the hem of her nightgown which was draped on the arm of the Turkish leather chair, then fixed the wires over her ears and settled the narrow, shell-tipped nosepiece into place.

All else but the note was out of focus. She held it to the lamp and read the heading: Etienne Renan Galleries, Salon: 630 Longchamps Boulevard, San Francisco. In even finer print appeared: Associate Galleries in Fresno, Los Angeles, Santa Barbara, and Forest Shores.

Forest Shores! It might be another piece of the puzzle, but she had no inkling of how it would fit. She put the note aside. Tomorrow perhaps she could learn more from it.

Laurie yawned and began to unbutton the dress. With the glasses still perched on her nose, she stumbled over the gold silk train. As she caught herself on the settee, she glimpsed her reflection in the wardrobe mirror.

For the sane instant she first saw it, she reasoned it was another trick of the poor lamplight and the faulty, crackled mirror. But as she looked again, neither light nor mirror could create the illusion that confronted her.

In the recesses of her memory she recalled the arrogant set of the head, the defiant thrust of the shoulders, the circlet of gold in the black hair.

Once before. . .on the train. . .

She tore off the dress, never knowing how she managed to unbutton it from her trembling body. Quickly she drew the nightgown over her head and stood before the fire, shivering. The coals were glowing red in the grate, with a bed of ash below, but she could feel no comfort from their heat.

"I must be mad!"

As if to bring herself back from the brink of lunacy, she quietly tidied up the room, stacking the accumulation from the attic neatly in separate piles on the floor. Her motions were automatic, controlled by habit. She lifted the teakettle, felt there was enough water remaining for a cup of tea, lighted the oil burner under it. She filled the infusion spoon with strong black tea, placed it in a cup and poured in boiling water.

Sitting at the table she looked about the large one-room apartment. All was orderly. Nothing was amiss. She was tired. That had to be it. And she had been terribly worried.

"Everything is quite normal," she repeated to herself. "Quite normal."

By ten past twelve, when she looked at the clock above the mantel, she had stopped trembling. By fifteen past, she felt strong enough to walk back across the wide room and go to bed. She was not sure she had the strength to look again into the crackled mirror.

Deliberately, slowly, she crossed the room, picked up the lamp from its stand by the wardrobe, and placed it by her bed. She watched her hand as she turned down the wick. It no longer shook, but she wasn't yet ready for the dark.

"I'll read a while," she said aloud. There was *The Tower of Taddea*, by Ouida, on the night table, and *Cameos*, by Marie Corelli, on the small desk beside the window. But the desk was too near the wardrobe mirror. She picked up the book from the night stand and climbed into bed, pulling the comforter up about her shoulders.

By one, when the little clock chimed, her eyes were drowsy and the type blurred as she tried to finish a chapter. The fire had exhausted itself and the last coals collapsed into ashes. Outside, the wind had picked up once more and rain splattered against the windows. A carriage with two horses had gone by on Shore Park Drive at twelve-thirty, but no human sound could be heard, only the storm and the ever-present roar of surf assaulting Point Piedras six blocks north.

Laurie turned the lamp a bit lower, but decided to leave a candle burning. She crawled out of bed and took a match from the iron holder by the fireplace to light the stub of candle on the night table. It wavered, then flared and steadied to an inch-high flame. She blew the lamp out and moved the candle to the center of the table before returning to bed.

As the girl turned her head she saw the old note, picked it up from the edge of the bed where it lay, and examined it once more, using the spectacles to read the tiny print. Inserting it to mark her place in the book, she put it on the stand by the candle.

She grasped the gold wire spectacle rims and grew cold with fear.

With a shock of horror she saw in the lenses, looking back into her own eyes, the eyes of a stranger. Blacker than the night beyond the windows, more intense than the storm's fury, the eyes stared out of the glass, searching, pleading.

Laurie flung the spectacles from her in panic. The small ovals of glass focused the yellow candlelight into two faint glowing patches on the soft rug beside the bed.

Terror, nameless and indefinable, possessed her. Thin gold wire bows caught the flickering light, reflected it into her eyes like a beacon.

Placing a hand on each side of her head, she squeezed until pain caused by the pressure brought a degree of sanity.

"No! It isn't possible!" She knew she whispered

the words, but they drummed in her inner ear as if part of the thundering storm outside.

"No! I saw nothing! It was my imagination! A trick of the light!"

Laurie collapsed into bed, overwhelmed by a feeling of terror. She did not know how long she lay there, immobilized, too frightened to move. Wind toyed with the French windows and fluttered the curtains as if to add to her fright.

"No one is on the balcony." She would concentrate on something familiar. "It's a straight drop of at least sixteen feet or more." By reasoning that there could be no intruder prying at the French windows, she would be able to put the spectacles and crackled mirror in logical perspective.

"Just a trick of the light," she repeated aloud, but remained unable to move. "Of course it was. I'm being utterly ridiculous." She forced herself to look at the glasses on the rug, then the mirror across the room. There was nothing at all unusual about either. "I've been worrying too much and this is what it does to me."

She relaxed back into her pillow and pulled up the quilt. For minutes she watched the flickering shadows created by the candle and listened to the wind and rain. As her eyelids closed in fatigue, she was brought upright again by a soft noise from the center of the room.

"Oh, Laurie, you are being so silly!" She rose and walked to the settee where the golden gown had slipped to the floor. After draping it securely across the back of the Turkish leather chair, she noticed a bit of white paper protruding from the side seam pocket of the skirt. As she pulled out the paper, something dropped to the floor beneath the chair. She crouched on the rug and felt for whatever had fallen, locating it with her fingers and holding it to the candle.

In the palm of her hand lay a large bee of yellow amber and jet. Wings of luminescent flat opals shimmered rainbow-colored in the wavering light. It was an earring, its gold mounting both delicate and bold, a remarkable fusion of the crafts of artist and jeweler.

The girl dropped the earring on the night table and investigated the paper—an envelope of the same stiff, heavy stationery as the note. She read the handwriting on the front:

'Mariposa Beach,
Forest Shores,
Gutierrez County, California.'

What caught the breath in her throat was the name of the addressee: 'Madame Mellona Jolais.'

Mellona!

Chapter 5

By Tuesday morning little remained of the storm but the damage it had done. Felled trees impeded through traffic in every neighborhood. More than one householder had found his roof insufficiently strong to resist the tearing winds. Split redwood shingles appeared on lawns, in the streets, and skewered into broken shrubbery. Enterprising boys were demanding a nickel an hour to clean up wet debris and haul it away in toy wagons. Their fathers consolidated effort with two-man saws. A steady metallic thud could be heard in all areas of town as mauls hit steel wedges. Aged pines which had fallen in the gale were utilized as split logs and kindling for range and fireplace.

Trains from San Esteban were still unable to get beyond Robles Canyon, where a slide had obliterated the rail bed. Suplies to Forest Shores were carted in by mule and wagon, much to the delight of small boys who were allowed to play truant from school and accompany their teamster fathers.

Bert Hutchins' Livery Stable was depleted of working stock well into Friday afternoon when the railway laborers sent from Sacramento finally succeeded in clearing rubble and mud from the narrow cut.

Along Main Avenue the streetcar had resumed full service once the branches and pine needles had been removed from its tracks. Laurie hailed it in mid-block, gave her fare to the driver and took a seat near the rear exit. Even the brace of horses seemed happy to be out in the sunshine, for they strained into their trappings as though eager to move again.

The sun was hot, the sky a brilliant blue intensified and reflected by the placid sea beyond Point Piedras. Gutierrez Bay spread northward like azure glass, with no frothing white-caps to disturb its surface. Most of the fishing boats had put back to Sand Town for the evening, but a few triangular stray sails in a cluster marked the spot where fish were still running.

Laurie felt guilty that Etta Korby would have to close the shop for her. Etta had promised to bring Fannie to the fiesta next day with the extra money Laurie had given her. There were just too many places Laurie needed to spend the cash, but she had heard Fannie with her mother, teasing to go.

Tonight, the night of the opening ball, would see most of Forest Shores' business and professional people attending in full costume, their one night of the year to be unabashedly romantic. That Mexican colonial attire did nothing to flatter paunches and thick waists of well-fed poseurs made no difference to them. Nor were their women-folk graced by their elaborate flounced dresses. It mattered little, as long as the costume was colorful and full of spirit.

When the horsecar stopped at Shore Park Drive, Laurie alighted and sped across the street. Pansy Hinshaw had all the first floor windows open, and from the music room came her tinkling piano rendition of *Crickets' Carnival*.

Roy Winbish was pruning broken branches from the mock orange shrubs which nestled between two bay windows. His wheelbarrow was heaped high with trimmings, although the Hinshaw place had fared better than most since it was somewhat protected by the heavy stand of timber to the west and south. Laurie waved and greeted Roy as she dashed into the house.

Olive Pickens was in the vestibule waiting for Thea who came running down the steps. "We're just leaving. We thought you weren't able to get away early."

"Etta's closing up for me, but Mrs. Arvidson came in at the last minute and couldn't decide which silk flower she wanted for her costume."

"Won't she let Etta wait on her?" Olive asked.

"They don't exactly get on together," Laurie replied.

"Who does with her? Knut Jepsen says Walt Arvidson died in self defense," Thea laughed.

"I wouldn't be a bit surprised. Myrtle Arvidson isn't a very congenial person, even when she's trying to do good. Look at all the fuss she makes at Board of Education meetings." Olive checked her nurse's cap in the hall mirror and tucked a stray wisp of hair beneath its gathered brim. "Well, how do we look?" She turned so Laurie could inspect their pinafores.

"Just like the real thing."

"Great! Just so they don't bring us any first-aid cases!"

"You'll sell out early. I know you will," Laurie said.

"I hope so. I don't relish standing around for hours in this get-up." Thea re-tied the wide pinafore bow in back and re-pinned her frilled cap. "If it weren't for the Well Baby Clinic, I'd never do it at all. Come on, Olive, let's go." The girls went to the door and over their shoulders called back, "See you tonight!"

Laurie climbed the stairs, left the door wide for air, and opened the windows of her one-room apartment. It was stuffy and warm after the full day of bright sunshine. Purple finches chattered in the Spanish moss and a woodpecker's scarlet patch flashed through dense green needles as it hammered bark for insects.

She threw open the French windows on the balcony and went outside for a few minutes to breathe deeply the soft, late afternoon air. It was still light, but lavender shadows were lengthening across the lawn. Beyond the road two slender does wandered at the edge of the trees, browsing in the thick grass. Down at Point Piedras the sea no longer roared among the rocks, but whispered and caressed. As far as she could see, neither blade nor leaf stirred.

What was it Elmer Hobart had said at the bakery the other evening? Something about how beautiful it is after the storm had passed. Laurie smiled to herself and silently agreed with Mr. Hobart. It truly was beautiful. The December afternoon had a magical quality. But perhaps the magic was Chace Creighton.

"I'll call for you at six, Laurie. And be sure to bring a warm wrap. It gets cold after sundown, even with the bonfires." Chace had stopped by the store around noon. Madge Hobart and Ethel Larcher had ceased their gossip when he entered. From the girl's face they had guessed the truth and exchanged wise looks—it would do the Creighton family a lot of good to have a fine, sensible girl like Laurie Mathews join it.

Laurie hesitated before the walnut wardrobe's mirror. There was no indication in its crackled surface that it could possibly hold anything more than a distorted image of whatever was directly in front of it. She had worked hard for the past few days to overcome her fear, and had even worn the tiny spectacles to read footnotes in one of her order catalogs. No pleading eyes had looked back into hers.

She pulled open the wardrobe door. The magnificent golden gown took up most of the remaining space inside, its ruffled train folded upon itself on the red cedar floor. She removed it and hung it on one of the French windows for a last minute airing, then laid out fresh undergarments and her patent-toed shoes with black ribbon ties. If she hurried, she would have time for a warm bath, providing none of the other women were using the bathroom. Undressing quickly, the girl threw on her robe and hurried down the hall, towel and rose-scented soap in hand.

Fortunately there was hot water remaining in the kerosene-fired heater, enough at least for her bath. The heater gurgled and thunked as she turned on the tap over the tub. There was a special joy in her preparations, joy and eager anticipation. The storm was over. From her mind she forced remembrance of the deadly carriage and convinced herself that she had seen in mirror and glasses nothing more than her own image distorted by anxiety.

Chace Creighton buttoned his brocade vest, checked the time by his watch and replaced it in the satin-lined waist pocket. His only concession to attending the fiesta in costume was to wear his own wide, flat-brimmed black felt hat and tooled-leather riding boots. He wore no spurs, nor did the boots bear marks of their straps, although the leather was chafed with considerable stirrup wear.

"Mother wants to see you Chace." Archibald wandered into the room without knocking, a dark panetela unlighted in his mouth. "She's going to make one hell of a ruckus, you know."

"I'm aware of that possibility." Chace coaxed his hair flat with engraved silver French military brushes, a gift from his father when Chace enlisted in '98.

"You'd better see her this time. She's really got the wind up." Archibald found a match above the fireplace and scratched it on the tawny stone mantel. "Are you deliberately trying to antagonize her with this girl of yours?" He wet the cigar between his heavy lips and set the match to it, rapidly drawing until it caught.

"Arch, you know better than that. You know damned well any girl we ever show an interest in, Mother disapproves unless it's one she's picked out. If she thinks she's going to hand pick my women, she's wrong.'

"I rather think she won't mention Aura Lee Striker again." Archibald chuckled, a mirthless, sarcastic sound that vibrated his stocky frame. "You will go down and see her before you leave, won't you?"

"No, I will not. I don't want to hear what she has to say, and I don't want to say anything to hurt her further." He buttoned his coat and transferred a handful of change from the dresser top to his pocket. "She's too possessive, Arch. It's a disease with her." He turned and looked at his brother. "You ought to get away from her, too. Live your own life while you still can."

"Shall I tell her?" Archibald asked.

"Tell her what?"

"That you refuse to see her."

"If you wish," Chace replied.

"Chace, you're the only one I can depend on, now that Father's out of the picture."

The oldest brother sat down heavily in a leather easy chair which faced the wide window. It was almost dark outside. To the west, through the fringe of trees that bordered the beach scrub, lamplight from Mariposa Beach cabins proclaimed that most of the artists from the colony would not be going to the festival in town. Archibald was incapable of wistfulness, but the expression on his face as he looked toward the cabins was eloquent of his wish to escape.

"Damn! Why do I have to go to this stupid affair tonight?" Archibald said. "Mother can handle it by herself and undoubtedly will. She always does. I'll be stuck up there on that ridiculous stand with all those silly women. I'm just window dressing for Mother—a token male Creighton!"

"Don't go. It's as simple as that." Chace stood in the middle of the room, waiting for whatever his brother really had come to say.

"My God, Chace, she won't let go of me! With Father the way he is, paralyzed, unable to do a thing, she's going to hang onto me more than ever. I feel as if I were going to be buried alive." Pungent smoke curled from the cigar in his fat fist. "What the hell am I going to do? I'm not like you. I can't just do as I please. I have responsibilities."

"Why? Because you're the oldest son? Rubbish! Father has enough salted away in those railroad funds to keep them in style as long as they live. And Mother has her own income. Take your shares of the company and dig out for yourself. Ralph Donner over in San Esteban still wants to take in a partner on the Aguilar Valley deal." Chace was patient with his brother, but privately deplored his lack of independence and initiative.

"Maybe I will." Archibald's voice carried with it no conviction.

"Look, I'm picking up Laurie at six. I've got to get

started.'' He put on the flat-brimmed hat and waited for Archibald to leave before he blew out the lamp and closed the door. The hallway was in darkness. Only afterglow through the end window lighted its length.

"Damn that Catalina! She never lights the lamps up here! Sometimes I think she'd like for us all to break our necks on the stairs." Archibald picked his way around the clutter of furniture in the hall and down the wide staircase to the first floor. Chace struck a match and touched the wick of the hall lamp, adjusted its flame and replaced the etched glass shade.

"Chase!" Sybil Creighton's voice rang through the lower floor, challenging her son.

"Goodnight, Arch. Have a good time." Chace strode to the door. "And, Arch, don't lend Duncan any more money, hear? He's in 'way over his head to a couple of sharps now. Don't encourage him by bailing him out. Let him sweat a little." He closed the door and walked around to the stables.

Laurie Mathews tucked the elaborately-carved tortoise shell comb into her hair above the chignon and moved her head about to see that it was secure, then draped the black lace mantilla over it. She stood back to view the effect. For an instant she recalled the vision in the train window and crackled mirror and cold fear stabbed at her consciousness. She looked again at the mirror. There was nothing unusual in it, only herself. Deliberately she shook her head at her foolishness.

"Hoo hoo, Laurie!" Pansy Hinshaw's thin voice called up the stairs.

"Yes, Mrs. Hinshaw?" Laurie's door was still open, for it had remained quite warm inside the house.

"May Roy bring you up something?" Pansy asked.

"Of course he can. I'm all finished dressing." Laurie went to the door and looked toward the landing below. "Besides, I want you both to see my costume."

"Oh, I'd like to. It must be lovely." Pansy preceded Roy, holding her skirts with both hands. The hired girl had lighted the small oil lamp and shined its reflector before she had left for the day. Its faint glow barely illuminated the wide central hall, but it showed clearly the excitement in the old woman's face.

"Come on in, both of you. I need your opinion—does it look all right?" The girl pivoted and turned toward them, lamplight shining aslant the gorgeous golden dress with its velvet chevrons and bows. The fragile headcovering fell to her forehead and draped about her shoulders, leaving the pale oval of her face softly framed in daintly black lace. Her brows arched in dark curves over eyes lustrous with happiness.

For a moment she waited, unsure. For that moment both Pansy Hinshaw and Roy Wimbish stood transfixed, staring. Pansy sat down in the Turkish leather chair, as if her legs suddenly were insufficient to hold her upright.

"What's the matter, Mrs. Hinshaw?" Laurie rushed to her and knelt by her side. "Are you all right?"

"I'm fine, dear. It's just that you look so like. . ." She glanced at Roy, shook her head and continued, "You just look so lovely in the gown. Like a picture out of a travel book." She groped for the words, her hands making ineffectual gestures. "Like a book on Spain, you know." She patted Laurie's hand and smiled reassuringly.

"You're sure you're all right?"

"Of course! I'm just old and sentimental. You'll have to forgive me." Then as if to settle the matter, she said "Roy, you brought something for Laurie."

"Yes, ma'am, Mrs. Hinshaw." He still stood in the doorway, seemingly unable to move further into the room. He stared, his jaw slack, making hollows in his browned cheeks. As though he were waking himself from a dream, he passed a rough hand across his face and tugged at his grizzled beard.

"Well, Roy?" Laurie took him by the arm and led him into the room. "Do sit down for a minute. Chace won't be here till six. We have that long, haven't we?" Laurie was alarmed by their reaction. "Do you like my costume? Is it suitable? I don't want to look. . .odd."

She recalled their expressions upon first seeing her.

"Miss Laurie, if you'll not mind my saying so, you're just about the prettiest young lady ever I seen. It's a grand dress on you." He nodded to emphasize his opinion, but his face retained the look of a man uncertain as to whether or not he had seen a ghost.

"Roy, you brought something," Pansy reminded him.

He stood up and handed Laurie a newspaper-wrapped parcel, one end of it tied tightly with white string. "They're to wear with the dress."

"Thank you, Roy. That's very kind of you." She took the package to the table and untied the string. "Oh, Roy, they are beautiful! Thank you!"

Roses, enormous yellow roses that deepened to golden centers, perfect in petals, stem, and leaf, lay within the dampened paper. They were of a different, more vigorous variety than those he had brought her previously. There was a wild strength about them, as if their exquisite beauty had not been bred in the strain but was wild and natural. The young woman held them by the lamp, then sniffed their fragrance.

"You're most welcome, Miss Laurie. Eusebio Villareal grows them special. They come a long time ago all the way from Wales, he says. Morgan Griffith give him some slips to grow on, twenty, thirty years ago."

"Oh, they are lovely." She held one bloom to the side of her head, seeing if it looked better with the rose beneath the lace, or outside. "You must thank him for me."

Pansy came to the mirror and watched for a moment. "I believe you're supposed to wear one over the right ear, if you are unmarried, and well forward."

"Like this?" The girl pinned the rose in much the same way as when she had gone to dinner at the Blue Roof Lodge.

"Ah, yes, that's it. Very pretty, too." Pansy clasped her hands and leaned toward the mirror as Laurie faced it. "I don't know if you have a shawl or not, but I recalled your saying you might borrow one from Thea's cousin. If you haven't, I have a very old Philippine shawl you might like."

"I was going to use my own knitted one, but I'd love to see yours," Laurie replied.

"I'll go get it. I seen where Hallie Mae put it." Roy abruptly left them and returned in a moment, the colorful shawl draped over his arms. "I didn't want to wrinkle it."

"It's a real Spanish shawl! It's beautiful!" Laurie took it and held it up to the dress material. "It matches the gold of my gown!"

"There was a special way to wear it. I remember. . ." The elderly woman folded the shawl and laid it across Laurie's shoulders. "The ladies of Seville have a different way of using it. They don't make a triangle of it, but fold it into an oblong and drape one end over each arm, like this."

"It's absolutely perfect! Now I really do have a genuine costume!" Laurie again inspected her image in the mirror, delighted with the addition of Pansy's shawl. "Wherever did you get this?"

For a moment, Pansy did not answer. When she did, it was quietly. "A very dear friend of mine loaned it to me many years ago on a chilly night. We never saw each other again. I kept it for her, always expecting her to come and ask for it some day, but I never heard from her. So there it is, and it is beautiful on you. She'd be happy to see it being used. She so loved gay, noisy, happy parties."

"Are you sure it's all right to wear it?" Laurie asked.

"Of course. I'm glad you can use it. It's been in the bureau, tucked away for years. I took it out and had Hallie Mae press it in case you'd like it." Pansy turned to go, giving Laurie one last long look. "You do look lovely, child. Have a wonderful time tonight. If you'd like to bring your young man in for a cup of chocolate, I'll be staying up late and shall be in the front parlor."

"That would be nice. I'll ask him, if it won't be too much work for you." Most of the cooking was done by

"I hope you're right, Mr. Creighton," Thea said, "But it seems to me we've been hearing that sort of thing in Forest Shores ever since I can remember. Harry young Hallie Mae Purdy, the girl from Sand Town, for Pansy had long since lost interest in food and its preparation.

"Not at all. And remember, Chace and I are old friends. We've shared many a cup of chocolate over the years." She smiled, remembering.

Laurie saw Roy's face in the shadow of the doorway. On it was the same expression she had surprised so often before. Now was not the time, but she must ask soon.

She had to know.

The grounds of City Hall's north plaza blazed with lanterns on lines strung from trees in the corner to the building's second floor balcony. Brilliant crimson and yellow banners fluttered above the milling crowds, while a rainbow of colored balloons bobbed on tethers from booths selling refreshments and games of chance. A platform had been constructed to elevate officials and speakers above the grounds, with bunting disguising raw wood and unpainted railings.

From the permanent bandstand in the square's northeast corner came strains of off-key brass and wavering woodwinds as the Saturday Music School students courageously tackled the intricacies of serenatas and fandangos. Missed notes and erratic tempi were small cause for embarrassment, for few of the merrymakers were intent upon the music.

Chace looped the reins over the dash and handed Laurie from the phaeton.

"Watch your horse, mister? Only a nickel!" The boy was too small to be out alone after dark, much less badgering for money. His nose was red and raw, and as he stood awaiting reply, he rubbed it on the cuff of his sleeve. "Just a nickel, mister!" He tried to smile, but his face couldn't quite make it.

109

"Hey, I know you!" Chace pointed a finger like a play gun and cocked his thumb. "Gotcha! Joe Deledda! What are you doing here at this time of night? Why aren't you home?" Chace touseled the boy's hair and gave him a coin before he dropped the buggy weight in the grass.

"Papa says us boys can make money watching buggies."

"Laurie, this is Joe Deledda. Joe, this is Miss Mathews." Chase pushed the youngster forward with his hand, conscious of the thin, bony shoulders beneath the ill-fitting coat.

"How do you do, Mr. Deladda?" Laurie took the child's hand, noticing how cold it was. She looked into his huge eyes and saw the blue circles under them. So this was one of Olive Pickens' children from Sand Town. "Have you had your supper yet, Joe?" She appealed to Chace with a glance.

"Yes, ma'am," he lied, shrugged his narrow shoulders and looked down at his feet.

"If you're going to watch the horse, you'll get hungry after a while, won't you?" Laurie asked. "Why don't you come with us and we'll stand treat for one of those big buns with sticky tops and some fried chicken?" The boy's face broke into a grin that was missing some front teeth.

Chace bent down to the child's level. "Now you've got to promise me you'll stay with the buggy. Is that understood?"

"Yes, sir, Mr. Chace. I promise." His face was solemn.

"Good boy! Come along then." He offered Laurie his arm and escorted her into the banner-and-balloon-filled midway. The child accepted Laurie's hand bashfully, his eyes wide with the wonders of the fiesta. She felt the tiny fingers within her own and realized for the first time why Olive was so concerned for the children of Sand Town.

"Let's go to the school's booth. Olive and Thea are

there," Laurie said. "They're selling box suppers with all sorts of good things." The boy skipped beside her for a few steps in obvious elation.

As they walked the far end of the midway where light was dim few people noticed them, but as they approached the center where gas lights and lanterns shone brightest, heads turned and stared as they passed—the tall man in black, the beautiful young woman in gold, and a small urchin from Oritz Lane.

"Laurie!" Thea greeted them across the makeshift counter decorated with red and yellow bunting. "Oh, you look marvelous in that costume! And you must be Chace Creighton. We've been hearing a lot about you the last few days."

"Thea, Olive, may I present Chace Creighton?" Laurie began the introductions. "Chace, my friends, Thea Harris and Olive Pickens."

"Ladies. . ." He doffed his hat in exaggerated deference and lifted the boy to sit on the edge of the counter. "I'm delighted to meet you both. Now in turn, I'd like you to meet Joe Deledda, a friend of mine." He coaxed the child to turn his head toward the girls. "Can you fix up a nice box supper for Joe? He's a working man tonight and needs something to see him through the evening." He turned to the boy and asked, "You're not a drinking man, are you, Joe?"

"No, sir," he giggled and swung his legs in embarrassment.

"Then a bottle of soda pop will do?" Chace suggested.

Laurie would have bet the child had never tasted soda pop before, not when every loaf of bread in Sand Town was dear. Olive dried her hands on a linen towel, came around the counter and took the child in her arms.

"Joey, what in the world are you doing out in this night air?" She cast an imploring look at Thea to put up the box meal. "Are your parents here, too?"

"No, Miss Pickens. Papa's packing fish and Mama's washing dishes at the cafe for Mr. Ferranti. Me and my brothers is watching horses and buggies for money." He rubbed his nose on his sleeve and looked grave, his long dark lashes veiling somber brown eyes. As he saw Thea packing his box with hot buns and cupcakes he turned to Chace and showed his toothless grin again. "Is that all for me? I don't have to divvy up with anybody?"

"Yes, sir, it is; and no, you don't. Now run along to the buggy, like a good fellow. You can pull the robe up and sleep in the seat if you want to. There'll be an extra nickel in it when we get back." He lifted the boy down and handed him the box, stuffing a few white paper napkins into the boy's coat pocket.

"Thank you, Mr. Chace. I'll stay right there so's nobody takes your rig. I promise!" He stopped and turned, coming back a few steps as if he remembered his manners at the last minute. "I'm happy to have met you," he said to Thea and Laurie. "Goodby, Miss Pickens." His smile flashed across his pinched face before he crossed the midway and ran toward the side street which was by now lined with carriages.

"Goodbye, Joey." Olive kept her back to them a moment, shoulders hunched and her head down. "He's too little and too frail! He shouldn't be out like this!" When she turned to them, her eyes were bright with anger. "The Deleddas have already lost two of their children! It isn't right!"

"Louis Deledda is a fine man, Miss Pickens. He loves his children far more than you realize." Chace's voice was low. "They're poor. The only way out for them is for the entire family to work."

"Do you really think that kid will wait for you?" Thea knew small boys were much more apt to scamper off clutching their nickels than to complete a tedious task.

"He'll be there. Joey's a good boy. All the Deledda kids are." Chace pulled his wallet from his coat and extracted a few bills. To Laurie he continued, "Children like Joey are the reason we hold this fiesta every year.

112

One of these days we'll have a good hospital right here in Forest Shores, with a clinic that doesn't put money first and care last."

"I hope you're right, Mr. Creighton," Thea said. "But it seems to me we've been hearing that sort of thing in Forest Shores ever since I can remember. Harry Eichner's still the only doctor who'll even go out to Sand Town. Every time he's approached either the City or the County for funds to help those people, he's been turned down flat." Thea could not forget that it was a Creighton speaking. "Seems there was a school that had to be built first!" She flushed red as Laurie frowned. "I'm sorry," Thea stammered.

"Don't be, Miss Harris. You have a right to your opinions. You should voice them. Next time the issue comes up at the town meeting, I want you to go and speak up. That's what we need to get the right things done." Chace looked over the large pan of fried chicken on the serving table. "You know, you might just find a lot of us have the same ideas."

"Can we sell you your suppers?" Olive interrupted.

"Laurie, how about it?" Chace asked.

"That would be fine. It all looks delicious."

"White meat for you, Laurie?" Chace asked. "And dark meat for me," he ordered and selected from the various displayed foods until the picnic box was filled. As Olive put them on the counter and totalled up the cost, Chace asked, "So Joey is one of your pupils?"

"Yes, they just registered the Deledda children in our school. He's a darling child, but I'm sure he isn't well at all. I don't know how he can walk that long way from the beach," Olive replied. She accepted the money, counted out change and placed the bills in a metal cash box beneath the counter.

"Keep me posted on how he does, will you? He's very bright—learns quickly. The whole family's honest to a fault." Chace pocketed the change then handed her an extra bill for the Clinic fund.

"How do you come to know them so well?" Olive was curious and not reticent where the welfare of her children was concerned.

"Louie and Marcella work in our home frequently. And the boys are a great help to old Eusebio and Catalina when they need extra hands. Good workers, every one of them." He put the boxes down on the counter. "You knew, of course, that Louie—Luigi—had been an attorney in Sicily?"

Thea and Laurie both turned to look at him in disbelief.

"No, I had no idea!" Olive said in surprise. "He must be an educated man, then?"

"He is. And so is his wife. University of Messina."

"Then why are they in Sand Town, of all places, doing menial labor?" Thea asked.

"Seems Louie dared run for political office against an entrenched and respected incumbent and offered the newspapers proof of his opponent's criminal associations and graft. It became more expedient for the officials to export the Deleddas than to clean up their politics, so here they are."

"How awful!" Laurie exclaimed.

"It isn't fair!" Olive agreed. "But I said that before, didn't I?"

Chace turned to Olive. "That's why we have to see they get a fair chance here, isn't it?" He picked up the boxes. "Nice to have met you both. I'm sure we'll see each other often from now on. Goodnight."

Picnic tables had been improvised on the lawn with long pine planks resting on wooden sawhorses. Bonfires blazed at intervals on makeshift brick hearths, where anxious parents shooed frolicking children from too near the flames. Strolling Mexican musicians from San Esteban wandered among the tables alternating sad, nostalgic ballads with gay, rhythmic tunes that could barely be heard above the happy noise.

A slight breeze had sprung up, swaying lanterns, animating shadows. Most families had settled beneath the lights, while couples found their way, two by two, into dim corners away from bonfires and lamps. Chace picked a table near the edge of the lawn where an arc of orange calendulas followed the plaza's circle.

"How's this? Far enough from the youngsters to be safe and close enough to the crowd to be respectable." He placed the boxes on the table and pulled the bench out for Laurie. "Here, let me put these paper napkins on the seat before you sit down. There, that's better."

She gathered her skirt and petticoats and slid into the narrow space. "Thank you, Chace. This is perfect. Listen to the music. What are they playing?"

"I'm sorry, but I don't know one song from the other. I'm afraid I'm one of those people who listens, but doesn't learn. Shall I call them over and ask?"

"Oh no, I'll just listen, too. But I intend to learn." She opened the boxes, laid out napkins. "We never had music like that in Chicago. Lots of German music, but not Mexican."

"Do you like it?" Chace asked.

"Yes, it's lovely. So sad and haunting sometimes, then all bright and gay." She smiled as she watched the players and the costumed crowds promenading in their finery.

"Which would you prefer? Coffe or tea?" Chace inquired, then added, "They had to ban wine and beer a few years ago. Got a little too exciting and began to draw the rowdy element. The ladies decided to make it strictly a dry celebration."

"Coffee, please," Laurie answered.

Chace motioned to Hoyt Larcher, who was selling hot coffee and lukewarm tea. The cumbersome wheeled cart could only be managed by a man of his size and strength. He rolled it to the table and extended his hand to the young man.

"Glad to see you here, Creighton. Evening, Miss Mathews. A bit chilly beyond the fire, isn't it? Too bad they don't set the date for this earlier in the year, maybe in summer. Falls in Advent season, too, and lots of folks don't like to come during Advent."

"You must suggest that to the planning committee, Hoyt," Chace said. "The ladies are amenable to suggestions—occasionally."

The men laughed. "Two coffees, please," Chace

ordered and dropped bills into the tin cup wired to the contraption. The butcher drew the black, steaming brew into heavy white mugs.

"Thank you, folks. Have a good time, hear?" Larcher trundled the cart along the walk, hawking his refreshments.

"He has a point there, about the time of year for the fiesta." Laurie nibbled at a bun drenched in maple syrup and sprinkled with pecans and cinnamon. "You truly want people to get involved in things—to speak their minds, even in opposition, don't you?"

"Certainly! Too many people complain, but never make any attempt to act. Your friend Thea is right—we've heard promises too long," Chace said.

"You intend to do something, though, don't you?" Laurie asked.

"I do. I'm working on a few things. . .but let's not talk about that tonight." He held up a drumstick and bit into it with relish. They smiled at one another and ate with their fingers from the boxes. The ludicrous incongruity of the *al fresco* dinner and her resplendent costume had not escaped Laurie. She laughed softly.

"What's funny?" Chace asked around the crisp chicken leg.

"Here I am, in fancy dress fit for a castle in Spain, and I'm eating with my fingers like a peasant!" She wiped her hands on one of the napkins and broke a roll in half, offering Chace a part.

"You do like it—I can see you do." Chace dared her to deny it.

"Oh yes! This is the most fun I've had for ages." She glanced away from his hazel eyes, for they looked too deeply into her very being. "I think I'd forgotten how to have fun."

"Someday you can tell me about it. Someday when it hurts less."

"How did you know?" She smiled and touched his hand. "But of course you'd know. It still shows, doesn't it?"

"Now and then. That's part of you, Laurie. That's

116

what makes you a woman." He tasted the coffee and put the cup down to hold her hand in his. "I don't want you to be unhappy again, ever. You know that, don't you?" He spoke quietly so only she could hear.

"Yes, Chace. And I love you for it." She said it before she had considered her words. Why, she wondered, must she always say exactly what she meant?

"There—you've said it." He raised her fingers to his lips and kissed them, oblivious to the snickering from a group of children at a table nearer the bonfire. "Marry me, Laurie?" He knew he did not have to spar and discuss their loving each other endlessly. He was a direct man who appreciated directness in return. "Marry me right away?"

Laurie sat back on the bench and closed her eyes, her lips curving into a faint smile. The lantern light was too dim to show much more than the smile, and as she opened them, her black eyes were moist, but Chace sensed her happiness.

"You only met me less than a week ago. How can you possibly know if I'm right for you?" She did not mean to parry. She was puzzled. "You know so little about me, Chace."

"Do you love me?" he asked.

"Oh yes, I do," she replied.

"Then that's all I need to know." He handed her a stalk of celery as if the matter were settled.

"But there's more to it than that!" she said.

He looked at her over the rim of his cup and grinned, his broad chin jutting forward as if daring her to dispute him. "Laurie, when I picked you up out of the street and held you in my arms for just those few moments I knew all about you.

"There something inside all of us that tells us what we need to know if we just pay heed to it. Most of us go rampaging through life making bad decisions, taking wrong turns, bloodying our heads, all needlessly if we'd just pay attention to our feelings, our inner promptings." He drank silently, waiting for her to assimilate his meaning.

"If you want to be prosaic," he continued, "Just say I noticed you didn't wear one of those atrocious rear-end pads. Most females today warp their bodies to conform to what is considered fashionable. They add rats and switches and pompadour wigs for the same reason. You don't. You have the courage and conviction to be yourself. You dress becomingly, as you please, not hiding the woman you are inside with trappings of ultra-conformity.

"When I held you, I held a real woman. My hands and eyes told me that much, but something within told me far more." He reached across the crude table and held both her hands. "I love you, Laurie. I want to share my life with you."

For a long time the girl sat quietly looking at him. "What shall I say to you?" she asked.

"Say you'll marry me. It's simple: I. . .will. . ." he prompted.

"I. . .will. . .marry. . .you," she whispered and gave his huge hands a squeeze. "Oh yes, Chace, I will marry you!"

On a low, raised floor of polished and waxed oak the dancers twirled and turned in time to graceful Spanish waltzes. The swaying, spinning crowd was a kaleidoscope of colors—vermilion, emerald, cerulean—with the men's somber black accenting the brilliant hues. The night was clear and moonless, with stars hanging low on the horizon, undimmed by fog or mist. Yawning, small children ringed the floor and watched the circling dancers. At one side was a small orchestra, its members attired in embroidered sombreros and tight, braid-edged vests. To their left, on a platform elevated from the floor, sat mayor, aldermen, and patrons of the fiesta.

Sybil Creighton, disdaining traditional costume, sat enthroned in splendid isolation to the right of Mayor Fulbright, her silver brocade gown glowing in the gas light. Archibald, feeling totally ridiculous in tasseled hat and tight-fitting Mexican breeches, sat one step below his mother, ill at ease playing the part of public benefactor.

"Disgusting!" Sybil hissed into his ear.

"What's disgusting now, Mother?" Archibald's temper was wearing thin after two hours of being civil and accomodating against his will.

"Don't be sarcastic with me, Archibald!"

"All right, Mother." He sat in petulant silence.

"Have you see him?"

"Who?" Archibald was not interested in his mother's conversation, but anything was better than sitting in silence, watching the dizzy gyrations of the dance floor, and not being allowed to participate. "Who should I have seen?"

"Chace, of course!"

"No, I haven't. Why should I have?"

"Myrtle Arvidson said they'd be here. Imagine, that common shop girl coming here with Chace!"

"It would seem to me that *he* is here with *her*." Archibald's sarcasm was overlooked by Sybil, who was much more intent upon the dancers than her son's rejoinder.

The orchestra finished the three-quarter tune and sounded a loud chord, the drummer striking his cymbal and beating a long roll on the snare.

"Ladies and gentlemen!" Mayor Fulbright strode from the dais and stood before the musicians. "I now have the great pleasure of awarding the prizes for the best, most authentic costumes in keeping with the theme of our fiesta." He seemed disconcerted in his role of master of ceremonies and ran his finger about his collar. The drummer struck a rapid tattoo and ended with a swat at the cymbal.

Sybil leaned forward, her eyes riveted on the couple walking toward the bandstand. Her breath, in short gasps through her thin lips, choked in her throat. With a cruel finger she jabbed her son in the back, unable to form the caustic phrases that came to her mind.

"What is it now, Mother?" Archibald refused to turn and look at her. He had attended with her, stood for over an hour accepting and giving felicitations, then sat on the dais interminably while others enjoyed the opening festivities. What more did Sybil want?

Anger and humiliation swept her like a flood, leaving her shaking, seething in its wake. Again she jostled her son's shoulder. This time he turned and saw in her face the fury of her ire. He followed the pointing finger, trying to discern its aim.

"Chace?" Archibald guffawed in ridicule. "Is that what's bothering you?"

"I will not tolerate your attitude!" she said hotly.

"Mother, you can't do one damn thing about my attitude. Unless you want to create a scene before the entire town, shut up."

"How dare you!" Sybil's eyes were glassy in their shock.

"I dare because you've got to depend on me from now on, Mother. And right here and now I declare my independence from you. I came here tonight to please you and to add a male Creighton to the affair, but from tomorrow on, I call my own shots." His eyes were like honed steel as he glared back at her. "And don't you forget it. Not for one minute forget it." His quiet tone was far more menacing than a shout would have been.

Sybil shrank back into her chair, a sick smile playing hide-and-seek about her mouth.

The crowd surged forward to hear the mayor, their press a melange of color and warmth in the lantern glow. In a daze Sybil Creighton heard Mayor Fulbright drone his usual preamble about worthy causes and charity beginning at home.

Finally when her endurance began to falter, he announced, ". . .Miss Laurie Mathews, proprietress of the Ribands and Roses Shoppe, the grand prize for the most elegant ladies' costume. . ."

Laurie's slim figure separated from the crowd and advanced to the bandstand, her golden, flounced train trailing on the dance floor. Chace stood at the edge of the stand, applauding, his dark face beaming approval.

As if seeing the presentation through an enveloping

mist, Sybil Creighton watched the graceful black-eyed girl approach the dais, her quick glance encompassing all there in a dazzling smile. The mantilla, shading Laurie's face in the lantern light, hid her expression as she turned.

A cold chill like the hand of a dead past clutched the woman as the girl's eyes flicked across her, paused and returned again to Sybil's gray face. The older woman's hand went to her breast as her breath strained in her throat. The golden gown with its dark chevrons, the oval face with its jet, piercing eyes, the yellow Welsh roses floated before her consciousness. She grasped the arms of the chair, her fingers tightening on the oak until she wanted to scream in pain. Then the vision vanished, the glistening, golden apparition took her place beside Chace.

Sybil's face in the faulty light betrayed some of the dread that suddenly encompassed her. She framed her smile, her pleasant repartee, to suit the impression she wished to create, that of the powerful and benevolent leader of her community. If she trembled, it was hidden. If she feared, it was obscured by her genteel laughter, but as she left the dais, she clung to the arm of Archibald, her steps faltering as they made their way to the street where Eusebio waited with their comfortable estate wagon.

"You must understand that I should return to my husband's side as soon as possible. He is so sorry he must miss the fiesta this year. Yes, I shall tell him you inquired about him." Sybil Creighton carefully formed the correct words.

"Why the devil don't you tell the truth, Mother? Tell them he's an imbecile—a vegetable! You'll tell him they asked about him? And he'll know what you're saying? Utter rot!" Archibald left his mother to Eusebio, who helped her into the upholstered leather seat.

Twin lamps on the front of the wagon lent little light to the rear of the carriage, but Archibald could see the desperate look on Sybil's face.

"I say, what's come over you? You look as though you'd seen a ghost!"

121

Sybil Creighton did not see her son's belligerent face beside her, nor his fat, gray-gloved fingers holding the dark panetela. She saw only the pale oval face surrounded by a lace mantilla, the shimmering gold of the chevronned gown, delicate, long-fingered hands holding an ivory and lace fan.

Perhaps she had seen a ghost.

Chapter 6

Etta Korby bent over the treadle sewing machine by the window, guiding a seam under the needle, inch by inch.

"There. That finishes Madge Hobart's skirt." She clipped the thread and took the garment to the pressing board. "I really didn't want to take a tailoring job, but it doesn't matter as long as we keep busy, does it?"

"I don't understand it, Etta," Laurie said.

"You mean business picking up like it has?" The iron sizzled as the little seamstress tested its heat with a wet finger.

"Yes. I know there's a Christmas rush, but I didn't expect anything like this. And so many tourists are coming in, too." Laurie poured a cup of tea and dipped a spoonful of sugar from the jar on the window sill. She sat on a stool just inside the workroom door where she could keep an eye on the front of the shop via the tilted mirror.

"Maybe word got around after the fiesta. About your costume and all. That sure didn't hurt, you know. And the paper printed such a nice story, too." Etta ran the hot iron over a pressing cloth laid on the new seam. Clouds of steam wafted from the board to the ceiling. "You notice how many younger women and girls are coming in? And lots of Mariposa Beach people?"

"Sure, but I don't understand it," Laurie admitted.

"As long as the bank balance shows in black, you don't have to understand." Etta hung the long, pleated skirt on a wire hanger by two snap clothespins. "Madge

Hobart said she'd be by to pick this up before closing time."

"Starting next week I'm going to give you two dollars a week more salary. You're helping the shop make money, so the shop can afford to pay you more." Laurie put the cup on the window sill where it made a patch of steam on the cold glass.

"I won't say I can't use it. You know better than that," Etta said. "Thanks, Laurie. It'll help a lot. And I sure thank you again for those nice old dresses you found at Mrs. Hinshaw's. You haven't seen the one I made over for Fannie, have you?"

"No. Her grandmother brought her by yesterday, but she had her coat on. She said she had a new dress, though."

"Well, to *her* it's new. She's never had a truly new one, although she doesn't realize it. But I'm a good sewer. She always looks real pretty, no matter how fast she grows."

"She's a darling child, Etta. You should be proud of her," Laurie said.

"Oh, I am proud of her. No doubt there. And she's all I've got. If I didn't have her. . ." Etta looked out the window at the bleak alleyway which was already enveloped in dusk.

"I know." Laurie put her arm around the young woman. "I know it's hard on you. Hard and lonely."

"Life doesn't end when one of you dies. It just isn't the same. It goes right on, but part of you doesn't. Part of you just won't ever be quite the same again, no matter how hard you try." Etta poured herself a cup of tea and sat on the sewing maching chair, elbows propped on the cabinet. "We muddle along, Fannie and me."

Outside they heard the grocer's delivery wagon returning for the afternoon. It clattered down the alley, its weary old horse plodding with resignation, knowing it was time to go to the barn. Laurie took the tea pot from atop the oil heater and slid a trivet beneath it on a shelf by the door.

"Is Chace taking you to the town meeting tonight?" Etta asked.

"No. He asked me to go, but I have too much hand-sewing to do for the shop. I want to finish those hat decorations, you know the ones—like satin fruit and berries. From the silk pieces Mrs. Hinshaw gave me."

"Sold to you, you mean," Etta corrected her.

"Well, practically gave to me," Laurie countered.

"Let me tell you—that dress you wore to the fiesta was worth it all! You can't even buy silk like that on this coast! I'd bet everything I had that it's French silk. You know they have a special way to moiré the silk and that color blend is unique. And the needlework—those seams are finished the way they do in the best fashion houses, like Worth's in Paris. I'm good, but I could never make a dress like that. It must have cost a fortune originally."

"Funny thing, that old hump-back chest put away like that all those years," Laurie mused.

"Say, speaking about funny things. My mother-in-law says you should have seen Sybil Creighton's face when she caught sight of you at the ball opening night. She was real close to the bandstand, just a few feet away from Mayor Fulbright and the rest of them. Mrs. Creighton was sitting right behind Archibald, her oldest boy, you know—the fat one," Etta said.

"Yes, I remember," Laurie said. "Chace was going to introduce me to them, but they left before he had a chance."

"Listen to me, girl—stay away from both of them, Archibald and his mother! The youngest boy, Duncan, would be nice enough if she'd just leave him alone. But he's spoiled rotten and is in and out of trouble constantly. His folks are figuring to send him back to some straight-laced blue-nose relatives in Boston if he doesn't toe the mark from now on," Etta said.

"You sound just like Thea," Laurie reminded her.

"Thea has a good right to hate the whole clan. I lost my husband but she lost her whole family, one by one."

"Yes, I know. She told me about her people and the way Zedekiah Creighton treated them." Laurie finished her tea and rinsed the cup under the basin tap in the tiny restroom. "What did your mother-in-law mean about Chace's mother?"

"She says if the old girl had seen the devil himself rise up out of the ground she couldn't have looked sicker. Said her face went pale; even in that light she could see it. Mother Korby says she probably couldn't stand the thought that Chace didn't let her pick his girl for him."

"Does everyone in town know about them?" Laurie was mildly annoyed that the Creightons' affairs were such public knowledge.

"Look—there are two factions here: pro-Creighton-and-his-crowd, and anti-Creighton-and-his-crowd. Most everyone likes Chace. He opposes his father and the rest of them all the time. Always has. But there it stops. Even the 'pros' won't say they like the Creightons, and most of the 'pros' aren't too fond of Chace because he isn't so crazy about them. Does that sort of give you a clearer picture?" Etta asked.

"Very graphic, I'm sure!" Laurie replied.

The polished brass harness bells strapped to the front door jangled as Madge Hobart came in. Etta saw who it was in the mirror and handed Laurie the skirt.

Standing to one side, invisible from the workroom, a young man with sandy hair surveyed the boutique, his pale blue eyes darting from the rack of pongee guimpes and Belgian lace blouses, past the small tree made from silk flowers, to the display of ribboned corsets and camisoles. At the boldness of his inspection, Madge Hobart drew away, her withering glance impugning his presence in the shop.

"Mrs. Hobart, how nice to see you." Laurie greeted the woman. "Etta has your skirt all pressed and ready. Would you like me to slip a paper bag over it?" Laurie halted as she saw the young man.

"No, dear. That will be fine, right on the hanger. I don't have anything else to carry and Charlie's going to

126

drive me home on his way down to the Shell Box." The woman handed Laurie thirty-five cents and took the hanger, draping the long skirt over her arm. "Etta, you did a beautiful job on this," she called to the rear of the store, knowing that the young woman could hear her. "Many thanks. Elmer would thank you, too. He didn't want me to buy a new one yet. I fancy he's buying me one for Christmas."

"Glad to help you, Mrs. Hobart," Etta said as she came from the workroom into the short hall. "I'll be happy to let out the waist of that suit you mentioned any time you want to bring it in. We can set on a new band and placket."

"That would be a great help. I'll have it seen to soon." Mrs. Hobart headed for the front door, stepped slightly aside as the young man removed his hat and opened the door for her with a graceful bow and flourish. "Goodnight, girls. Thank you, Duncan. Very kind of you, I'm sure." Her disapproval of him was obvious. She cast a backward glance at Etta and Laurie as if to warn them. The door jangled musically as it shut behind her.

"Ladies. . ." Again he affected a deep bow, and held his hat in his hand.

"Just what do you want, Duncan? Last I heard, you weren't up to wearing sateen bloomers or silk roses behind your ears." Etta folded her arms and shifted her weight to her right foot, belligerency in every line.

"Etta, you look enchanting as ever," he said. Turning to Laurie he smiled and stepped toward her. "I'm sure Etta won't introduce me, so I shall do so myself. I'm Duncan Creighton, Chace's brother."

"I'm happy to meet you, Duncan." Laurie extended her hand, which he accepted and held a bit longer than necessary. "Chace has mentioned you. You're the brother who knows horses, aren't you?"

"Ah. . .yes. You might make that statement about me. I am a good judge of horseflesh, but not of winners!" His laughter was the infectious mirth of a child reminded of its naughtiness before company in the

127

parlor. "Did Chace say kind things about me? I want to know how I stand in your affection before I proceed."

"As a matter of fact, he did. He seems very fond of you. I think you're lucky to be his brother," Laurie replied.

"That is a matter of some dispute—but not with you, Miss Mathews." His pale blue eyes were suddenly animated; a bit of pink came into his white face. "Since he said nice things, I shall deliver his message to you verbatim."

"You mean you wouldn't have, had I said he told me terrible secrets about you?" Laurie immediately liked young Duncan and found it easy to spar with him on his own level of banter.

"Probably not, dear lady, probably not. I am not reliable in any way, and when miffed, completely irresponsible." He leaned on the counter and looked up into her face. "Do you really want to know his message, or may I make up one of my own?"

"Duncan, we're about to close the shop. Why don't you tell Laurie what you're supposed to, then run along home or wherever it is you go to at this time of day." Etta's face was stony and hostile.

He frowned at her like a small boy deprived of a pleasure. "Very well: Chace wants you to wait for him. He'll come by for you about six-fifteen and either take you home right away or escort you to dinner. Your choice. He's sorry he couldn't get by himself earlier and invite you, but he had some business in San Esteban and then at City Hall. He got tied up a whole lot longer than he intended."

"That's very kind of you to let me know." Laurie was almost glad the shop had no telephone, for it allowed her to meet at least one member of Chace's family.

"He wants you to go to the town meeting, too. Wants to show you off to the aldermen, I guess. Can't say that I blame him, either." He spoke almost in a whisper, "If you'd rather go right now with me, I'd be delighted to take you to dinner."

"No, thank you! I'll wait for Chace." Laurie

suspected there was more than casual banter in his invitation, for his pale eyes were suddenly serious. She had heard strange things about Duncan, but not from Chace. Now she would believe at least part of them.

"Then, dear ladies, goodnight." He opened the door and chuckled. "Etta, Miss Mathews, it's been a pleasure." He mounted his huge black gelding in one easy movement, his long thin fingers barely holding the reins in check. As he urged the horse into a smooth walk, he turned and flourished his hat once more.

"So that's the notorious Duncan Creighton. I like him. He's a bit too forward on first acquaintance, but he's nice." Laurie hung the 'Closed' sign across the glass and pulled the green fabric shade over the window display.

"I suppose he could be, really, but the way he treats poor little Rosa Cantu I just can't even be civil to him." Etta emptied the small trash basket from under the counter into a larger one in the workroom.

"Is she the girl who lives over Bert Hutchins' stables? The pretty Mexican girl? Seems Mrs. Hinshaw has mentioned her."

"Yes, she's the one. He set her up in an apartment in San Esteban a few years ago, but his folks just put a stop to it and she moved over here, just to be near him. Bert lets her stay there in return for doing a little cooking and cleaning for him. It's so pitiful. Her own folks disowned her when she took up with Duncan. They're an old, respected family, very religious. The scandal hurt them terribly."

"Why doesn't he marry her?" Laurie asked.

"Oh, Laurie! You don't have to marry a girl if you're a Creighton! You can get what you want without all that bother." Etta threw open the back door and dumped the trash into the metal bin. "Now Chace is different, of course. It's almost as if he didn't belong the family."

"But Duncan's so young to have a. . . a. . .mistress," Laurie said.

"That's only part of it. He tried to enlist in the ar-

129

my in '98 when Chace did. Wanted to see action in the Philippines or Cuba. 'Fight the Spanish and free the colonies. . .' All that idealistic, patriotic jingoism.'' Etta sat on the edge of the counter and ran a comb through her wiry hair.

"Did he? Did he go to Cuba?" Laurie asked.

"No! Never got beyond Sacramento!" Etta replied. "His parents both threw a fit. They say old Zedekiah camped at the telegraph station fourteen hours straight. Sent wires to everybody in the War Department, the State Department, probably even the janitor in the White House basement!"

"What happened?"

"They weren't going to have their baby serve in anybody's army. No, sir! They pulled every trick in the book to get him out. Some say his mother arranged to pay off a couple of people. That would be like her, all right, and old Zedekiah, too. Duncan came back home like a whipped pup. Began raising hell and hasn't quit since. Guess that's his way of getting even with his folks,'' Etta concluded.

"But what about Rosa Cantu?" Laurie wondered.

"She loves him so much it's sad. And he isn't faithful to her. He chases after anything in skirts—even married women. You'd be surprised at some of his lady friends! It's a pure wonder some husband hasn't shot him yet. Guess only his family name protects him. But how he can treat Rosa the way he does is beyond me.'' Etta shook her head and thrust long black wire hairpins into her dark topknot.

"She must love him very much."

"Yes, I suppose that's what love can do to a woman.'' Etta hopped down from the counter, pinned on a flat, feathered hat and wrapped her russet-colored shawl about her shoulders. "Take my word for it, he's a wrong one, that Duncan. He's sweet and lovable on the surface, but he's poison.'' She opened the front door. "Goodnight, Laurie. Have a lovely evening.''

"Thank you, Etta. Goodnight.''

Laurie looked at the small clock recessed between

displays of glacé kid gloves and wool challis scarves. She had not planned on seeing Chace this evening. Perhaps she could wear the cerise scarf to brighten her sober gray dress. She could borrow Etta's hat with the pink and cerise ribbons. And there were her long, five-button gloves of black silk. She could be conservatively chic.

She thought of Chace, of being with him, having dinner with him, sleeping beside him, raising their children. The prospect filled her with happiness. Etta's admonition about Duncan annoyed Laurie. Not that she doubted the little seamstress. It was just that she wanted nothing to impinge upon her present joy. Such knowledge of itself was unwelcome and a harsh intrusion.

Laurie pinned the hat at a saucy slant and resolved to ignore all she had heard. Across the street Emmet Lauder turned out the gas light in the front of his tailoring shop, closed the front door, rattled it to check the lock, then headed south toward Glasgow Avenue. For the few minutes he was in sight Laurie watched his gaunt figure in the street lamps' dim glow. As he turned the corner Laurie caught her breath.

The shadow of the building concealed a darker shadow. No movement betrayed its presence. Only a sharp eye could distinguish the outline of the carriage. From Main Avenue a canopied automobile sporting a battery lamp made its way toward the halted vehicle. In the light as the car passed Laurie spied the glitter of a fancy brass whip socket on the buggy's dash. What filled her suddenly with fear was the sight of a gloved hand grasping the whip—an ivory handled whip.

Etta's warning drummed in her head. Surely there could be no connection between the carriage and Duncan Creighton! She had convinced herself that her recent accident had been the result of a drunken driver losing control of his horse. Even now as she adjusted the blinds in the display window and extinguished the gas lights at the rear of the shop she told herself she had to be imagining things. She was being ridiculous to suppose anyone in Forest Shores should wish her harm.

Laurie buffed the toes of her shoes with a patch of flannel from the workroom and secured the ungainly hat with another pin. In front of the shop Chace's light phaeton pulled to a stop. She recognized the sound of his footsteps in the recessed entry. Quickly she tied the cerise scarf about her throat and ran to meet him.

As she raced to the door she could not see the other carriage emerge from the shadows, wheel about and speed down Glasgow Avenue out of sight.

Sybil Creighton pulled aside the curtains that surrounded her husband's bed.

"Has he shown any signs of improvement today?" She might have been speaking of an inanimate object. It was a routine, dutiful question that carried no real concern. Nor was her attitude lost on the nurse.

"No, Mrs. Creighton. I did manage to feed him some scraped beef and broth, but it's so difficult for him to swallow." Nurse Althea McMurray smoothed the pillow beneath Zedekiah's head and gently pushed his shock of white hair from his forehead. "He's perfectly aware of everything, I assure you. Nothing's wrong with his mind." She looked down at the man, pity in her glance.

"Leave us alone, Nurse. I'll come for you when I leave," Sybil commanded.

"Yes, Madam. I'll be in the hall outside should you need me." The nurse was reluctant to leave her patient.

"You've been in attendance a long time today. Why don't you go down to the kitchen and have Catalina fix you some chocolate?" It made no difference to Sybil that Catalina had already retired for the night. Her whim was reason enough to rouse the elderly house servant.

"Oh no, thank you. It's much too late. I'll be right outside." Althea McMurray seethed at the lack of consideration the mistress of the house had for those who served her. The belief that old money made truly genteel people was given the lie by Sybil Creighton.

The diminutive nurse left Zedekiah's capacious

bedroom and seated herself outside the door near a burnished cherrywood hall table containing a small night
lamp. She was weary, not from physical effort, but
from constant watching and listening. Sometimes it
seemed as if the old man's very breath depended upon
her conscientious vigilance. Leaning her head back
against the rose damask head cushion, she closed her
eyes and in a few minutes was fast asleep.

Sybil sat on the edge of the bed, half sick at the
sight of the sunken cheeks and gaping mouth. She moved the candle toward the corner of the table so that its
light fell upon their faces.

"Zedekiah, I want you to listen to me. Open and
shut your eyes so I know you hear me," she ordered.

The old man's eyes, his only feature evincing life,
bored into hers. The eyelids closed, then slowly reopened.

"Yes, you understand me. Good! That girl—how
dare she come here and make trouble for us? Do you
realize what is happening? Chace is not only seeing her,
but actually had the temerity to inform me he intends to
marry her!"

She rose from the bed and began pacing the
delicately-hued Aubusson carpet that covered the dark
oaken floor.

"I've made inquiries. No one seems to know a
thing about her or who she is. Came from
Chicago—which gives us no information at all. She even
had the effrontery to engage that. . .that. . .very same
room at Pansy Hinshaw's!"

The woman wrapped her arms about herself as she
became conscious of the cold, but made no attempt to
stir the fireplace embers or replenish wood in the grate.

"I forbade Chace to continue this affair. After all, I
do have voting stock in the company. It isn't as if I had
no power to enforce my wishes in such matters." She
returned to the side of the bed and looked at her husband's face. "You do understand, don't you?" As his
eyelids closed and reopened, she nodded.

"Of course you do. It's your concern, too, isn't it,

Zedekiah?'' Her voice carried a viciousness that made him close his eyes and not open them again until she had stalked across the room and stood before the fireplace.

"It's not possible for the dead to reincarnate in flesh and become Nemesis!'' She stretched her cold hands to the dying fire. "And yet. . .''

"You've made your point, Mother!'' Chace threw his napkin on the table. "Just how do you propose to malign this girl who's done you no harm? I already know you've instructed your friends not to trade with her, instructions which I devoutly pray they will ignore.''

"No harm? How can you utter such a foolish question? She deliberately caused your father's stroke! No harm? Had she taken an ax she couldn't have done a more thorough execution upon him!'' Sybil Creighton was incensed.

"That's insane, and you know it. He'd never seen the girl before that night at the Lodge. And you can't tell me he was so set on my escorting Aura Lee Striker that just seeing me with another girl caused him to have a brain hemorrhage. That's rubbish. More than likely you'd badgered him into too much food, too much drink, too many arguments.'' Chace's indignation was at the limits of his control.

"I can see it's useless to discuss it with you, Chace,'' Sybil said.

"Are you going to the board of aldermen and request they burn her at the stake as some kind of witch?'' Chace persisted. "Or maybe you'd prefer they strangle her, something typically medieval? What's it to be, Mother?'' The anger in his face brought a chill to the woman.

"I have my good reasons for being adamant. Reasons that are none of your concern!'' she replied.

"Damn it! *She* is my concern! Everything that touches her is my concern!'' Chace shouted.

Archibald looked around to see if Catalina were listening. "For God's sakes, if you must carry on so, can't you at least lower your voices? Do the servants have to hear everything so they can spread tales all over town?''

"Let them! It's time the town heard the whole truth!'' Chace drained the last from his wine glass and restrained his urge to dash it against the toile-covered wall.

"And as for your moving out of your father's house, I shouldn't advise it, Chace. That architect you're working with at San Esteban—he's almost finished with the plans for your precious projects,'' Sybil said quietly.

"What about him?'' Chace demanded.

"He's had an attractive offer from a firm in Santa Barbara. Someone might increase the salary to make it irresistible,'' Sybil said. "You have him under no contract, you know. You placed everything on a gentleman's agreement basis. Very unbusinesslike of you.''

"He wouldn't quit before the job is done.''

"Oh he wouldn't? Go see him tomorrow if you like. And while you're in San Esteban go to the Court House and see if they've decided to allocate funds for the waterfront improvements at Sand Town—the ones you're so determined to get financed by the county.''

Sybil poured black coffee from the ornate silver pot and passed the cup to Archibald. "I still have considerable influence, especially now that your father is in no position to oppose me. Ask your brother if I have managed to convey my doubts as to the merit of your project.''

"She's right, Chace.'' Archibald sipped the thick coffee and wrinkled his nose in distaste. "Dreadful! Why must we have this stuff? Even the White Front Cafe and the Shell Box serve much better.''

"Because it is traditional and fashionable. You should become accustomed to it:'' Sybil tasted the demitasse and put it down again. "You are Creightons, not trail tramps who drink from tin cans.''

"What do you mean, she's right?'' Chace asked Archibald.

"There's a lot of pressure for improving the pleasure boat harbor down at Point Piedras. Seems most of the votes will go to that rather than to the Cove breakwater or straightening La Gaviota Creek. Sorry!" Archibald was not only sorry that Chace's proposals were in danger, but sorry that their mother had brought it about. He had hoped Chace would win, for it meant a lucrative, long-term contract for Creighton Development. With Zedekiah out of the way, Archibald would be in control, his prestige and power greatly augmented. He had not counted on their mother's interference.

"If you persist in seeing this. . .this. . .shop girl, I shall see to it she regrets the day she decided to come to Forest Shores!" Sybil's wrath was quiet—and certain. "Please believe me, Chace, I can do it, and I shall," she added.

Her eyes narrowed, her thin lips set in a line of cruel determination. "You have paraded her before this town and have flaunted her in sheer defiance of the wishes of your own parents—a girl who deliberately came here to destroy this family!"

"What a filthy thing to say, Mother!" Even Archibald was surprised at her venom.

"If the truth is filthy, then filthy it is. Take my word for it, she is a scheming, devious young woman." She reached over the immaculate linen cloth and stroked Chace's arm. "It is difficult for you to believe, but that is the truth. She is far more dangerous than you realize. I'm an old woman, but my years have given me a modicum of wisdom, doubly so where my own sex is concerned. Your Laurie Mathews has an ulterior motive in her liaison with you, Chace."

Disagreeable as it had been, dinner was less unbearable than the loneliness of silence in his own room. Chace looked out the west window toward Mariposa Beach. Lights twinkled as the pines swayed in cadence with an inshore breeze.

Life at the small art colony was free and open, with renown and success of one person being cause for rejoicing by all. Not that the Bohemian element was totally accepted by Forest Shores. Far from it. Their lack of piety, their disdain of convention and social ritual had from the beginning more than thirty years ago brought them castigation and opprobrium. That the colony had survived despite criticism and ostracism was due to those few in the town of Forest Shores who appreciated their talents and their business patronage.

It was still early enough in the evening that he would be welcome beside their hearths with a glass of red wine and kisses from the girls. Chace blew out the lamp and made his way to the stables. Eusebio came limping into the stall.

"Can I saddle her up for you, Mr. Chace?"

"Thanks, Eusebio, but I'll do it." He tightened the girth and caressed the sleek belly of the enormous gray mare. She nickered and nuzzled the old man's shoulder as he stood by, ready to help.

"I don't have to tell you, be careful with her. Not like Mr. Archibald. Some day Linette here, she throw Mr. Archibald right on his head, if he's not careful." The old Mexican put an arm around the thoroughbred's lowered neck and stroked her white-blazed forehead. "She's a real lady. Gotta be gentle with her, treat her nice."

"I don't want Arch riding her at all, Eusebio," Chace said.

"I know, Mr. Chace, but he come out here and say for me to saddle her up for him. What'm I going to do? I say 'no' and he go up to the house and make trouble for Catalina and me." His aged brown face pulled into lines of worry around white-fringed dark eyes.

"I know. But you send him to see me next time, hear? If he can throw a saddle on her without her knocking him down, you can't stop him, but I can stop him if I'm around." He led the rangy horse from the stall and out through the stable door. "I don't want Arch to fool with this horse at all. She's dangerous, but as you say, she's a lady."

"Yes, sir, Mr. Chace. Next time, I tell him go see you." Eusebio released the horse's head with a caress.

"Come on, Linette. Let's go see what's going on down at the beach." Chace held the reins more tightly than if they had been travelling by daylight, for given her head, the great gray mare would break into a gallop and race blindly along any trail simply for the joy of movement. He checked her in the moonlight, but let her pick her own way down the trail which wandered through heavy pine, into scrub, and to the sand along Mariposa River. As she caught the seaweed-and-salt-scented night air drifting upriver from the ocean half a mile northwest, she snorted and pranced her delight.

"Easy, girl, easy!" He reined in on her exuberance. "If Arch ever takes you and gives you your head, you'll kill him!"

Laurie Mathews took down the last garland of twisted crêpe paper and handed it to Olive. The room, now bereft of gay red and green Christmas decorations, once more was plain and efficient. Pine cones and boughs had been placed on a pyre of wrappings and boxes outside in the rear yard and added their crackling smoke to the crisp evening air. A wind had sprung up from north-north-west carrying clear, bright cold thousands of miles from Alaska and the Bering Sea. Curtains at the French windows moved slightly as the door across the hall opened.

"Now that you two are all finished with the work, I'll volunteer my help." Thea's head was turbaned with a blue striped towel. She stood in the doorway, her robe hanging unevenly about her ankles. "I have some magazines you might like to read. Last month's *Munsey's* and *Smart Set*. Would you like to see them, Laurie? Olive's already had them."

"Sure. Whenever you're through with them." Laurie dropped the paper into a cardboard carton.

"Is that everything? I'll take it down for Roy to burn, if we have it all." Olive wiped her hands on her calico apron.

"No—just one more thing." Laurie brought a small, brightly-decorated teak and ebony box from the night table by her bed. She held it with both hands and gazed at it before she stuffed it into a corner of the trash.

"But Laurie! That's the box Chace sent you from Sacramento! Why on earth are you throwing it away?" Olive was aghast.

"I don't want anything from him!" She covered her eyes with both hands and turned her back to them.

"Surely it's not as bad as that, Laurie." Thea, mystified, came into the room and put her arms around the girl.

"Yes, it is! Hasn't he made it very clear?"

"Just because he went away on business for a week or so? All men have responsibilities, Chace Creighton included. He's the working end of their company, remember? He wrote you letters and he'll see you the minute he gets back." Olive sat down at the dining table and toyed with the Brittania-ware tantalus. She was experienced in pacifying small children, but not her close friends.

Laurie turned to Olive, tears wet on her cheeks. "He's been home for three days! Three whole days! Etta Korby's mother-in-law came over from San Esteban on the same train with him when he came back. Etta wasn't going to tell me, but Mrs. Korby let it slip this afternoon when she brought Fannie downtown for her ice cream treat."

"Was that why you ran out of the drugstore so fast? I looked up just in time to see you fly out the door. I thought then something must be wrong." Thea pushed the girl to a chair and sat her down. All three said nothing for a few moments.

"Maybe something is wrong. Maybe his father. . ." Olive began.

"No! Althea McMurray is nursing him, and she's a good friend of Madge Hobart's. She says there's no change in Zedekiah. He's even a bit stronger—no worse." Laurie held her head in both hands, her black eyes filled with tears. "No, he's just had second thoughts about me and decided to end it where it was."

139

"Did he tell you that?" Thea asked.

"No, but he sent a note to that effect," Laurie replied.

"A note? That's not like Chace. Any of the rest of them, but not him," Thea protested.

"Well, if he doesn't want to keep me company, his brother does! And I intend to cultivate his acquaintance." Laurie sat back, dabbing her eyes with the handkerchief.

"Oh God! Not fat Archibald! You couldn't!" Olive groaned.

"No, not Archibald. Duncan," Laurie said.

"Oh girl, you don't want anything to do with him! Not Duncan! Did he ask you out?" Thea's disapproval showed in her face.

"Yes, he did. And I'm going. He was honest enough to admit he'd only withheld his attentions because he was afraid of Chace."

"Afraid of him? Nonsense! Chace has got him out of trouble ever since he was a toddler. From what I hear, he's even been paying off Duncan's gambling debts," Thea said. "I just don't believe that."

"Regardless of the truth, I'm going to a New Year's Eve supper with him at the Shell Box." Resolution was in Laurie's voice. Her eyes flashed determination.

"Just how did all this come about?" Olive asked.

"Chace had Duncan bring me a note this afternoon. He came by with it just as I was leaving the shop," Laurie said.

"I thought I heard a carriage before you came in. Did he bring you home?" Thea wanted to know.

"Yes, he did." It was as though Laurie were prepared for all their objections.

"And if I'm not being too inquisitive, what did Chace's note say?" Olive was reluctant to believe Chace would ever take such an indirect way of contacting the girl. Should he do so, he would have good reason.

Laurie went to the wardrobe and reached into the pocket of her cape. "Here—you can read it." She handed a folded note in its envelope to Olive, who opened it and read slowly.

"But Laurie, all he says is that he isn't going to see you for a while, that he can't explain anything right now, but will as soon as he can." Olive could neither understand Laurie's reaction nor Chace's enigmatic note. "Surely you must give him the benefit of the doubt. If he says a serious situation has developed to prevent his seeing you, you can be sure something really has happened." She found herself defending the man. "Chace Creighton is not a liar."

"Nor is he the sort to send his no-good kid brother around with a note if he wanted to break off his engagement!" Thea was positive even though it was a Creighton she was championing.

"What did Duncan have to say?" Olive was suspicious.

"He as much as told me Chace was through with me."

"You didn't believe him, did you?" Thea was shocked that Laurie would give credence to the word of such a man. "He'd lie to anybody just for the fun of it. He can't be trusted. Everybody knows that."

"What exactly did he say about Chace?" Olive asked, then quickly apologized. "I'm sorry. I know it's none of my business, but this whole thing just doesn't sound like Chace at all." She recognized the girl's distress. "We won't even talk about it if you'd rather not."

"You're my friends—of course I don't mind talking to you about it. How does the old saying go. . .troubles shared are troubles. . .?"

"Troubles shared are still troubles and they won't automatically disappear," Thea put in abruptly. "What else did Duncan say?" More Americanized than the rest of her family, Thea had no qualms about asking personal questions when Duncan was involved with one of her friends.

Laurie walked to the French windows and parted the curtains. To the south and west a bit, dim lights

141

from the main house on the Creighton estate flickered through the pine tops. Perhaps the lamplight was coming from Chace's own room.

"He said Chace finally knew on which side his bread was buttered," Laurie said softly.

"How very trite!" To Thea it sounded typical of Duncan.

"What did he mean?" Olive asked.

"He said their mother demanded Chace not see me again. It seems she thinks I came here purposely to insinuate myself into their family for some nefarious reason or other. Or worse—to ruin the Creightons." Laurie turned a puzzled face to Thea and Olive. "I asked him why I should want to do that, but he said he knew it was ridiculous, that his mother was just like that. Always dramatic, always suspicious of everyone's motives."

"And don't forget: Sybil Creighton insists on picking their women friends and running their lives," Thea said. "She wants to hang on to her sons."

"Well, she sure doesn't have much of a grip on Duncan! And as for Chace abiding by Sybil's dictates—if he didn't want to, he wouldn't do it." Too late Olive realized what she had said. Laurie left the window and sat down on the settee beside her.

"See—you've said exactly what I've been thinking ever since I learned he'd come back three days ago and didn't let me know. He wouldn't behave like this if he didn't want to." She tried to laugh, but the sound held no gaiety. "Besides, if he feels he must abide by his mother's word, he's not the man I thought he was, is he?"

"You should wait until you can talk to him, Laurie." Olive tried to mend her gaffe. "I know he says in the note not to write him, but you could get word to him. Maybe Roy could tell Eusebio or Catalina."

"No! I'll not go begging! Obviously his mother convinced him I'm some sort of predatory Delilah. And she openly blames me for her husband's stroke. I thought Chace cared—it's plain he doesn't care

enough." She jumped up and poked at the blazing log
in the grate, stirred the red coals and added another
piece of wood. "They can think anything they like. It
isn't important anyhow, is it?"

Olive knew it would be futile to discuss the matter
any further. The hurt was too deep, the wounds too
fresh. Nor could she offer remedy, she who had never
been in love or courted by any man. The school teacher
realized with a pang that while love could bring pain as
well as joy, she had known neither. She picked up the
carton of wrappings and boxes and went to the door,
not knowing what to say to the girl.

"Don't be too hasty. Give Chace a chance to explain and make things right. You'll find it isn't as you
think." She turned the knob and opened the door. "I'll
run along now. I've arithmetic and spelling papers to
correct. I've been putting them off too long and school
starts again in a few days." Olive would wait until she
was out in the hallway before she retrieved the bauble
box from the trash. She could keep it for Laurie and
return it when the proper time presented itself.

"Goodnight. Thanks for helping take down the
decorations." Laurie washed her hands at the sink and
dried them on a small towel hung on a peg by the stove.

"Would it do any good if I said I agree with
Olive?" Thea asked.

"You mean I should try to see Chace, maybe get
word to him through Roy?"

"Something like that, yes. Or wait until he can explain," Thea said.

"No, I guess it wouldn't do much good. My pride
can survive rejection, but it couldn't survive my going to
anybody on my hands and knees. Not even to Chace!"
Laurie replied with a toss of her dark head.

"You're angry right now, angry and hurt. Don't let
that make you do something you might regret." Thea
was remembering Rosa Cantu, who had lost everything
because of Duncan Creighton, and in the end lost him,
too.

"I'm going with Duncan to supper. He asked me,

143

and I accepted." She was not testy or argumentative, but merely reaffirming her decision. "If their mother forbids Duncan to see me, too, I'll just have to deal with that when it comes."

"All I can say is if you go with Duncan, you'd better tell Guido Ferranti to keep an eye on you, and you'd better have a way to get home safely. I think you're being very foolish, but it's your affair." Thea rose to leave. She was annoyed at Laurie's determination to believe Duncan. "I've got to dry my hair and press my waist and skirt. I may have to work late helping Knut take inventory, so I probably won't see you before you leave tomorrow night."

Thea was too concerned not to speak her mind bluntly. She turned at the door and looked hard at Laurie. "Duncan runs with a pretty wild bunch. You're not used to his sort of crowd. Remember what I said about Guido. He runs a respectable place and is a good, decent man. Just in case you need one in an emergency." She smiled, but was not convincing. "Have fun, but please, Laurie, be very careful."

The Shell Box Cafe crowned an outcropping of granite thrust up on each side of La Gaviota Cove. Like mighty fists on encircling arms, gargantuan heaps of rock protected the small harbor and made navigation hazardous for all except shallow-draft vessels. Larger ships and lighters anchored well off the coast and unloaded or took on cargo with utmost caution.

Guido and Teresa Ferranti had used wide slabs of native redwood to construct the restaurant, and had glassed in an observation deck as business warranted expansion. Collections of opalescent abalone and clam shells encrusted the cement walkways, vertical reinforcements, and broad buttresses which extended to the waterline below. Although it was fragile in appearance, the restaurant had been built by Ferranti to be almost as solid as the rock upon which it rested. Smashing tides had more than once dampened the terraces and occasionally a rock had been flung explosively against the glass windows, but it remained unscathed over the years to become one of the prime attractions of the area.

In the lee of rocks and a stubby stand of gnarled cypress, a sandy field had been cleared and graded to make a lot in which carriages could be left. For the few automobiles which dared the trip to Sand Town, a corduroy parking lot had been made with stripped poles and planks south of the cafe. While diners enjoyed salmon and sand dabs or robust beef and lamb, their horses were protected from blowing sand and stinging salt wind off the bay.

Geraniums bloomed year-round inside the dining room in tall, blue and yellow painted earthenware vases, and wooden baskets trailed rose oxalis and cerise and purple fuchsias. The floor of random width planks was covered with clean sawdust from the lumber mill at the other end of Sand Town, and candles in the necks of empty wine bottles flickered on every table.

On mild evenings after dinner, customers could stroll across sand dunes and climb up into the hills directly west of the restaurant. There the view of the Shell Box and Sand Town made a pleasant foreground for La Gaviota Cove, Beach Park, and Forest Shores beyond. Below the cafe, ranged on both sides of two flimsy docks, were small fishing craft. Staring eyes were painted on the prows - saints' names on the sterns. The boats swayed with rhythm of tide and swell, their lines alternately taut and slack. Lacy edges of sea froth danced across the top of the water and pushed several hundred yards into the arrowhead-shaped cove where it met sweet water from La Gaviota Creek.

New Year's Eve at the Shell Box was not the dignified celebration of the Blue Roof Lodge, but if more noisy, it was also more enjoyable. Wines were not from as fine a cellar, but they were good natives that complemented simple, hearty fare. Donning white aprons and bustling about with carafes and clearing the tables were the Deledda boys, hired for the special night.

Laurie rested her arm on the window ledge and leaned toward the glass. Etched in faint outline against dark water were rocks and fish-packing sheds. The vague uneasiness which had pursued Laurie all evening had grown steadily until conversation had become difficult.

"You've never been here before?" Duncan had interpreted her distraction as boredom. He snapped open a flat, gold-embossed morocco leather case and extended it to the girl. She shook her head, surprised that he would offer her cigarettes in a public place.

"No, I've never been here until tonight," Laurie replied, vowing to throw off the pall of premonition for Duncan's sake. The dinner of veal in delicate lemon sauce had terminated with rich, yellow zabaglione, tiny macaroons and black, fragrant coffee.

"You must come here often, judging from your reception."

"Oh, you mean Guido? Yes, I guess he considers me a good customer. I wasn't too sure of my welcome tonight, however." He struck a match and lighted a long, gold-banded cigarette.

"Why is that?" Laurie asked.

"I got drunk a few weeks ago and broke up his private dining room over there." He motioned toward the opposite side of the restaurant with a jerk of his head. "Sometimes I'm like that. Never remember a thing when I'm sober again."

"Why do you do it? Do you enjoy doing destructive things?"

"I wish I knew why I do it. I truly wish I knew," Duncan replied. "It would tell me something about myself, wouldn't it? It's as if there's a devil inside me, driving me to perdition." He drew deeply on his potent Russian cigarette and exhaled slowly. "Going to hell in a hand-basket! Isn't that the usual phrase for it?" He settled into the wicker-backed chair and signaled Guido Ferranti.

"I've heard the phrase, but never knew anyone it fit." Laurie liked the sandy-haired young man in spite of his self-deprecation.

"Well, now you've at last met one it does!" As the short wiry Sicilian came to the table, Duncan turned to Laurie and asked, "Would you care for a liqueur, perhaps a brandy?"

"No, thank you. I'm fine." To Ferranti she said, "Everything was perfect. I've never had that dessert before. It's delicious."

Beneath his oversized walrus-moustache Ferranti smiled. "Thank you, young lady. I'll tell my wife. She's in charge of the kitchen. Sees to everything personally." He turned to Duncan. "What can I bring you, Mr. Creighton?" He looked apprehensive.

"Don't worry, Guido. I have a lady with me. I promise I won't break so much as a glass tonight." His laugh was strained, as if he were not sure of himself. "Bring me a brandy, please."

"Yes, sir. Right away." He scurried away, paused to look at the time shown on the shelf clock over the central fireplace.

The crowd was getting noisy, especially a group keeping to themselves in a corner near the entry. Their dress was a gay hodge-podge of style and rags, satins and rough canvascloth. Along the window sill beside their tables they were lining up wine bottles as they emptied them. Their tables remained strewn with dishes which were passed about, shared and tasted by each in turn. Several large loaves of twisted, crusty bread and a heavy crock of fresh butter were carried to them, along with a board of cheeses and olives.

A tall, aristocratic man, clad in hand-loomed tweed and red foulard, sat at the head of one long table facing across the room. During dinner Laurie had become aware of his scrutiny. His expression reminded her of Roy Wimbish's—the same wistful look of remembering. He could be of an age with Roy or younger, for in the deceptive candlelight it was impossible to guess if he were as youthful as the laughing, joking people surrounding him or much older.

Mounting apprehension clawed at her as she felt

147

the intensity of his stare. To overcome the uncomfortable feeling, she tried to focus her attention on Duncan.

"Who are the people in the corner?" Laurie asked but did not look toward the man across the room. "I noticed some of them seemed to know you."

"They're from the art colony down at Mariposa Beach. The man with the red cravat facing us is Morgan Griffith, the famous portrait artist. He must be quite taken with you." Even Duncan had noticed the man's staring.

"Oh, I've heard of him!" She glanced at Griffith. "They don't look especially arty, do they?"

"How do you expect them to look?" Duncan was amused. "They're just like anybody else. And they are different in only one way—what they do, they do openly, honest and above board. Best bunch of people—except you—in this whole rotten place." His tone was bitter, but as he looked at the boisterous group his pale eyes softened. "They are kind and generous, and not a one of them puts money above people."

"You must know them fairly well," Laurie ventured.

"Fairly well."

"Especially the pretty girls?" To counteract her increasing anxiety Laurie resorted to teasing Duncan.

"What girls do you mean? I see only one girl in the whole place here." He gestured broadly with his white, long-fingered hands. "There has never been any girl but you—ever!"

"You're too young to be such a fantastic liar! Shame on you."

Guido Ferranti interrupted with a small snifter of brandy which he placed before Duncan. "May I bring you anything else?"

"No, Guido, that will be all, thank you," Duncan replied.

"Champagne at midnight?" Ferranti asked.

"Not tonight. I promised the young lady I'd abstain and behave myself." He reached across the table and patted Laurie's hand. "So far, I'm doing remarkably well and I don't want to spoil my record."

At the far end of the enclosed terrace, the wide double doors to the outside opened. For long moments there was a lull in the noise. Revelers turned to see who had joined them, and seeing, fell silent. A murmur, low in pitch and out of key with the happy tenor of the evening, followed in the wake of the newcomers. It swelled till it drowned conversation and laughter.

Duncan Creighton scraped his chair backward. His cigarette hung forgotten between lips suddenly colorless. His eyes darted about the room like a mouse seeking to escape a pride of stalking cats. He grasped the edge of the table, his knuckles white with tension. Even the rejoicing celebrants in the corner became still.

"Laurie, I have to leave," Duncan whispered. "Don't ask any questions. Tell Guido to get you a carriage and go home." He threw several bills on the table and pushed one into the girl's hand. The couple at the next table watched with growing alarm. "I love you, Laurie. You're the only good thing that has ever happened to me!"

He turned abruptly and ran from the cafe, taking the side exit down the shallow steps that led to the lot where he had left his buggy.

Quickly he maneuvered the horse about, clapped the little mare smartly on the rump, and drove through the collection of rigs which had been left at odd angles. The mare picked her way to Shell Road and began to trot.

Four figures ran down the steps leading from the cafe to the road, dodging couples who were on their way into the Shell Box. One of the figures, younger and more agile than the others, sprinted and caught the mare's bridle, ran with her a few yards and halted her.

"Whoa! Whoa!" He grabbed the reins and forced the buggy to return to the steps. "You don't want to leave the lady, do you, Creighton? Not on New Year's Eve! That's no way to act."

"Laurie?" In the darkness Duncan could see only a

149

long-skirted figure beside the road. As the carriage stopped, he could discern who it was. "What are you doing with her? Leave her out of this!"

The couples who had been going into the cafe stopped at the door to listen, two of the young men hesitantly advancing toward the bottom of the steps.

"Duncan, what's wrong?" Laurie screamed in terror. "Who are these men? What do they want?" The tall man held her tightly by the arm, his fingers digging into her flesh. As he shoved her toward the phaeton, she stumbled in the darkness and fell to her knees in the sand.

"Laurie!" Duncan leaped from the carriage and ran to her side. "You shouldn't have come with them! Oh God! I'm so sorry!" He held her to him, then helped her onto the cement pathway. "Are you all right?"

"Yes, but tell me what's wrong!" Laurie pleaded. Two of the men stood behind Duncan, their faces indistinguishable in the darkness.

"Tell her, Creighton! Or do you want us to?" The taller figure moved closer. They could see the flash of a heavy, silver head on his cane as he tapped it into the palm of his hand. "I gave you two weeks, Creighton. I told you I meant business. You didn't want us going to your family so you set that sheriff on us in San Esteban. Pretty cute trick!"

"We're here to collect. . .one way or another." The man behind Duncan moved in. "You double-crossed us after we trusted you. We aim to get even."

"I have only part of the money! You can have what I've got. Just leave the girl alone!" Duncan said.

Creighton's voice was husky with fear as he took out his wallet and handed it to the tall man.

"Why should we? Maybe she can give us some good entertainment. That might make up the difference, wouldn't it, boys?" The man's quiet laugh sent chills of terror through the girl. "You're a sporting man, Creighton. I guess you got yourself a sporting woman, eh?"

With quick movement, so fast that he caught them

unaware, Duncan brought from his coat pocket a small revolver and fired once, point blank.

"Run, Laurie! Run!" he yelled.

He wheeled and shot again into the darkness behind him, stumbling over the tall man who pitched forward into the sand. In the gun's flash the face of the man on his right was white with sudden horror. As the bullet ripped through him he screamed.

The man to the left stooped to the ground as if to dodge Creighton's aim. He lifted something from the sand.

Before Duncan could fire again, the silver head of the tall man's cane slashed through the damp air and with a dull, sickening thud caught Duncan behind the left ear.

Chapter 7

Henry Fulbright pulled himself up with dignity, his red face livid with the control he was having to employ. He was not accustomed to being accused of obstructing justice. Had the accuser been a man, instead of Sybil Creighton, the man would have been half-way across the room looking up from the floor. As it was, the mayor clenched his fists while the veins in his temples bulged and pulsed with rage.

"That is a most unfounded and dangerous imputation, Mrs. Creighton. You know as well as I do that Mayor Fulbright is as anxious as anyone else to bring Duncan's killer to justice."

Ed Sickles was not a diplomat and had risen to the woman's challenge with anger. "People have to back that sort of talk either with proof or defend themselves in court." His rumpled clothing was dusty and in the stuffy office smelled strongly of horse sweat. Spurs of ancient make jangled on his high, laced boots, attesting to his night in the saddle.

"You say dangerous, Chief Sickles. May I ask to whom it is dangerous?" Her face was white with contained emotion, but no evidence of tears stained her face, nor were her eyes red-rimmed as might be thought normal.

"Mrs. Creighton, if you want a debating society, go over to the High School Forensic League. They'll be happy to give you a good argument. This is a police station. I don't want arguments here. I want facts—things I can act on legally. I don't want suppositions or fancy charges leveled at anybody unless there's truth in what's said. Do I make myself clear?"

Ed Sickles was a plain-spoken man, capable in all areas of his work except handling privileged citizens with delicacy. His dark auburn hair bushed from under a wide, flat-brimmed hat. Since he had not removed his hat in his office, it meant that he was on official duty, uniform or not.

"I realize you're overwrought, seeing as how you've just lost your boy, but that doesn't give you the right to accuse people of complicity unjustly. That's libel, defamation, and as such, Mrs. Creighton, it comes under the law. Now if that's all the business you have with me, I'll get back to work."

Sickles rose from behind his desk, his huge frame blocking the gray light that sifted through the window behind him. He had been up all night and was weary after organizing a mounted posse and directing its efforts. The sheriff in San Esteban was glad to relinquish some of his authority to the local police, especially when it came to trailing the fugitive in the Santa Margaritas. Sickles hesitated to see if Sybil Creighton would leave, then crossed the room in front of her. Without excusing himself, he said, "Mayor, soon as you get time, I'd like you to see what you can do in contacting the sheriff down at San Luis. I tried to get hold of him again just now, but they had some ruckus down there and he hadn't come back yet. If our bird keeps flying south, he'll make San Luis in a day or so. I want a welcoming committee all set up when he gets there."

"Sure, I'll keep on the telephone till I get him," Mayor Fulbright agreed. "You going down yourself?"

"No, I'll have one of the boys go collect him. I've got too much to do here."

"If you'll excuse me, Mrs. Creighton?" Mayor Fulbright bowed and followed Chief Sickles into the hall.

"See what you can do with her." The policeman motioned with his thumb to the closed door. "My God! You'd think she'd be home bawling her eyes out instead

153

of down here bawling us out! Keep her out of my hair, will you? I've got twenty-three men out on the south trails and the sheriff's deputized a dozen or so. We're doing all we can, without her making it harder. I've got enough on my hands without some woman demanding I arrest you and that poor Mathews girl." He ran a hand over his unshaven face and rubbed his eyes. "By damn, if I don't get me some sleep pretty soon, I'm going to fall over."

"I'll do what I can, but it won't be easy, Ed. And you saying she can't make accusations like that will only make her more determined. She's one vicious female. She'll get her gossip mill going and we're both apt to be looking for jobs come election." Mayor Fulbright's bird-eyes glittered irately between puffy red pouches.

"Why the hell doesn't she get on a horse and go after him herself?" Sickles exploded. "She can put a thumb-screw on him and have herself a good time!"

"That's not quite the point," Fulbright said. "She'll crucify that girl—and us! Just to satisfy herself that something's being done." They walked a few steps down the hallway. "You talked on the telephone to the chief in San Esteban last night, didn't you?"

"Yeah. And notified every town down the line. I figure if he goes to the railroad, they'll nail him sure. Those that don't have a telephone, I telegraphed. You better be ready for some mighty big communications bills."

Fulbright glanced down the hall to make sure the door remained closed. "Now don't you repeat this, Ed, but I'd say some folks hereabouts would just as lief that killer got a medal instead of a rope!"

"Nobody deserves what Duncan got. Not murder." Sickles shook his head.

"Duncan Creighton's been asking for what he got for a long time and you and me know it. Why, Guido Ferranti told me Duncan tore up his place something awful a few weeks back. His brother, Chace, paid for the damage, like he usually does. That's why Guido didn't come to you about it."

"Hell, Frank, if a few more people had come to me about that kid, maybe he wouldn't be dead right now!" Sickles complained.

"You couldn't stop him any more than his folks could. He'd have laughed at you for your try," the mayor said. "Look at him—keeping that nice little Cantu girl on the string all these last few years. And her a good, church-going girl before he ruined her. It's just luck her brothers didn't take care of him long ago."

"That'd put them on a level with him, and they aren't the kind to do that. I know the Cantu boys, and they don't come any better," Chief Sickles explained. "They'd be afraid of their pa, too. He's a proud old man, proud of his family name. Why, they go back into the late seventeen-hundreds. Did you know that?"

"I heard it, yes. But even if they didn't do it, somebody else was sure to sooner or later."

"Look, Hank, I'm going on home and eat, shave, take a bath, sleep a couple of hours, and get right back here. Then I'm going to talk to a few of the witnesses again. It's just possible one of them may have remembered something since last night that could help us get a line on our man."

The policeman started down the steps to the foyer, his spurs chinking on each riser. He raised a hand in farewell and threw open the swinging door.

Fog swirled through the pine tops, blanking out the highest branches. It was as if the first day of the year had gone into mourning for its beginning.

Moisture dripped in desulatory patter from every exposed surface. Three mongrel dogs ambled along the picket fence which surrounded the old Hinshaw place. One lifted his leg to the gate. The other two investigated with their noses and followed suit. Then, as if there were insufficient cause to continue their late afternoon prowl, they slunk away down the alley, bypassing garbage pails and trash bins.

From somewhere in a live oak came the scolding shriek of a scrub jay, but no answering chatter replied.

Even the birds were subdued by the intimidating mist.

New Year's Day in Forest Shores was a quiet holiday with families celebrating modestly at home. Christmas had seen as much feasting and visiting as most people wanted for a while; after dutifully attending church services in the morning, they went home to roast beef or crown of pork and an afternoon of pinocle.

Olive Pickens pulled the shades and tiptoed to the bed. In the dim light of the candle Laurie's face seemed as pale as the muslin pillow case, her hair still pinned in its formal arrangement from the night before. Her arm, extended on top of the hemstitched and embroidered sheet, was discolored with dark bruises.

"If that Chace Creighton had any heart at all, he'd come to her now when she needs him!" Thea spoke aloud.

"Shh! Let her sleep!" Olive said.

"She won't wake up. That hydrated chloral will keep her under for a long time yet." Thea pulled the drapes across the French windows. "Why didn't she listen to me? Why did she have to go out with Duncan? I tried to warn her, didn't I?"

Olive laid kindling over wadded newspaper, piled on a few pieces of small wood, then struck a match to it. She adjusted the damper so the draw was sharp and waited until the wood blazed. She sat on the hearth with her arms clasped about her knees.

"You warned her, but the poor thing was so hurt by Chace..." Olive began.

"I thought he was different from the rest of the Creightons, but I guess I was wrong. Maybe they're all alike after all." Thea curled up in the Turkish leather rocker and watched the fire. "For her sake I'd hoped he was different."

"It just isn't like Chace. What I really don't understand is why he would propose to her, then end it like he did. There must be a good reason, but I know it isn't Laurie." Olive looked toward the high-posted bed. "She's too sweet and honest; I don't care what that horrid woman says! We know Laurie—she doesn't."

At the sound of someone coming up the stairs, Thea went to the door and whispered, "Come on in. She's still sleeping. Hasn't moved."

Pansy Hinshaw walked to the side of the bed, her face frowning in commiseration. Her light blue eyes were reddened, their lids swollen. "Ed Sickles stopped by just now. Wanted to know if she had anything more to tell him. Maybe something that had slipped her mind last night. I told him Doctor Eichner gave her a sleeping draught. Ed's downstairs in the front parlor. He wants to see you both for a minute." She turned and stood by the fireplace, twisting her apron nervously. "I'll watch Laurie while you go talk to him."

Olive placed a small log in the grate and pushed the chain mesh across the opening. "We'd better go. Come on, Thea."

The two girls descended the staircase and turned to the left into Pansy's front parlor. Chief Sickles rose as they came into the room and held out his hand to Olive, his face breaking into a wide grin.

"Hello, Olive. Haven't seen you in some time—since the last school supper, to be exact." His red-brown eyes were circled with fatigue, but his delight in seeing the young woman was evident.

"That's about right, Ed. Last November, before Thanksgiving."

"Yes, ma'am. You wore a brown dress with something frilly and blue here." He pointed to his neck, but his eyes remained on Olive.

"Did I? I don't recall what I wore." She fibbed, but was elated that he remembered. Olive felt his broad fingers close over hers, almost expecting a crushing grip, surprised at his gentle touch. "Thea, may I present Ed Sickles? Ed, this is Thea Harris."

"How'd do, Miss Harris? I knew your folks over in San Esteban. Your granpa Orozco was one of the finest men I ever knew." He held her hand long enough to feel its chill and saw the deep worry in her face. "You girls sit down. I won't keep you long. This has turned out to be a pretty poor holiday for all of us, hasn't it?''

Thea and Olive sat beside each other on the upholstered chaise by the bay window. A large silk-shaded lamp shed rose light through the room, its warm glow a comforting contrast to the gathering night outside. Ed Sickles perched on a small side chair which was dwarfed by his bulk.

"Did Miss Mathews say anything to you girls that might help me? She hardly made sense last night," he began. "I know Doc Eichner gave her something, but did she say anything at all about what happened? Who the men were? Did she know them before? Or were they strangers to her?"

"Oh no, I can assure you she didn't know them," Thea spoke up quickly.

"How can you be so sure of that?" Sickles queried.

"She's just not the kind who'd be acquainted with that sort!" Thea answered.

"I'd like more assurance that that. Not that I don't believe you, but I've got to have facts, not opinions. You understand, don't you?" His voice was as gentle as his touch, much out of character with his rough appearance.

"Yes, I do understand. But there's more: when we were bathing her and trying to get her warm—we had to heat bricks and wrap them in paper and put them in her bed, she was so icy cold. Well, she said she'd never laid eyes on them before. Had no idea who they were or what they wanted. They just came to the table, told her Duncan was in trouble and for her to come with them. When she refused and said she intended to take a carriage home, they jerked her to her feet and practically carried her out of the restaurant. It all happened so fast no one had a chance to do much. Guido Ferranti was down in the cellar, and the other waiters just stood around and watched, thinking it was just one more of Duncan's escapades and didn't want to get mixed up in it. After all, they didn't know Laurie." Thea stopped, not wanting to admit aloud that she felt responsible for the whole event. She had, of course, warned Laurie, but she could have stopped her.

"That's right, Ed. Laurie said they forced her to go outside," Olive continued the story. "The tall man hurt her arm where he held her. It's covered with black and blue marks. He must have pushed her, because she fell down, too. Evidently Duncan tried to defend her. She had no idea he was carrying a gun or that he needed to carry one. She'd never have gone out with him had she known."

Olive leaned forward to emphasize what followed. "She's a good girl. Not like those other creatures Duncan Creighton was fooling around with. She'd been told he was no good, but she'd only met him a few times and liked him. He fast-talked her, and, poor thing, she didn't realize how wild he was. That's the simple truth of it. I'd swear to it on the Bible that she didn't know any of those men."

"Who were they? Did you find out?" Thea asked.

"Their identification was pretty sketchy. Probably fake. We may not even have their right names. Two dead ones were mixed up in some shady gambling over in the valley. Seems Duncan blew the whistle on them for robbing some well-to-do Armenian farmer from Fresno. He'd won a sizable pot in a private game in San Esteban. They waylaid him outside of town and beat him up. He couldn't identify any of them, but Duncan was to blame, you can be sure."

"Duncan would do that?" Even Thea was shocked.

"That and a lot more, too, Miss Harris," Sickles answered. "He was even trading in girls over in the valley, if you'll pardon my frankness. Only trouble was, he was dealing with some mighty mean fellows, and when they found out he'd sicced the sheriff onto them, they came looking for him. The big one seems to have been the ringleader. He gave Duncan time on what he owed them. Duncan set up the Armenian, but it didn't net enough to pay off. They came over here to collect and get even."

"How dreadful! We'd warned Laurie he was bad. I

159

suppose she thought it was just hometown sour-grapes gossip about the local rich boy. She was so willing to believe the best about him. What an awful way to learn the truth!'' Thea shifted in the chaise and looked away, wondering if she should tell Ed about Chace and Laurie. And she still blamed herself for not convincing the girl about Duncan.

''She said they made some sort of threat about her, to the effect that since Duncan couldn't pay them, they might make Laurie pay—the implication was horrible. That was when Duncan began shooting. He was trying to protect Laurie. It was probably the only decent thing he did in his life.''

Ed Sickles got back into his buggy and let the horse take its own way down the darkened street toward Sand Town. Every instinct in him rebelled at Sybil Creighton's accusation, but there was always a possibility that she was right. Perhaps the girl had lured Duncan to his death.

Sunday afternoon brought a deep blue sky unsullied by either fog or cloud. The sun burned down through the pines which enclosed Bert Hutchins' pasture from West Main Avenue and Shell Road. Gauged by the way the horses and mules kept to the shade, standing close together, nose to rump with tails whisking at tiny black flies, the day was unseasonably hot. Even a few pioneering bees hovered around the brush, searching for early blooms, their undulating hum and solemn dance informing others of their kind where nectar lay hidden.

Laurie Mathews walked behind Roy along the dusty edge of the road, following as best she could in his footsteps, and breaking her stride only when they reached the bridge over La Gaviota Creek. They had walked in silence from the house, with even Thea Harris unwilling to disturb the peaceful quiet.

''Mind the droppings, ladies,'' Roy cautioned them as they crossed a trail which led south through the forest. Fresh manure lay drying in the sunshine, with great buzzing flies shimmering iridescent blue-green about it. La Gaviota Creek, high to its brim with winter run-off, gurgled and complained on its way to blend with the sea in the cove.

Circling in slow, graceful arabesques were two red-tailed hawks, their creamy white bellies flashing against the indigo above. Their piercing shrills seemed to warn the colonies of ground squirrels to cover, for only a few twitching noses emerged from holes in low, overhanging bluffs above the creek.

"You pick us the horses, Roy." Thea gathered her skirts about her knees as the man handed her over the stile which gave access to the pasture just beyond the bridge.

"Be glad to, Miss Thea. Bert Hutchins wouldn't be above giving ladies a star-gazer now and again. No sir, I'll make sure you get nice Walkers." He knew Bert would see to it they had the best in the stalls, purely as a favor to him and Pansy Hinshaw, but it suited him to pretend not to trust the wily horse trader.

A covey of quail burst from heavy brush along the path, their black plumes bobbing in their frightened whirr. Laurie started at the noise and watched in amusement as the hens ran along the ground refusing to take flight.

"You be sure to give 'em their heads going down that bank at Mariposa Beach. They can slip around in that sand a fright. They aren't pan-footed like most of Bert's horses. If you've got the reins choked up on 'em, they don't get their footing right good. They know the way, you just let 'em go. Same coming back to the stables, 'specially if you come back by the lighthouse and them sea cliffs."

Dogs, spaniels only in their long, multicolored coats and silken, drooping ears, came on the run, their barks announcing visitors to Hutchins and his stable hands. Yapping in excited welcome, the dogs dashed up to Wimbish for ceremonial pats and caresses, then dashed off to convey their message.

"Roy, you're keeping a sight better company these

161

days, I see.'' The livery stable owner came from the blacksmith shop, his leather apron flapping. ''How are you, ladies?''

He was a short man, heavy of build, with muscle and large bones. His face was almost of a hue with his apron, his eyes white and gray depressions shaded by bristling white brows. He gazed with calm shrewdness at the trio, sympathetic in his appraisal of the girls.

''They want to take a ride down Mariposa Beach way. Be gone most all afternoon,'' Roy said. ''You got Sally and Dora available?''

''Now you know I don't rent them two out to nobody, Roy,'' Hutchins protested.

''Sally and Dora it's got to be.'' Wimbish picked up one of the young mongrel spaniels and scratched its ears, cradling it to his chest, the puppy's pink wet tongue flicking at his beard and ears. ''I don't want Mrs. Hinshaw's ladies coming back along them cliffs at sundown on none of your spooky old crocks. It's them Walkers or none.'' He put the pup down and patted its sister, who promptly sprinkled the dust in her excitement.

''They're for sale, Roy, not for hire.'' Hutchins had already nodded to a small Mexican boy who waited just inside the barn door.

''I know; I know.'' Roy looked up and grinned at him.

''Lady-dandy saddles, side-wheelers, or honest ones? Got your choice. I'd suggest stock saddles if you're going down the west trail. Got something to hang onto.'' He was certain they were both inexperienced riders, and assuredly incapable of using side-saddles.

The boy had disappeared into the cool darkness of the barn and took down the two best double-cinch western saddles from the rack.

''Much obliged, Bert.'' Roy sat on his haunches, cuffing the dogs who gnawed playfully at his sleeves and trouser legs. He smiled at Laurie. ''You'll be safe as in a rocking chair on Sally and Dora. They're genuine Tennessee Walkers. Don't you worry none about them being for sale. Bert's had 'em ever since they was yearlings. That's why they know every inch of the trails hereabouts. They're his babies, them two big bays." He looked up at the girls, his face serious once more as if to impress upon them the honor they were being accorded. "Bert don't let just anybody take 'em out. No sir, just people he's real fond of."

Dora took the lead down the west trail, picking her way with dainty steps along the sandy path. Laurie leaned back into the high, flaring cantle and let the reins hang almost slack from the bit. The mare knew her way, for Bert Hutchins visited the beach colony frequently, and as often as not the mares had to take him home on their own. Hospitality at Mariposa Beach usually included plenty of stout wine or Kentucky rye.

For the better part of a mile neither girl spoke. Hurt was still too near the surface for either of them to chance idle talk. As they rounded a sharp bend they came out of the forest into a meadow dotted with tree lupine and yarrow. Dried seed heads and stalks rustled in the slight breeze and small birds flitted into hiding at the horses' approach. A few sand dandelions bloomed in sheltered pockets, their yellow blossoms nodding on slender scapes. Unseen to the west and north, the ocean created a low sound like distant thunder which could be heard from the entire point of seaward-jutting land. Always behind the chatter of birds and raucous gull cries was the deep rumbling as surf nibbled at narrow beaches and dashed against algae covered rock.

"Have you been down there before?" Laurie turned in the saddle and looked back at Thea. "I hope we're going in the right direction."

"Only once, many years ago. My father helped build some of the newer cabins and took us down to see them when they were finished." Thea stood up in the stirrups and shielded her eyes with her hand. "This is the right trail, all right." She pointed due west. "Through that bunch of trees, beyond the rocks."

"It's a whole little town. I had no idea there'd be so many cabins." Laurie looked about the sloping meadow, startled at how primitive it had remained. "No wonder they picked this area for their colony."

From the minute they entered the stand of trees west of Shell Road they had left civilization behind, with intersecting trails and the two rutted wagon roads leading toward Mariposa Beach and the government lighthouse the only signs of man's trespass.

"It's beautiful out here. So quiet and peaceful." Thea pulled up beside Laurie in the clearing. "Are you sure it's all right if I came along today? Morgan Griffith asked you to come see him—not me."

"But Thea, I would never come alone. He certainly knew that," Laurie answered.

Griffith had been the first to reach her side after the shots rang out the night Duncan Creighton had been killed. He had carried her up the stairs into the cafe, away from the awful carnage in the road. It was he who had driven her home in his spring wagon and had gone for Doctor Eichner.

He had taken a long look at her as she lay back on the cafe bench, her simple gold silk splattered with darkening red. He had not even asked her name. It was as if he already knew her. As he raised a shot glass of brandy to her lips—what had he called her? "My sweet lady of the bees," he had whispered.

"He won't mind one extra. He just said they were having a little get-together down on the beach. Nothing special, a fish fry and roast potatoes," Laurie said. "He wanted me to come and meet some of the young people who live there."

"It'll do you good, Laurie. You've been working at the store pretty steady. And you need to make friends," Thea wondered if the girl knew what she meant.

"Get Chace off my mind? Is that it?" Laurie was not offended.

"Something like that, yes," Thea replied.

"You're right, of course. But surely Morgan Griffith can't know about Chace and me," Laurie ventured.

"Mariposa Beach is a tight little community, and Morgan Griffith is the equivalent of mayor, banker, patron—everything. He's undoubtedly heard something. After. . .after. . .'' Thea could not bring herself to mention New Year's Eve.

"Yes, I suppose after what happened to Duncan he must have heard the rest. It wasn't as if I'd tried to keep it a secret,'' Laurie said.

"Mrs. Hinshaw says he wants to paint you. That's quite an honor. He's so famous he doesn't have to paint anybody he doesn't want to. Knut Jepsen says Griffith was rich when he came here over thirty years ago, and has made nothing but money ever since.''

"Why does he live down here?'' Laurie couldn't help wondering. "And why should he run a general store if he already has enough to live on?''

"His idea of fun, Knut Jepsen says. Everyone comes in and gets whatever he needs and signs a bill for it. They just help themselves and pay when they can. Funny way to run a business, but for Mariposa Beach it works,'' Thea explained.

"I'm not sure I'd want to live out this far.'' Laurie was somewhat awed by the wildness.

"You'd have to be self-reliant, but then you'd have neighbors close by.''

They rode along the edge of a sharp bluff cut by the Mariposa River through soft, tawny sandstone. Along the precipice the trail snaked among boulders worn smooth by waters of an ancient sea. Dora and Sally eased their way down the steep path, with the girls holding tightly to the saddle horns.

By the time they had reached the bottom, a tall thin man appeared on a spit of sand near the broad mouth of the river. A wide smooth beach stretched north toward steep sea cliffs. From the shore farther inland rose wavering columns of smoke and shouts of hilarity and horseplay.

"Halloo! I see you found us with no trouble.'' Morgan Griffith waved a narrow-brimmed tweed hat, motioning them south along the sand. "We're up river a bit, away from the tide. You're just in time! We've a marvelous catch of cod and salmon.'' He led them to the picnic, tethering the Walkers to a stunted cypress and slipping their bits so they might browse. "Come, I'll introduce you to our hive."

Laurie wiped her hands on a wet towel and dusted sand from her skirts. The sun was dipping toward the southwest and far out on Gutierrez Bay a lavender haze heralded the approach of fog. Gulls wheeled overhead, begging for bits of fish and bread crusts. Some, braver than the rest, alighted and waddled near to catch tossed tidbits in their beaks. Crested jays, lured from the treed area, hopped about the picnic baskets, sneaking bites from dishes and plates until shooed away, only to return and repeat their brazen offenses.

A fat, spotted hound ran after the birds, creating havoc and scattering sand. The jays scolded from adjacent brush and returned the instant the dog collapsed, his tongue lolling.

Laurie laughed and stooped to pat the exhausted animal's head. "Poor old dear, you just can't win, can you?" For the first time in many days, she felt young and happy once more. There was gaiety and exuberance in the gathering, and she liked the people whom they met. Living had once again become bearable.

Morgan Griffith shaded his eyes and looked toward the source of new laughter. From a rise where cabins nearest the beach were located a man and slim blonde young woman headed down the path to the river. In the haze of smoke from the cook fires he could not be sure at first. He looked at Laurie. She had not yet seen the couple.

"I'd like you to see my home, ladies. Since this is your first visit to Mariposa Beach I think it fitting and proper you should see a working artist's studio, too." He held out his hands to the girls and pulled them up the slope, skirted gnarled, grotesque cypress and led them back into the forest. Below them on the beach the new couple was greeted by welcoming shouts and peals of laughter.

In a large clearing among giant pines was a long,

two-story structure, more lodge than cabin, for its front extended a hundred-twenty feet across the width of the open space, with an ell toward the back of similar proporations. A wide porch supported by smoothed tree trunks sheltered its entrance. At gable ends huge windows took full advantage of the location. Wide windows tucked under the low overhand of roof flooded the interior with cool, green-tinted light. The outer door was carved into a fantastic, twisted bas-relief imitating the cypress forms. Stained glass inserts in the high windows splashed multi-hued patches of light over rugs and furnishings, adding color to an otherwise neutral decorating scheme.

Morgan Griffith threw open the unlocked door and ushered the girls inside.

"My menage, young ladies." He swept his arms toward the room. "May I offer you a sherry while I give you a tour?" From a built-in cabinet along one wall he took a cut-glass decanter and several thin-stemmed glasses.

"Yes, thank you. That would be nice," Laurie answered.

"You, Miss Harris?" Griffith asked.

"Yes, please." Thea was awed by the splendor of the cabin. Tapestries of delicately woven fabrics hung below the balcony railing with primitive wooden dance masks; an entire wall displayed brilliant watercolor sketches and oil paintings of countless sizes. From the high, open-beamed ceiling hung chandeliers in the shape of black wrought-iron wheels with oil lamps in sockets at the spoke ends.

Lining the open redwood staircase were small etchings and prints, all exquisitely matted in colored linen and framed in gold-leafed mahogany. The furniture, constructed from slabs of natural wood fastened with wooden pegs and bound with leather thongs in the mission style, was littered with comfortable cushions in clear, singing colors to match the stained glass. It was not a room fashionable decorators would wish to claim as their own creation, for it was simple and clean of line, free of fussy embellishment. It was not a showplace, not a monument to wealth and affluence, but a warm home, with choice, loved objects and collections of sentimental trophies, all blended with the sure skill and knowledge of a great artist.

Griffith filled the small glasses to the brim and handed them to his guests. Into his own glass he poured clear gin. He was quite aware of the effect his lodge had on first-time visitors. His eyes twinkled over his drink. Thea, he was sure, had never seen anything like it, although the Orozcos before her time had enjoyed an equal luxury. Laurie, he felt, would be at home in it, could add to it her own touch of beauty.

"It's lovely! I didn't expect..." Laurie blushed and stopped.

"A bit surprising in the midst of the forest primeval? Is that it?" His quiet laugh was not ridicule, but gentle understanding. He took her by the elbow and guided her to the left where a door stood open beyond a short passageway. "Miss Harris?" He grabbed her hand and tucked her arm in his.

The north window extended to the high ceiling, with a panorama of sea, beach, and cypress grove seen through the pines. Several hundred feet of clearing sloped northward, its grass lush and deep. A shallow brook trickled through a corner at its far end.

"Usually at this time of day I have deer out there to keep me company. I suppose they heard or saw us as we came in, but if we wait long enough they'll return. I keep that spot of lawn cleared and toss a bit of seed on it before the winter rains each year. They in turn do me the courtesy of keeping most of the brush cleaned out from about the place. Just a precaution, in case of fire. Most accommodating, and I have the pleasure of their beauty." His speech contained the musical intonation and lilt of his native Wales which lent grace to the most commonplace conversation. He sat in a tan leather window seat and glanced at the girls' faces as they stared out, fascinated by the sight. "Lovely view from here, isn't it?"

168

He studied Laurie's face as she gazed across the small meadow, the light falling evenly over her black hair and smooth ivory skin. He had painted this face so often before—he knew from memory each plane, each shadow, where the richness of deep color would add warmth to the pale skin, where soft blue highlights would add luster to the jet hair. In the loft at the far end canvasses of the studio were stored, portraits done over thirty years ago, showing the same lovely oval face, the same high brow and intense dark eyes. For a moment he considered the wisdom of letting the girls see them. Could Laurie accept what the old portraits would reveal?

He turned from her and downed the gin at a gulp. He glanced at the stairway to the loft and shook his head. For a while longer the secret would have to wait.

"You've been very kind, Mr. Griffith. Thank you for a wonderful afternoon." Laurie gave him her hand, happy to count him as her friend.

"I'm delighted you could join us," the artist said. "I do hope you'll consider my offer. Just let me know if you decide to agree. You can send word by Bert Hutchins or Roy Wimbish if you like. I join them almost every Friday night for cut-throat pinocle at the livery stable."

His black hair, blown awry by the beach wind, stuck out from under his hat like unruly thatch. A red scarf loosely tied into a cravat gave him the rakish appearance of a man much younger. His sunburned face could be forty or seventy, for as with all faces constantly exposed to salt air and sun, it had the wrinkled, weathered aspect of tanned leather.

"I must admit I am flattered," Laurie admitted. "To be painted by you would be an honor. I've seen your work at the Lodge Gallery."

"Do say you will. But first think it over. It would tie you up on your weekends, I'm afraid. And you know posing is a job, just like chopping wood or scrubbing floors." He untied Sally and Dora from the cypress and looped the reins over the saddle horns.

"I promise I shall think about it. My shop takes up most of my time, but I'll consider it," Laurie said.

"Fine! Now up you go, my dear." Laurie vaulted into the saddle and took the reins. "And Miss Harris, allow me." He boosted her by the waist and straightened her skirts about her legs.

"I needn't tell you how I've enjoyed your visit today," Morgan Griffith smiled. "Miss Harris, may I call on you Tuesday at the pharmacy? I should like very much to lay in a few toiletry items—scents, cosmetics, things of use to my female customers. Next time you come down, we shall go see my store and I shall have your ideas on improving it. Agreed?"

Thea smiled and nodded, as if suddenly too shy to speak. Color rose in her dark cheeks and her eyes grew round with genuine surprise.

"I shall see you Tuesday, then. And please inform your Mr. Jepsen that we shall be discussing our business over luncheon at the Lodge." He smiled and scratched the bay's black poll. "Best be on your way, ladies. Don't want that fog bank to roll in and catch you on that beastly cliff trail. Here you go." He took the bridle, turned the horses into the trail, and slapped Dora's sleek rump.

The girls clung to the saddle horns as the horses scrambled up a slight incline and took to the trail which ran along the bluff overlooking the picnic beach. Below them several people called and waved farewell. As Laurie twisted in the saddle to return their waves, she noticed the tall man standing by the broiling rack of fish and potatoes. His arm was about the waist of a slim blonde girl, his head thrown back in laughter.

Thea nudged Sally to a trot behind Dora, hoping to distract Laurie's eyes from the beach. The horse sidestepped in protest and Thea caught herself with a gasp and grab at the horn. The great Tennessee Walker fell back and shivered her indignation.

They rode on in silence, the blooming of the surf below growing louder as they neared rocks immediately south of the cliffs. Below on the sand, small birds darted out with the water, scrabbling in the sand with long, thin bills, then dancing back on wire-like legs with the bubbly surf edge running races with them. Their glides bouyed by wind, white pelicans sped low over the water, barely moving their wide wings to alter course.

Thea caught the glisten of tears on the other girl's face as she turned to watch a flock of band-tailed pigeons explode from scrub near the trail.

"I saw him," Laurie said.

"I was afraid you had." Thea had hoped in vain.

"Now I don't have to wonder why, do I? Do you know her?"

"I couldn't tell who it was from such a distance, but I don't believe I do," Thea replied.

"But there was no mistaking him, was there?" Laurie sounded hopeful that Thea would dispute her.

"No. It was Chace."

Chapter 8

Pansy Hinshaw took the glass-bottomed wicker tray into the kitchen. She had missed Laurie's company at her Sunday entertainment. The other tenants had been there as usual, but Laurie had kept to her room, saying she was not feeling well. Pansy knew it was not the fish served at the beach picnic, for it had been freshly caught; nor had it been too much to drink, for Laurie was not overindulgent. Thea had given no hint as to what might be the matter, but Pansy was certain something had happened during their outing at Mariposa Beach.

Had she been so easily upset at Laurie's age? She tried to remember, but of course Adam Hinshaw had been with her to soften the blows and hold her hand.

"Oh, Adam..."

Pansy breathed her husband's name aloud, as if by its utterance she could cross the barrier between them. Her ladies kept her comany. She was not lonely in that respect. But she had never been able to accept his absence. She sighed and went to the cooler for the tall bottle of sauterne. "You do understand, don't you, Adam?"

The old woman looked at the fog outside the kitchen window. She could barely see the holly bushes beyond the brick walk. She had been worried that the

172

girls might get caught on the cliff trail by the fog bank, and had been much relieved when she saw them crossing Shore Park Drive toward home. Even then wisps of mist were curling through the tree tops, presaging the complete blanking out of everything farther than fifty feet distant.

In the music room Olive was playing the piano, a simple children's song with several of the women singing along. Ed Sickles was coming to take Olive to late supper at the Blue Roof Lodge, and the young school teacher had mended and pressed her best wool challis for the occasion.

"Adam, I may be losing one of my girls before long," Pansy said wistfully. "You should have seen Ed looking at Olive! You used to look at me that way, too." She refilled her glass and stood by the narrow window that gave onto Shore Park Drive. Roy Wimbish was crossing the lawn from the street, passing by the holly. She hid the glass in the cupboard and cranked down the cage of the cooler.

"Come in, Roy." She smoothed her hair and straightened her apron. "We've just finished, but would you like a cup of tea and some sandwiches?" She could see by the redness of his face that he had been indulging in something a bit more warming than tea and put the pot aside.

"No, ma'am, Mrs. Hinshaw. Thanks all the same. I ate with Bert and Rosa at the stables." He stood in the doorway to the summer kitchen, not wanting to change his shoes to come into the house.

"How is she taking Duncan's death?" Pansy asked-ed.

"Right bad," Roy answered. "It's a pity, too. He ain't worth all the carrying on she's doing. She's a nice girl, too good for the likes of him."

"I know, Roy. Maybe with him gone she'll find some nice young man and get properly married."

"Not many young fellas want to marry a girl that's

173

been kept.'' Wimbish shook his head sadly.

"Well, perhaps she'll move away from here and make a new life for herself.'' To the elderly woman anything was possible.

"Bert's hoping she'll stay. He'd be in a bad way if she up and left him now.'' He shifted from one foot to the other, trying to think of how to tell the old woman what he had learned at the livery stables. "Bert let Miss Thea and Miss Laurie have them Tennessee Walkers of his today.''

"That must have been your doing, Roy. I can't see him renting those two bays out, not even to the girls.''

"Yes, ma'am. I told him it was them or none.'' He fidgeted with his hat in his hands. "Morgan Griffith come up to see Bert a while ago.''

"In all this fog?'' Pansy was shocked at such a risk.

"Oh, that old pinto of his knows every step of the way. He can go along as if it was bright day. I think it's got cat eyes,'' Wimbish said with a chuckle.

"This isn't your pinocle night. What did he want?'' Getting Roy to the point took time and patience, but Pansy was accustomed to his slowness.

"Miss Laurie seen Chace Creighton down to the beach with one of them modeling girls.''

Pansy turned around and stared at Roy. "Oh, I knew it was something like that! She didn't come down after she got back. That's not like her at all. You say he was there?''

"Yes, ma'am. They'd already et and when Morgan seen Chace coming he hustled the girls up to his place. He hoped to keep Laurie from seeing Chace, but when Thea and her left by the cliff trail, she seen him.''

"Is he sure?'' Pansy asked.

"No doubt of it. Morgan says she slumped in the saddle like somebody'd hit her, then just kept riding on north.'' Roy hung his head as if the girl's pain were his.

Pansy sat down on the stool by the cupboard, her flat heels caught on the spreaders, hands in her lap.

"What's happened between those two? I don't understand it. Do you know who the girl was?"

"Morgan says it's the daughter of one of them new fellas down there. Come from Ohio, he says. Girl poses now and again for Morgan. Nice enough girl, too. He says Chace ain't seeing her steady—ain't nothing like that. Just drops down for a visit now and then."

"That's a comfort anyhow," Pansy said.

"Time Chace found out Laurie'd been to the picnic and gone, it was too late for him to go after her. You know how it is at one of them things—they's so many there you'd miss your own mother 'less she bumped into you."

"Should we tell Laurie?" Pansy thought a moment. "No, best leave things alone. They've got to work it out for themselves. They're both too independent to like anybody butting in."

"Yes, ma'am, you're right about that." Roy was not quite through, but Pansy could see he was having difficulty phrasing his thoughts.

"Was there something else, Roy?" Pansy prompted him.

"Morgan Griffith seen it—just like us."

"I'm not a bit surprised. He of all people would have spotted the resemblance." She twisted the frilly apron in her hands.

"Roy, I'm so afraid for Laurie!"

"There must be something wrong with me, Etta! There just has to be. You know Roy Wimbish, the man who lives at Mrs. Hinshaw's in the cottage south of the main house?" Laurie put the broom in the utility closet and shut the door.

"Sure. I know Roy," Etta said. "He's a very nice person. Not too bright, maybe, but a fine man. My father was a good friend of Roy's. What's he got to do with yesterday?"

"Not just yesterday—the first time Roy saw me,

the day he moved me from my room at the Lodge, he looked at me so oddly.''

"Not old Roy Wimbish! He's not that kind!" Etta protested.

"No, no! Not that way at all," Laurie said. "It's as if I remind him of someone. I catch him looking at me that way all the time. Just something out of the corner of my eye. And he is so sweet and good to me, brings me flowers and extra firewood, little things like that. And very protective. It's his whole attitude toward me.'' She leaned against the workroom door, keeping an eye on the front of the shop.

"Have you asked him?" Etta looked up from her sewing.

"No. I felt it wasn't my place to," Laurie admitted. "But that isn't all. Pansy Hinshaw once was on the point of telling me that I reminded her of someone she knew long ago, when her husband was still alive and working for Mr. Creighton.''

"She didn't tell you?" Etta was intrigued.

"No. She just said, 'But that was such a long time ago, I shouldn't be bothering you with my reminiscences.' That's as far as she went." Laurie turned and glanced into the alley beyond the grilled window. "And New Year's Eve at the Shell Box, when Morgan Griffith took care of me after...after...''

"Say it Laurie. You have to live with it, so you have to learn to speak about it. After...''

"...Duncan was killed...''

"Good! We've gotten that far at least. Now what about Morgan Griffith?''

"Well, I must have fainted. I don't remember much of what went on, but when I was lying on a bench inside the cafe, he gave me some brandy to bring me around.'' Laurie wrinkled her brow trying to remember. "I vaguely recall what he said to me—and it doesn't make any sense at all.''

"What did he say?" Etta asked.

"It was what he called me," Laurie said.

"Well?" Etta was becoming exasperated.

"He said, 'My sweet lady of the bees'!" Laurie was baffled.

"That's odd." Etta snipped the threads from the end of a seam. "I wonder what he meant by that?"

"But that's not all: he refers to the colony at Mariposa Beach as 'the hive.'"

Etta put down the scissors and looked at Laurie, alarm growing in her eyes. "But that doesn't mean there's anything peculiar about you."

"No, but look what happened to Zedekiah Creighton! He took one look at me and fell down with a stroke. And then Duncan... His mother blames me, and Chace must, too." Laurie gestured her helplessness. "I'd never seen any of these people in my life before I came here! None of them!" She was becoming agitated and desperate. "It's just something about me..."

"You said the woman who owned the old trunk in Mrs. Hinshaw's attic had the same name as old Zedekiah called out when he fell?" Etta wanted to start Laurie on a different track.

"Yes! That's odd enough, isn't it, to make you wonder?" She fished in the pocket of her dress and handed Etta a small object. "This is even more odd!"

Etta turned the amber and jet bee about in her fingers. The opals caught the light from the window in rainbow pools. "It's an earring. A bee!" Etta was frightened. "Oh, Laurie, you're right. This *is* odd!"

Laurie wanted to tell sensible, level-headed Etta Korby about the woman in the crackled mirror and darkened train window, the stranger's eyes which peered back into her own from the old-fashioned spectacles. And then there was the carriage that almost ran her down, the carriage with an ornate whip socket and ivory handled whip. But she'll think I'm insane, she thought.

"Did you go through everything in the trunk?" Etta asked.

"No, not really," Laurie said. "It was so personal: letters, photos—tintypes, daguerrotypes I guess you call some of them. And all sorts of sketches and drawings. I wasn't sure I should disturb them."

"What did Mrs. Hinshaw say about them?"

"She said it didn't really matter, that she didn't expect the owner to return after all these years to claim them. She told me to use my own judgment, whether to burn the letters or not."

"Then I'd go through it all. The letters might explain a lot of all this queer business," Etta scolded. She looked at the golden bee in the palm of her hand. "Something is very odd, Laurie," she said. "Suddenly I'm afraid, too. I have the feeling you'd better be very careful till you know what this is all about."

Laurie took the bee from Etta's hand and replaced it in her pocket.

Laurie placed the candle on the chimney offset and opened the large hump-backed trunk. She was resolved to discover what sort of ghost she might be. The answer had to lie within the collection of memorabilia.

Carefully she untied the faded blue ribbons from a packet of envelopes with letters enclosed. She fanned the collection out, comparing the various handwritings, the penmanship quite obviously from several foreign countries. The crisp, heavy paper bore addresses in English and French. She hesitated before opening them, unfolding the sheets one by one.

"Nothing!" She flung the letters aside impatiently. Although her schoolgirl French was sketchy, she could read enough of the contents to discover they held no clue that bore upon her mystery. They were, instead, affectionate pennings from friends abroad.

If Mellona Jolais had received letters from lovers, she had been exceptionally discreet, for there were no compromising missives in the collection.

Even more importantly, there were none of a threatening nature. If there were to be clues, they were not to be found in her correspondence.

A black, pressed cardboard sketch folder lay flat where she had left it atop the albums of photographs. Laurie lifted it out and spread it on the lid of one of the wooden crates, then set the candle beside it. As she untied the faded black ribbons which bound it, they fell apart in her fingers. Inside, carefully separated from each other by tissue paper, were ink sketches done on buffine paper in shades of sienna, umber, and black. The sheets, all standard size, were illustrations of beach and forest scenes, with sure, precise strokes and clear washes, the work of an accomplished artist.

Written in black ink with a fine crow-quill pen were legends and dates, so deftly blended into the design they were barely legible by candlelight. The illustrations seemed to be a consecutive series, all in the same style, inks, paper, and subject matter. One by one she turned them.

The first sketch depicted a wide stretch of beach, with rocks and crashing surf against a bright, cloudless sky. The second was pine forest and cypress grove as seen from the beach, with birds and deer hidden in brush. Next came a close-up of a clearing in the trees, with small cabins, and several men grouped about one woman. Her dress of striking banded design, was shown in a brilliant gold wash, her hair by india ink. Fourth was a couple embracing in the sunshine beside one of the cabins, the golden woman and a tall, broad-shouldered young man.

Into each sketch was incorporated what appeared to be insects, all clustered about a wild hive.

"Bees!"

Laurie turned the sheets quickly. "Why, it's illustrating a romance." The poses became more intimate, the motif of love reaching an emotional crescendo explicit in the curves that focused attention on the

179

central couple.

Suddenly the backgrounds became full of distorted clouds, the forest tortured and writhing. With a feeling of growing horror, she turned to the next picture.

Sketched into the background, peering from cloud, tree, and rock was the face of a woman, her lips set in rage, her face contorted in violent hatred. In the foreground the couple, lying in each other's arms behind a sheltering dune, were unaware of the pervasive fury so near. Each further design made more vivid the menacing motif. Something about it seemed vaguely familiar, and yet was frighteningly strange.

In the last picture the golden woman walked alone—toward the female Gorgon.

Laurie stared at the final sketch, chilled by a growing sense of fear. With its portrayal of impending violent confrontation, the series obviously was intended to tell a story. But whose? And what did it mean? Somehow she felt it was she, herself, portrayed as walking to her own doom.

Hands shaking so she could hardly gather together the sheets, she jogged the sketches back into the folder and set them aside, then bundled letters and photos into one large box and placed them on top of the folder. By the better light of the reading lamp downstairs perhaps she dared examine the drawings more closely, perhaps to decipher their message.

She desperately hoped neither Olive nor Thea would wish to join her, for she wanted to go over the contents of the trunk in solitude. To do so had become a necessity. She must know its dread secret.

The small apartment had grown cold. In the fireplace a half-consumed oak log smoldered above a dully glowing bed of ash. As she spread the sketches on the floor in sequence, the same chill of abject foreboding came over Laurie. Trembling, she held the inscriptions to the lamp, but was unable to read the infinitely small writing. From the night table she took the gold-wire spectacles and fitted their slender bows over her ears.

The series of dates began with 13 May 1870, and ended with 19 September 1871. Sixteen months and a few days. The beautiful, romantic drawings—up until the motif of the second woman obtruded—were lovingly executed. From there on, the style, obviously the same artist, but under a different emotion, had shown dread and courage as well as tender love. But why was there no man in the last sketch? Where had he gone? And why was the golden figure going to meet the Gorgon alone?

Laurie placed the sheets on the seat of the Turkish leather rocker and took out of the box a green, smooth leather album with small heart-shaped brass lock. She tried to open it, but the lock had been set. There was no key. Taking a wire hairpin from her chignon, she jabbed futilely at the ornamental lock. Her fingers clumsy with fear, the book slid from her grasp as if snatched by an unseen hand.

A subtle noise made her start with sudden panic. The sketches slid to the floor from the chair and spilled across the floor. Recoiling from them as from some unnameable menace, the girl cowered near the dying fire, unable to derive from it either solace or warmth.

One sheet had separated from the rest, its corner caught beneath the hearth rug. Summoning her last reserve of courage, she stooped to pick it up, and suddenly froze in terror. It was no trick of the light this time.

Inside the glasses were another's eyes staring back into her own.

Whatever strength she had fled. This time Laurie could not remove the spectacles, but collapsed onto the hearth, the sketch still clutched in her hand. As if robbed of a will of her own, she stared past the alien eyes at the picture on the paper. The sketch grew sharper in focus, drawing the girl into its depths.

Laurie slowly became aware that she was on a low dune, sea behind her, sand whispering softly in the wind. Salt grass and scrub brush rustled as she walked the sun-warmed shore. In the distance appeared grotesque gray cypress, crowns flattened, limbs twisted landward. Slowly she passed them and crossed a slight rise covered with blue broad-leafed asters and lavender erigeron daisies. To the right was a wide patch of bluff lettuce, its pale yellow spikes of bloom alive with bees. The scent of late summer was in the air, sweet and lush. A mystic warmth flooded through her as she seemed to glide over the sand. No longer was she afraid; gone was the paralysing fear, replaced now by a gentle sadness.

Tiny phoebes darted from twigs after insects and flitted back to their perches, tails spread and twitching. Dusty green chaparral cloaked the next rise where twittering bushtits scattered in alarm before her.

As if someone had spoken, Laurie halted, turned, and saw the ancient blasted tree, its roots contorted about a heap of boulders and clinging to the edge of a low cut. A water course, dry in the fall of the year, ran below the leafless tree.

"This is a special place," she thought. "I must mark it—remember it!"

Distant gull cries caused the girl to turn her head; suddenly she was back in her small apartment by the dying fire.

She picked up the drawing and took it to the lamp. In the corner the legend grew clearer: 'La Barranca, Mariposa Beach, 19 September 1871.'

The signature seemed to expand and glow with luminescence—'Mellona Jolais.'

Mellona!

Mellona had been an artist and had lived at Mariposa Beach! The illustrations were her record of her love affair with some man—strong, virile, handsome. They were the records, too, of something more sinister. And somehow, someway, Laurie knew they also held a special meaning for her.

The girl reached for the album. If only she could force it open perhaps it might tell her more. She again slid the button on the lock. With a sharp click it fell open on its strap.

Quaintly posed tintypes and daguerrotypes were inserted behind ovals cut into the heavy leaves. Clothing of half a century past, children with kittens and puppies long dead, distinguished elderly men and women in stovepipe hats and hoop skirts, pillared and porticoed houses—the history of a human being, with relatives, friends, the homes they lived in, even small, beloved pets.

One face appeared repeatedly. A tiny girl in voluminous skirts and fluffy petticoats and bows gradually became a voluptuous young woman modishly attired in light colored gowns. The contrast between the somber, dark clothing of the rest of the women in the album and the young woman's paler gowns set her apart from them, as did the ever-present flowers which she either clutched in her hand, wore upon her attire, or tucked into her dark locks.

The last picture in the album was a formal portrait of the lovely, jet-haired young woman, with pale Welsh roses at her breast.

Laurie stared at the photograph. It was as if she were looking into a mirror.

The differences were subtle—in the slightly arrogant tilt of the head, the self-assured and world-knowing arch of the brows, the sensuous curve of the lips. It was herself in other circumstances and another age.

With the album in her hand, Laurie sat on the baise settee. The eyes within the spectacles still remained, pleading, begging her to understand. She held the book to her, as if trying to clasp the woman to her heart.

"Mellona, I know you're here," Laurie said softly. "I'm trying to understand, but you'll have to help me.

You loved him very much, I know, just as I love Chace. Something dreadful happened down at Mariposa Beach, didn't it?'' Tears came to her eyes and spilled unchecked down her cheeks.

Roses and lilies, wild sweet broom—the room was filled with fragrance. Laurie now felt no fear, no terror.

"Oh, Mellona, I want so much to help you, but I don't know how!'' She looked into the spectacles. There was no trickery in the light.

"You always wore the same shade of gold as I do, didn't you? Is that why Zedekiah Creighton had a stroke when he looked at me?''

It did not matter if anyone came into her room or not. Laurie could never make them understand.

Chapter 9

San Esteban dozed in mid-day heat. Laurie stood on the station platform, uncertain what to do next. To whom could she turn?

"Your shipment just hasn't arrived, Miss Mathews. If your shipper says he sent it, it's obviously been delayed somewhere along the line. All we can do is send a tracer after it. We'll know in a few days and drop you a notice." The station freight agent had been indifferent, his answers evasive.

"But don't you see, I need that merchandise! I've been waiting now since before the holidays. You chose to ignore my inquiries about it—that's why I had to make the trip over here myself. I simply must have those shipments!" She had wanted to stamp her feet and pound on the counter. Anything to wipe the complacency from his smug face.

"I'm sorry, lady, but there isn't one thing I can do about it. These things happen. Human error. You've got to allow for it in business." He had actually turned away from the counter and had begun to eat his lunch. The interview was at an end. She was supposed to go away and not bother him further.

"Then I insist you send a tracer today!" She was furious. He looked up at her and slowly went to the counter and pulled out a sheaf of forms from a file drawer. Butter from his sandwich smeared on the sheet of paper, but he continued to fill it out, the pencil slipping in the grease.

That was that. It was all she could do for the time being. She had to wonder if the agent would even file the tracer, but what more could she do? The impotency of her position filled her with such rage that she even thought of consulting an attorney. But they cost money. Even the least competent of them was too dear for her purse. She had increased the number of her customers, but without goods to sell, she could soon be out of business.

Laurie walked the few blocks to the commercial district and found the post office empty. At the high writing table she addressed several postal cards, wrote quick notes, and dropped them in an outgoing-mail slot. Perhaps firms in San Francisco would let her buy from them on credit. It was worth trying. It was all she could do.

Laurie would turn her mind to her other reason for coming over to San Esteban.

Across the dusty street was the San Esteban Daily Dispatch, its wide double doors open for air. Thea Harris said her cousin worked for the newspaper and would know if they had copies of their editions going back over thirty years. Thea had given Laurie a note of introduction to the woman.

"I should like to see Miss Lucia Orozco, please." The young man at the front desk grinned so broadly Laurie wondered if she had forgotten her petticoats. She moved her foot to reassure herself she was properly attired and smiled back, handing him the note addressed to Thea's cousin.

"I'll go get her. Won't be a minute." The rolled shirt sleeves and pencil behind his ear indicated he was not apt to prevent their interview. In a few moments he returned and sat back down behind a battered oak desk piled high with spindled copy.

Lucia Orozco was short, very fat, and dark as mahogany. Her black eyes were shrewd and calculating with the wisdom of her people. She had been a great beauty in a day when too much intelligence and ambition in women destroyed their appeal no matter how lovely their face and figure. When she moved, it was with the grace many heavy people have; her clothing, although plain and unadorned, was tasteful without being drab. At her throat a small locket on a golden bow pinned a maroon grosgrain ribbon to her severe dress. As she smiled in greeting, her teeth flashed white in her dark face, belying her sixty-six years.

"You are Laurie! I'm so happy to meet you. Thea has told me about you so often I feel I already know you." She extended her plump hand and grasped the girl's. "Thea writes I may be able to help you with something." The woman glanced toward the young man who had not taken his eyes from Laurie. "Why don't we go across the street and have some coffee and talk about it?"

"Are you sure it's all right?" the girl asked.

"She runs the paper, girlie!" The boy chuckled and winked.

"Oh, I didn't know." Laurie was embarrassed. Thea had been vague about what her cousin did. Perhaps she had not wanted it to sound like bragging. The Orozcos had retained the exquisite Latin manners of old Spanish California.

"I'll be right back, Richard. If you should need me, send someone over to the cafe," Lucia said as they left.

When they were seated in a corner, away from the noisy pressmen who dominated the place, Lucia asked, "Now, Laurie, how may I help you?"

"Does the paper have copies of its publications from 'way back?" Laurie asked.

"Way back how far?"

"Over thirty years," Laurie replied.

"Yes. They're down in the basement storerooms, but they're easily accessible. Any special year?" Lucia Orozco looked at the hand-printed menu and replaced it in its coiled rack on the table.

"1871. The last two weeks of September, 1871," the girl replied.

"I'm sure we'd have those. A bit musty by now."

The waiter stood by their table, his respect for Lucia apparent in his deference.

"Laurie, if you're hungry I can recommend their lamb stew or chicken paprika with egg dumplings. Very good."

"I'm really not hungry." Laurie was still too angry to be interested in food. "A piece of the lemon meringue pie and coffee would be plenty."

"Fine. We'll have lemon pie and coffee, Sam. Bring us a pot, please." It was clear Miss Orozco was used to giving orders, but without overasserting herself.

"Yes, ma'am. Right away. Thank you." He didn't wait to write up a ticket, but ducked into the kitchen.

"You undoubtedly have a definite story you'd like to see," Lucia said. "Do you care to tell me which one?"

"I'm trying to find out what happened to a woman who once lived at Mariposa Beach. She was one of the artists there." Laurie hesitated, then added, "I don't want to go around Forest Shores asking too many questions. I don't know what to make of it myself yet. And I certainly don't want to stir up trouble for anyone if it's just a mare's nest."

"And this woman's name?" Lucia Orozco was already suspicious, her eyes intent upon Laurie.

"Mellona Jolais."

For a long time Lucia looked at Laurie, her piercing black eyes attempting to obtain some indication as to the girl's reason for the inquiry.

"Is something wrong?" Laurie asked.

"No, child, not as you mean it right now. Something was wrong, terribly wrong, when Mellona Jolais disappeared. And believe me, it is no mare's nest!" She shook her head as she remembered. "I've often thought about her in the past thirty-odd years and wondered what became of her, where she went—*if* she went."

"*If* she went? Then you must think the same thing I do, Miss Orozco." Laurie shuddered despite the heat of the cafe.

"Lucia, dear. Just Lucia. 'Miss Orozco' is only for business, and I do grow tired of it. Not that I didn't try to change the 'Miss' part several times!'' She sighed and smiled. ''But to get back to Madame Jolais...''

''Was it in the paper then?'' the girl asked.

''Oh my, yes! The reporter who wrote the story was let go. Couldn't get another job anywhere around here. Yes, indeed, I remember it well. I was already an old maid by then, but we had made plans to be married.'' She sighed again and looked across the street at the publishing company. ''When he couldn't get work and his money ran out, he drifted away. Nobody around here ever heard from him again.''

Laurie knew only too well the pain of losing a sweetheart. ''I'm so sorry,'' she said.

''Don't be. He was a regular rake-hell. Cheated on me with some of those girls down at Mariposa Beach. He wasn't cut out to be a one-woman man. He liked the Bohemian, arty crowd over there, and I was prim and proper, set in my old-fashioned, respectable ways. We wouldn't have lasted long married. But I often wonder what became of him.''

The waiter brought their pie and coffee, leaving a small metal pot on the table beside the woman's cup. She nodded and took the check.

''Why was he fired?'' Laurie asked.

''Unfortunately he wrote and we published a news story that someone didn't want printed,'' Lucia answered.

''I don't understand. What happened?'' Laurie asked, then added, ''And what was the story?''

''Well, let's see if I can keep it brief, but still give you the entire picture: Mellona Jolais was half French, half Welsh, a true artistic combination if national heritage has anything to do with beauty and talent. Several years before the war between France and Prussia, she fled Paris with a few friends who had been caught up in the political turmoil aimed against the emperor, Napoleon the Third. They were a radical sort, full of idealism and brotherhood, all that lovely but impractical philosophy so unpopular with entrenched and privileged bureaucracy. They found it was not very wise to espouse their cause on French soil, so they emigrated, hoping to return someday. But the Prussian army eventually occupied the Empire; then came the bloody violence of the Commune..." Lucia tested the coffee, made a face and put the cup down to cool.

"They had heard of California from some of their friends who had traveled the West. Something about its vastness, the freedom it offered, appealed to them. They wanted to experience it for themselves.

"It was a difficult journey for them, because in those days it meant going 'round the Horn. Eventually they established an artists' colony at Mariposa Beach. Before long, the group became quite famous. Some of them were already renowned painters and sculptors—Morgan Griffith was one of the founders of the place. He was a cousin of Mellona, about the same age as she. They adored each other and since they were all the family either one had, they stayed together. He had a darling little wife who loved Mellona like a sister, but Gwenllian died a few years after coming here. She had tuberculosis. The climate at the beach literally killed her. The scenery may be spectacular, but it's not the place for anyone who has lung troubles.

"Mellona had a friend, Etienne Retan, an old lover, who'd started a chain of fine galleries here in California. He'd been a wealthy man, a patron of the arts in France, but he was also an ardent and outspoken opponent of Louis Napoleon. One of his close friends warned him of a pending move by the emperor's secret police to arrest him and confiscate everything he had. Rather than risk being sent to a penal colony he raised what cash he could and booked passage on the first available ship. It was bound for San Francisco, and there he settled.

"He was exactly what the newly wealthy of those days wanted. He brought a touch of old world culture to their homes. They wanted the arts and fashions of Europe - he provided them. Naturally, the doors of the best society were open to him, and he was enormously successful. Through him, the group of artists at

Mariposa Beach soon were doing very well. He had an agreement to handle most of their work and frequently advanced funds to keep the retreat going.

"For Mellona he arranged a prestigious showing of the group's work to be held in the fall of '71. He'd even sold a few of the best paintings before they opened the exhibit.

"That was the reason for the picnic at the beach, as I remember it. Anyhow, to celebrate, they organized a fish fry. Since one of Retan's galleries was in Forest Shores, in what eventually became part of the Blue Roof Lodge, they invited guests from there—some of their patrons. It was well attended, too, for they were popular even though some blue-stockings disapproved of their free and easy behavior."

The woman had forgotten her pie and coffee as she recounted the story, and looked down almost in surprise, then tasted the tart yellow filling.

"Everyone referred to the colony as 'the bee hive,' because they were so industrious. Always building and painting, sharing communal chores, trying to put into practice the philosophy they had been forever preaching. It was idyllic, but the work was taxing and left less time to pursue art than they might have liked. Perhaps it was the novelty, the exciting strangeness that appealed to them. They were a strange lot, themselves. Childlike, emotional, loving, and trusting, always doing their best to stick with their original plan. I can't help but feel every member loved Madame Jolais and kept on working at it just to please her. She was like that, you know.

"Mellona was probably the most beautiful woman I ever saw." She looked at Laurie, turning her face to the light with her finger to the girl's chin. "You so strongly resemble her it is amazing! You aren't a relative, are you?"

"No, not a relative," Laurie admitted. "I guess you could call me a friend. I've just discovered I look like her and decided I wanted to know about her."

Lucia Orozco paused in her recitation. There was

far more to the girl's interest than casual curiosity. She wondered if she would be doing her a favor by opening the old files. Perhaps she would be leading her into danger by doing so.

"Madame Jolais was the widow of an older man, some officeholder in the French government. He was a member of the petty aristrocracy. When he died, he left her well off financially, but she neither particularly enjoyed her position in society nor used it to unfair advantage. She much preferred life at Mariposa Beach with its freedom and camaraderie. The only occasion on which she displayed any claim to her husband's title was when she'd be dealing with San Francisco society. They were simply fascinated by anyone with titled background, so Mellona would don her gold tiara and go do battle for the sake of her little colony.

"She was pretty successful in promoting her friends' work, too, especially through the Retan Galleries. And she was a fine artist. Mostly etchings, engravings, small prints—usually of nature, animals, small children, things like that. Monumental, overblown themes so popular at that time didn't appeal to her at all. Her things were intimate, warm, loving. I have several in my home. Quite charming."

For a few minutes they ate in silence, the hot coffee restoring Laurie's flagging spirits. Lucia refilled their cups and waved greetings to the men who by now were returning to the newspaper.

"As I said, they had this fish-fry party at the beach," Lucia resumed. "Mellona, according to some of the guests, was acting a bit strangely, as if she were expecting someone who never came. About dusk she said she was going up to her lodge for some champagne she'd been saving." The woman paused, then said, "That was the last anyone saw of her."

"Just like that?" Laurie was astonished.

"Just like that," Lucia replied. "She'd packed no bags, taken no clothes, told no one of any immediate plans to leave Mariposa Beach. It was as though the earth opened up and swallowed her."

"Didn't anyone search for her?" the girl asked.

"Oh yes!" Lucia said. "Search parties were formed late that night. But at that time Mariposa Beach was a wild, desolate place, impossible to search thoroughly without an army. A heavy rain fell that night and by the time the sheriff was called in next day, hounds brought over from San Esteban couldn't get the scent at all.

"Late that night—the next night after her disappearance—an old Italian fisherman who lived along the beach where Sand Town is now, began telling everyone he had taken a woman matching her description out to a lumber boat that was lying off Point Piedras. It was bound for San Francisco and the sheriff sent word for the authorities to meet it when it put in there. Some woman did get off the ship, hired a carriage—and that was the end of the trail. She eluded them completely. A sailor on the ship said she'd given out the story she was getting away from some man who meant to do her harm. She'd paid them well to take her to San Francisco, so they took her—no questions asked.

"The Italian fisherman gave the sheriff a gold silk chiffon scarf the woman had tied about her head as he rowed her out to the ship. Morgan Griffith recognized it as one he had given Mellona a short time before. As far as the sheriff was concerned that was it."

"You mean he dropped it right there?" Laurie asked. "Didn't anyone look for her?"

"Morgan Griffith hired people to follow up on several leads, but they found no more," Lucia replied. "She—whoever it was—covered her tracks effectively, but no one who knew Mellona ever believed it was she on the boat."

"What happened to the fisherman?"

"A short time later he inherited money from an aunt's estate in Sicily and returned there to live. I heard from his family in Forest Shores that he died many years ago. By their standards, he was a rich man. Strangely enough, they knew nothing of the aunt who had willed him her property."

Laurie began to see sinister facets in the disappearance. "Do you believe he was given a good deal of money to tell that story?"

"It looked pretty suspicious," Lucia said.

"Why did your young man, the reporter, get fired?" Laurie was now more certain than ever that Mellona had never left the beach alive.

"He wrote the original story with the usual flambouyant lead that was the style then. The headline read 'Goddess of Bees Flees Hive.'" She smiled recalling the article and the sensation it made. "I can see it now! What a stir it caused that day! He intimated foul play, which was certainly reasonable. What got him into trouble was that he insisted the rumor of a married man being involved was the truth. And he further said that Mellona was pregnant by this man.

"My friend was undoubtedly given that information by some of the girls at the beach—he was popular with more than one! You know how gossip is in a small group like that. It was tantalizing—just enough to sound like the truth, but no names to go with it.

"Mellona's cousin, Morgan, was sure she was having an affair with someone, but she was very discreet about it. Even he didn't know who it was, although I'm certain he must have suspected someone.

"It was strange that Mellona didn't confide in Morgan Griffith. They were so close. Had Morgan not been at the party all day and well into the evening, his time accounted for by many witnesses, he would have been the logical suspect himself. As it was, he was above suspicion. And he never got over her disappearance, poor man. He'd come to a new world, and lost both his loves," Lucia sighed.

"You said the reporter headlined the story with something about the goddess of the bees," the girl said. "What did he mean?"

"Madame Jolais always wore a certain shade of gold, in what would have been an affectation by most women, but for her it was as natural as breathing," Lucia answered. "She was herself spectacular. The gold enhanced her complexion and hair, just as it would yours, Laurie. And she always had her gowns banded with black and brown in some fashion, a deliberate visual reference to bees."

"I'm still not sure I understand," Laurie said.

"An elaborate play on her name, dear—Mellona," Lucia explained.

Laurie's knowledge of folklore and mythology was the rudimentary sort to be had from most public schools, and quickly forgotten. The name meant nothing to her.

"You see, Mellona was the name of an obscure ancient rustic goddess of the bees!" Lucia said. "She was the *numen*, or special divinity, whom beekeepers invoked for the protection and fertility of their hives and bees."

"Oh, now I see! That fits in with the 'bee hive.'"

"Mellona Jolais was the goddess of that particular bunch of bees, the cohesive element that held the retreat together. Indeed, it held together a long time after she was gone, until homesickness drove most of the French artists home once again. It isn't the same now, but then it was Mellona's own hive, with Mellona protecting her own adoring bees."

They finished their pie and small pot of coffee. Lucia led the girl to the basement storage rooms and searched for the yellowed newspapers covering the last two weeks of September, 1871.

"That's odd. They should all be right here in sequence." Lucia Orozco rummaged through the collection, one by one, to no avail. She checked the year before and the year after, and adjacent months', in case they had been misfiled.

At the sound of furtive movement outside the storeroom door she looked up in alarm. A door at the end of the passageway closed softly.

"Come into my office. I must speak to you." Lucia took the girl by the hand and slammed the storeroom door behind them, not waiting to relock it, and quickly led her up a flight of stairs at the rear of the building. When they reached her private office, she shut the door and indicated a chair for Laurie. She inspected the adjoining rooms which opened into hers, making sure no one was near enough to overhear their conversation.

"You're getting involved in something I don't like, Laurie," she said. "Someone has taken those papers from our files. Very deliberately, too. To my knowledge no one has ever gone back that far looking for an old edition. And I've been here ever since that time. Those copies have probably been gone for a very long time. Somebody wanted the story hushed up when it happened. We ran only two stories on it before orders were passed down not to print another line. I thought then, and I think now, that Madame Jolais was murdered, and the murder covered up. God only knows where her body could be, but I think you may be endangering yourself if you go too far, asking questions and trying to find the truth.

"Someone very powerful was back of my friend's being dismissed and unable to obtain work anywhere on the west coast. Someone with friends in authority who owed him favors. Am I making myself clear?" She perched on the edge of her desk, her brown face contracted with worry.

"Yes, Lucia, I understand," Laurie said. "You mean Zedekiah Creighton, don't you?"

In spite of the heat inside the little office, Laurie shivered. It was clear why Zedekiah had fallen with a stroke upon seeing her with his son—the gold color, the raven hair, the face that so resembled Mellona's.

Laurie smoothed her gray business dress beneath her as she sat down on the station bench. The afternoon train to Forest Shores would be forty minutes late due to a delay on the run from San Francisco. She had hurried from the Daily Dispatch to the depot and arrived breathless and hot.

The great disparity between climates of the coast and San Esteban was pronounced. The January day had been warm even before she had left home. Afternoon sun slanted under the porch roof, making the wooden benches uncomfortable places to wait until departure. Sparrows fluttered in shallow depressions in the ground, their dry ablutions sending miniature clouds of dust skittering along the road. The girl watched in amusement as the drab little birds gyrated and fussed among themselves.

At the far end of the long porch she heard the sound of a man's heavy boots on the wooden flooring. A crowd at the center of the platform was slowly disbursing after the agent posted arrival time in white chalk on the schedule board. There was enough time for a bit to eat or a drink down the street at the saloon.

Laurie did not have to count the cash she had in her handbag to know that she would have to wait until returning home to eat. Business had been flourishing, but her wish to add new lines to her merchandise required advance payment. Credit was seldom extended to a woman shop owner, and never to one so young and inexperienced. The fact that cash had been paid but goods never received was beginning to pinch.

"Miss Mathews?" The man's voice was a nasal drawl.

Laurie turned to look at the stranger. "Yes?" She relished no conversation with anyone at the moment. Her thoughts were too jumbled and confused. She had looked forward to the trip home alone to try to put her new information in some sort of perspective.

"Arch said to look for the prettiest girl at the station and I'd find you." His blatant inspection of her brought a flush to her face, a flush the man mistook for modesty instead of resentment. "May I?" The question was unnecessary for he seated himself beside her without allowing an answer.

"I'm Ralph Donner." It was as though he expected his name to bring a smile to her face and an utterance of delight to her lips. Her stony face caused him to shift a bit from her, ostensibly to cross his long, thin legs. "Arch thought I might do you a favor if I passed by this way."

Her only response was the raising of her left

eyebrow. There was not even curiosity in her glance. He was obviously puzzled by her indifference.

"Arch Creighton!" He seemed to think she should respond in some way. "Say, if you're not interested in a favor. . ."

"I am not acquainted with him," Laurie told Donner.

"No?" He was not aware of the fact. "Well, it makes no difference, does it?" Donner dusted his highly polished black boots with his hand and flicked at his trouser legs with his fingertips. In his usual experience with San Esteban girls they either gushed enthusiasm for him or worshipped in respectful silence. The Mathews girl was an altogether different sort, and far lovelier.

"Arch is over here seeing my Aguilar Valley development. You've probably heard of it." He seemed deflated when she showed no signs of recognition. "Arch is thinking of becoming a partner in it himself." Still she gave no indication of interest, but continued to watch the sparrows in the dust. It became clear he intended to deliver his favor even if she were not willing to receive it.

"Word got back to Arch this afternoon that you've been over at the Dispatch to see Lucia Orozco, that Mexican woman they've got managing the paper." His tone implied disapproval of a woman—especially an Orozco woman—in such a position.

"Seems you were having her dig up stories of some old scandals having to do with Forest Shores." At this Laurie turned to look at his tanned, bony face, and remembered the furtive visitor in the basement of the Dispatch. "He thought it would be a kindness if somebody dropped you a word of advice."

"I don't see how my visiting a friend has anything to do with either you or Archibald Creighton—or anybody else, for that matter." The flush became crimson and her eyes narrowed in anger. The man could no longer confuse the reason for it.

"Now he knows you're a newcomer to the area and can't really appreciate what it's taken to build up these towns around here, attract settlers, businesses, industry, shipping facilities. Took an awful lot of initiative and hard work.''

"How does that concern me today? I'm sure it's all very interesting if you're a buff on history and origins. I'm not!" she declared.

"Well, it wouldn't hardly do to go raking up old scandals best left buried. A lot of people might get hurt, innocent folks suffer embarrassment, that sort of thing. Now Lucia Orozco being with the paper makes it even more dangerous. She'd like nothing better than to print slanderous articles about some of our most respected citizens. It'd be sure to stimulate circulation and that'd make her look real good, wouldn't it?" Donner smiled at his reasonableness.

"I have nothing to say to you. And I don't want to hear whatever else you may have to say to me." Laurie left the bench and stalked into the station. The tall man rose and followed her. A few passengers were seated on the long benches in the waiting room, their curious glances falling on the couple entering.

"Miss Mathews, it's for your own good I tell you this," Donner insisted. "You're in business for yourself, and there's lots of people who might not like to trade with you if they thought you didn't have the good of the community at heart. They might think you were deliberately trying to start trouble." His voice had the irritating quality of a whine and could be heard a distance away.

"Are you threatening me?" Laurie raised her voice.

"Nothing of the sort!" Several people looked up and now openly listened.

"Please leave! I have no wish to create a scene, Mr. Donner, but if you don't leave me alone I shall call the stationmaster or a policeman!"

Heads turned from every bench and three men in rough laborers' clothing came into the waiting room from the freight platform. "And please do me a favor: tell Archibald Creighton to attend his own business! I don't require the sort of favors he wants to impose upon me! And as for the good of the community, perhaps its good might better be served by someone other than the Creighton family and their lackies!''

The imperious tilt of her head, the defiance in her blazing black eyes caused the man to halt in mid-step. If he were not so anxious to have a Creighton in the Aguilar Valley project, he would beg the lady's pardon and retreat as best he could, maybe send her flowers with a note of apology. But he needed Archibald Creighton.

''Miss Mathews, you may not take it kindly, but I'm duty bound by my word of honor to deliver the rest.'' He was not a man to fumble in any transaction, but he found himself doing so as he faced the young woman.

''Then you aren't speaking for yourself at all!'' Laurie exploded. ''Do all the Creightons get someone else to speak for them? Even a mongrel dog does its own barking!''

At that the crowd in the waiting room roared approval. The three workmen edged nearer, their eyes measuring the tall, thin man, their fists gripping crowbar and pick a bit tighter. Ralph Donner became aware of their advance and stepped back from the girl. He saw they were not San Esteban workers, but from the line up north. The name of Donner had no power to intimidate them.

''I'm sorry you don't take it in the spirit it's. . .'' he began.

Laurie turned her back on him and walked to the side of the room where two solid doors were labeled in red letters 'Gents' and 'Ladies.' She put her hand on one knob and turned to face Donner.

''I'm going in here, where I presume you wouldn't have the gall to follow.'' The passengers guffawed. ''When I come out in a few minutes, I expect you to be gone.''

As he stood in front of the restrooms, his face growing livid with humiliation, the crewmen began barking in ridicule. He turned and strode quickly from the station, his heels pounding angrily into the plank flooring. His anger was not with the girl, but with his prospective partner.

Ralph Donner was a good judge of people and their motives. This was one woman against whom Archibald Creighton would not win. She had spirit and temper, and in her black eyes Donner had caught a glimpse of something beyond anger. He was sorry he had earned her enmity, and pitied Archibald.

Chapter 10

Etta Korby held the bill of lading out to the teamster. "What are we supposed to do now? This stuff is ruined! How do we get replacements?"

"Lady, all I do is deliver it—don't take my head off!" the man protested. "Only thing I can suggest is you take it up with the railroad and your shipper. They've got insurance to cover accidents. They'll make good on it if they're to blame."

"I'm sorry, I know it isn't your fault," Etta said. "It's just that we've waited so long to get it, and now it's ruined." She sat on the top step and looked at the water-stained silk blouses. "There's no way we can even wash these and sell them half-price. I just don't know what we'll do!" She wanted to weep, but she had learned long ago it did no good. "Laurie!" Etta called in to the Ribands and Roses.

"Yes, Etta?" Laurie came to the rear door and stood beside her seamstress. "Oh God! Is it all like that?" She knelt in the alleyway and lifted the damaged clothing from one of the crates.

"They're all like that. We opened them all. Been left out in the rain, I'd say." Etta held up underdrawers, caught the man grinning and threw them back into the box.

"You can tell by them stains on the sides and bottoms of the crates. Probably been left on a loading dock somewhere," the deliveryman said. "I'm awful sorry, ma'am, but it wasn't my fault. That's just what I been trying to tell the other lady here. You got to file a claim with the railroad." He added almost apologetically,

202

"And I still got to collect my freight charges." He rubbed the right-hand lead horse's muzzle and adjusted the blinkers around its eyes. It whinnied softly and butted his shoulder.

"Etta, get the cash from the drawer and pay him. He has other deliveries. We mustn't hold him up." She unfolded the silk blouses and guimpes.

"Thank you, ma'am," he said. "I'll be glad to sign your claim and swear to the condition of the merchandise. That's why I told the other lady she'd best take a look right away."

"Yes, I'm glad you did. Thank you," Laurie said.

When the hauler had gone, Etta sat down on a crate just inside the back door. It was useless to even keep the material, for it had mildewed and was covered with vile-smelling dark specks.

"What do we do now?" she asked.

"I'll have to go over to the depot and file a claim," Laurie replied.

"But that won't give us the merchandise. We need it right now." Etta was worried. It meant her own livelihood as well as her employer's.

"I can telegraph a few companies we've ordered from before. Maybe they can expedite shipment." She went to the small desk and riffled through receipted bills.

"But you don't have a line of open credit with them," Etta reminded her.

"Maybe I can get a short term loan if necessary," Laurie said.

The claim with the railroad would have to wait. Laurie collected the addresses from her records and composed brief telegrams to wholesalers, pleading for immediate consideration. As soon as she had finished the last one she grabbed her shawl and ran down Birch Street to the telegraph office.

On the morning of the third day she received special-rate replies to her urgent inquiries. Before the delivery boy could pocket his nickel tip and wheel his bicycle from the curb she had torn open the first yellow envelope. As Etta watched Laurie's face, her heart fell. There was no need to ask the messages' contents. One by one the girl read the strips of large type and tossed the sheets into the trash basket.

"All bad?" Etta asked.

"You can read them."

"I don't want to!"

"They say they can't do business with me because another store—unnamed—in this area carries their lines. It would amount to breach of their agreement with this store if they continued to supply me when they had promised exclusivity to this other store." Laurie collapsed onto the high stool behind the counter and covered her face with her hands. Once again she was forced to the conclusion that she had made a terrible mistake in coming to Forest Shores, and doubly so in attempting to go into business on her own.

"That's pure hogwash!" Etta exploded. "They've shipped to us before. I'm sure they didn't just discover their exclusive arrangement in the last day or so! The only one it could be is Chambers in San Esteban. Nobody here in Forest Shores has those same lines." Etta retrieved the telegrams from the trash basket, looked at them and threw them down in disgust. "I smell a rat of some kind, Laurie."

"If we had more time I'd go to San Francisco and see what I could find," Laurie said. "As it is, I don't know any other course than to go to Chambers and see what sort of deal I can make with him."

"Humble yourself like that?" Etta considered and reluctantly agreed. "I see what you mean. You're right, of course. Business is no place for a high-horse. Besides, that may be where the trouble is coming from in the first place."

"I'll go over to San Esteban and see if Chambers will let us have something on 30-days' account. We can't last next month if we don't get another shipment right away." Laurie had no time to be emotional. "Can you look after the store the rest of the day?"

"Sure. I can bring my handwork out here and do it."

"Close at noon for your lunch," Laurie ordered.

"I'll do no such thing! I don't want to miss even one customer. Not the way things are right now," Etta objected.

"Etta, you're a darling and a wonder!" Laurie pecked her on the cheek with a kiss and dashed to the workroom for hat and cape.

"If I hurry, I can just make the morning train. I'll be back before you close this afternoon. See if you can get Charlie Hobart to put this stuff in that storeroom behind the bakery. Madge Hobart said we could rent it if we ever needed storage space. Won't amount to more than a dollar or so, and maybe fifty cents for Charlie. We'll have to keep everything so it can be inspected." Laurie brushed her gray dress and pinned on a small, feathered pearl gray hat.

"You're going right now?" the little seamstress asked.

"I've got to, Etta." The girl shot her arms through the straps of the cape and scooped up change and a few bills from the cash drawer. "And if Mrs. Arvidson comes in, ask her for something on account. We need it!"

Although the sun was shining and the sky a cloudless blue, the north wind was cold. Gutierrez Bay lay like a blue-gray slate with shallow, foaming chalk marks. In exposed spots geraniums were blackened at the tips, fuchsias shriveled and frost-blighted. Grass tufts growing in cracks and along the curbs glittered with dew drops which an hour before had been crystaline frost.

Laurie's breath blew in white puffs as she rushed to the depot. The early train was stoking up for the run back to San Esteban. A small knot of passengers waited on the platform, staying in the patches of sunlight and out of the shade. Laurie nodded to several acquaintances and ran to the ticket window, clutching her cape against the cold.

Chambers Department Store filled three lots on San Esteban's Union Avenue and rose four storys high, a monument to pioneering enterprise. Jonathan Chambers, although in his seventies, was still on hand each business day to open the store and greet personally the first customers of the morning. That his shrewish wife made lingering abed less desirable than rising early and walking five blocks to his store was well known, but the elderly man maintained the pretense of enjoying his routine.

"Now, Miss Mathews, what may I do for you?" Chambers asked. "My secretary tells me you are here on a matter of considerable urgency. Do sit down." He pulled up a comfortable damask upholstered chair. "There we are."

"Mr. Chambers, I won't waste either your time or mine," Laurie replied. "I'll come right to the point: I need your help in getting merchandise for my shop in Forest Shores."

The old man sat behind the wide, burled-walnut desk, his elbows on the arms of his chair, fingers steepled before his chest. He nodded as if he were already aware of her problem.

"I have a small ladies' accessories store called the Ribands and Roses Shoppe," Laurie explained. "Many weeks ago I placed orders for a considerable amount of new lines and paid cash in advance of shipment. I haven't been able to establish extended credit—I understand a woman is assumed to be a poor business risk." Her voice raised just enough to convey her indignation. Again he nodded.

"First of all, the shipment was delayed somewhere, and held up for weeks," she continued. "Then a few days ago when it was finally delivered, it had been completely ruined by water. I've filed a claim, but that doesn't supply my shop. I applied to several wholesalers and manufacturers by telegram, firms with whom I've done business before, and this morning I received their replies. I want you to read them." She opened the small, ribbon-tied manilla folder she carried and handed him the yellow papers.

"Very well." He took them, put on his pince-nez spectacles and began to read the telegrams, handing them back to her as he finished. "Yes, I see," he said.

"Is Chambers Department Store the one they refer to?" Laurie asked.

He looked squarely at the girl and hesitated a long time before answering. "Yes, it is. And we have enjoyed just such an agreement as mentioned in the replies."

"Then why have these firms all at once seen fit to stop shipping to me? Did you just recently instruct them to live up to their word? And why? I'm no competition to Chambers!" Laurie flushed red with anger.

"I'm willing to admit I did remind them of their arrangement with me. It has been so for many years," the old man answered.

"But the area is growing every day! My customers don't come over here to buy from you, nor do your shoppers come to my place in Forest Shores. Surely, Mr. Chambers, there's room for two such stores, your very big one and my very small one!" She was close to tears, but refused to indulge in female histrionics. Jonathan Chambers had carved out a small commercial empire for himself in the valley and was not amenable to such tactics.

"What exactly would you like me to do?" he asked quietly.

"Contact your suppliers and let them do business with me, too," she answered.

Again he waited before replying. "I can't do that, my dear, for reasons I'm not at liberty to divulge."

"But I must have the supplies—you are destroying my business!" Laurie exclaimed. "I must support myself and I have a seamstress who has a small child to keep. We at least deserve the opportunity to make a living for ourselves!"

"I'm sorry." His face showed he was concerned.

"Then sell me the merchandise on a 30-day account," Laurie bargained. "At a percentage above wholesale and shipping costs."

"As you've admitted, you have no line of credit yet," he reminded her.

"And precisely how am I to establish credit if I'm not to be given a chance to even supply my shop and prove my reliability?" she asked heatedly.

The short, baldling little man walked to the window, hands clasped behind him, head pulled down into his high, inflexible white collar. He was irritated by her outburst, angered and annoyed that she should be so persuasive in her questions. He stood looking down at the bustling street corner four floors below, where carriages clattered over streetcar tracks and several automobiles jockeyed for right of way. Laurie knew she had piqued him and had sense to halt for the moment. He turned and walked back to the desk, paused, looked at her, then went to the frosted glass door which partitioned his private office from his secretary's. After opening it and satisfying himself that no one could be eavesdropping, he pulled his chair close to the girl's.

"There are certain elements we businessmen must sometimes deal with—elements with which we may find ourselves at odds, you understand," Chambers began. "We may not agree with them, but we must accede occasionally to. . .suggestions."

"Do you mean demands? If so, please call them that and be honest about it, Mr. Chambers." She was already beginning to see the broader picture of her distress.

"Very well, I shall: demands," he affirmed. "While I can't help you myself, I may be able to do so—indirectly."

"I'm not hesitant to ask why you aren't supposed to. I'm in no position to remain polite." Timidity was not in her character, and tact had given place to frankness. "I'd like to know the reason."

"In order to finance recent improvements on my property, bring it up to date, so to speak, I had to avail myself of funding from private sources."

Laurie cut through his evasiveness. "You mean you had to obtain a loan from individuals rather than through a bank. Your bank refused to loan the money so you had to go elsewhere."

"Ah. . .yes. You're very perceptive," he said. "The bank thought at my advanced age the risk wouldn't be advisable." He looked at her, his forehead wrinkled in appreciation of her directness. "It seems the people from whom I secured the loan are of the opinion you're not a proper sort of young lady and shouldn't be encouraged to continue on in Forest Shores." A broad smile softened his revelation. "As I've said, I don't have to agree with them."

"But they hold your note, which they may call at any time, and you must do as they say or be in trouble yourself. I see! Oh yes, indeed, I see!" Laurie aimed at the heart of the matter. "Then I must look elsewhere for help." She rose to leave and tucked the folder under her arm.

"Just a moment, Miss Mathews." Chambers caught her sleeve and indicated for her to resume her seat. "I think I may be able to help you, as I say, indirectly. I have a good friend in San Francisco who's a wholesale distributor. He's the west coast representative for a number of dry goods and accessory lines. I conduct a certain amount of business through him, although my store as a rule is supplied directly. Now, if you take a note from me and explain the situation, I feel he'll back you one-hundred percent." Chambers adjusted his pince-nez and looked at the girl.

"You know, I took a good many chances when I was a young man," he said. "And the odds were great against me, too; I know how it is to be starting out on your own. And I know the desperation of failure. I'm willing to take a chance on you, Miss Mathews. I'll ask that you respect my request to keep my name to yourself. Is that agreed?"

"Certainly!" Laurie leaned forward, lips parted in an expectant smile.

"Only the three of us are to know I referred you to

him or that I've guaranteed your credit."

"Would you do that?" Laurie's joy was evident.

"I shall. There are times, my dear, when what we find we're compelled to do goes against principle, but, just as you say, you have an employee with a child. So have I—only there are dozens depending on me and the management of my affairs. Should it ever come down to it, I'll never deny aiding you, but I'd rather it didn't come to that." He gauged her reaction, then continued, "If this is agreeable to you, I think it may solve your problem and ease my conscience a good deal."

"Oh yes, Mr. Chambers!" Laurie agreed. "I'd be so grateful. And I promise to keep your kindness a secret. Thank you!" She relaxed back into the chair as if a spring had broken, releasing the tension that had held her rigid during the interview.

"Then I'll get on with it, if you'll excuse me." He dipped an old-fashioned steel pen into the antique cut-glass and pewter inkwell, pulled a sheet of stationery from a drawer and began scratching at the paper, looking up and smiling at the girl between sentences.

It was too early to return to Forest Shores when Laurie left the department store with Jonathan Chambers' letter in her manila folder. The Daily Dispatch offices were only a few blocks away, but she took the new electric trolley to the corner and almost ran to see Lucia Orozco.

As she burst into the office the same young man whom she had encountered before rose to greet her. His face was not full of his customary good humor, nor did he smile when she rushed up to the counter.

"May I please see Miss Orozco?" Laurie asked.

"I'm afraid she isn't here, Miss Mathews," he said.

"You remember my name?" She was flattered.

"Of course I do. Who wouldn't remember everything about you?" He was not being fresh, merely sincere. But something had happened. Laurie was alarmed.

"Is she ill?"

"No, ma'am. Not ill." He seemed so reluctant to

say anything further that she was frightened.

"What is it then?" Laurie demanded.

"She isn't with the paper anymore. She's been let go."

Hallie Mae lighted the rose-shaded lamp and placed it on a cherrywood table before the north window. It was her favorite lamp in the old Hinshaw place, and her favorite window. From it one could watch passing carriages, streetcars, wagons, and the few preposterous, noisy automobiles which used Shore Park Drive to gain access to San Esteban Pass Road.

Pansy Hinshaw's home was the most elegant place the Purdy girl had seen in her young life, and just to be able to work there set her a bit above the other girls of Sand Town. And, too, it was nice to do little things for the ladies and receive tips in addition to her regular pay. She had never revealed to her parents that she earned anything extra. That way she could at least have a bit for herself instead of turning it all over to them. She did not consider it lying, but the thought that it probably was selfish bothered her.

Over and over she would count the money in the little metal bank Pansy had given her. It was hidden in a corner of the kitchen cabinet's silverware drawer. She was mystified when every so often she would find a dime or so more than she had counted the last time, until she spied Pansy drop a coin into the brass slot. The bank remained their secret for Pansy well knew Hallie Mae was not allowed to use her own money. Most Sand Town people, even those who did not spend on liquor, barely managed to feed and house themselves and their broods.

"If there's nothing else today, I'll be going home, Mrs. Hinshaw." She straightened a crocheted table runner and dropped the burned match into the fireplace grate.

"That's fine, dear. You run along now before it gets dark." They both worried about her walk home on West Main. Shell Road was lined with houses within whistling distance of one another, but Main extended a quarter of a mile through thickly wooded forest which only thinned out at Bert Hutchins' livery stables. The city still refused to route the horsecar out to Sand Town and thus provide transportation for those most in need of it.

"Goodnight." The girl hung her apron on a peg in the summer kitchen and wrapped her shawl around her shoulders and head. The wind was still blowing from the north, and even with the heavy woolen shawl she was frozen. Just beyond Shore Park Drive to the right was the forested part of Beach Park, a section of trees, bluffs, and sandy shoreline that bordered the east side of La Gaviota Creek and Cove. Hallie Mae Purdy was a tall, buxom girl, with the large-boned build of her County Mayo forebears and quite capable of defending herself, but only when she reached the livery stable would she slacken her pace. It was not the people she might meet she feared, but the threatening atmosphere of the spot itself. It seemed malignant, a place apart from the rest of the area.

As Hallie Mae neared the bridge over La Gaviota Creek, she could hear the roar of white water below. It had been raining in the high country and the creek was rising steadily. It was too dark on the road to see the torrent, for although the sky overhead was still light, the gloom of the dense forest on either side muted that light to an ever-present dusk. The girl did not linger on the bridge, but crossed quickly, her steps on the wooden planking drowned by the tumult of rushing water.

"I must tell Pa how high the creek is," she thought. "We'll have to move the pigs and chickens up to higher ground." She rounded the corner of Shell Road and faced into the bitter wind. She might be colder now, but she could slow down and enjoy the rest of the walk home.

The rose lamp cast a warm glow through the window as Laurie got off the horsecar. It was a welcome sight after her trip to San Esteban. It meant home - a place where she was secure from the threats of Archibald Creighton and Ralph Donner. Tomorrow she must again make a trip to the valley, but would continue on to San Francisco. With the note from Jonathan Chambers she might be able to salvage her business despite what she now knew was a conspiracy against her.

She opened the door and peeked into Pansy Hinshaw's front parlor. The woman was not there, so Laurie continued upstairs. She would warm herself with a glass of sherry and eat the remainder of a pork roast with horseradish in a sandwich. There were so many things she must do tonight that she could waste no time on cooking.

After throwing her cape on the bed and unbuttoning her patent-toed shoes, she lighted the kerosene heater and put the teakettle to boil. Etta Korby had gone over the list of merchandise they needed with her, so that chore was done, but she must talk with Pansy and then pack her valise for the trip. And she must tell Thea about her cousin's dismissal from the paper. It was all so incredible she could not believe it was happening.

If Archibald Creighton saw fit to actually threaten her, albeit through Ralph Donner, and had intimidated Jonathan Chambers into being party to his scheme, it followed that Chace, too, imagined he had reasons for avoiding her. If Sybil blamed her for Duncan's death, unfair as it was, Chace undoubtedly did also. Laurie had made up her mind not to grieve over him and had instead transferred her thoughts and energy to fighting back. Partly from pride, partly from principle, she would fight them all. If disaster came, she then at least could not blame herself. Only when she was alone in the stillness of the night did she think of Chace. Only then would she quietly weep.

By half past seven she had again brushed and pressed her cape, laid out a gray and gold Cheviot tweed suit, clean petticoats and underdrawers, and hung her black lisle stockings to dry on a line above the oil heater.

Tonight she would be too busy to even think of Chace except as one of the Creightons.

"Mrs. Hinshaw, may I come in?" Laurie called out as she tapped on the hall door.

"Oh, Laurie, of course. I've just made tea. Do sit down and have some with me." The old woman, always glad to have company, puttered about collecting her best porcelain and pouring thick cream from its pail into a dainty blue glass pitcher. "Tell me what you've found out about your shipments for the store."

Laurie was tired, her body slumping in exhaustion against the fruitwood and plush settee. She had taken her hair down and it fell about her shoulders in dark, wide waves. Before she answered, she allowed Pansy to pour the fragrant tea and get settled into a chair opposite her.

"There—we're nice and cozy and can have a good chat." Pansy's ruffled skirts spread over her feet, giving her the appearance of a diminutive elderly doll perched stiffly upright in a disproportionately large chair.

"I must go to San Francisco tomorrow morning on the early train," Laurie began. "I've had quite a day."

"To San Francisco? Whatever for?" Pansy could not imagine how the trip would solve the girl's problems.

"You remember our shipment the other day was ruined?" Laurie asked.

"Yes, I recall you said it was water damaged," Pansy replied.

"Well, I immediately telegraphed several companies to get other shipments right away. This morning we received their replies. They said they could no longer do business with my shop. It seems they had agreed to sell exclusively to Chambers Department Store."

"In San Esteban?" Pansy handed a plate of wafers to the girl.

Laurie sampled the cookie and tasted her tea. "Yes, that's the one," she said. "I took the early train over to see Jonathan Chambers himself this morning. He refused to sell me anything at discount or permit his

214

suppliers to sell to me, so I have to look elsewhere. I may be able to get something from a wholesaler in San Francisco.'' Laurie remembered her promise to keep Chambers' efforts secret. She nibbled at the crisp vanilla wafer and sipped from the fragile, forget-me-not patterned cup. Pansy waited for her to continue. ''But what's more important is that I went by to see Lucia Orozco at the paper and found out she'd been dismissed from her job! After all these years—it's so unfair!''

''But why on earth would they let her go? She *is* the paper and has been for almost forty years,'' Pansy said in surprise.

''Because someone found out what I went to see her about!'' Laurie said.

''Now how would they know?'' Pansy asked.

''When we were in the basement storeroom, we heard a noise outside. Then a door closed down the hall. Someone could easily have heard us talking. Lucia acted frightened, too. She warned me I might be getting into something unpleasant.''

''Do you want to tell me about it? What you were looking for?'' Pansy asked.

''Yes. And I want to ask your help, too.'' The girl waited for a reply.

''If I can, I'll be glad to,'' Pansy said.

''Who murdered Mellona Jolais?''

There was no mistaking the shock her question elicited. For a moment Laurie thought the frail old woman might faint, but she drank several swallows of scalding tea and put the cup down resolutely, as if she had come to a difficult decision.

''Then you've found out?'' Pansy asked.

''Yes—that I look enough like Mellona Jolais to cause a man to have a stroke when he saw me—and to make you and Roy Wimbish stare at me as if you were seeing a ghost.'' Laurie spoke gently to ease the woman's distress. ''And I know she was murdered, regardless of the sheriff saying she just left Mariposa Beach of her own accord. I'm involved, perhaps against my will, but I *am* involved, and I want to know the

215

truth."

Pansy collected herself, her hands clasped tightly in her lap. It took a while for her to begin.

"Mellona Jolais came here with some friends from France—before the war with the Prussians, you know—and founded the art colony at the beach. She was so beautiful! And so kind.

"My husband and I had her staying with us for a while in 1870, the year before she disappeared. Her lodge at the beach was destroyed by fire—almost burned the forest and cabins, but fortunately it began to rain that night. Adam, my husband, suspected it had been deliberately set. He could tell by the way the wood charred. Oil and turpentine had been splashed about and set fire.

"We always figured it must have been some drunk from town who sneaked out there and thought he would rob the cabins. She and Morgan Griffith were financially well off, so we supposed the thief had the idea they'd have valuables lying about. No one ever found out who did it, but since there were a lot of drifters at that time, it was put down as their work.

"Mellona stayed with Adam and me here, in the very same room you have now. She loved the little balcony up there. Many afternoons when it was nice she'd sit there and work on her sketches and drawings. And she'd dry her hair in the sunshine."

Pansy laughed quietly as she recalled, "She was appalled at the way American women washed their hair so seldom. I remember her sitting there in the sunlight, combing and brushing that long black hair of hers.

"Everyone who knew her loved her. And she loved in return. She was always doing things for other people, arranging showings of her friends' work, selling their pictures, loaning them money when they needed it. She was the very heart of the colony. She and Morgan Griffith—he was a cousin, you know—had the money to keep things going. They could have settled anywhere, but they'd heard of the coastline here, how wild and unspoiled it was, and decided it would be ideal for their retreat.

"There were some people here, though, who didn't approve of her or her artist friends. I think they really envied them for their freedom and the joy they had in their work. Most of us are very quick to condemn the very thing we might wish for ourselves.

"Zedekiah Creighton had married Sybil that June in Boston and brought her back here to live. Then in July he and my Adam began building the Creighton place over there on the north boundary of Mariposa Ranch. Sybil refused to live any farther from town and as it was, spent most of her time in San Francisco.

"She was so. . .so. . .repressed, I guess you'd say. Never relaxed and enjoyed herself and wouldn't let Zedekiah, either.

"You know, Laurie," Mrs. Hinshaw continued, "Sybil never did forgive Zedekiah for selling off the beach section to 'those horrid foreigners' as she called them. He did that, of course, before he even knew Sybil, but she always resented it. She would have nothing to do with anyone there—refused to see them socially—even when Zedekiah was making a great deal of money building their lodges and cabins.

"Well, Zedekiah had only been back here a few months when Mellona's cabin burned. And as I said, she stayed with Adam and me for a while. Then when Adam and Zedekiah had finished building another, and even larger, lodge for her, she moved back down to Mariposa Beach.

"I always thought Zedekiah might have known who set fire to her place, for when they'd built the other one, he swore she'd not be burned out again.

"My Adam and Zedekiah were close friends, and had been for a number of years. They pioneered this area. I suppose Adam was the only real friend Zedekiah ever had in his life. Most people either feared him or hated him. Adam accepted what he was, and always did a good, honest job when it came to building for the

Creighton company. He stood up to him, and Zedekiah respected that. Adam said if he were to do the job, it would be done right and at a fair price, no pirating.

"It was shortly after Mellona disappeared that Zedekiah began to change. Adam could still handle him—they remained as close as ever—but Sybil drove him to the limit. Always the biggest, the finest, the best. Yet nothing ever satisfied her. I never got to know Sybil. She's not the sort anyone can really know. I've heard her family has a brain-taint from too many close marriages over the years. That's what comes of too much pride!"

Pansy paused before she gained enough courage to begin again. "Then after Adam's accident. . ." The words were stifled as if she were loathe to form the memory into words. "After that, Zedekiah became more violent and irascible. In earlier days he had an unsavory reputation, but it grew worse the older he got.

"But you wanted to know about Mellona, not Zedekiah. All we ever knew was that she was at the beach party, went up to her lodge, and was never seen again, at least by any of us. We searched for her, but some old Italian man said he took her out to a lumber ship bound for San Francisco. Ships used to anchor off the coast beyond the Cove and it was no big chore to row out to one if the sea was calm. The authorities looked into it, and a woman did get off the ship and go ashore. And, too, they had a scarf that was Mellona's. The Italian said she left it in his boat, but no one ever saw her again. No trace of her ever turned up. Morgan Griffith hired men to find her, but they had no luck."

Laurie interrupted with a question. "Lucia Orozco told me Mellona was wealthy, the widow of some French official. Surely an estate was left. Didn't anyone try to check through that way?"

"She never tried to draw against the estate, if that's what you mean. When she was declared legally dead, finally—and I understand that is very difficult to do in France—the estate reverted to another branch of her husband's family, but there was no indication that they

218

needed the money. They certainly had no reason to harm her." Pansy waited to see if the girl had more questions, then resumed the story.

"A few weeks after Mellona disappeared, Adam drove up into the side yard here, in one of the springwagons they used at their building sites, and had his men take that hump-backed trunk up into the attic and leave it there. I was curious and asked him about it, but all he said was that it belonged to Mellona, and that if she never came back for it, he'd ask me not to open it so long as he lived. He said it was just things he thought she'd like kept." Laurie had to respect the willpower Pansy had exercised over three decades with the mysterious trunk in her attic. As if to signify that her recitation was finished, Pansy scooted back into the chair and poured a fresh cup of tea for them both.

"What do you think really happened to her?" Laurie asked.

"I didn't want to think she was so capricious as to just leave that way," Pansy said. "And later I didn't want to think she'd met with foul play."

"But you do?"

"I'm sure of it!"

"But who? And why?" Laurie had so many questions. "Didn't the sheriff try to find out?"

"In a desultory way he did. But when it was confirmed that a woman in a gold dress had gotten off the ship in San Francisco and took such pains of eluding pursuit, he said it was just like a flighty, immoral woman. He didn't know one soul down at Mariposa Beach, but to him all artists were like that!

"Adam thought it more probable he was afraid to carry his investigations much further. He was up for re-election, and a lot of money had been put into his campaign by businessmen around here. They didn't want any notoriety or scandal. They were trying to attract the railroad and investments in land. If it got out that a group of Bohemians were involved in a terrible scandal—and even worse, a murder—it might have dampened their plans a bit."

Laurie suddenly realized she had just heard such an argument only hours before, at the station in San Esteban. Could there be a connection?

"Did your husband have his own suspicions?" Laurie asked.

"We both felt Mellona was secretly keeping company with some man, and the fact that she kept it quiet meant he must be married. No woman like Mellona could live without being in love. It's like breath and food to women like her," Pansy replied. "With suitable gentlemen courting her as they were, surely she would have formed some sort of serious attachment, perhaps not the kind sanctioned by our very proper and conservative community at that time, but she would have fallen in love with someone, had she not already been in love."

"Could it have been Morgan Griffith?"

"No, I really don't think so. They were close all right, but not like that. Morgan had been so happy with his little wife, poor thing. Gwenllian, her name was, but she died soon after settling in at Mariposa Beach. Morgan never got over her. Never has." Pansy sighed. "That's why he lives alone in their big lodge down there. He's had affairs, I've heard, but that's just gossip. I'm in no position to know. Some of the Sand Town women have gone down there to pose for him, and I don't imagine it stopped at just posing. He was—and is—a very attractive man."

"Do you have suspicions?" Laurie felt the old woman was circumventing the main question, as if by a direct answer she might in some way do an injustice.

"No, I honestly don't know who it could have been. Oh, I've mulled it over a thousand times, and thought of reasons a lot of people might have had, and who might have done it, but none of it makes any real sense when it boils down," Pansy admitted. "I just do not know."

"But why would anyone want to harm her, if Mellona was so well liked?" That question seemed to Laurie to be the key.

"Mellona was a woman, and we women, when thwarted or deceived, once we've set our minds to something, can become harridans," Pansy said. "She was no different. She had a side to her that was so opposite her usual self that you'd wonder it could be the same person."

"In what way?" Laurie asked.

"She was part French, you know, and some blamed her temper on that. Others said it was the Welsh in her that did it. Still others said it was because she was an artist. I say it's just part of all of us, the bad side of the coin, so to speak, and has nothing to do with where we come from, who our parents were, or what our calling in life may be. Mellona was no exception." Pansy paused, reflecting. "I've thought about it so often since it happened! Perhaps she became angry, irrational. If it were a married man, maybe he struck her, or she fell."

The two women sat in silence, their heads turning on that fatal day long ago. Laurie took another wafer and broke it into pieces, eating it bit by bit. She hardly knew what to say or ask next.

"Laurie, is that what you went to see Lucia Orozco about?"

"Yes, it was," the girl confessed. "I wanted to read the newspaper accounts."

"Did they agree with what I've told you?" Pansy was certain they would.

"Your account agrees with Lucia's," Laurie said. "But I never got to read the papers—they weren't there. That's what makes the whole thing so sinister now. Somebody had taken the copies of those papers out of the files. Lucia said they'd been forbidden to write any more than the original two stories. And her young man, the one she was going to marry, was let go because of the stories. Not only that, but he couldn't get another job on the west coast. He'd wanted to follow up on what happened that day, but someone didn't want him to. Lucia didn't know who it was, but said it had to be somebody with a great deal of influence. And then there was the sheriff, too. He dropped the matter too

221

quickly."

"And now thirty years later, it's come to this!" Pansy was worried.

"Mrs. Hinshaw, please be honest with me," Laurie begged. "You wanted me to have Mellona's things, didn't you? You and Roy saw that I looked like her, and you wanted me to find out what happened to her. Isn't that so?"

Pansy placed her cup and saucer on the marble-topped table, her hand trembling enough to make the china chatter on the hard surface. She was afraid the girl would be angry with her.

"That's true," Pansy admitted. "Perhaps I shouldn't have, but it seemed as if it were fate, your coming here to my house, living in the very same room she lived in, even wearing the same odd shade of gold that she always wore, doing your hair the same way. Roy and I have carried this in our hearts all these years. If anything can be done at this late date, we felt you'd be the one to do it."

"I'm not at all sure I should thank you, but I know you thought it best." Laurie reached across the tea table and patted the old woman's hands. "And of course it was best." She held her cup out for more tea to show she was not angry. "Tell me, what was Roy to Mellona?"

"Poor, dear Roy." Pansy shook her head sadly. "He was never a very smart boy. Never got farther than fifth grade at school before he had to go to work. Never had a cent to call his own, just hand to mouth. Mellona was good to Roy. She was always kind to those who most needed kindness. She saw how miserable his life was, how he'd been taken advantage of by so many people just because he wasn't as bright as most. His own folks made him support them and wouldn't even let him court a girl. Some of his early employers worked him like a dumb animal and paid him just enough to keep him alive. By the time Mellona came here, Roy was working for my Adam, and of course he was a lot better off. He was our handyman and gardener, and did odd jobs for Adam on construction sites. His folks had died in the cholera epidemic and he was living in our caretaker's cottage out back, where he is now, and was getting a decent wage.

"Mellona, when she was living here with us, had him pose for her many times. She used him for a lot of her paintings and drawings. Adam and I bought several of them, but I've never had the heart to put them up, not after what happened to her.

"Roy was big and handsome, sunburned and robust, a real frontier type. When pictures of him began showing up in the Retan Gallery here, and word got around town that pictures he posed for were winning prizes in competitions and selling at fancy prices, all of a sudden he was somebody to look up to. Folks who'd snickered behind his back began to ask him to their homes. Deacons at the church asked him to join, although they made it plain they didn't approve of the Bohemians at the beach. Lots of folks tried to get him to take a shine to their daughters, but he never did more than look at them. He'd already fallen in love for the first and only time in his life. And it stayed that way—still is that way.

"Mellona had seen to it that he gained the respect due him. He was a fine young man, honest, moral, hardworking, a man worthy of respect. She made people see it.

"Roy fell in love with Mellona the first time he saw her. Never could do anything about it. He was too shy, and he had nothing to offer a woman like her. Oh, but he loved her very deeply, and he still does. Like Morgan and his little Gwenllian, Roy just never got over Mellona Jolais." Pansy was near tears as she finished.

How cruel people can be to one another, Laurie thought. Poor old Roy Wimbish, still pining for the woman he could never have, and never being tolerated as a worthwhile man until the scandalous Mellona thrust his image at the scoffers. She drank the last of her tea and placed the cup beside the blue glass creamer and forget-me-not pot.

"What do you know about Archibald Creighton and a man named Ralph Donner?" Laurie remembered that Chace and Pansy were old friends, and that Archibald had at one time enjoyed the hospitality of her kitchen, too.

"I guess it's sinful not to love all little children, but I could never learn to love Archie. He was never a very nice little boy. He was sullen and sulky and couldn't always be trusted to tell the truth. I never really blamed the child—his mother expected far too much from him. He was her first boy, and had to be perfect. If he did something naughty, he'd blame Chace or Duncan. He simply couldn't stand to have his mother know he wasn't what she wanted him to be. He was always frightfully jealous of the other boys. If he thought they had a toy or an apple better than his, he'd either grab it away from them or run to Sybil and throw a tantrum. As far as I know, he hasn't changed. He's been involved in some shoddy dealings here and there, not the sort that got Duncan killed, but things like his father had done. He's evidently acquiring a lot of money for himself, but he isn't helping anybody but himself when he does it."

"And Ralph Donner?" Laurie persisted.

"I only know of him by reputation. I can't tell you first hand. I've heard he bought out some Mexican landholders—the Aguilar family, I believe it was—over in the valley and is breaking the property up into truck farms, putting in irrigation and canals. He builds the houses and barns, the storage sheds, all that, and then sells the whole farm. It's bringing in immigrants from everywhere—Iowa and Minnesota, even from Denmark and Switzerland. I hear his places sell the minute they're completed."

"But what about him personally?" Laurie wasn't sure whether she should bother the elderly woman with the rest of her experiences or not. It might unduly alarm her.

"He's a good, honest man. Not too likeable from what I hear. Much too selfish and egotistical. Thinks he's a real card with the ladies," Pansy confided.

"Guess any man with his money and prospects is considered a card by people who stand to gain from him. He belongs to the Masons and Commercial Boosters, but nobody's ever been able to get him to head up a fund drive or donate much to their charitable events."

"You mean he's a cheapskate?" Laurie asked.

"Yes, you could put it that way," Pansy replied. "What he's made, he's going to keep and he doesn't feel he owes a handout to anybody. But if he promises a thing, he's as good as his word. He's proud of his reputation and he'll bend over backward to protect it. He could be a very nice young man, I guess, if he'd learn there are more things on earth than his money."

"He's not the sort to make threats?"

"Threats? I don't understand," Pansy said.

"I don't either, Mrs. Hinshaw." Laurie hesitated, then decided to reveal the advice Donner had delivered. "If he's careful about his good name, he must be in urgent need of more money. Otherwise he wouldn't have said what he did—it had to be Archibald Creighton's idea."

"I don't follow you at all, Laurie." Pansy Hinshaw was puzzled by the reference to threats.

"When I'd gone over to San Esteban earlier this week to see about our shipment, and then went to talk to Lucia Orozco, this Ralph Donner came up to me and introduced himself; I was at the station, waiting for the train back home. He told me he'd been asked by Archibald Creighton to do me a favor. And I must say it was some favor!" Laurie was angry; Pansy looked at her in growing alarm.

"Donner said they had heard why I'd gone to see Lucia—he must have been the person out in the basement hallway—and that no good purpose was to be served by digging up old scandals that were best left buried," the girl said. "The implication was very plain: either I stopped trying to find out about Mellona Jolais, or they'd see I lost my business and got run out of town. It wasn't worded exactly that way, but his meaning was quite clear!"

Pansy was speechless, indignation written on her small features. Her mouth formed a word, but refused to articulate it. She sank back into her chair, her head back and eyes closed. When she could speak, her voice was full of anger.

"How could they? How dare they say such things to you?" Then as if a thought had struck her, she suddenly leaned forward and tapped Laurie's knee. "Ah! But why should either of them be afraid of what you might find out?"

"Perhaps they just don't want any bad publicity about this area, now that they are both involved in that development in Aguilar Valley."

"No, no! That won't do at all! Aguilar Valley is too far from Forest Shores and Mariposa Beach for an old scandal to make any difference. Donner has people waiting in line for his big farm plots." Pansy Hinshaw sat back and squinted her eyes in thought. "Archie must know it would bring the Creighton name into it somehow. That has to be it! And how like him to have this other man deliver his message. No, he hasn't changed one bit since he was a child. But one thing, Laurie, when he meets his end, he'll have to do it all alone. That's the one thing he can't have somebody else do for him!"

Chapter 11

Olive Pickens slowly leafed through the sketches, admiring the artistry and intricacy of design. "They're really fine illustrations. I'm no expert, but to me these are magnificent. I can see why Mellona Jolais' work brought high prices in the galleries. Just see the marvelous sweep of movement, and the way she's emphasized detail only where she wants to stop the eye." Olive paused at the introduction of the menacing woman in the background. As she turned to the succeeding sheets, her face mirrored the subject matter. "These are frightening!"

"If we can interpret them literally, Mellona knew who it was, and went willingly to meet someone," Laurie said.

"But there's no way to know whether it was the woman in the sketch or not—it could have been anybody at all. That's what is so dreadful. And pen and ink sketches hardly constitute an indictment, do they?" Olive scrutinized the final drawing. "And, too, these may have absolutely nothing to do with her murder."

"The date on the last one is 19 September 1871. Since she'd finished and dated it, the meeting obviously had been planned well ahead of that afternoon. No, I'd say they tie in to her murder, all right." Thea's mind was made up by the dating.

"Yes, but she meant to return from that meeting," Olive said. "Otherwise she would certainly have left more definite evidence, maybe a written document of some sort. And if she'd thought she were going to be killed, she certainly would not have been so esoteric about her message—it would have been explicit, with names and reasons.''

"I think she made the last one, feeling she'd continue the series, but had to wait for the outcome of their meeting.'' Thea picked up the illustrations and looked through them once more.

"I agree,'' Laurie said. "Had she thought she'd be in real danger, she either would have refused to go, or would have told someone—left word as to whom she was meeting, just to protect herself.''

"From what Mrs. Hinshaw says, Madame Jolais was not the sort to behave in a stupid manner. And these sketches show she was not stupid. What they do show is that she was stopped abruptly,'' Olive said.

"Stopped abruptly is one way to say she was murdered!'' Thea could reduce all things to essence. She shuddered. "And to think it happened right down there on the beach, maybe along one of those trails, or up in the woods. It makes me all quivery just to think about it.''

"You aren't going to let what Arch Creighton said scare you, are you?'' Olive asked.

"Of course it scares me! Wouldn't it you?'' Laurie had no reluctance in admitting fright.

"I guess you're right. It would scare me, too.'' Olive stacked the pictures and placed them on the bed where she was sitting.

"But you're not leaving it where it is, are you?'' Thea had hoped for more.

"I don't really want to, but I don't know what to do next. How can I ask the police or sheriff to re-open a case that was considered closed over thirty years ago? I have nothing at all to go on.'' Laurie could tell no one of the golden apparition or the haunted spectacles, and certainly not about the more tangible but equally unprovable carriage which had almost run her down in the street. How could she? Who would believe her, or if believing, would not think her mad?

"Want me to put more wood on the fire? It's get-

228

ting chilly in here." Thea didn't wait for Laurie to answer, but selected two split chunks of pine and placed them on the grate. "Should I go down and get more from the woodshed?"

"No, Roy will bring some up this evening," Laurie replied. "He never likes to bring it unless I'm here. Pansy says he's afraid we might think he was snooping if he came up when we're not at home." Laurie lighted the small lamp which rested in a metal socket over the cooking stove. "I've enough milk to make us a cup of cocoa if I put a dash of water in it."

"I've got some milk. Wait a jiffy and I'll go get it." Thea opened the hall door and called back, "Here's Roy now, Laurie. I'll leave the door open for him."

Laurie poured the milk from its wire-handled pail and measured sugar and cocoa into the pan. "Roy, will you have some cocoa with us?"

The grizzled man pushed into the room, his arms loaded with split logs and a bundle of kindling tied with a string.

"No, thank you. Just come up to bring your wood." He spilled the chunks onto the hearth and stacked it in the brick bin. He straightened up slowly, a concession to his years.

Too late Olive remembered the sketches on the bed. Laurie had said she did not want Roy and Pansy to see them yet for fear it would upset them further. Should they be ineffectual in bringing the truth to light, why should they bother two elderly people?

Even as she turned from the saucepan of cocoa, Laurie saw the expression on Roy's face. Olive had seen it, too, and looked helplessly at Laurie.

The man stared at the illustrations, evidently recognizing at a glance the technique of the artist. He might have been alone in the room, for he uttered no sound, nor did he take his eyes from the drawings. Slowly, as though he were a somnambulist swimming through the thick ether of a dream, he took the top sheet and set it aside, looked at the next, and the next, until he reached the motif of the second woman.

Laurie set the pan off the burner onto the cabinet and went to his side. She waited for him to turn to the last drawing, unsure what she should do or say. This was the man who had loved Mellona, the man whom Mellona had lifted from the ignominy of his menial existence.

"I'm sorry, Roy. I hadn't wanted you to see these. . ."

He looked at Laurie, his eyes clouded with remembering. For an instant she was not even sure he recognized her. The blow had been struck and he was reeling, the stunned expression on his face much like that of a steer in a slaughter-chute.

"It's my fault! I shouldn't have left them there on the bed! I should have put them back in the folder!" Olive took the man by his arm and led him to the leather rocker. "Go into my room and get that brandy bottle from the cupboard. Quickly!"

Olive loosened the man's shirt collar which had been buttoned against the cold wind, and unbuckled the belt around his middle. She went to the hall door and called downstairs. "Mrs. Hinshaw! Please come up here! We need you!" Although not covered by any manual of classroom procedure, the situation was not too foreign to her experience.

Laurie burst into the room with Thea and splashed a bit of brandy into one of the cocoa cups and handed it to Olive. Thea stood bewildered at the development, but saw the disturbed drawings and realized what must have happened.

"Here, drink this," Olive told the man, and tipped a spoonful between his lips and waited for his reflexive swallowing. "There. That's better. Come on now, another sip." Her hand was behind his head, her face near, reassuring him. "Yes, that's fine. You'll be all right. And another little bit. Good!" To Laurie she continued, "Heat up the cocoa. It'll do him good to have something warm in his stomach besides raw brandy."

Pansy Hinshaw came into the room, a gasp choking in her throat as she saw Roy. "What happened?"

She wrung her hands as she stood before him, looking in anguish at his gray face.

"He's all right," Olive said. "He's just had a shock. It's all my fault, too. I'm terribly sorry." She rubbed the back of his neck with her fingers, her other hand resting on his arm.

"No, no, it's all right. Don't feel it's any your fault." Roy's voice was weak and hollow, its usual deep resonance gone.

"But what is it?" Pansy insisted.

"Show them to her, Miss Laurie. Please." The brandy was bringing back the color in Roy's face and the dullness fled from his eyes.

"If you think I should. . ." Laurie hesitated.

He nodded, but made no attempt to get up. Laurie gathered the sketches and handed them to Pansy Hinshaw as she sat across from Roy.

"These were in Mellona's trunk," Laurie said. "I didn't know whether to have you and Roy see them or not. I was afraid it might upset you both." She returned to the stove, turned up the wick and waited for the milk to heat. She tested the temperature with her finger and poured two cups which she took to Roy and Pansy. He drank slowly, with no protest, his eyes on Pansy and her reactions to the illustrations.

Pansy turned the sheets, her expression changing as the meaning became clearer, sketch by sketch. By the end of the series, her mouth was set in a rigid line, her eyes narrowed with suspicion. She straightened the drawings and placed them in the black folder Olive handed her. She tasted the hot cocoa, automatically putting the cup to her lips.

"You both know what they mean, don't you?" Laurie sat on the floor between them.

"Who was it Mellona went to meet? Who was her lover? Why was she murdered? Surely these told you something." Laurie gestured toward the drawings.

Thea sat cross-legged before the dying fire. She yawned and tapped a finger on the black cardboard folder beside her on the floor.

"Why won't either of them admit they read the meaning of these?" Thea was impatient with the elderly pair. "Why, after all these years?"

"You should have seen Roy's face when he was looking at them - he turned gray as a ghost!" Olive said.

Laurie finished packing her valise and felt the lisle stockings which were still not dry. "Of course they knew—or at least they must have some pretty good ideas."

She laid her necessary belongings in a line on the narrow library table so she would miss nothing when leaving early next morning. She walked to the French windows and opened them a few inches for fresh air. As she did so, she saw a movement below on the lawn.

"There goes Roy now," Laurie said. "Guess they had a little conference after they went downstairs. Maybe we can get the truth from them later."

"I think they're just plain scared stiff!" Thea turned-ed the sketches over to the very last one. "Just look at that face! It's as if the whole forest and every rock and blade of grass were imbued with all that fury!" She slapped the folder closed and twitched her shoulders as if a cold hand had touched her.

"But who is it?" Olive asked.

"Maybe you could show it around to some of the other long-time residents," Thea suggested. "Surely someone will recognize the face—maybe even who the man is. Let's see, who else do we know who's been here that long?"

"I know a lot of people," Olive said, "But I have no idea how long they lived here."

"Nor do I," Laurie said.

"And besides, if Laurie started to do that, Arch Creighton wouldn't like it, would he? And he does have one point: what earthly good will it do thirty years later?" Olive was practical from years of dealing with school boards and parents' committees.

"But nobody should get by with murder! Nobody!" Thea was indignant. "Even if they get by with it for eighty or a hundred years it isn't right!"

"Notoriety really wouldn't help the reputation of Forest Shores, would it? Especially when people like Chace Creighton are doing their best to get county and state funds for improvements in our area." Olive knew, too, how sensitive to scandal all governmental bodies are, if only to keep their own records free of it, since mere association brings with it taint.

"Perhaps it won't help, but that isn't the question, is it?" Thea asked. "We're all thinking the same thing, aren't we? It was old Zedekiah, wasn't it?"

"Don't go around making that accusation, Thea! It could get you into an awful lot of trouble, believe me." Olive also had a nodding acquaintance with the laws on slander and how quickly gossip in a small town sped to the wrong ears.

"You're right," Thea agreed. "I hate to admit it, but you're very right. And there's not one shred of proof, nothing to base it on."

"But it looks as if Mellona meant to confront her lover's wife—a jealous wife, from the looks of the drawings. I think he stopped her before she could meet her. If Mellona were pregnant by him and intended telling Sybil Creighton, you can just bet Zedekiah would want to stop her. Can you imagine how Mrs. Creighton would react to that bit of news?" Olive could only suppose what occurred. "Still, what good would it do now? Zedekiah's never going to recover from his stroke."

Laurie had to hold her tongue. She wanted to tell them she'd made a promise to a phantom. She glanced at the tiny spectacles lying on the night table by the bed. Olive saw her glance and misinterpreted.

"You've had a long day and there's another one ahead. We'd better let you get some sleep or you might miss your train." Olive stood up and waited for Thea to join her. "You know we both wish you the best of luck."

"We'll be rooting for you all the way," Thea said. "Your battle is now somewhat our battle, too."

Olive hugged Laurie. "This is one battle we've got

to win! I'm going to dinner tomorrow night with Ed Sickles. Shall I mention any of this to him?''

Laurie thought for a moment. ''No, not yet. It would be my word against two respected businessmen, remember. And who'd be believed? Can't you see the peculiar position I've been placed in?''

''All right, but I'll nose around and see how Arch stands with Ed. He may know something about Arch and Ralph Donner,'' Olive said. ''But I won't say anything about what's going on, or what went on thirty years ago, either. I can be pretty devious if I want to be.''

''I'll trust you to be. Goodnight.'' Laurie went to the door with the two young women.

''Good luck tomorrow, and a pox on the Creightons!'' Thea said.

Laurie laughed and closed the door. She was bone weary. Tomorrow would be worse. She put the cups in the dishpan and blew out the lamp. The log fire had made the room very warm, too warm for comfortable sleeping. She opened the French windows wide and stood on the small balcony for a few minutes, relishing the fresh, cold night air.

A stealthy movement beyond the white picket fence caught her eye. The moon was low in the sky, its light still too wan to distinguish things at a distance, but as the furtive shadow moved west toward the road she knew it was Roy Wimbish by the lumbering, easy gait and slope of his broad shoulders. As he angled south the moonlight glinted dully on the heavy Stevens deer rifle he was carrying.

''Oh dear, I hope he doesn't ask me if I want some venison!'' Twice before she had turned him down, repulsed by the thought of the graceful, sloe-eyed creatures having been shot and butchered. With a start she realized Roy only hunted raccoon and opossum at night, not deer.

She must have mistaken the rifle. It must have been the .22, for after all, she knew nothing of guns and had only looked at Roy's to be polite. Yes, he must be going into the forest for coon and possum. As she watched him, he crossed Shore Park Drive and headed south through the pines.

By midnight the wind had died down and frost had set in. Morning dawned bright and cold, with frost lying white on rooftop and lawn. The streetcar stopped at Catalpa Street and Laurie got off, its driver helping her with her valise as she stepped down into the street.

"I'm sure we lost all our geraniums last night." Elmer Hobart was just opening the bakery, but had already put in hours of work. "Hardest frost we've had in a few years. When I came to work about four-thirty I could see how bad it was. Madge'll have a fit when she sees that pink Martha Washington she's been coddling so long." He cranked down the frosted awning which began dripping as soon as the sun hit it. "Now what can I do for you?"

Laurie didn't spend much time looking over the case full of freshly baked rolls and cakes, gingerbread and cookies. "I'd like a dozen of the raisin rocks and a half a dozen palm leaves, please. And would you pack them in a box for me?" She and Etta could have a breakfast roll and coffee before she had to leave for the depot; the cookies would tide her over until she reached San Francisco. The dining car was much too costly for her thin purse.

"Say, I bet you haven't heard the news, have you?" Hobart selected the honey-crisp rolls and placed them in a box with wax paper to separate them.

"I haven't spoken to a soul yet today," Laurie said as she stifled a yawn. "What news is that?"

"Old Zedekiah Creighton died last night! Ed Sickles came by for a bite with me about six o'clock. I always have coffee hot in the back and he stops in now and again when he's up that early." He was obviously proud of his association with the police chief. "He says they called him in the middle of the night, but it wasn't a job for him. After all, old Zedekiah had a severe stroke. Ed sent for Doc Eichner right away. Said he couldn't figure out why the heck they called him instead of Doc anyhow.''

He looked up from tying the box. "That be all?"

"Yes, thank you." She counted the change and closed her purse. "When did you say this happened?"

"Doc Eichner says he figures it must have been about midnight, give or take a bit. Nurse says she was down in the kitchen getting him his usual hot milk and brandy. When she came back, there he was, stone dead.''

"I'm sorry to hear he died." Laurie wondered if she really was sorry. She felt no grief, no regret, for the old man had been nothing to her, and yet she was as sad as she always was when she learned of someone's death. They always left so many things undone, so many loose ends. Like Lawrence Bowen when he marched off to war in Cuba, and Duncan Creighton who tried to run away from evil of his own making. Now Zedekiah had died. What had *he* left undone?

By the time she reached the Ribands and Roses, she was glad Etta Korby would have the coffee made. Even with her gloves on, her fingers ached with cold as she held the bakery box and her valise. She tapped on the glass of the door and waited for Etta to unlock it and admit her.

"Brrr! It's really nippy this morning." Laurie dropped her luggage on the counter and took the bakery box to the workroom where a pot of coffee was already boiling.

"Have you heard about old man Creighton?" Etta stirred the pot and took it off to settle the grounds.

"Yes, Elmer Hobart just told me," Laurie replied.

"Not a minute too soon, either!"

"What not a minute too soon?" Laurie pulled off her silk gloves and held her cold fingers to the pot.

"Creighton dying, of course! He should have got on with it a long time ago. Would've saved a lot of people from trouble. It's a wonder somebody didn't help him do it a long time ago." Etta took the cups from the shelf and sniffed the half-pint bottle of cream to see if it was still sweet. "We'll have to go without cream. It's gone blink."

"As long as it's hot, that's all I care about."

"Do you have your list?" Etta asked.

"Yes, and the address." Laurie could not tell Etta that she also had the note from Jonathan Chambers.

"Here's your ticket. I picked it up last night on my way home as you asked." Etta handed Laurie a long yellow envelope with the railway timetable.

"Thank you, Etta. I don't know what I'd do without you." She snipped the string off the box and offered Etta one of the sticky palm leaves, then took one herself and bit into it hungrily.

"I think it should be said the other way 'round: I don't know what *I'd* do without *you*. Me and Fannie, too," Etta said quietly.

"We're a company, aren't we?" Laurie reminded her seamstress.

"Well, we're trying to be—if Arch Creighton doesn't mind too much!" Just repeating the man's name made Etta angry.

"Now do you remember who to give credit, and who not?" Laurie asked. "And who to ask for payment on account?"

"Yes, I made a note of it so I can tuck it into the cash drawer." Etta held up a strip of paper covered with names and coded little marks beside them.

"Good. And please, if Mrs. Arvidson comes in, try to be nice to her," Laurie pleaded.

"For you, I'll try. For her, I wouldn't." They laughed together as Etta poured coffee into their cups. "Sorry about the grounds, but if we wait for them to settle, the train'll go without you." She took down the sugar and handed a spoon to Laurie. "I don't think we'll have to worry about Mrs. Arvidson."

"Why is that?"

"Mother Korby—you know how she hears all the gossip whenever she goes to the church suppers—well, she says Sybil and Arch Creighton are trying to persuade people not to patronize us. Myrtle Arvidson is busy relaying the suggestion, but nobody seems to be paying much attention to it. I have a notion folks around here have just about had enough of them." Etta took the spoon and helped herself to the sugar. "I just heard about it last night."

"I hope you're right." Laurie could not let Etta know she was beset with misgivings and concerned about the effects of Sybil Creighton's influence on their business.

"You've just got to get that man to help us," Etta was suddenly serious. The prospect of being without a job and none other available had filled her with anxiety. Her mother-in-law was too poor to help her out, and Fannie would not understand if she had to be sent away to live with relatives.

"I'll do the best I can—for all of us," Laurie promised.

"I know you will." Etta considered herself too old to cry, but she was close to it as she stirred the sugar in her coffee. She quickly looked away and took her cup into the front of the store. Laurie followed her and put her arm around Etta's waist and hugged her.

"It'll come out right, just you wait and see," Laurie said, as much for her own benefit as for Etta's.

Laurie stepped from the victoria and waited for the driver to hand down her bag. She had his pay counted in her pocket, plus a coin for the tip, and dropped it into his upturned palm. He tipped his hat and mumbled his gratitude. Too late she realized she had given him a bit more than necessary.

She was alone in the street, except for teamsters and dock workers busy with their loadings. The area was lined with brick and board warehouses, their few windows placed high above loading docks recessed into the buildings. Wagons hitched to heavy draft horses were lined up, waiting turns to either deliver or pick up merchandise. She had seen similar places in Chicago near the rail yards so it was not new to her. Only before she had not been there on business.

An ornately painted sign with curlicued letters in black and red was blazoned across the top floor of the building for which she headed: 'Meister's Wholesalers—Ladies Wear and Notions, Aaron Meister, Prop.' She clutched the note from Jonathan Chambers in her hand and rechecked the name and address which she already knew by heart.

Since her hands were full, she had to mince carefully up the steep steps to what appeared to be the main offices. Behind a long oak counter were a battery of men at individual desks, each one seemingly engrossed in stacks of papers which apparently had no system of arrangement. There was a great deal of noise, with much shouting back and forth. Two young boys were busy with boxes of more papers, collecting and distributing a few here, a few there, in rather disorderly fashion. One of the men near the counter looked up and smiled over his thick glasses.

"Yes, Miss, may I help you?" He got up and came to the counter as if he were stiff from sitting in one position too long. His trousers were shiny on the seat, and elastic sleeve garters held his cuffs out of the way of posting and figuring.

"I should like to see Mr. Aaron Meister. I have a note of introduction, if you'd take it to him, please." Several men turned to look her over, their eyes lingering on what they saw. Across the room a row of girls at typewriters made such a staccato clatter that conversation was difficult.

The man took the paper, and was gone only a few moments before he returned to usher her into the office which occupied the far end of the long room. "You may go right in, Miss." He held the door open for her and stood aside as she entered, then closed it after her.

"Come in, Miss Mathews." The man was small and very dark, his clipped beard and moustache so covering his face that only his eyes were definable. They were intensely black behind small, round spectacle lenses. He had a distinctive foreign look about him, even in the cut of his clothing, and his accent was decidedly German. "Won't you please sit down?"

He waited for her to become comfortable, then gestured with Chambers' note in his hand. "I shall sell you anything you like—anything at all!" he said before he seated himself.

"But you haven't heard what I have to say!" Laurie was surprised by his abruptness.

"I don't have to hear any more unless you care to tell me. Jonathan Chambers called me personally, long distance, yesterday and told me all about your situation. I am not in sympathy with such tactics as your two gentlemen acquaintances are using. If Jonathan had not guaranteed your credit, Miss Mathews, I should still consider it a pleasure to see that you received whatever you needed to continue your business." Meister was an impulsively decisive man.

"That's very kind of you, but wouldn't you be taking a great chance?" Laurie asked.

"No, I should not be taking a chance." His look was enigmatic as he shook his head and smiled. "Do you have your list of merchandise?"

She extracted from her purse the list and held it up, a simple, childish gesture that amused the man. He laughed softly, his dark lips parting over small white teeth. "Good!" He pressed an electric button on his desk and somewhere in the outer office a buzzer sounded, summoning a young man in shirt sleeves and green visor.

"This is our Mr. Feldman, Miss Mathews. Tell him what you need. He will show you samples, and write up your order. We shall expedite shipment to see that you get it as soon as possible." He smiled at her bewilderment. "Is that satisfactory?"

"Oh yes! How can I ever thank you?" Laurie said, then added, "I don't even know for certain if my shop can survive long enough to pay you. I promise to pay eventually, no matter what happens, but if..."

"You shall succeed!" Meister said it with determination. "I know you shall! But even if I didn't feel so certain, I should take the chance anyway." The mer-

240

chant tapped the top of his desk to emphasize his point. "I do not approve of such methods in dealing with competition or opposition. I'm not aware of your particular problem; Jonathan did not go into the more personal details, but to threaten a young woman who is trying to earn her own living in a respectable manner is barbaric."

Aaron Meister rose from his desk. "You must pose a very serious threat to them, must you not?"

"I hadn't thought of it in that way, but you may be right. How that can be, I don't know—but yes, you're right!" Laurie had not considered her position as a threat to either Creighton or Donner; the enlightenment fired her with more determination than ever.

Aaron Meister escorted her to the door, his hand on her elbow. "I should be delighted if you would accompany my wife and me to dinner." He bowed stiffly and held out his hand to her, taking hers gently. "I'm sure she would be most happy to meet you." He had sensed her hesitancy. "Do say you will."

"Yes, thank you. I'd like that very much," Laurie said.

"Now run along and get your orders written up. Mr. Feldman will see to it they're packed and carted to the depot for the overnight freight. That should get them to you late tomorrow afternoon."

Meister glanced again at Chambers' letter. "If you will allow me, I shall inform a railroad agent whom I know of your problem with your previous orders. I shall request that he personally see this one to your door. I'm sure he will agree to investigate the incident himself. If so, you may get an insurance settlement within a week or so."

Laurie's head was in a whirl as she listened. Why were first Jonathan Chambers and now Aaron Meister so interested in helping her? She hazarded the question.

"Zedekiah Creighton's reputation extends far beyond Forest Shores. If his son is intending to follow his example, there are many who will oppose every step of his way." The black eyes snapped with repressed anger. "If many of us must join forces to thwart his ambition, so be it. It is our pleasure to help you, Miss Mathews, because your battle is ours."

The words were familiar. Olive and Thea, even Etta Korby, had used them, too. She was not alone, Laurie realized, and drew renewed courage and hope.

"I think you should know that Zedekiah Creighton died last night," Laurie said. "I heard about it early this morning before I left." She did not expect a show of sympathy and none came.

"What a pity he did not live to atone for past transgressions." There was no smile on the man's face. His eyes behind their spectacles were hard. Thea Harris had mentioned that Zedekiah Creighton had tricked some early German settlers out of valuable riparian rights in the valley and had cost them their farms, the most prosperous ones of the region. Laurie knew from her German acquaintances in Chicago that they considered personal questions ill-mannered. She would not ask Aaron Meister, but felt there must be a relationship between his hatred of Creighton and the ruined farmers.

Mr. Feldman escorted her from the office and took her into a wide showroom on the second floor. Directions were given and the shipment began to accumulate box by box before fifteen minutes had passed. In a daze she checked off the items on her list and added a few more. There were silkateen underwear, black mercerized-silk waists with tucks and buttons, detachable oxidized silver and enamel buckles, web and satin hose supporters, lawn guimpes embroidered with pink and green rosebuds, Amsterdam silk gloves, linen mesh dress shields, and for the coming warm season, the latest Belfast mesh linen undergarments. She would remain in business at least for a while. Etta and Fannie would not be parted yet, not so long as Laurie could still fight back and had Aaron Meister on her side.

"I don't know what's come over Roy! I haven't heard him hum or whistle like that in thirty years!" Pansy closed the summer kitchen door after him and returned to the parlor. "I did hate to turn him down, but I can't abide the thought of eating those dear little animals. I do so love to watch them out in the yard late at night."

"I'd heard of people eating raccoon and possum back in Illinois, but I've never tasted any," Laurie said. "I know they're thought to be quite good stewed, but I'm just like you. I had to turn Roy down on venison, too." Laurie watched out the bay window as Roy crossed the lawn and headed for Bert Hutchins' livery stable and their inevitable Friday night pinocle game.

"I've always been soft-hearted when it came to wild game. Poor little creatures." Pansy had to smile as she looked at Roy. "I haven't seen such a spring in his walk for years. Just look at that! He almost looks young again, doesn't he?"

"He does seem pretty cheerful." Laurie could still hear him whistling the chorus of *The Missy Bubble* two-step until he was out of sight in the dusk.

"If I didn't know Roy as well as I do, I'd almost think he'd got himself a lady friend." Mrs. Hinshaw pulled the drapes across the window alcove. "You must be exhausted after all the excitement today. Now tell me exactly what the railway agent said." She settled herself on the settee and spread her skirts primly about her feet.

"He says I'll have my money within a week. He found out who left my crates out on the loading platform. He agrees it was all the railroad's fault. I've more than a suspicion that it was done on purpose—the man was just a day laborer and some of the other men say he had a good deal of money when he took off. Nobody's seen him since."

"No one knows where he went? That's a pity. He should be reprimanded for his negligence," Pansy said.

"But it wasn't just negligence, Mrs. Hinshaw. He seems to have been paid to leave the crates out in the rain." Laurie could discuss it calmly now.

"All the more reason he should be made to answer," Pansy huffed.

"There's nothing I can do about it, but perhaps the railroad will," Laurie said. "I doubt they will, since it's hardly worth the trouble, and I really don't care about him, now that I've got the shipment from Meister's. I'll let the agent take care of it."

"I don't suppose you've had time to hear about Zedekiah." It was more question than statement from the elderly woman.

"I'm not sure what you mean," Laurie said.

"You know that old Mexican couple who's been with the Creightons for years?" Laurie nodded and Pansy continued, "Well, they say when the nurse found Zedekiah he had such a look on his face she almost screamed with fright."

"I still don't understand." The girl was puzzled.

"Catalina and Eusebio told Roy about it," Pansy explained. "They said Zedekiah was sitting up in bed, just like always, with his robe on and the sheets pulled up around him, but it was the expression on his face that was so terrible. Catalina said his mouth was wide open and his eyes staring, like he'd seen a ghost. She said it was the worst thing she'd ever seen. She's helped bury most of her own family, but had never seen anything like it."

Pansy relished the macabre account and went on, "Eusebio said when the nurse found Zedekiah like that, she ran down the hall to tell Sybil and Archibald and had to break in on a regular donnybrook they were having. When Sybil came in and saw him, she let out a yell that brought Catalina and Eusebio running. They couldn't imagine what had happened. Poor Archibald almost collapsed. Eusebio said for the love of God to straighten the poor man out and shut his eyes and mouth, as any good Christian would, but Miss McMurray, the nurse, said not to touch him until the doctor got there." Pansy made a deprecating face and added, "But Sybil didn't want the doctor—she demanded Ed Sickles come out and see to things."

"Why would she have wanted the police?" Laurie asked.

"Catalina said it was the expression on Zedekiah's face! But Ed Sickles sent for Harry Eichner, since he was Zedekiah's doctor, and he says there was nothing amiss about the death. He'd had one stroke and probably had another. And of course his heart wasn't too good, either." Pansy added as if it were significant, "He was a good deal older than I, you know."

"Do they hold an inquest or have an autopsy in a case like that?"

"No, I don't believe so. There was nothing questionable. He died right in his own bed, after all, and not a mark on him. He was just a sick old man and he died. No need to have an autopsy." Pansy shook her head sadly. "Doctor Eichner hadn't expected him to last this long."

"How...how is Chace taking it?" Laurie found she could pronounce his name without too much pain, just so long as she reminded herself that he was another Creighton.

"They got word to him in Sacramento, but he wasn't coming back until today. He probably came on the same train that brought your shipment over on the afternoon run."

"He's been in Sacramento?" That was news to Laurie.

"Yes, for some time, now," Pansy replied. "He's been trying to get the Legislature to allocate funding for a sanatorium here. The County said it will authorize an addition to the county hospital, but it seems it won't put up monies for a tuberculosis wing. That was something Creighton Development has always opposed. Said it would damage the image of our climate here if we were to build a sanatorium, never mind how badly we need one. Archibald still holds with that, but Chace has been doing his best to push it through, now that Zedekiah hasn't been active in the company." Pansy was glad to speak of less ghoulish matters.

"I didn't know." Laurie looked up as the front door opened and Olive came in, her arms burdened with school papers and groceries.

"Hello, you two! Oh, it's nice and warm in here. I think we'll get more frost tonight." Olive's nose and cheeks were red from her walk home.

Laurie was glad Olive had interrupted, for she felt she could not speak of Chace for long without giving way to the emotion that tormented her night and day.

Laurie did not intend to go to Zedekiah's funeral, although most of the town's business people were sure to attend. Since it seemed that her very existence was anathema to the entire Creighton family, her presence would hardly be welcomed. And now that she had obtained her merchandise and flouted Archibald's warning, she deemed it prudent to remain as inconspicuous as possible.

Friday evening Olive devoted to grading her student's test papers. By eight-thirty, her chore completed, she tapped on Laurie's door.

"I just had to find out how you made out at San Francisco." The school teacher's robe and slippers made a garish costume with the towel wrapped about her wet hair. "If you're too tired, I'll talk to you tomorrow." She saw Laurie had not yet unpacked her valise, but had left it on the table.

"No, no, please do come in. Thea's here, too. I'm going to bed early, but not yet. Besides, I have to tell you the good news."

"Before you say one word I want to tell you *my* news!" Thea was still in her business suit which smelled of aromatic herbs and pharmaceutical chemicals. She had stayed late at work, inventorying stock for Knut Jepsen. Her one concession to being off duty was to remove her pointed-toed, laced boots and don her old felt bedroom slippers. She had flopped back across the bed and was talking toward the ceiling, her hands behind her head. "I told Knut about what was happening to you, Laurie, and he's damned mad about it. You know how active he is in the Masons—well, he's putting out the word!" Thea chuckled wickedly. "I have a feeling old Arch and Ralph Donner will have good reason to regret what they tried to do. It isn't just with

246

you, either."

"You mean someone else had been digging into the paper files?" Laurie asked in alarm.

"Oh, nothing like that," Thea answered quickly. "I meant Arch Creighton has been trying to pressure other people the same way. Maybe not for the same reasons, but he implies he'll see to it they lose business one way or the other. And being in a good position to do just that, now that he's in the catbird seat, they got pretty scared. And tales like that get around." Thea sat up and unbuttoned her suit jacket.

"The obvious question is, what are they going to do about it?" Olive, as well as Thea, had a very practical turn of mind.

"They're going right to Chace!" Thea spread her hands to signify the reasonableness of their decision. "He's not head of the company now that the old man is dead, but he has a certain interest in it. And he's the only one who's ever been able to do much with Arch."

"Don't bet any money that he can stop Arch!" Olive was doubtful of Chace's influence now that his brother would head up the powerful company. "This is Arch's big chance, and don't think he won't make the most of it. Ed Sickles says he's about to take over the Aguilar Valley project in San Esteban. Seems Ralph Donner went in way over his head and ran into financing problems—something to do with extending the irrigation system and connecting canals. He needs money to complete the project and someone to represent him in Sacramento. Unfortunately, Archibald Creighton fills both needs."

"Knut Jepsen says he's heard Arch has taken it into his head to run for governor in a couple of years! Can you believe that?" Thea snorted in contempt. "Seems he's made all sorts of plans, all with Sybil Creighton's approval and backing. Knut says those two would really be the pair to run the state all right!"

Laurie suddenly realized those rumors must also have reached the ears of Aaron Meister in San Francisco. No wonder he had sworn to oppose Creighton every step of his way.

"There'll be plenty of people against that proposition. Too bad women can't vote! Maybe we could form a coalition and see that he's kept out of politics," Olive said.

"But will the men around here have nerve enough to oppose Arch?" Laurie wondered. "If he's already throwing his weight around, wouldn't it be dangerous to work openly against him?"

All three young women were silent, each thinking of the possible reprisals in store for those daring to cross Archibald and Sybil Creighton in their ambitions. California was an immense state, but the Creighton influence extended its breadth and length.

"No, you're right," Thea agreed. "Chace won't have an easy time of it now that Archibald's in control."

Chapter 12

No one but Pansy Hinshaw was aware of the old piano's need of tuning. Only her sensitive ear noticed the fraction of a tone many of the strings were off. She played a portion of a Chopin sonata, her stiff fingers finding the keys easily, but striking them with difficulty. The plaintive melody, repeated in variations, was sweet and haunting, reminding her of Adam, who had so loved to hear her play. Pansy could pretend she was playing for him, too, instead of just her ladies.

Thea, Olive, and Laurie, together with several other tenants, had joined the elderly woman in her music room and parlor. It had not been planned, as were their Sunday afternoon parties, but was an impromptu gathering. As usual, they took turns playing, singing, reciting, and telling jokes, some of which elicited blushes along with laughter.

Pansy finished the graceful ending and straightened the music, reminding herself to put fresh candles in the brass holders hinged to the rack. At the sound of a horse turning from Shore Park Drive and halting before her house, she went to the bay window and parted the drapes. By the street light she could see the huge gray mare and thick-set rider. Over her shoulder Olive recognized the outline of the man.

"Now who in the world can that be coming here? Excuse me, ladies." Pansy turned from the window and headed for the door as a man's heavy boots scraped and pounded along the walk and up onto the veranda. Before he could twist the nickel-plated key which sounded the doorbell, she opened the door. In the parlor and music room her visitors were silent, for at Olive's hissed announcement of who was coming, they remained quiet to listen.

"Why, Archibald! Do come in!" Pansy was surprised and genuinely delighted to see the man.

"Thank you, Mrs. Hinshaw. I won't take up much of your time. Can't stay but long enough for my intended business."

"Oh, it's business then, is it?" She sounded a bit disappointed, but still happy to see him. "We can step in here, if you like." Pansy was puzzled by his attitude, which usually was one of polite effusiveness. She parted the velvet portieres and led him into the back parlor where a small lamp was burning on a side table. "Won't you sit down? I want you to know how sorry I was to hear about your father. I expect you'll have a heavy burden on your shoulders from now on, considering all the responsibilities he had that will now be yours."

"Yes, I thank you for your sympathy." It had the ring of a rehearsed and pat response, as if it were some sort of verbal ritual to appease the dead. "Mrs. Hinshaw, I'll come right to the point."

"Please do, Archibald." She saw from the corner of her eye that several ladies had tiptoed close to the door to overhear the conversation, their animosity at his intrusion evident in their faces. She was not offended at their action, because it lent her a bit more courage as she sat opposite Creighton. From where he sat, the man could not see them, nor was he aware of their presence. Had he known, he would have lowered his voice.

"It's been brought to my attention that you've never applied for a business permit to run a commercial hotel or apartment house, as city ordinance requires," Archibald Creighton began. "Moreover, there seems to be some question as to the suitability of your house as such an establishment." As he shifted position in the uncomfortable straight-backed chair his spurs, with elaborate rowels of finest worked silver, clinked against the highly polished oaken floor. At the sound, Thea's face contracted into a scowl aimed invisibly at his back.

"Creighton Development Company has underwritten the offer made by the Civic Club to buy your property, and is willing to add five-hundred dollars to the original proposal, seeing that values have gone up somewhat."

Pansy started to say something, but he put his hand up as if to prevent her. "Reports are circulating about some of your tenants, as to whether they are desirable in the neighborhood. I'm sure you're aware..."

"Archibald! I'll not have you say one word against my ladies! Not one word! If you want to spread your insinuations elsewhere, I can't stop you, but in my own home, I most certainly can—and I shall! Not one word more, do you hear?" She stood up, her old eyes blazing defiance. Her silk petticoats rustled as she flounced to the door in indignation.

"Sit down, Mrs. Hinshaw." His tone was surly and insulting. "I'm not finished yet, and I won't go until I am. Understand that!" He made no attempt to rise, but sat insolently looking up at her small white face.

"Get out this minute! You are not welcome here! No, sir! You are not welcome at all!" She stood in the doorway and held back the portieres for him to leave.

Instead, he sprawled with his arms folded across his chest, his roweled boots gouging into the floor. "You have no living relatives, have you?" he asked. "You don't need to answer—I'm already aware of that fact, just as Father was. The only difference was that he tried his best to protect you, prevent the city from taking action against you. They could, you know." He seemed to gloat over the assertion.

"And since you have no relatives who might act as conservators of your estate, I intend to request that privilege. When you display such incompetence as to rent the premises to women of dubious reputation—shall we say—you bring into question your ability to handle your own affairs. That coupled with your obstinate refusal to accept a substantial offer for your property, and in view of your age and health, the court may see fit to appoint someone to see that your situation is taken care of. Someone who is responsible.''

"And...and...you would dare to present yourself as a responsible person? Responsible for me? How dare you?'' Pansy flew back into the room to confront him. "I'll see you in hell first, Archibald Creighton!'' She went to the door leading into the front parlor and brought in Thea Harris. "You heard how he threatened me, Thea?''

Olive and Laurie stood behind them, the other women grouped about the door. "Ladies, you all heard this...*gentleman*, did you not?'' Olive was disgusted with the man, and her expression conveyed the emotion clearly.

"You see, I have witnesses, Archibald! Now you go right ahead and file for conservatorship. We'll just see who's responsible!'' Pansy almost shouted in her anger.

His visage contorted with shocked surprise as the women filed into the room, their faces glowering with disdain. Without a word he rose to go. Thea moved forward, every line of her expressing her loathing.

"I see you're still trying to wear my grandfather's spurs. After that stallion almost killed you for using them, I'd have thought you'd give up.'' She sidled in front of him, blocking his exit from the small room. "You're going to goad the wrong horse one of these days, and God help you.'' Thea placed her arm protectively about Pansy and led her from the back parlor, followed by the other women.

"Credit him for this much: this time he didn't ask Ralph Donner to come lodge his threats for him.'' Laurie, fury igniting her black eyes, dared the man to remain in the house another instant.

He fled from them as from Harpies. The door to

the veranda slammed shut behind him and a moment later they heard the huge gray mare whinny her anger as the silver spurs dug into her sensitive flanks. Creighton whirled her about and headed south on Shore Park Drive, posting awkwardly as the mare broke into a trot.

"His mother's put him up to this! She's teaching him some of her tricks." Thea helped the shaking Pansy to the damask settee and sat beside her, holding her withered hands in her own.

"But it's me they're after!" Laurie's face was white with rage. She turned to Pansy. "I should move away. I'm so sorry..."

"You'll do nothing of the kind! We won't let them win this battle! My ladies and I..." Pansy looked about at their angry faces. "My ladies and I will stand together!"

At eleven-fifteen no one had yet decided to leave the parlor. If there had been a spirit of unity before in the old Hinshaw place, it was militantly doubled this evening. With the threat against Pansy, they were all threatened, and in their danger were even more unified and determined. Although terrified that Archibald might actually do as he said, Pansy would not be intimidated. That time had passed when she had been forced to take in tenants long ago.

As he emerged from the forest across from the house, Roy Wimbish noticed the downstairs was still lighted, and through slits where the draperies did not quite meet, he could see motion inside the front parlor. His first thought was of Mrs. Hinshaw. He hurried to the door of the summer kitchen and let himself in. At the sound of laughter from the front of the house, his anxiety was allayed. Nothing had happened to his elderly employer. He stooped and untied his heavy boots, left them by the outer door and slipped on the old shoes kept in the kitchen for his use inside the house. He rapped loudly on the kitchen door and called aloud.

"Come on in, Roy." Pansy rushed to the dining room and beckoned him to join them. "We've having our Sunday party tonight."

"Oh no, ma'am. I just wanted to know if there was anything you needed before I go to bed." It was quite true, but he was also curious about the unusual gathering.

"I insist you come in and at least say hello to the ladies." She took him by the arm and pushed him through the dining room into the parlor. He lumbered into the brightly lighted room, nodded shyly at the assembly of women.

"Arch Creighton paid Mrs. Hinshaw a visit this evening. We're celebrating our declaration of hostilities." Olive was glowing from her second glass of Pansy's sauterne. She took him by the hand and pulled him to the table loaded with sandwiches and sweets collected from all their rooms. Into his huge, rough hand she thrust a glass of wine and filled a plate for him.

Within a few minutes Roy had learned of Creighton's latest threat. His face grew hard, his eyes flinty, as first Olive, then Thea, then the others told him of the night's events. Muscles of his jaw bulged beneath his beard and veins in his temples throbbed with his quiet anger.

Laurie remembered he looked the same way a few nights before, when he had taken his rifle into the woods for raccoon and opossum. She had to wonder if he would go hunting again tonight.

"...and you should have heard that big mare of Chace's! Arch put my grandfather's spurs to her. You remember those fancy spurs of his, don't you, Roy?" Thea asked.

"Yes, ma'am. But I never knowed him to use them except for show. He'd never treat a fine horse that way. He was a mighty fine man, your grandpa." Roy could recall old Orozco sitting tall and proud in his silver studded saddle, his dappled roan pawing daintily at the ground, the jingle of silver spurs and bridle trappings marking their progress down the dusty streets of San Esteban.

Olive began tinkering at the piano, children's songs alternating with simple old ballads. She struck several loud chords for their attention, then began a rousing version of *Battle Hymn of the Republic*. By the middle of the first verse they were all singing the brave words, Roy's defiant baritone rising above their sopranos and contraltos.

"Glory, glory, hallelujah!" It was not his winning at pinocle tonight which made him throw back his head and smile as he sang. "Glory, glory..."

Laurie Mathews awakened early Sunday morning to the rattling of the French windows in their sills. She opened her eyes slowly, letting them adjust to the cold daylight filtering through curtains beneath drawn blinds. It had been well past midnight when their party had ended. She had been tired from her excursion to San Francisco, but had risen to do battle once more when Archibald Creighton had arrived. This morning she would sleep late, she decided, but the wind buffeting the old house made further rest impossible.

She yawned, stretched beneath the comforter and lay looking up at the ceiling, watching the flickering pattern of dull light and shadow as shades and curtains fluttered in time to the wind. This morning it had a changed sound. She listened and wrinkled her forehead in bewilderment. What was so different about it that frightened her now? She sat up and reached for her plush robe at the foot of the bed.

It had grown colder during the night, the wind still blowing from the northwest. She thought of Madge Hobart's yard full of fancy geraniums and wondered if they could have survived the drop in temperature. The light coming in was peculiar yellowish-gray, a darkness that should have been accompanied by rain or hail, but was instead merely heralded by a new moaning note in the gale. There were no sharp gusts that shook the house with their violence, but a steady, hard blow that seemed to have increased in velocity overnight. From six blocks north came thunder that should have been part of a storm, but was only the sound of a tremendous surf pounding against Point Piedras and the breakwaters at the foot of Hawthorne Street and at La Gaviota Cove.

"Why don't you go with me tomorrow?" Olive had asked Laurie. "I have to give a short talk at the old school house in Sand Town. I'm supposed to induce non-English speaking families to send their children to some of the special classes the school board insists they must attend. What makes it ridiculous is that if the parents don't know English, then how can my speech convince them of anything?"

Olive was insistent Laurie go with her. The girl had not been too enthusiastic about returning to Sand Town after her experience at the Shell Box on New Year's Eve. She finally agreed, feeling herself a coward if she refused.

"Good, then that's settled. I intend to sleep late, but we must be down there about one o'clock. It will be quite a long hike, so wear walking shoes."

Laurie put the coffee pot on before she opened her room to the day. She stood and looked out the French windows at trees flexing in the wind. As far as she could see, every leaf and needle was turned from the gale. The lawn below was littered with leaves and twigs torn from low shrubs and live oak trees. She had not realized before how strong the wind had become.

She had heard Thea leave to catch the early train to San Esteban, where she would go to mass with her relatives and spend the day with them. Laurie wished she had not promised to go with Olive, since it would probably be miserably cold down by the cove. She bathed in cold water at the sink and combed her hair down over her ears for warmth.

A little before noon Olive rapped at her door. "Ready?"

"All set." Laurie pulled a heavy woolen beret low over her forehead and wraped her throat with a flannel scarf. "I've got a sweater under my cape. Do you think that will be warm enough?"

"Ought to be. You'll get warm walking." They called a greeting to Pansy Hinshaw and young Hallie Mae Purdy, who were having their Sunday lunch by the bay window.

"It's getting real bad down at Sand Town, Miss Pickens,". the little maid said. "Got terrible trouble with the water rising all the time. The cove's full and the creek's overflowing its banks. Guido Ferranti says it's still raining in the mountains and we'll be getting a lot more water yet." Hallie Mae was glad to be warm and dry in Mrs. Hinshaw's home, with cold roast lamb and hot tea. "Pa had to put all our animals 'way up on the hill, up from the beach. Can't stand to lose them or we don't eat." She speared a bit of lamb with her fork and dunked it in tart-sweet vinegar and mint sauce.

"We'll look in on your family before we come home and let you know how they're doing." Olive had read the girl's concern in her face.

"Thank you. I'd like that. Mrs. Hinshaw says I can go home if they need me, but I'd much rather stay here. I'm afraid of water." It was clear the girl was very worried.

"We'll let you know the minute we get back," Laurie promised.

"Do be careful, girls." Pansy's admonition was almost unheard, drowned out by wind as they opened the front door. The enclosure of the veranda had been constructed to withstand the abundance of wind on the jutting peninsula, but even those thick panes were straining in their heavy redwood sashes. As soon as the girls left the porch, the full force of the blow hit them.

"Ed says if the wind doesn't change direction we're apt to have a lot of damage," Olive said. "Builds up something like a tidal wave along this part of the coast. Buell Spencer out at the lighthouse sent word in for Ed to come see him yesterday."

"It hasn't changed for days! It's blowing harder than ever, and still from the northwest." Laurie snuggled her face down into the scarf and clasped her loose cape about her.

The wind sweeping down Shore Park Drive drove at them as they crossed into the forested section on Main. Neither girl spoke. It would have required more energy than it was worth. The steady, odd-pitched howl that Laurie had been aware of in the early morning had increased once they continued down the road toward the bridge. By the time they reached it, they could hardly believe the roar of water down the steep-sided canyon. There was no patch of placid water, only froth and white foam. For a few minutes they stood in the center of the timbered bridge, absorbing some of the wild fury of wind and water. The enormous squared logs that made up the roadbed over the bridge vibrated with the violence that assaulted the supporting stanchions and beams. Spray blew upward defying gravity, like rain gone mad.

Both girls kept their heads down, faces averted from the blast. By cutting through Bert Hutchins' pasture they would have some shelter. They helped one another over the fence stile and followed the pathway toward the livery stable.

Through the trees they could see Bert's dogs and a group of boys herding horses and mules from the lower pasture and corrals which fronted on La Gaviota Creek. Shouting, yelling, barking, they circled the panicked animals and drove them up into the high pasture where the carriage horses milled about, too frightened to put their rumps to the wind. Bert Hutchins was busy taking down several sections of fence along Shell Road and replacing them with lengths of rope.

"What's he doing that for, Olive?" Laurie had no knowledge of rural emergencies.

"So they can evacuate the horses instantly if they need to." Olive stood in the lee of a pine tree and watched the hectic procedure. "His dogs are so beautifully trained. Just see how they keep the horses moving."

"But why are they doing it?" Laurie again asked.

"He must expect the creek to flood more. I don't know what else it could be." Olive grabbed the girl's hand and pulled her along after her. "We've got to get down to the schoolhouse." They crossed through the collection of livery stable buildings and almost ran the few blocks remaining to the one room school.

Both sides of Shell Road were clustered with excited residents, some with personal belongings packed into quilts and baskets and pulled on children's wagons or makeshift sledges of boards. Children, their faces etched with fear, clung to favorite toys or to pet animals who struggled to free themselves and return to the shelter of the squalid shacks lining the lanes off the road. Here and there a wagon loaded past capacity would creak past, heading for higher ground.

"Mr. Ferranti, what's going on?" Olive was breathless as they ran up the dilapidated board walk to the schoolhouse. "What's the matter?"

"It's the high tide in a few hours, Miss Pickens," the man said. "Last one came right up to the houses. Broke some of the boats loose from the docks. Next one will be a lot worse." He gestured toward the cove which lay slate gray down the sloping sand bank to the east. "Look how high it is now!"

"What's being done about it?" Olive asked.

"Nothing much can be done," Ferranti said. "Can't get the boats out of the cove. Too dangerous. Ocean water pours in through the slot at the east end of the breakwater and whirls around in the middle of the cove. There—you can see how it is, out in the center. See where all that white water is?"

"What about the rest of the people?" Laurie asked.

"We've tried to get them to leave their houses, but we can't make them understand!" Ferranti explained. "My God! They just sit there and watch that water get closer and closer." Two of the older Deledda boys carried boxes of food into the schoolhouse and ran back toward the Shell Box. A small child, too little to run with his burden, stumbled and fell as one of the boards in the walk slipped beneath his foot.

"Joey!" Olive ran to pick him up. "Oh, Joey." She hugged him to her and brushed sand from his pinched face. "Where are Mama and Papa?"

"Helping Mr. Ferranti." He added with a note of pride in his thin, high voice, "I'm helping, too."

"Yes, dear, I see you are," Olive said. "You're a big, brave boy. How'd you like to stay with us and keep an eye on things here?" She took a handkerchief from her pocket and wiped his red nose. The child looked to Guido Ferranti, who nodded and patted him on his bare head.

"You stay here, Joe," the man ordered. "I'll go tell Papa and Mama where you are. You watch my things here, eh?" Guido's face was haggard with worry, but he smiled at the boy.

"Is there no organized evacuation plan?" Olive was now alarmed; she remembered what Ed Sickles had said about the possibilities should the wind not change direction.

"I tried to warn everybody—so did Ed Sickles yesterday. Sent the kids out, hammering on doors, telling everybody. But who listens? Always it's somebody else it happens to!" Ferranti said with exasperation. "Only I've been talking to old Buell Spencer, the lighthouse keeper down at Calabasas Point, and he says this whole area's bound to go." He edged away, anxious to return to the Shell Box and get on with salvaging as much as possible from his restaurant.

"What about the children?" Olive asked.

"I tried—God knows I tried!" he replied. "Maybe you'll have better luck. They know you. I'd best get back to Teresa..."

"Certainly, Mr. Ferranti." Olive understood his impatience.

"You'd better get on back home, ladies. This is no place for you right now," he called back over his shoulder.

Olive turned to the child, who stood as close as he could to her skirts, his hand still nestled in hers. She knelt beside him, wiped his nose again and gave him the handkerchief. "Joey, will you go with me and try to get your little friends to come here and stay with us for a while?"

"Yes, Miss Pickens. I guess I know 'bout every kid in Sand Town." Joey Deledda took Olive by the hand and led her down the battered wooden walk.

"Laurie, you stay here and take care of the children as we send them in. Something has to be done. Ed Sickles says..." Olive stopped as she looked at Joey's upturned face. "Never mind, I'll tell you when we get back."

Within minutes several small children, bundled up against the cold and wind, ran toward the schoolhouse and bashfully followed Laurie into the classroom. Piled high in one corner were supplies from the Shell Box Cafe.

"How would you like to draw some pictures for me on the blackboard?" Laurie had no idea how to amuse them and wished Olive had made some suggestions before she left. She found pieces of chalk in the trough that ran around the room under the blackboards. "I'll bet you can draw boats and fish and horses. . ."

Another child rushed in the front door and stood timidly in the hall. "Come in, we're in here." Laurie led the girl into the classroom and pulled a chair up to the blackboard. "There, that makes you just as tall as the others, doesn't it?" she said as she lifted the small girl to stand on the chair. "Now you can draw me some fine pictures, too."

The Purdy children, the Deledda girls, the Ferrantis, the McBrides, the tiny, dark-eyed Chew boy—one by one, by twos and threes, the children came, some carrying babies in their arms and leading toddlers by the hand. Olive's arguments had been more persuasive than Guido's, possibly because the children loved her. The seats filled, then the seats held two, then the aisles filled,

261

and still they came, round-eyed with fright, too afraid to either question what was occurring or to fight among themselves. In their childish wisdom they sensed a danger which grew moment by moment. So subdued were they that the sound of wind and water could clearly be heard inside the classroom, even with doors and windows firmly shut.

Olive burst into the outer hall and ushered Joey into the room to join the other children. She frowned as the child went into a spasm of coughing. "Joey, you are not to go back to the Shell Box! If your Papa or Mama come for you, all right; otherwise, you're to stay here." She felt of his forehead and cheeks which had become flushed. He sat on a box in the corner, his solemn eyes large and unusually bright.

Guido Ferranti returned, pulling an improvised sledge made of crate tops loaded with boxes piled high. He rested in the cloakroom, panting from his exertion.

"Why aren't these people leaving their houses? Don't they know what's coming?" Olive was shocked and exasperated at the risk they insisted upon taking.

"Just what is going to happen?" Laurie, already alarmed, was now as frightened as the children who packed the small schoolhouse. "You've never told me yet! What is it?" She steered Olive to one side of the door so their conversation could not be heard inside. Guido joined them, his chest heaving to catch his breath.

"Ed Sickles says one of the dangers of this stretch of coast is that a huge storm surge can build up on the ocean when the wind stays in the northwest for a long time. Even the Indians were aware of the phenomenon. It takes several straight days of blow, but if the storm system that feeds the wind becomes static and doesn't veer from the northwest, the tides become very high. It has something to do, too, with the alignment of the earth, sun, and moon. During the full moon, which is tonight, a spring tide builds up. And with the wind coming from the northwest like it has been, by surface friction it builds up and pushes the waves this way, toward land." She halted, unable to explain more clearly and turned to Ferranti.

"When it all happens together," he said, "...as it's doing now, something like a tidal bore can hit the coast along here, sweep into the cove, and take everything in its path." He smiled wryly. "The Indians were smarter than we were: they didn't build anything here! Old Grandma Rodriguez says they only fished in the cove and cooked on the shore. They lived up on the hills, out of reach of the tides." Guido slumped against the door, exhausted.

"A tidal bore?" Laurie had only heard of the term, but the name alone held terror in its sound.

"That's right! Buell Spencer calls it a storm surge. But call it what you like, that's exactly what's happening." Guido gasped between great breaths.

"Ed says it can build up into one huge wave, roll up over the beach and into the trees, sweep everything away—boats, houses, everything!" Olive continued. "He tried to tell people over in Forest Shores about it, too, because if it comes, the wave will damage the breakwater and the shorefront homes there. But nobody would listen! And of course, there's no way to guarantee it will happen at all—or if it does, exactly when it would hit. No one wants to believe it will happen."

"Buell Spencer rode over early this morning from the lighthouse and told me to start getting out of my place right away," Ferranti said. "He's from Maine, you know, and he can read the sea just like most of us read a book. He says the water's building and likely to hit next high tide. He's safe up on the rock where the lighthouse is. They put it up high like that on purpose. He can't speak anything but English, so he couldn't warn many families down here. I went around and tried, God knows I did, but they don't understand." He shook his head. "I couldn't make them understand."

"Do you have a telephone in the cafe, Mr. Ferranti?'' Laurie asked.

"Yes, but the lines may be down by now. Every time we have a blow like this, they go out," he answered.

"Olive, I know he would never listen to me, but maybe if you called Archibald Creighton, he would send down his construction wagons and get these people and their belongings out of here. They could at least save their furniture and pots and pans," she said hopefully. "It's worth trying, isn't it?"

"But Arch has no reason to love me, either! Not after last night!" Olive had no doubts as to how she stood with the Creightons.

Guido looked mystified, but did not ask what they meant. "If it works, it's the only way to get these folks out of here. They just won't leave all they have in the world, not just on the chance the water might rise." For the first time, Ferranti also had hope.

"They did send their kiddies with me," Olive said. "I can take the children up into the hills if it looks like it will get this far. But what will become of the youngsters if they have no homes or no parents?" As Olive opened the door to leave for the Shell Box a vicious burst of wind whipped through the frail building, shaking the whole structure. "I'll see what I can do."

Down toward the foot of Ortiz Lane, Laurie could see the crash of water as it exploded against boulders that marked the water's edge. In a short time it would be lapping at the houses themselves. And still the wind did not veer.

Olive doubled over with the wind at her back, her headscarf flapping wildly in front of her face as she returned from telephoning. Laurie opened the door and closed it behind her quickly. Sand sifted through every crack and crevice.

"Will he send the wagons?" Laurie asked as Olive entered the schoolhouse. "What did he say?" Some of the children trooped after Laurie as she met Olive.

"I won't repeat exactly what he said, but in

essence, no, he will not." Disappointment clouded her face as she looked about at the children's faces.

Guido Ferranti came from the classroom where he had been stacking supplies against the wall. "He flatly refused?"

"He did! And he ridiculed me for even asking. When I told him it was not for me, but the people who live in Sand Town, he was utterly contemptuous. Why should he risk wagons, horses, or men? If these people want to live in such a place, then they have to assume the risks." Olive sat down on one of the desk tops and unbuttoned her coat. "I even tried to speak with his mother, thinking I might persuade her to do a humanitarian act, but she hung up in my ear."

Joey Deledda slipped off his crate in the corner and came to stand by Olive, his feverish face turned to her. Laurie caught the look of helpless trust in his eyes, her anger welling hot within her. "What do we do now?" she asked.

"I just don't know." Olive sagged in defeat.

Laurie stood at the window, looking down Ortiz Lane. In only those few minutes the water had advanced. Three mongrel dogs who had been staying in the lee of one of the shanty-houses abandoned their position, slunk up the lane, crossed the road, heads down, backs humped to the wind.

"Mr. Ferranti, do you have a good, fast horse? I'm not an expert rider, so the horse has to be a good one—bridlewise, I think you call it." Laurie turned from the sand-and-spray-spattered window, resolution grim upon her face. "If you don't, I'll have to go back to Bert Hutchins' stables and get one."

"I have a nice, gentle, lady-broke gelding. He's as much for harness as riding, but he's good if you don't want to do anything fancy with him." He understood what she intended to do, and was already opening the door. "You wait here and I'll have one of the Deledda boys fetch him. Can you ride all right in this wind with those skirts and petticoats? I can lend you a pair of my trousers."

"Fine! Yes, it would be easier with trousers."
Laurie looked down at her full, heavy skirts. "Tell me,
if I take that trail by the bridge, the one that leads due
south from the road, will it take me directly to the
Creighton place? I think I've heard Roy say it goes right
through the trees to their construction yards and on up
to the house. Is that right?"

"Yes, ma'am." Guido grinned. He was liking her
plan better and better. "There's a latched gate, about
half a mile south, but you can unhitch it from the saddle. You won't have to get off to do it. It's just to keep
the cattle in that north pasture from wandering off.
From where the fence starts, it's not too far to the yard
and barns."

"Will this tide hit Mariposa Beach, too?" Laurie
asked.

"Yes, but not with the same force as here.
Calabasas Point breaks most of the force. But it will run
'way inland, up the river there, especially since the
river's already pretty high." Guido saw what she meant.
"I'll see if I can get some of the older boys up to Bert's
and have them ride out to the colony. Buell Spencer has
told them already, but it won't do any harm to let them
know what's happening here so they can be prepared."
He was already pounding down the board walk, his
head down, into the blow.

Olive shut the door, having to lean against it to
make it latch fast. She put her arms around Joey and a
tall, thin boy of about eleven. She did not feel confident, but from her face the children did not know.
"What are you going to do?" she asked Laurie.

"I'm going to ride up to the Creighton place and
see Chace!"

Laurie's borrowed trousers were clammy with
horse sweat as the cobby gelding scrambled up the trail
leading from the forest edge to the clearing that crowned a low foothill. The sky by now was black and

ominous. The wind had picked up, moaning through the trees and rocks with a high, hysterical wail that rose and fell with fluctuations of velocity. Twice along the way the girl slid from the shallow saddle and almost fell, grasping desperately at the horn and hugging the beast's lathered belly with her feet in the stirrups.

As the little horse strained into an easy gallop the last few hundred yards, old Eusebio Villareal came running from the greenhouse south of the stables. Since it was Sunday, the other hired men were spending the day in their small cottages hidden in the stand of pine directly north of the main house.

Almost before the horse had stopped, Laurie had swung down from the saddle, her knees buckling with fatigue. She grabbed the cantle and held on until strength returned. Eusebio, his brown face pulled into wrinkles, threw down his watering can and ran to her side.

"Where's Chace?" Laurie spoke with great effort. "I've got to see him! Something terrible is happening down at Sand Town! He's got to help us!" Her own voice as she listened to it had the same hysterical overtone as the increasing wind. She tried to walk toward the house, but found her legs would not move more than a few steps.

"Here—you stay here." The old man eased her to the stump of a tree which had been leveled and whitewashed to serve as a table upon which rested clay pots of frost-nipped geraniums. "You be all right for a few minutes? I'll go get Mr. Chace, but you wait right here." Old Villareal held her arm and watched the color return to her face before he shuffled away toward the main house, his feet raising clouds of dust that sped southeast with the wind.

The girl looked into the barn behind her. The high-wheeled station wagon and phaetons had been polished, their axles greased and leather freshly enameled. Back of them, barely discernible in the dark interior, were other carriages, testimonials to the wealth of the family.

Ranged in box stalls on the opposite side were horses brought in from open pasture before the storm. Even as Laurie looked, the huge gray mare raised her head and nickered nervously. One of the stable dogs came around the corner of the barn, spied the girl and ran to her, its plumed tail wagging, ears flapping in the driving wind. He snuggled against her knees and made whimpering noises of welcome as she scratched his pate.

"Poor puppy, do you know something's coming, too?" She held his chin in her hand and caressed his long, shaggy fur. As he whined and danced his joy, Laurie heard a door slam from the direction of the house, followed by the pounding of running feet. Eusebio hobbled down the steps behind Chace, with Catalina trailing them both.

Chace Creighton stood for a moment looking at Laurie, then caught her up in his arms, his lips finding hers, his arms holding her body to him until he could feel the beating of her heart. Within his embrace Laurie forgot the long, painful days of silence, the threats of his brother, the hatred of his mother, and knew only that this was her man, warm, tender, loving. Instinctively she knew he had never ceased loving her. His mouth upon hers, his hands pressing her tightly, the look in his deep amber eyes told her it was so.

He guided her into the shelter of the barn and held her, his face buried in the fragrance of her hair which had come undone during the hectic ride and hung loose below her scarlet beret. She pulled away only far enough to look into his face. He started to say something, but she placed a finger on his lips.

"Chace, there's no time to talk about us!" Laurie began. "You've got to send your wagons down to Sand Town! The people there won't leave their homes. Everything they possess in the world is in them. They can't move their belongings and they won't leave them! The water's rising fast, but Guido can't get them to abandon their houses. The children are with Olive at the old schoolhouse..." The words came tumbling out with no order, but he at once grasped their meaning.

"What is it? The tide?"

"Yes! Ed Sickles and Buell Spencer tried to warn them, but they can't make them get out if they don't want to. All the fishermen know what's coming—they understand the sea—and so does Guido Ferranti. But the others... Chace, you're our only hope!" He loved her all the more for including herself in their plight.

Laurie did not tell him that Archibald had already refused assistance or that his mother had scorned Olive's plea. It was apparent he had known nothing of the emergency until now. They could speak of all that later. It was not important—only getting the wagons to Shell Road was important now.

"Eusebio, get all the men together. Send someone over to town and round up those who live there. Have them all meet me at the yard. Tell them not to bring any volunteers— there won't be room on the wagons. I'll start harnessing the teams. And if Arch or Mother try to stop you, tell 'em to come see me." To Laurie he said, "I'll have Eusebio drive you home later."

"No! I'm going back to help Olive with the children!"

He was a man used to giving orders and taking action. Eusebio headed for the workers' houses. Catalina watched from the kitchen garden, her apron wrapped about her arms for warmth. "When's high tide expected?" Chace asked.

"Less than three hours from now," Laurie answered with a shudder.

"We can make it! We'll have to go on up into the Calabasas Hills there, but they're high enough. What about Mariposa Beach?" He had also thought of the isolated colony.

"Guido Ferranti sent some boys there, but Buell Spencer says it won't be nearly as bad there as at Sand Town. He says the water will just run up river and fan out over the salt marshes, but La Gaviota Creek is running full and beginning to flood already. When the water rolls into the cove..." She did not finish. The thought chilled her.

"Laurie, you can't ride that horse back down to the beach. He's too spent. Let Eusebio walk him out, cool him off, and put him in a stall for now. I think you should go home. You look as bushed as that horse." He hurried through the length of the barn and opened the door at the far end which looked out onto crowded storage yards. Two long, low structures spread west down the slope; one was a barn, and the other a warehouse for concrete, plaster, and building materials.

"I won't leave those children and Olive alone! I've got to go back and do whatever I can!" Her thighs and back ached from her jolting ride, but she felt stronger, more invincible than ever before in her life. Chace still loved her, and that gave her strength. He hugged her and looked back to the house.

"I wish I could say go up there and keep out of this, but we both know that's impossible. You just go tell Eusebio what to do with Guido's horse." He called to Catalina, "You'll let her stay with you until I get back, won't you?"

"Of course, Mr. Chace." Catalina smiled at them.

"No! I'm going with you! Or give me another horse and I'll go back by myself!" Her eyes were defiant. She had seen the helplessness of the children and the water lapping at the foot of Ortiz Lane.

"I won't try to stop you." He buttoned his short coat and headed for the wagon barn. "But only on condition you go with me." It was a command, not a request.

"Fine! I'll come right back after I've seen Eusebio!" Laurie ran back through the barn, halting for a moment before the stall of the great gray mare. Roy Wimbish had told her of the beautiful thoroughbred, the one Chace had forbidden his brothers to ride. She wondered if Chace knew Archibald had used it last night. The mare snorted and stamped the strawed floor with impatience, as if she sensed excitement and wanted to be part of it. Laurie reached over the stall and patted the horse's white blaze.

"Linette...what a pretty name. Good girl, Linette." The mare arched her long neck and nuzzled the girl's shoulder. "How hateful of that man to use spurs on you!" she whispered. The stable dog pranced on his hind legs for attention and yelped happily as Laurie ran to find Eusebio.

Unnoticed by the girl, a curtain dropped back into place at a second floor bedroom window of the house. Indistinct movements of a hand quickly rearranged the lace into precise, straight alignment.

Chapter 13

Laurie clung to the wagon seat as she looked down into the maelstrom of La Gaviota Creek. Water was now only a few yards below the roadbed. Great chunks of earth and rock were scoured from the banks on either side. Boulders collapsed into the stream with a roar, then battered their way along the canyon bottom.

"Think she'll hold up?" One of the teamsters motioned, indicating the bridge, as he yelled to Chace over the howl of wind.

"For a while at least. It'll last, unless the run-off gets worse." The wagons were driving two abreast. Huge draft animals lunged into stinging spray, muzzles protected by burlap hastily attached to face straps, ears flattened back to their skulls.

The men had agreed on their pattern of deployment before leaving the yard. Chace wanted no confusion, for there would be only minutes to spare. Should some of the wagons become mired in sand—but he couldn't worry about that beyond equipping each wagon with narrow wooden planks and gunny sacks to use beneath the wheels in case of necessity.

Overhead, clouds had lowered. Wind-whipped spray fogged the outline of anything beyond a few hundred yards. By the time the wagons rounded the turn at Bert Hutchins' livery stables, the danger was apparent at a glance.

Great surges of black water swelled in a semi-circle, curling into La Gaviota Cove and well up onto the beach. Already the houses located at the lanes' lower ends were inundated, with water sucking away flimsy foundations and outbuildings.

Without further instructions, the Creighton crews took up their positions. Within minutes the wagons were filled with the meager possessions of the residents. Family pets were tossed atop the lumbering vehicles where they clung in terror or jumped off and sped wildly into brush opposite Shell Road.

Men hammered at doors with their fists or kicked them in to search for anyone reluctant to leave. It was no time for ceremony. Frightened Chinese women, cowering from the burly drivers, were lifted and carried screaming to the wagons, smiles and soothing foreign words doing nothing to allay their fear.

Chace halted his wagon and helped Laurie down from the high seat and into the old schoolhouse. By now the children were too quiet. Some huddled together sniffling, their eyes red. Others sat at desks, their hands folded as if Olive were about to instruct them on deportment.

"Take the children up into the trees, clear to the top of that ridge. Keep together and don't get separated." Chace turned to the youngsters. "You older ones, look after the little fellows. Don't anybody wander off. Your folks will be all right, but we don't want them to have to worry about you. Does everyone understand?" He looked too big in the small classroom, as if he had been constructed to a different scale. The children murmured assent, some knuckling wet eyes to look at him. He jammed his hat down over his forehead and slipped the knot of its leather tie tight under his chin.

For no reason other than their long faces, when he reached the door he said, "How about singing a song for me? I'll bet I could hear it 'way down on the beach if you sing loud enough."

"Thank you, darling. I'll stay with the children and Olive." Laurie felt his hand about hers, but her eyes were too full to see him clearly as he ran back down the board walk to Shell Road. "Be careful!"

273

As Chace reached the street he heard the shrill, high voices begin, "Once there was a rabbit, A very tiny rabbit…"

He snapped the lead horses and flicked the wheelers, urging them on toward the Shell Box Cafe and the breakwater.

Olive shut the pendant watch which hung about her neck on a gold chain. She signaled five older children to bundle up the smaller ones, then began to lead them up the slope of the Calabasas Hills behind Sand Town. On the eastern seaboard the rise of land would have been termed mountains, but with the towering Santa Margaritas in the background, these could only be called hills.

Laurie trailed the children, urging the slow and laggard to hurry, coaxing stronger boys to carry toddlers and larger girls the babies. The path was smooth and sandy until it left the beach scrub, then became a twisted, steep trail hardened by countless years of use. Here and there it detoured about huge outcroppings of granite worn to rounded contours by the winds and rains of centuries.

"Go straight on up," Chace had instructed Olive and Laurie. "Don't linger on the trail. Try to get on the other side of the ridge as soon as you can. They can't see Sand Town from there - only Mariposa Beach." Chace had been concerned at what they might see. "Explain to them what's going to happen. That takes some of the scare out of it."

Laurie marveled at the way Olive could maintain discipline among the youngsters as they toiled up the hillside. Some were still weeping, but as the trail grew steeper, they saved their breath to climb.

"Olive!" Laurie called as they reached a narrow switchback. She put down the three-year-old she was carrying and ran up the path to Olive's side. "Where's Joey?" She had suddenly missed the small boy and could not see his bare head with the group of children ahead on the trail.

"Have any of you children seen Joey Deledda as we came up?" Olive asked.

No one had. Laurie looked back down toward the schoolhouse but could see no motion in the brush that indicated the child was moving through it toward them.

"Carlo! Carlo Deledda!" Olive summoned the boy's brother from the vanguard of the group. "Joey isn't with us. Did you see him go back to the beach?"

"No, Miss Pickens," the boy replied. "I didn't see him. But he might."

"Why on earth would he?" Olive could not imagine a reason for the child to slip away and endanger himself.

As if it should explain Joey's actions, Carlo said, "Papa."

"Papa? I don't understand," Olive said.

"He always has to be with Papa." Carlo, next to Joey in age, flinched under the eyes of the other children. Joey was an embarrassment to him, always hanging around the men, never wanting to play games or join in escapades like the rest of them.

"He's Papa's pet," Carlo added. It wasn't said with any bitterness, but as a statement of fact and a concession to Joey's station in the Deledda household as the youngest son.

"I'll go back for him," Laurie said. "He must have slipped away and gone back to the Shell Box. That's where his parents are."

Olive could not argue the point or the wisdom of Laurie's decision, nor could she protest, because she had the remainder of the youngsters to look after herself.

"Do be careful, Laurie." Olive did not trust herself to say more, for below in the cove she could see the massive build-up of waves, each successive one washing higher ashore. Already wreckage was drifting about in the frothing edge that was devouring the village yard by yard.

"I'll get back just as fast as I can," Laurie reassured her. "I'll find the way up, don't worry."

Horses, carriages, and wagons from Bert Hutchins' stables were making their way up the hillsides along precarious trails ordinarily used only for logging and hunting. Light runabouts and surreys were loaded to the spilling point. Even the heavier, less maneuverable broughams and landaus had been put to use and sent up the more reliable road on the south slope of the range where the carriages' high centers of gravity would be less apt to result in their overturning.

Women walked behind, leading goats, sheep, calves, heifers; some struggled along with crates of goslings and chicks, having loosed the hens and geese to fend for themselves. Dogs patrolled in businesslike fashion, nipping at cows and nannies who wanted to stop and nibble grass, barking in circles around ewes and lambs to keep them headed for high ground.

The tops of the Calabasas Hills, densely covered with pine and strewn with a jumble of gray, barren rock, were slowly disappearing into lowering clouds. The steady soft mist gave way to light drizzle as the refugees climbed higher, adding physical misery to their burden of fear. Few turned their eyes back to the village below, but kept plodding upward, lungs bursting from unaccustomed exertion. There was little noise, considering the extent of the exodus. Over all was the incessant howl and shriek of wind and the thunder of the incoming tide.

Laurie made her way down the trail behind the schoolhouse, passing a few people, none of whom had seen the Deledda child. She was glad she was still wearing Guido's old trousers. With skirts on, it would have been impossible to run down the rough trail and through the chaparral. Below she could see Chace's wagon at the end of Shell Road. Figures of men and women shuttled back and forth to the restaurant and neighboring fish-packing sheds, loading furniture, utensils and food supplies into the heavy vehicle.

Already surf was beginning to spill over the tops of rocks which formed the breakwater base. Gulls that usually congregated in uncountable numbers near the rocks and gutting troughs behind the packing sheds were nowhere to be seen. No seals or sea lions, no playful otters or ground squirrels remained sprawled about the rocks. Not a living thing could be seen but the people around the wagons and the teams of drays.

"Chace! Chace!" Laurie shouted over the wind.

"Why aren't you with Olive and the kids?" Chace boosted Marcella Deledda and Teresa Ferranti into a springwagon and tossed in an unwieldy roll of bedding. Guido signaled the last of Bert Hutchins' runabouts to leave with the older Deledda boys who had been helping evacuate the cafe. Their eyes, round and frightened in their dark faces, followed the small buggy as it started up the nearest logging trail and was soon out of sight behind a stand of timber.

"Joey came back down!" Laurie had to yell to make herself heard. "No one going up saw him and he isn't with the other children! Did he come here?"

"We haven't seen him." Guido Ferranti looked scared as foam trickled onto the upper terrace of the cafe. That meant the water was well over the breakwater. "We thought he was with you and Miss Pickens."

"His brother Carlo says he wanted to be with his father all the time," Laurie said. "We thought he must have tried to get back to him here at the cafe."

"But he didn't get here." Guido considered for a moment. "He could have seen his father go over to their house a while back. Louie went over to get blankets and extra clothing. He figures we may be up on the hills for a night or two and might need all the warm things we can manage."

"Then Joey would have seen his father come back here, wouldn't he?"

"Maybe not," Ferranti replied. "Louie cut through behind the packing sheds. If Joey had been watching from up on the hill, he might not have seen Louie come back here. He'd think he was still at the house. And once down on the road, he has no way of knowing where his father went."

"Guido, take the wagon and start on up the hill," Chace said. "We can't wait any longer. The lead horses are the best of the lot—they know what's expected of them. Give 'em plenty of head when it gets steep, but keep the reins firm, just so you can feel their mouths. The wheel horses are greener, so keep them checked pretty close. Think you can handle it?"

"Let me go look for Joey..." Ferranti began.

"No! You've got your family to take care of! I know where the house is—I'll go." Chace lifted Laurie and put her in the high seat beside Ferranti.

Laurie was too frightened to do anything but watch. Water was washing through the door of the third house from the foot of the lane. Pieces of lumber from smashed privies and makeshift dry-docks were cast up onto the sand for a moment, only to be swallowed again.

Guido Ferranti, unused to driving four-in-hand, flicked the lead horses with a long whip, then sorted out the reins as the animals leaned into their harness and began laboring up the road into the trees. Accustomed to inexpert drivers, the horses assumed their usual gait, heads down and bobbing with their effort.

"Let me go with you!" Laurie pleaded.

"No! I can move faster alone!" Chace was firm. "They need you up there with the kids!" There was no time to argue. He darted off toward Ortiz Lane, cutting between packing sheds on Fish Row. After a few yards, he was ankle deep in white froth that splashed around corners and over rocks as he ran toward the Deledda home.

"Chace! Chace!" Laurie was horrified as she watched. A surge, swift and silent, rose from the very edge of the beach, rolled higher and higher, tumbling small boats torn from their moorings, lumber, brush, rock and sand in a deadly mélange that crashed up Ortiz Lane.

She started to leap from the wagon, but Ferranti caught at her loose cape and pulled her back onto the seat.

"It's no good! You can't help them! You'd only make it harder for him—he'd have to rescue two!" Guido's face was bloodless as he watched helplessly, the reins in his hands forgotten. He crossed himself and closed his eyes for a moment as if he wanted to blot the scene from his sight.

"Oh dear God, keep him safe!" Laurie moaned as the water crashed high against the houses, obscuring her view of Chace with foam and wild spray.

Guido firmed up the reins and urged the horses faster up the slope. Buell Spencer had warned him the storm surge would probably not follow an exact time schedule, but could be ahead of the usual twelve-hour, twenty-five-minute tidal rotation. They must get to high ground as soon as possible, even if it meant leaving Chace and Joey to the mercy of the water. He knew he could not have stopped the young man any more than he could have halted the incoming tide.

The wagon lurched up the logging road and passed behind an almost vertical upthrust of granite which blocked the village from view. Ahead of them they could see several surreys and another large construction wagon heavily laden with women and household effects. Above the noise of wind and pounding surf came shouts of drivers, dogs barking, and an occasional loud peal of laughter as one of the teamsters flung a bawdy joke into the teeth of danger. Ferranti would have liked to put a comforting arm about the girl, but responsibility for horses and wagon prevented more than a reassuring look and words of encouragement, which even he did not feel.

"He'll be all right," Guido said. "He'll probably beat us getting up the hill."

Laurie could not respond. The picture of Chace enveloped in the sudden surge remained burned into her consciousness. To lose him now would be losing her whole world. If he perished, there was nothing left for her.

They drove in silence as the trail steepened and the horses strained with their load. Guido remembered Chace's instructions and gave the lead horses their heads and kept the reins a trifle firmer on the wheelers. He did not have the 'good hands' of an experienced hostler or teamster, but he could feel the tug and ease as they trudged upward. As they rounded a bend he could see ahead of them the gaily painted red and yellow springwagon with Marcella and Teresa, their faces grim and set. Louie was walking beside the wagon, leading Purdy's cow by its halter. Beyond them were several light carriages, and farther on the small runabout with the Deledda boys. Guido could breathe easier now. His own children were safe with the school teacher, and he had managed to save some of his property. They would survive.

Suddenly they emerged into a wide, barren, rocky space hemmed in by buckthorn and poisonous rattle-weed which clung to crevices and wedged into debris-filled clefts. Above and to the west of the trail were tracts denuded of timber and given over to thick grass and low shrubs. Vehicles of every description had crowded into available spots between stumps, with drivers frantically trying to bring order from a milling chaos of wheels and animals. Women sat immobile, faces taut with dread and fear.

Below spread a vast panorama that encompassed the village of Sand Town, La Gaviota Cove and Creek, Beach Park to the east and open sea to the north. Forest Shores, farther east, was invisible in wind-driven mist.

Ferranti pulled up beside the springwagon. "Don't tell Louie and Marcella about Joey yet. We don't know anything, so no use in alarming them, is there?" He touched Laurie's hand. "I won't tell you not to worry. That would be foolish. Chace is a strong man. He'll make it on foot. You'll see." He patted her hand and jumped off the wagon.

Teresa Ferranti stood up in the wagon bed and looked toward Sand Town. A movement at sea to the northwest had caught her eye. She pointed, unable to speak.

Mrs. Purdy, her ruddy Irish face paled by fear, crawled erect on the seat of a neighboring surrey to look in the direction Teresa was pointing. Her hands went to her face, smothering a shriek of terror.

"Look! Oh my God! Look!" Those too far toward the summit to see ran to the edge of the clearing, their eyes focused on the destruction below in fascinated horror.

At a distance from shore a towering black wall of water was building, racing so fast that even as they turned to look it engulfed breakwater and rocks. The Shell Box was swept away as if made of paper. Inexorable, it sped on, its eastern current curling as it met resistance in the sloping beach, building ever higher, the crest far above roofs of the village, smashing, bursting, crushing, sweeping away on its mighty crest everything in its path. High-prowed fishing craft were lifted like children's toys, their gaudy painted eyes looked down into the deep for a moment before they tumbled from that awful watery height into an abyss of crushing fury. Shanties exploded, roofs born aloft for a brief interval, then sucked under by the relentless water.

The mighty bore drove on, tearing at stands of giant pines, threshing them about, racing through the cove, up into the wide, sloping creek canyon. Its thundering violence shook the granite mountain top. On and on it swept, carrying all before it.

As they stood watching, stupified by the horrible display of unleashed power, many turned away, white with disbelief and shock. Others, too fascinated by the sight, gazed almost unseeing, unable to comprehend the awesome devastation.

Then, as if by some perversity of intent, the water swirled and returned to obliterate everything that remained of the village. Where rutted lanes had been, where modest houses and shanties had sheltered the people of Sand Town, only violent, turbulent sea remained. The cove was a heaving mass of wreckage. Nothing alive could have survived the dreadful onslaught.

As they stood watching, a curtain of rain began to fall. Too stunned to do much more than look in numbed despair at one another, the residents of Sand Town clustered in hushed groups about the wagons and carriages.

"Mr. Ferranti, we've got to rig up some kind of shelter for the ladies and children. By the looks of it, there ain't going to be no going back for a long time." Bert Hutchins' hostler gestured with his thumb toward the cove. "Me and some of the Creighton men brung along our tools. If you can round up some men to join us, we can put something together before dark."

Guido was quick to recover his wits. "You're right. It's already getting cold." The wind was slackening a trifle, but the temperature was dropping and rain becoming heavier. He turned to the springwagon and helped the women down.

"Teresa, you see to Miss Mathews." He whispered in her ear that Chace had gone after Joey, his look conveying the need for secrecy to spare both the Deleddas and Laurie. "I'm going to help the men make some sort of camp for us." He kissed her tenderly and held her terrified face in his hands. "We'll be fine. We have enough to start again."

As he followed the hostler, he could only wonder what would become of his neighbors.

Olive Pickens warmed her hands by the open fire. The melancholy chill of the mountain pervaded their improvised camp. Talk was subdued. Even the usually boisterous children clung near their parents and spoke in monotones or whimpered desolately under the shelter of the wagon beds. The Creighton crews went from one slope to the other, reuniting families, making a list of the missing, carrying word from one camp to the other.

Bert Hutchins rode up on one of his huge Tennessee Walkers, leading the other behind. "Where's Guido? I got us some things out of the schoolhouse. Little bit damp, but saltwater ain't as bad as going hungry, I guess." He set his kerosene lantern on a stump by the fire, turned the wick down and extinguished the light. "Better save what oil's left. Can't never tell when we'll get more."

"Is the bridge out?" Olive knew Mrs. Hinshaw would be sick with worry by now.

"Can't tell, ma'am. Water ain't down yet. I seen my barn roof out in the cove so I reckon the bridge went, too." He swung down out of the saddle and removed a bag of flour strapped to the Walker's rump. "I ain't so bad off, though. Far as I can tell, I didn't lose no animals. Course, getting back my mules is going to take some doing. Nothing in this world's as plain cussed as a runaway mule."

Commonplace talk of runaway mules substituted for the grim reality of the moment. He turned to Olive and whispered quietly, "Few folks can't be accounted for yet. Kevin Purdy ain't been seen. Neither has that little Chinese lady, Henry Chew's wife. You know the one—he's got a little store down on Fish Row? I mean, he *had* a store there." Olive nodded and he went on. "Chace Creighton and that littlest Deledda kid..."

"Chace?" Olive would have wept, but the children were watching her face for signs of alarm. She dared not show fear or despair as long as their trusting eyes were on her.

"You'd best tell Miss Mathews." He wiped rain from his face with the back of his hand. "I just don't have the heart to do it, and that's a fact."

"You can't be sure, though, can you?" Olive pleaded. "I mean there's no way to know for certain yet, is there?"

"Well, put that way, no. But if anybody survived down there when the water hit, it'd be a plain miracle." Hutchins unpacked pails of leaf lard and a drum of salt.

"Let's not panic anyone yet." Olive was thinking of Laurie as well as Bridget Purdy and Henry Chew.

"You may be right, ma'am. I'll leave that up to you." Bert Hutchins tipped his hat and attended to the pack on the second horse.

Guido Ferranti and Teresa, arms white with dough, came from the shelter of the cook tent and took the stores in out of the rain. The smell of baking biscuits wafted through the trees as children lined up bashfully to take the warm bread as it came off the griddles.

"Is there enough left so we can feed these people a day or two?" Guido caught Hutchins by the sleeve as he was unloading the last of the staples into a dry patch beneath one of the large wagons. The Deledda boys were elbow deep in dough, kneading in lard and salt, patting flat cakes to bake over the fire on the salvaged kitchen equipment.

"Reckon so, but won't last long with this many folks. Come daylight, you'd best send out a couple of good shots with rifles. A few deer can make a sight of stew. Get the old Rodriguez grandma to look for wild things—she'll know what's fit to eat and safe to put in the pot. Don't you let nobody else go telling you it's good unless she says so. She knows every blessed plant and creature in these parts."

"But she's not here," Teresa said.

"I know. She's over the ridge, but I'll see she gets here in the morning, first light. She's too old and crippled up to make it tonight, but come morning, she'll be here. She's that kind." To Bert Hutchins the elderly half-Mutsun, half-Mexican woman was the one authority to be trusted in such an emergency. That she had been kind to Rosa Cantu after Rosa's own family disowned her had forever endeared Mrs. Rodriguez to the wily horse trader; it was her ancient knowledge of the land and its provender that they needed if they were to survive on their isolated Calabasas hilltops.

Laurie crawled out from under the wagon, pushing a basin of steaming water before her. "It's a nasty cut, but I think the bleeding's stopped." She stood up and poured the bloody water to one side of the wagon. "Mrs. Purdy got him to drink some whiskey and he's so groggy now he doesn't feel too much pain."

"Where are the boy's parents?" Olive asked.

"One of the drivers says they're on the next rise, but they can't get over here until daylight," Laurie replied.

"Will he be all right?" Olive spread her wet skirts in front of the blaze to dry them a bit.

"Yes, it's a clean wound. Mrs. Purdy says there'll be no danger of lockjaw or gangrene. Not like the man." She shook her head and glanced under the canvas flap that protected the injured man and boy.

"The one with the broken arm?" Olive poured a tin cupful of coffee from the pot which rested in smoldering coals at one side of the fire. The rock ledge which jutted protectively over them was blackened with smoke and soot from centuries of Indian campfires. The young teacher wrapped the cup's hot handle with a scrap of torn sheeting and handed it to Laurie.

"He just lies there, looking up, not saying a word," Laurie said. "Mrs. Purdy says he'll get gangrene unless we can get him to town or get a doctor over here." They sat under the protection of one of the wagon sides which had been swung down to make a rude lean-to closed with a blanket at one end to retain the heat of the fire. Serafina Ferranti snuggled into Olive's lap, her solemn, dark eyes heavy with sleep, but too frightened to yield to it. The child's thumb went to her mouth as Olive rocked her in her arms.

Laurie warmed her fingers about the cup. "Did Bert Hutchins know anything about..." She found she could not finish the question.

"No," Olive said, hoping Laurie would not look at her and discover she was lying. "It's too dark to see anything. There are probably a dozen or so sitting around in the brush down there, waiting for daylight so they can see where they are."

"But they could see the lights up here," Laurie persisted.

"They wouldn't want to stumble around in the dark and risk getting hurt." Olive removed Serafina's thumb from her mouth. The child looked at it a moment, then closed her eyes and slept. "It's much too dangerous to try to climb up here at night."

Laurie nodded, trying to accept the idea, afraid not to. She sipped the hot coffee which was full of unsettled grounds. "The bridge?"

"They don't know yet," Olive said.

"Mrs. Hinshaw must be wondering what happened to us."

"I doubt if anybody in town knows what's happened over here. Ed Sickles wanted the paper to print a warning about the possibility of the storm surge or tidal bore, call it what you will."

"Why didn't they?" Laurie asked.

"It seems Arch Creighton disapproved!" Olive answered. "Arch said it would unduly alarm the town and might be picked up by other papers elsewhere and scare off investors. Can you imagine?" Olive was indignant that the man would block the warning, and then refuse to aid Sand Town when disaster struck.

"You know, if even one life is lost," Laurie said, "it will be his fault and he ought to be tried for manslaughter if not worse!"

Behind them a man's voice rumbled, "Arch Creighton's going to answer for a hell of a lot before this is all over!" The muscular driver knelt at the rear opening and crawled into the warmth of the shelter to have a look at the injured man. He was wet through and shivering. In the firelight Laurie could see him eyeing the steaming coffee.

"Here, you need this more than I." She handed him the tin cup. "Let me see if I can find you something dry to put on. We can dry your things by the fire."

He drank the coffee and crouched near the opening which faced the fire. "Many thanks." He took off his wet hat and wrung it out. "No use of me putting on dry clothes yet. I'm tending the horses down there." He pointed east down the logging road where they had left the animals so their excrement would pose no problem to the camp. "Much obliged all the same."

Carlo Deledda handed the man biscuits hot from the griddle. "Mama says this is all they've got to eat. Papa's got soup making, but it ain't..." He looked at Olive and blushed. "It..isn't done yet."

"Tell your Mama I appreciate that." He handed the tin cup back to Laurie as Carlo dashed back to the cook tent holding his coat over his head to keep off the cold rain.

"You're the girl tending my buddy, ain't you?" The driver sat down and chewed on the biscuits.

"The man with the broken arm?" Laurie turned to look at him.

"Yeah. How's he doing? He won't look at me. His eyes is open, but it's like he don't see me."

"Mrs. Purdy says he's in shock. It's a very bad compound fracture. She's keeping compresses on it so it won't fester, but she says he's got to be taken to where they can tend him properly and set the bone. She got him to drink a lot of whiskey and that dulled the pain, but that's about all we can do here for him." The girl looked at the dark stains on her cape and borrowed trousers. "Mrs. Purdy says he's in very bad shape and we'll have to get him to the hospital in Forest Shores as soon as we can."

The rugged driver squatted with his face to the heat, steam rising from his wet clothing. "I promise you ladies one thing: Arch Creighton's going to wish to hell he'd sent them wagons when you called him the first time."

"How did you know who it was that called him?" Olive was surprised that their attempt was known.

"I guess everybody on the hill knows who they've got to thank." His smile was slow and included them both, but behind the smile lurked a hint of the promise

287

he'd not lightly made. He took another look at his friend who lay motionless in his agony.

"And by damn," he said before rising to go back to the horses, "We all know who we're going to see gets his!"

Chapter 14

Bert Hutchins slouched in the saddle, his back bowed under the waterproof poncho that spread over his legs to cover the tops of his leather chaparejos. He rode south from the summit of the Calabasas Hills with Sally, his rangy Tennessee Walker, picking her way step by step along the treacherous, slippery trail. Toward morning the wind had veered south and rain settled into a steady soft drizzle that was far more depressing than a relentless downpour. Behind him the camp was stirring to life. Guido and Teresa began preparing breakfast for the refugees who clustered in groups along the logging trails which bisected the hills above Sand Town. Pine smoke curled through the tree tops and hung low over the camp like an ineffectual umbrella.

No one had as yet been able to get down to the bridge over La Gaviota Creek. How extensive the damage was, remained unknown. That his buildings were demolished, Hutchins already knew. That everything else in Sand Town had been swept away, smashed like so many toy match-box houses, had been apparent even last night. At first light groups of men would fan out and begin combing through wreckage cast up and abandoned by the water along the lower slopes of the hills. Successively diminishing surges had continued throughout the night. As the storm disintegrated, surface water became less agitated, until only long, monstrous swells broke over the ruined breakwater and curled into the cove.

That no vast loss of life had occurred was small consolation to those who were now bereft of home and—

shelter. Hutchins hoped enough of his stable equipment had survived for them to repair the creek bridge. A means of supplying the people of Sand Town with food was their immediate problem. Without the bridge, that would be impossible.

It was, of course, possible that the old logging bridge on the upper Creighton property had escaped intact. That was the closest connecting point to the mainland from the peninsula. There the steep canyon narrowed, and the bridge, high above the creek bed, may have remained unscathed.

The horse's breath drifted in white puffs as she clambered toward the beach. After the storm, which even now seemed to be breaking up, would come another hard frost. That at least would somewhat reduce the danger of pestilence.

Hutchins let Sally find her way parallel Shell Road, keeping to the brush and secondary trails. The sound of the water told him the flood tide was receding, although a steady, low undertone from where La Gaviota Creek entered the cove told him it was still too high for fording. Wet chaparral slapped against the horse's belly and his leather-clad legs. The pungent scent of wet sage and tarweed was sweet and good, but was mingled with a sour, salt odor of seaweed, out of place on the hillslope.

As the horse relaxed into her customary smooth walk along a flat deer trail directly above what once was Castillo Lane, her ears pricked up, her head turned east toward the beach.

"What you hear, girl?" Hutchins reined in slightly. "Whoa up now," he said aloud. He leaned forward in the saddle and looked in the direction the horse's head was turned. The eastern sky was brightening, with silver gaps in the overcast, but below toward the cove all was shadow and gray drizzle. The horse nickered softly, tossing her sleek head, her ears still pricked forward.

"You hear something, Sally girl?" The man strained to hear what the animal with its more sensitive ears was obviously hearing. All around him was the monotonous dripping of wet sage and lupine and a faint soughing of pines higher up on the hill. Suddenly above the sound of water came a cry that sent a shudder of joy through the old man.

"Come on, girl!" He guided the Walker down an adjacent path and coaxed her closer to Shell Road.

"I'm coming! Keep yelling so's I can find you!" He hoped the child would hear him above the sucking, lashing swirl of water.

"Keep hollering!" he shouted. From far above him he could hear men calling to each other as they began their descent to the cove in search of the missing. He urged the horse on, trusting her to find solid footing in the wet sand.

Halfway between where Castillo Lane and Stable Road had been, the spot now recognizable only by huge granite boulders which of all things remained unmoved, a peaked roof rose and fell at the edge of foaming surf. Strewn across what had been Shell Road were pieces of siding, bits of furniture, empty window frames, shrubs with torn roots washed clean and bare—pitiful remnants of modest dwellings which only hours before had lined the narrow, sandy streets.

Hutchins let Sally find her own way among the pieces of wreckage left on the slope by the receding tide. Fearing broken glass hidden in the sand, he dismounted and looped the reins on a shattered tree branch. His prized animals were too valuable to risk severed arteries. He patted the horse's shoulder and watched her ears.

"That way, Sally?" She shivered her muscles against the sand flies that had emerged from cover. The stench of the beach was strong in his nostrils as he walked through debris, following the direction of his horse's listening. Sound at such a time can become distorted, its echo and reverberation misleading to human ears.

"Where are you, Joey?" Hutchins yelled. He strained to catch the child's cry. From up on the hill came shouts of the men who had heard him calling the boy. Louie Deledda came running from up the trail.

A faint noise, so unlike a human voice that he

thought he was mistaken, issued from near the floating roof. Hutchins turned to look at the horse once more. Her ears pricked forward, to the place where the roof was lodged.

"I'm coming, Joey!" On the trail above he could see movement in the brush indicating he would soon be joined by the rest of the men. "Where are you, boy?"

Wading knee deep in water, he caught at the ornamental gable trim and hoisted himself atop the shingles. As a wave crashed into the wreckage the child screamed. Hutchins struggled to gain his balance on the steep incline. Holding to the ridge beam he inched his way toward the top. Another surge of water lifted the roof crazily and spun it sideways, the opposite side dipping low into the water while the gable swung high onto the sand. He grabbed the beam and waited for the roof to settle, then crawled up over to the other side.

"Hang on, son! I'll get you off!"

Clinging with both hands to one of the rafters exposed by a gaping hole was Joey Deledda. Beside him, his legs dangling in the black water, lay Chace, one arm still clasped about the boy, the other hanging through the hole as if he had tried to anchor himself.

"Over here! On this side!" Hutchins called to Deledda who had followed him. "Bring me a rope from my saddle!"

"Is he alive?" Louie Deledda had not heard his son's cries.

"Boy is," Hutchins answered. "Can't tell about Creighton. He ain't moving. We'll have to pull 'em up and over. Can't chance losing them down on this side. We'd never get 'em back again. No in that water!"

"I'll help." Deledda started over the beam. The roof groaned ominously and Hutchins could feel the rafters shift beneath him.

"Stay where you are!" Hutchins shouted. "It'll cave in any minute! Just heave me the rope and pull when I say to!" He knelt beside the boy and loosened Chace's arm from about him, bending back the fingers which gripped the child's clothing. He felt for a pulse

"Alive?" The men called from the beach.

"Yes, but by the looks of him, just barely. We idn't get here any too soon. This thing's going to break p. I can feel it giving." Another man hurled one end of he rope over the ridge beam and secured the other to a eavy log, then waded close enough to hear Hutchins' nstructions.

"When I yell, you pull the boy up, then throw the ope back to me and take Creighton up. It'll take 1ore'n one of you to pull him. And don't waste no ime!" The section of roof upon which they waited reaked and settled a few inches lower. Below them vater slapped and pulled at the broken rafters.

Bert tied the boy and signaled his retrieval. Slowly he men pulled him ashore, unfastened the rope, and hrew it back up. As they did so, the rooftree sagged and roke with a loud crack, buckling the entire roof. Hut-hins slipped halfway into the water, but managed to rope his way back to Chace. The rope dangled just out f reach.

"Give me another two yards of line!" Hutchins rdered.

"We'll have to unhook it from the stump!"

"Then do it!"

"Move, boys! Unloose it and you come hang onto here. Bert's got to have more rope. Hurry!" The man elayed his instructions. The rope slithered down to Iutchins once more. Quickly he secured it around Chace's shoulders and yelled, "Pull!"

As the men eased Creighton up and over the beam, Iutchins clambered beside him, making sure his Iothing didn't catch on the shingles. As the men took Chace and carried him to the beach, Hutchins jumped lear of the heaving roof. Behind him the rafters gave vay and splintered, demolishing the fragile float. The ieces broke apart and were sucked back into the cove y an ebbing wave. He was shaking as he waded ashore.

"Much obliged, fellas." He could smile, but his egs trembled under him.

"Take my coat for the boy." One of the drivers

took off his melton and handed it to Deledda. Louie had put his own coat about the child.

"Thank you, but no." Louie shivered in the cold morning wind, but he knew they must continue their search for the others who were still missing. "You'll need it yourself." He looked at each man, then at the wreckage in the cove. "Thank you," he breathed. He hugged the boy to him as a gathering wave rose high, hovered for one improbable moment, then toppled with a roar, smashing the remnants of the roof.

"I'll take Louie and Joe back up to camp and bring down something to make a litter for Creighton." Bert Hutchins looked at Chace lying inert at their feet.

"Why don't we just dead-man carry him on your horse? Tie him on?" One of the men asked.

"Look at his head," Hutchins said. "Bad bruise—might be concussion. If he hung head down all the way, it'd most likely kill him." Bert took the boy from Deledda and placed him astride the big bay's withers in front of the saddle. The horse sidestepped at the unaccustomed position of her rider. "Whoa! Easy girl. Grab her mane, Joey. Hang on tight. We'll have you back with your Ma in a minute." Wordlessly, Joey obeyed, his fists clutching the black mane, his eyes round with terror. Hutchins handed Louie Deledda up behind the saddle, then mounted and turned Sally back toward the trail.

"I'll get back as soon as I can. If Creighton comes to, don't let him move around or try to get up." The horse trader reached into the saddle bag and took out a small flat whiskey bottle which he tossed to one of the men. "Here. Give him some of that if he comes to. Might pull him out of the wind, beyond that tree over there." He motioned with his head toward an uprooted pine which spread across Shell Road and could provide some shelter.

The Deledda's son was safe, but what could Bert Hutchins say to Henry Chew and Mrs. Purdy? While they rode up the west slope he tried to think of how best to tell Bridget about the roof. Kevin Purdy had been proud of that gable ornament. It was the only part of their house that regularly received a bit of paint. Only last month he had loaned Kevin the tall barn ladder. Kelly green he had painted the fancy carved wood. Now bits of kelly green floated at the water's edge.

Bridget Purdy wrapped the hot blanket about Joey's small form and tucked it around his clammy feet. His eyes followed her movements for a moment, then returned to his mother's face. Marcella Deledda dipped a spoon into the steaming soup and tested it with her lips, then gave it to the boy. He swallowed with difficulty, his throat constricted and raw from exposure and shouting. The redness of his cheeks was unnaturally brilliant against his pale skin. He made a motion with his mouth as if to speak, but his mother shushed him and stroked his wet, touseled hair.

"We should get him to the hospital," Mrs. Purdy whispered to Bert Hutchins. "He's got a terrible fever." She took crackers from the wooden barrel by the cook tent and handed them to Mrs. Deledda, then returned to the livery man's side. "Isn't there any way we can get over the creek yet?"

"I wish I could tell you we could do it, but there just ain't no way. Lord knows they're trying hard enough, but there ain't nothing left of that bridge. Not even the stonework's standing. Washed clean away."

"Then he'll not last the day." She sat down heavily on the wagon tongue. Two of her own children stood near, too fearful to venture questions. Bridget Purdy looked hopefully at Hutchins. "There's no word of my husband? No sign?"

Bert wished he could avoid the straight, direct look in her eyes that said she already knew the truth. He knocked some sand from his chaps and boots while he tried to decide how to answer the woman.

"No, ma'am, Mrs. Purdy, there ain't no word yet." The woman's eyes never flinched. He slapped at imaginary mud traces on his trousers and continued, "You mustn't think the worst. Just like Joey and Chace here, your husband might be down there somewhere, stuck on a roof or lying around in the brush with a clout on the head, just waiting for somebody to find him."

"If you were a betting man, would you bet all you had on that?" Bridget Purdy refused to delude herself that her husband could have survived the water. Her life with him had been hard enough with some hope for better days, but now with her nine children to care for she did not dare pretend to herself. There wasn't even their shanty left, nor the boat from which to catch enough fish to feed themselves. "Tell me, Mr. Hutchins, would you bet your fortune on that?"

He saw the depth of strength in her clear gray eyes and could not lie to her. "No, ma'am, I wouldn't bet on it." He turned away as he saw the faces of her two youngest children as they stared in fear at him. "I'm awful sorry, Mrs. Purdy. But I can't in conscience tell you nothing else. That'd be a terrible cruel thing to do. I can't let you get your hopes up."

Hutchins took a step or two toward the central fire. "Anything I can do, I'll be glad to. I'd say you and the youngsters could stay in one of the barns, but there ain't any barns left. We'll get something figured out. Do you mind if I send little Rosa Cantu over to give you a hand with the kids? She's awful scared and lonesome. She'd be a sight of help to you."

"I'd like that. Yes, that would be nice," Bridget Purdy said.

"Good. Then I'll send her along. She can keep you company." The man seemed relieved that the two women could support one another and call on each other's strength. "I'll let you know right away what we find out." He touched his hat and nodded before he fled. Mrs. Purdy sat immobile on the wagon tongue, gathering her children to her arms as if in touching them, feeling their reality, she could cope with the worst.

"Did Chace come to yet?" Bert asked Guido Ferranti, who stood stirring soup over an open fire before the cook tent.

"Not yet. Louie Deledda says he's probably got concussion. Took a hard hit on the back of the skull. Terrible bruise and swelling." Guido took a pail of water his oldest boy brought from one of the springs on the west side of the hill. "I can thin this soup just so much, Bert. How soon can you get some lines across the creek so we can get supplies over here?"

"Soon's the tide goes out we maybe can find some way. I still don't know how we can get across. We may just have to go 'way south, below the Creighton place. Can't go by the beach yet. No way to ford the creek to the other side."

"The boys say most of the deer's been spooked down toward the river," Ferranti said. "Too much commotion, I guess. Got a couple young does so we'll have meat. And water's no problem. Old Mrs. Rodriguez took the kids with her to look for things. She says there's plenty of cattails in a boggy spot down there on the other slope, but I'm worried about her overdoing."

"What we got to do is get help from over to Forest Shores." Bert dipped a cupful of soup from the pot and blew on it before he tasted it. "One of my men rode back up a while ago and said they seen Ed Sickles and a couple other riders down by the bridge. Couldn't hear what he was trying to yell—not over the sound of the creek—but you can bet he's going to try something."

Hutchins squatted on his heels near the fire, his leathered face collapsed into a frown. "We got to get them that's hurt over to town or we're gonna lose 'em sure." He motioned toward the lean-to where Laurie kept her vigil.

"What time is it?" Laurie's black eyes never left Chace's face.

The school teacher snapped open her pendant watch and closed it again. Time suddenly seemed so important to them all. "Just past two o'clock. Why don't you go walk around a while, get some exercise before you go stiff from sitting in one position too long? I'll stay right by him and call you if there's any change."

"No. I want to be here when he comes to." She would not let herself say 'if he comes to.'

"All right, but let me get you some dry clothing to put on. We've finally managed to get some of it dried." Olive felt the trouser legs that were doubled under Laurie as she sat beside the improvised pallet. "These are still wet. And you're soaked to the skin."

"Do you have anything I can wear?" Laurie asked.

"I tucked your skirt and petticoats into one of Mr. Ferranti's boxes and brought them along," Olive replied. "They got wet and are pretty wrinkled after we dried them on sticks, but at least they're warm and dry. Will you change if I bring them?"

"Yes, I'm cold to the bone, but then everyone else is, too." Laurie looked across the clearing at Bridget Purdy and knew the cold she felt was more than damp and chill.

"I'll hold the blanket for you at this end and you can change right there." Olive understood her reluctance to leave. "I'm sure we can find you a shirt to put on until your waist and camisole are dry. The men say the storm's over. That's something to be grateful for." She crawled out of the lean-to and returned with Laurie's rumpled clothing.

"Now I'll hold the blanket up outside here. Ready?" Olive asked.

"All set," Laurie replied. "This shirt feels wonderful." It was sizes too large, but it was dry and warm from the fire. "Whose is it?"

"I've no idea. It was just extra, so I took it," Olive said.

Laurie put down the canvas horse blanket which protected the end of the shelter, then pulled her wet blouse off and tossed it outside. She loosened the narrow blue ribbon which secured the top of her camisole beneath her arms and across her breasts. It was damp and clung to her as she pulled it over her head, and then struggled into the rough red flannel shirt. The heavy nap, warm and smelling of wood smoke, felt comforting in the cold of the makeshift tent. She wriggled out of the trousers, then donned the dry petticoats and wrinkled woolen skirt before discarding her knee-length underdrawers and stockings. Her shoes, thoroughly wrecked by sand, mud, and water, were beyond repair, but she thrust her bare feet back into them.

"Do you have a comb, Olive?" she asked. When Chace regained consciousness Laurie wanted him to see her as presentable as she could make herself. It mattered little that the shirttails hung down over her soiled skirt.

"I don't, but I'll go see if I can find one. Surely somebody brought one along." Again Olive understood and had to smile to herself as she left to search for the comb. Laurie removed the pins from her hair and let it fall about her shoulders, running her fingers through it, loosening the damp locks. She crawled back to her place beside Chace and sat close to him. As she bent near his face, she saw his lips curve into a faint smile. The telltale flutter of his eyelids made her heart leap.

"Oh, darling, please wake up." She took his hand in hers and brought it to her lips. "Please be all right, Chace." She bent and kissed his mouth.

The amber eyes raised their heavy lids, and focused on the girl's face. He laughed softly and whispered, "Laurie. . ."

"You were awake just now. . .all the time I was. . ." She held his hand to her cheek and flexed the strong fingers with her own.

"Don't be angry with me. . .you're so beautiful, darling." His fingers closed on hers, the grip weak, but their response brought a smile to her lips. He was alive and conscious at last.

"No, Chace, I won't be angry." Tears welled in her eyes and spilled over, moistening his fingertips.

"Don't cry. . .don't cry. . ." he whispered.

"Oh, Chace, when I thought I'd lost you I wanted to die."

"Sweetheart. . ." He moved slightly beneath the blankets and winced with pain. He fell back, his eyes closing. "Joey?" The name was a question.

"He's all right. He's with his mother in one of the wagons," Laurie assured him.

He tried to nod his head, but grimaced with pain.

"Chace, I love you so," Laurie breathed in his ear. "I've never stopped loving you for one instant. I don't know what happened between us, but it doesn't matter. Not anymore—not ever." She spoke softly so only he could hear.

"I want to tell you. ." Chace began.

"Not now," she hushed him. "Later. When you're stronger, then you can tell me. All that matters is that I don't ever want to be away from you again. Down there on the beach, before the water came, I died a little when you ran to look for Joey. I stopped living then. Not until just now did I begin again. Oh, darling, I do love you so."

He touched her wet face with his fingers, wiping away the tears that she could now shed in happiness. His head swam dizzily, his eyes seeing only her face, her jet black eyes and tumbling dark hair. He drew her to him and held her close, kissing her reddened eyelids, the blue shadows that circled her eyes, the full red mouth that tasted sweet and warm on his.

"I'll not let you go again, Laurie. Not for any reason. I love you too much." His fingers tangled in her hair and pulled her head to his chest. "Not for any reason. . ."

"Shhh! Later. . ." She could hear the beating of his heart, feel the throb of his breast beneath her cheek. "You must rest now. We'll get you over to the hospital as soon as we can."

"The bridge?" Chace asked.

"It's gone," Laurie replied. "But Ed Sickles and some men from town are fixing some sort of temporary crossing. We can't get any word across yet. Bert sent some of your drivers up to see if the bridge beyond your place—the old logging bridge—is still intact. We may be able to use that."

"Wagons can't make it up there." Chace knew the road.

"Don't you worry about it right now. Will you try to drink some broth? Guido has coffee and soup. There's biscuit and crackers." Laurie hoped the warm food would help restore him.

"See if Guido has some whiskey," Chace said.

"And we'll get you out of those wet clothes. I'll get Olive to help me." Laurie smoothed back his unruly hair and kissed him. "I'll hurry back."

Chief of Police Ed Sickles swung crazily in the basket-swing over the torrent of La Gaviota Creek. Bert Hutchins steadied the ropes to stop the swaying. Inch by inch the jury-rigged conveyor neared the west side of the steep canyon.

"Don't let her go slack there, boys!" Hutchins stood at the pulley and eased the line around a tree trunk. Sickles signaled to continue and the journey across the chasm resumed.

"Good! Good!" Hutchins directed his men as they pulled the policeman up onto the bluff.

Before they could secure the lines, Sickles had jumped out and grasped the horse trader's hand. "Good work, Bert." He could waste no time on niceties. "What's the situation here?" He swung up into the saddle on Dora while Bert took Sally and led Sickles up the trail toward the temporary town.

"We got some people injured. Couple of 'em real bad. Best to get them over to the hospital first off. Got a few folks still missing. Men are down to the cove looking for 'em now, but we ain't likely to find 'em alive. Gives the men something to do right now; keeps them busy till we can get better organized."

"Food? Water?" Sickles asked.

"Got some. Guido Ferranti's taking care of that. Had some meat on hand at the cafe and salvaged a good deal of the staples. Dressed out a couple deer and old Mrs. Rodriguez found some edibles to put in the stew pot. Stream's running good just over the hill, so there's no problem with water. Got latrines set up down in that level patch on the east side. Reckon it's healthier there in

301

that loamy soil for drainage. We can keep it covered. Plenty of soft earth to do the job. Got some tents rigged up, but if it comes rain again, it'll be bad." Bert knew they could not live beneath wagonbeds for long.

"We could see it was pretty bad," Sickles said. "The heaviest surge smashed over the breakwater. Wrecked most all the pleasure craft. Slammed into a lot of houses, but the force wasn't as strong along there once it'd hit the rocks. I could tell it was bad over here." Sickles fended off a low branch as they entered the pines. "I sent word to Sacramento and San Esteban right away, but they've got to know the facts before they'll act. Hell," he swore impatiently, "that's always the way of it! Facts first, then they decide if they'll help!" He bent over the Walker's withers as she passed under low branches that hung dripping over the trail.

"I think you ought to know there's a mighty lot of talk about Arch Creighton up at camp." Bert rolled a cigarette between his fingers, licked the paper, pinched it shut and put it between his lips. He had no dry matches, but from sheer habit he kept it there.

"How's that?" Sickles was alert to trouble, for during catastrophes tempers can become explosive and actions violent.

"Arch wouldn't send no wagons down to help folks get out," Bert explained. "That young girl—the one bought the ladies' shop over on Birch Street—she rode up to the Creighton place and got Chace to bring wagons and drivers. It was the only way. Folks was leery of leaving all their goods and houses, even after Guido done his best to give 'em fair warning. I reckon most of 'em would be floating in the cove right now if Chace Creighton hadn't took matters into his own hands. Just went right ahead and moved everybody out."

"Yeah, but what's that got to do with Arch?" Sickles asked.

"Some's saying they're going to see Arch gets paid back in full. Olive Pickens, that school teacher who lives up to the Hinshaw place, she tried her best to get Arch to send help down here, but he turned her down flat.

And so did old Mrs. Creighton. Hung up on her, she did. Seems Arch had got his back up about something that happened last night—Pansy Hinshaw and her ladies had a run-in with him." Bert twisted in the saddle to look the policeman in the face, as if to stress his point. "Now there's plenty Sand Town folks talking lynch."

Ed Sickles knew that lynch talked about was often accomplished. He resolved not to disclose the fact that Archibald Creighton had also tried to keep rescuers from reaching the bridge on the Creighton property. "Lynch? That's pretty strong, Bert."

"You be sure to tell the fellas that!" Hutchins laughed. "And you keep telling them when they find Kevin Purdy and that nice little Chinaman's wife and when they see how bad off Joey Deledda and Chace and one of his drivers is!" Bert was angry. "And you just be sure to keep on telling me, too!"

"You say Creighton's been hurt?" Sickles asked.

"Bad hit on the back of his head. Miss Pickens told me he comes to, then drifts off again," Bert said.

"I heard from a couple of my men that he'd brought drivers down from the construction yards. I didn't know if they had it straight or not. I didn't contact Archibald or Sybil Creighton to check on it." Sickles did not need to add his reasons for not doing so; Bert understood. "I'll have to let them know Chace's hurt as soon as I get back to town."

"Best ask Chace before you go doing that," Bert advised.

Sickles nodded. He knew he'd have another bad time with Sybil Creighton if he delayed informing her of her son's injury. But in deference to Chace, he would wait and talk with him first.

As the two men rode into camp, solemn-faced youngsters watched, then fell in behind them on the muddy trail. Their elders looked up in surprise as the burly police chief swung down from the saddle before the cook tent, which had become the hub of camp activity. Forest Shores had incorporated Sand Town within the city limits in order to increase revenues, but other than forcing the children into a new school several miles away, none of the city officials had shown more than election-time interest in their welfare. Ed Sickles, known to them for his fairness in dealing with their erring citizens, had earned their increased respect merely by being the first man over the creek.

Shadows were lengthening, spreading blue-purple darkness under the pines and across the old logging-camp clearing. Cold was edging in around the fires, and the line of those waiting for food was growing as it filed past Guido's open kettles. There was little conversation as the exotic stew was ladled out. Louie Deledda, a torn sheet tied about his middle, calmly directed the serving of their meal, quietly supervising the older boys who replenished the bread and kept the stew from burning.

Silence had descended on the camp after Sickles left. He would get what he could and expedite their relief, but as to where they would live, and how they would live, he could not say. Emergency funds would have to be voted and appropriated for county aid. Much could be raised locally with the help of churches and fraternal groups, but every person in Sand Town knew the ignominy and humiliation involved in accepting such largesse. Whispered despair could galvanize the refugees into a dangerous faction. They would trust Ed Sickles to obtain help for them, but they warned him they would not be put off any more by the city. Reform must begin with the rebuilding of Sand Town.

Laurie Mathews, her incongruous red flannel shirt and stained navy woolen skirt warmed by the bonfire, took her place in the long line. The brisk air and knowledge that Chace was safe whetted her appetite. To the girl it seemed as though she and Olive had walked to Sand Town a year ago. Only a bit longer than twenty-four hours ago they had left Mrs. Hinshaw's and headed into the howling wind. Could so much happen in such a short time?

"I'll take some plain broth for Chace, please," Laurie said. Carlo Deledda handed her a small granite bowl and spoon, then ran to the wagon for a cup.

"Will this do for him? Can he drink from it all right?" Louie brought utensils from the wagon and stacked them on a plank by the fire. "We have some saucers, if that would be easier."

"No, this will be fine," Laurie replied.

"Can he eat some stew? Meat's pretty tough, but it's more nourishing," Guido Ferranti suggested.

"Mrs. Purdy thinks he should just have broth and crackers," Laurie said.

"Yes, she'd know best. She's very good with the sick." Guido dipped into the stock pot, poured liquid into a heavy restaurant cup, then ladled stew into the granite bowl. "Here, I'll send the boy with coffee. There's no milk right now, but we sent someone to milk Purdy's cow. And we're saving the sugar for cooking." There was no apology, just explanation. "Do you want to wait for the milk?"

"No, thank you. This will do." Laurie juggled bowl and cup, and held the spoons between her fingers as she made her way through the hungry crowd to the lean-to. Olive moved to one side as the girl gave her the food to hold until she could crawl under the shelter.

"It's a lot better tasting than it looks. With plenty of garlic and onions, it could pass for beef." Olive looked at Chace, who lay propped up against one of the wagon wheels. "I've got to run down the hill for a minute," she said with delicacy. "Then I'm going to talk to Mr. Hutchins and see how soon we can get you over to the hospital." She would leave Laurie and Chace alone, giving them an opportunity to say things they might hesitate to say in front of her. In her mind she went over some of the phrases that had occurred to her when she thought about Ed Sickles.

Olive Pickens did not bother to tuck up her skirts as she walked through the muddy, trampled grass toward the latrines. Clothing did not matter on their mountain-top aside from keeping them warm. Somehow she would have to squeeze ten dollars from her next pay for a new suit. By summer perhaps she could manage four more dollars for a chiffon and lace blouse in which to be married.

She smiled as she looked at the children. There was hope for her after all; she would be married before she was thirty. Ed Sickles made it clear he did not wish to wait until the school term was out, but she had her obligation. Such a ridiculous place for a proposal! Not at all as she had pictured to herself a thousand times in her imagination. They were both dirty, her hair blown to a stringy, wispy tangle, and at least a dozen youngsters laughed at him.

"You're going to marry me so I'll know where you are! Scared me half to death yesterday when Roy Wimbish told me where you'd gone to! Damn it, Olive, don't you know what I imagined might have happened to you?" It was as if Ed were eager to blame her for his worry. He sat down on his haunches with the children so he could look her right in the eyes. She said not a word, but her smile told him all he needed to know. "I already told Roy what I aimed to do. He thought it was a good idea. So must Pansy Hinshaw—seems some gal from the telephone exchange was by looking for a place to stay and Pansy told her she might have a vacancy real soon." Sickles waited for her to respond and little Serafina Ferranti, thumb in mouth, grinned as she looked from one to the other. The disheveled teacher took the child on her lap and hugged her. Hugging Ed could come later.

"I think it's a splendid idea," Olive agreed.

It was not the acceptance she had rehearsed over and over in her dreaming, but it was from her heart.

Ed Sickles had heaved himself to stand towering above her and the children, his seamed face showing relief and personal happiness. The expression faded quickly, however, as he looked toward the blanket-tent where Mrs. Purdy hovered over Joey, and Marcella Deledda quietly wept.

Sunday afternoon Pansy Hinshaw and young Hallie Mae Purdy had watched with growing apprehension as the surf exploded against Point Piedras, shooting spindrift and salt spray high above the roofs of shoreline houses. Elevated on its hill as the old Hinshaw place was, there was little danger, but even as they kept their vigil by the window they became aware of the gravity of the situation.

Inured to troubles, the hired girl busied herself about the rambling old house, filling lamps, emptying grates, helping Roy bring in firewood.

From the bay window Pansy could see across a stand of pine at Beach Park to the hills of Calabasas Point. Even before darkness fell she had spied flickering orange lights of campfires atop the ridge. A few blocks north of the house, at Point Piedras, came a muttering undertone of surf clearly audible inside the parlor. Built to take advantage of its location on the crest of the hill at the town's western limit, the Hinshaw place afforded a sweeping view north and northwest. Until the drizzle became too heavy, Pansy sat looking out upon the disaster.

"I'll not hear of you trying to go home in this storm," the elderly woman said. "It might not be safe for you. If Olive and Laurie haven't come back yet, it must mean the road's bad. You'll stay here tonight. Your parents will know you're here with me and won't worry." Pansy did not need to voice her fears. The girl's young face mirrored her own anxiety.

By late afternoon Shore Park Drive had been thronged with sightseers. On foot and by carriage, crowds came to gape at the devastation and to wonder at the fate of Sand Town. The carnival atmosphere disgusted Ed Sickles as he directed his men to their various patrols and instructed volunteers in their special duties. From her veranda Pansy Hinshaw watched the procedure, then retreated to the warmth of her front parlor. Hallie Mae brought in a tea tray, fresh cut bread, jam, butter and cheese.

"I think I see Roy coming back now. Shall I ask him to step in for a minute?" The girl pulled up a small serving table and placed the tray close to the woman.

307

She had arranged the food as enticingly as possible to tempt her elderly employer.

"Please do. Maybe he can tell us what happened." Pansy was too upset to worry about eating. That a catastrophe had occurred was obvious. She had seen Ed Sickles ride west down Main Avenue with his men, and later with wagons carrying emergency equiment. Hallie Mae buttered a piece of bread and poured tea, pushed it to the edge of the tray, and placed the blue glass pitcher of cream near the pot.

"Do try to eat a bit," the girl coaxed. "I'll go get Roy." She removed a brightly colored lap robe from the warming rack before the fireplace and draped it about the woman's shoulders. "There, that's better, isn't it?"

"Yes, thank you. It is getting chilly." Pansy wondered how it was on the other side of the creek in Sand Town. It would be very cold up on the hills. That surely must be what the fires were for, but what had happened?

Pansy spooned raspberry jam from the marmalade bowl onto her bread and tasted it, all the while keeping her eyes on the activity beyond the window. By now some of the curious, wet and chilled, began to leave the stricken area. She stirred her tea and dutifully sipped it. Since Hallie Mae had fixed the tray and insisted she eat, she could not disappoint the child. What had become of Hallie Mae's family? And of Laurie and Olive? The questions chilled her more than the cold.

Roy Wimbish, muffled to his ears, changed his boots in the summer kitchen and followed the girl into the front parlor. His beard and face were glistening with drizzle and his clothing was wet through.

"What is it, Roy?" Mrs. Hinshaw asked anxiously. "We've seen such a commotion all afternoon!"

"Tidal wave, I reckon you'd call it. Ed Sickles says it's more proper a storm surge. Big wall of water pushed up by the wind. And then the tides is extra high, too." He shook his head as the girl pulled up a straight chair for him. "No thank you, Hallie Mae; I'm just too wet to sit down. Would ruin the finish on the chair. I'll be getting home and drying out if there's nothing more you ladies need." He stood awkwardly with his oiled-felt rain hat in his hands.

"No, Roy, there's nothing we need. And you mustn't keep those wet clothes on." Pansy hoped he could tell her more. "Like a tidal wave, you said?"

"Yes, ma'am. Run right up over the breakwaters," Roy said. "Smashed up all them boats at the foot of Hawthorne Street. Damaged some houses along the waterfront. Nothing too bad here in Forest Shores, but looks like Sand Town was pretty near wiped out. From what folks say that lives along Shore Park Drive, a big wall of water slammed into the cove and climbed right up through Sand Town, taking everything in its way."

Hallie Mae gasped. Roy touched her shoulder in sympathy. "Now don't you worry about your folks, girlie. Your papa's a right smart man. He'd have taken care of things before it happened." To Pansy he said, "You know that old retired sea captain that bought Hap Cruller's place on Dunbarton? Right on the corner of Shore Park?"

"I've heard of him," Pansy said.

"Well, he's got a turret built up on top of the roof with windows all the way 'round and he's got a telescope up there," Roy went on. "Uses it to watch ships and whales. Well, he was looking out to sea—the tides was getting so bad he pretty well knew what to expect, what with the wind from northwest. He seen that water coming and used that glass to see close up what was going on. He says it was awful. Just picked up boats, barns, packing sheds, the restaurant—everything—just like they was nothing. Got too drizzily right afterward to see much, but he says a man could walk across the cove on the wreckage. Roofs and sheds floating around. . ."

"But what about the people?" Pansy asked in dismay.

"Reckon they got out beforehand. Folks saw a bunch of wagons come down out of that stand of trees that fronts on Main just this side of the bridge. You know, on that old logging road that runs down from the Creighton property?''

"Yes, I recall there's a trail there," Pansy said. "Comes into Main right where Beach Park Lane does."

"That's the one. What they seen must of been the Creighton wagons and crew going along to Shell Road. The captain figures everybody got out. Says he seen all the livestock being moved up the hills first, then later all sorts of buggies and wagons took to the logging roads. Went up to the top of the ridge."

Roy seemed impatient to leave, but he continued, "Bridge over the creek's washed out. Not a stick of it left." He did not wait for Pansy to dismiss him, but headed for the portiere-draped doorway to the dining room. "Soon's I get dry clothes on and eat me some supper I'm going down to the bridge. Ed Sickles says that's the first thing we got to do—get a bridge across the canyon. We can jury-rig something to work. Some of the men went on to scout out the old bridge that's on the logging road farther up the creek. Seems Arch Creighton tried to keep them off his property, but they called his bluff and went anyway."

"He wouldn't let them use his road?" Pansy was shocked at such callousness.

"Didn't want 'em to, but Elmer Hobart and a couple of the deputies had on side arms and Arch didn't have the nerve to dare 'em." He parted the portieres. "If you don't need nothing more, I'll be going and see what I can do to help."

"Yes, run along, Roy. Thank you for coming to tell us." Pansy hesitated a moment and called after him, "Do be careful."

"Yes, ma'am. I'll be careful." He crossed through the kitchen to the summer porch, changed back into his heavy boots, and headed for his cottage. Somehow they'd have to get a line across the canyon and get over to Sand Town. He only prayed there had been no lives lost. As he lighted a lamp and began taking off his damp clothing he eyed the gun rack over the fireplace. The blued-steel barrels shone with a dull reflection of the yellow light. His face set with hatred as he thought of Arch Creighton.

Monday had been a day of consternation for the entire town. There was no way to assess the destruction beyond La Gaviota Creek. Elmer Hobart and his men had found the logging bridge in bad condition. Long before it could be made safe, one could be strung across the Main Avenue crossing. The intersection of Main and Shore Park Drive was the scene of frantic activity as men and machinery concentrated on bridging the canyon.

The antiquated grandfather clock in the hallway chimed the quarter-hour just before Ed Sickles stopped by the Hinshaw place. He was not only wet, but dirty, his face and clothing smeared with black grease and mud. Hallie Mae opened the door and stared with dismay at the tall, burly man who stood on the veranda.

"Yes, sir?" Even had the girl known him by sight, she could not have identified him.

"May I see Mrs. Hinshaw?" He could not repress a smile as he saw the look of suspicion cross her face. "I'm Chief Sickles."

"Oh?" The girl squinted into the dark beyond the door, doubt showing in her expression. "Wait right there, please." She closed the door and Sickles chuckled as he heard the turnlock click into place.

"Some terrible looking man is out there!" Hallie Mae whispered to Pansy. "He wants to see you. I latched the door."

"Who is it?" When she saw the girl was frightened, Pansy put down her crocheting and led the way back to the front door.

"He says he's Chief Sickles, but he doesn't look like a policeman to me!" The girl stood to one side as Pansy opened the door cautiously.

"Ed! Do come in." To Hallie Mae she said in a whisper that made the man laugh, "It's all right, dear. It really is Chief Sickles."

He grinned and edged into the lamplight. "I just

wanted to tell you your girls are all right."

"Oh, thank God for that! I've been so worried!" Pansy stepped back and motioned him inside.

"I'm too filthy to come in," Sickles said. "I'm going home and get a change of clothes and a meal. By that time the crew'll have a line secured over the canyon. Then we'll see if we can bring the injured across the creek and get them to the hospital."

"Hallie Mae and I've just finished supper. There's plenty left over. Do stay and tell us all about it." She was eager to learn of the disaster.

"No, thank you, Mrs. Hinshaw. I've got too many things to attend to, but I'll take you up on that in a day or so." He turned to go, his hand on the door knob. "I just thought you'd want to know about your young ladies. They'll have quite a story to tell."

"Oh yes, I'm sure they will. Thank you, Ed. That's a relief to know they're safe." She touched his arm and moved close to him. "What do you know about the Purdys? Little Hallie Mae's terribly worried about her family."

"They're all fine," he said reassuringly. "Mrs. Purdy's been pressed into service as a nurse, and a good one she is, too." Sickles lowered his voice so only the elderly woman could hear. "Kevin Purdy's missing." At her look of concern he added, "That doesn't mean much right now. Men are searching the wreckage. He could still be found. Use your own judgment about telling the girl." He opened the door and stepped out onto the veranda.

"Maybe I'll wait until you know for sure. Yes, I'll wait," Pansy decided.

When he had gone, Pansy stood for a long time in the cold hallway, listening to the monotonous ticking of the walnut and brass clock that towered a full foot above her. She watched the shiny pendulum as it marked off the seconds, back and forth, back and forth. *Tick-tock. Tick-tock.* How many seconds make up a lifetime? How many tragedies can be played out in those seconds?

She heard Hallie Mae in the kitchen washing the supper dishes. The clatter of pans was a comforting, familiar sound. The girl's childish voice rose in a wailing Irish ballad of unrequited love and parting.

"I'll wait till tomorrow. Tomorrow will be time enough." Pansy resolved. She turned down the hall lamp and wandered through the quiet parlor and music room. She still had not replaced the guttered candles on the music rack of the piano. Pansy reminded herself to have Hallie Mae do that tomorrow.

Standing at the west window, she looked across the road where lanterns bobbed at the barricade and men's figures milled about the wagons. They would keep working through the night. Some things would not wait until tomorrow.

Chapter 15

Doctor Eichner ushered Laurie into the stark room. Shades had been drawn against brilliant south light, leaving the interior in semi-darkness. "Don't stay too long. He looks fine, but he'll have to rest and take it easy for a while. I don't want him tired out." He pulled up a chair for the girl and placed it by the bed. "You heard me, didn't you, Chace?"

"I did. But I'm not making any promises." Chace held out his hand to Laurie and enfolded her slim fingers in his. Their eyes met, ignoring the doctor and Nurse McMurray, both of whom found reasons to leave the room and close the door behind them. For a moment Laurie stood by the high bed, appalled by the paleness of his face and swath of bandage about his head.

"Darling!" No words were sufficient. Only her lips on his, her face soft against his unshaven cheek could convey her message. Her jet eyes opened and caught the golden glint deep within his. His wide hand pressed her head close, his arms held her body to him.

"There's so much we must talk about, Laurie. There's so much you need to know." He let her go, but held her hand as she perched on the side of the bed. "For your own sake, you must listen."

She was surprised by his seriousness. She placed her other hand on his and bent to kiss him. "Then I shall listen."

"I didn't stay away from you because I wanted to. You do believe that, don't you?"

"Yes, I believe you, Chace," she said.

"I heard about the problems you had with your shipments coming through San Esteban. It was all my fault, and I've had to live with that knowledge the past couple of months."

"I don't understand. How could you be to blame?" She pulled her knee up under her and spread her skirts so they would not wrinkle.

"I brought your troubles down on your head. God, I'm so sorry!" He caressed her face with his rough hand. "I thought I could let things stand as they were until such time as I could get them straightened away. When you came to me Sunday I realized I couldn't wait any longer."

She started to interrupt, but he stopped her.

"No, let me finish. For some reason—unknown to me—my mother took exception to my seeing you. It's true she was trying her best to get me involved with a girl of her own choice, the granddaughter of an associate of Father's, but there was something else, too. Something I still don't understand.

"We've never been close. We've never hit it off. Her values have never been mine. She disapproved of my enlisting in the army in '98; she disapproved when I insisted on learning the building and construction business by working with my hands. Even my choice of friends. . .wearing apparel. . .what I like to eat. . .

"When I told her I intended to marry you, she demanded I stop seeing you. I refused." He twisted in the bed to see her face more clearly in the half-light. "You must already know our family's influential, and not always for the best. Mother threatened to make things difficult for you. I saw she really meant to do what she said. There was no way I could stop her. I agreed to stop seeing you, to wait until we gave our love the test of time and separation. One of her conditions was that I should not tell you, not communicate with you in any way.

"Please believe me, I didn't make such a promise lightly. I didn't want you hurt by her; I wanted you to

315

succeed. I didn't want her to ruin your business or drive you away. She's quite capable of doing such things, I assure you.

"Maybe you think it was weakness on my part, agreeing to her demands, but, Laurie, her influence extends far beyond Forest Shores. As spokesman for my father, she had—and still has—the ability to coerce powerful people to do as she demands. Father taught her well! And she wouldn't hesitate to use any means to gain her ends.

"I've been working hard for several years to bring improvements to this area, improvements that will mean jobs, security, increased economic expansion based on sound commerce and industry. We need that for all the people who live here—workers, shopkeepers, tradesmen—everybody. I've always hoped that if I'm remembered someday, it will be for my efforts in that direction.

"Mother can destroy all my work, all my plans, and those of every other businessman in the community who's gone along with me in this. I was beginning to see the results of her machinations, but there is absolutely nothing provable—she's much too subtle. Ralph Donner, over in San Esteban, got into trouble financing his Aguilar Valley project. When I was in Sacramento last December I found out why. Mother had very cleverly maneuvered Donner into the position of having to take in Arch as a partner. Now the project is completely Arch's—and Mother's.

"Businessmen right here in Forest Shores are finding capital money harder to get. They're being forced to turn to Creighton Development for funds. I've backed a few with my own money, but I can't take care of them all, not until I can get my own projects approved and started. And if I make the wrong moves, a lot of people, good, hard-working people, would be financially ruined.

"I had a poor choice to make. . ." He turned away from her intense black eyes as he castigated himself for his decision.

"Chace, darling, you did the right thing." Laurie pulled his hand to her lips and kissed his rough fingers. "You had to agree for the sake of all the others. I understand."

"Do you?" He could not bring himself to look back into her eyes.

"Of course I do. I only wish I'd known. . ."

"Duncan?" He need not ask a further question.

"Yes. I was so angry, so hurt, not knowing." She turned away from him and buried her face in her hands. "I'm so ashamed! I should have trusted you. He might be alive today if. . ."

"Don't, sweetheart, don't!" He raised up on one elbow and pulled her to him, turning her face to his. "Duncan was lost before you ever met him. He courted his own end. Nothing anyone could say or do would have changed him or what he did. He was determined to destroy himself, Laurie." He pushed back a stray wisp of black hair that fell across her forehead. "You mustn't ever blame yourself for him. Never!"

He embraced her and held her close. When she was calm once more, he continued. "I can't stay away from you. Not any more. Do what she will, Mother will have to accept it. I hope I've pushed my plans far enough along that she can't damage them too much. Even so, we have a right to be together."

"As long as I know you love me, I can wait," Laurie told him. "We have all our years ahead of us. It isn't as if we'd have to wait forever."

"We shouldn't have to wait. We mustn't!" Chace said.

"But she holds me responsible for your father's death—and Duncan's. And now, because of me, you almost lost your life. She'll never accept me!" There was despair in Laurie's voice. She knew Sybil Creighton would never be reconciled.

"We'll just take it one step at a time." Chace tried to sound confident, but he knew the viciousness of which his mother was capable.

"And even your brother is against me!" Instantly

317

she regretted saying it.

"Arch? Why?" Chace demanded.

"Believe me, he is!" She considered whether to tell him the whole story or not. He was not, after all, to get upset or agitated.

He shook her and frowned. "Tell me! What has Arch done to you?" There was supressed fury in his deep voice.

"When I was over in San Esteban trying to get my shipments straightened out, I went to the newspaper to see Lucia Orozco. There was something else I had to find out about, too. Archibald had Ralph Donner meet me at the railway station. He had Donner give me a message." Her face flushed with anger as she remembered the encounter. "He intimated my business would suffer if people in Forest Shores learned I was digging up old scandals at the paper, especially with the help of Lucia. They'd look upon me as an undesirable element!"

Chace was silent. His mouth set in a hard line and his eyes narrowed with anger. "That bastard!" He swung his legs over the opposite side of the bed, braced himself and stood up, unmindful of the hospital shirt that fell short of his ankles.

"Chace, what are you doing? Please get back into bed!" Laurie ran to him as he swayed unsteadily. "You're not able to get up yet! It's dangerous!"

"I'll horsewhip the bastard!" he swore.

"No, Chace, you mustn't! It doesn't matter anymore!" She forced him to sit down on the bed, then ran out the door and down the hall, returning with Althea McMurray.

"You'll fall flat on your face if you try that!" The nurse threw back the bedding and straightened out the sheets. "You're getting right back into that bed. I'll take no sass from you! Now!" She eased him into the bed, lifted his legs and pulled the bedclothes up around him as he fought to regain his feet. "No more of that!" He was no match for the nurse's experienced strength. "You're not as foxy as you think, young man."

His face was pale, his eyes unfocused as he collapsed back into the pillows. He reached for Laurie's hand, and held it as he tried to keep the room from slipping away from him. What was it she had said? Something about old scandals. . .and something about Archibald. . .

"I'll kill Arch for that!" he whispered as darkness came.

Lanterns warned of the barricade at the intersection of West Main Avenue and Shore Park Drive. Yellow-orange sawbucks, hastily borrowed from the railway, clogged the road in a semi-circle. Crews from the road maintenance department alternated hours around the clock to throw a temporary bridge across La Gaviota Creek. A swaying, unstable rope bridge was superceded by one of planks across which the injured were taken to the hospital in Forest Shores and supplies transported down to Sand Town.

Burros and mules plodded docilely on the crude footing, but few were the men brave enough to test the bridge with a horse. The planking resounded with a hollow echo over the roar of the flooded creek and supports creaked with every movement. Only emergency traffic was permitted on the structure, although the exodus on foot continued sporadically. There remained nothing in Sand Town to hold most of its residents. Those who had relatives or friends willing to give them refuge filed dejectedly along the road and over the narrow bridge. By dark the emigration ceased. Travel in the stricken area was still dangerous.

Roy Wimbish poured kerosene into one of the red-glassed lanterns, wiped a spill from its brass base and handed it to Hiram Perry.

"That fills 'em all." He swung the five-gallon oil drum into the back of a wagon which was turned at right angles to the roadway. "There's plenty oil left. Not more'n half of it's gone." He latched the tailgate and took out his pipe.

"Good, that'll save me a trip back to town

tonight." The man was weary and sat down on one of the sawhorses, his shoulders slumped with fatigue. "Reckon you heard they found Kevin Purdy late this afternoon."

"Ed Sickles sent a boy by the house to tell us they found Kevin. Ed wanted Mrs. Hinshaw to be the one to tell Hallie Mae. That's the oldest Purdy girl—works steady for Mrs. Hinshaw." Roy sifted tobacco into the bowl of his burl pipe and tamped it down. "Got time for a smoke? Genuine North Carolina plug. Just come in at Jepsen's." He passed the tin to the crewman, then struck a match with his thumbnail and drew on the stubby mouthpiece.

"Thanks, Roy. Believe I will." Perry extracted a pipe from his coat pocket, held it in his fist and filled it. "I've been working since before sunup. My wife's gonna wonder if I'm ever coming home. Brought me my supper in a basket a while ago. Give up on me getting back, I reckon." The match flamed as he lighted the tobacco. For an instant his face was visible, then disappeared again as he flicked away the spent match.

"Too bad about Purdy," Roy Wimbish said. "He was a right good man. Worked awful hard, he did. Turned his hand to any honest thing he could." Roy could think of no finer praise for any man. "Nice bunch of youngsters he's got, too." Smoke curled about the two men in the still night air. From down the road where the crew still labored on the bridge came sounds of sledge hammers and bucksaws.

"I hear tell a couple more's still missing. A Chinawoman and that old Italian fella that worked in the fish-packing sheds." The watchman pulled his collar up against the cold. "We can praise the Lord it wasn't no worse. Hoyt Larcher told me there ain't a boat left undamaged behind the town breakwater. Smashed up like so much kindling wood."

"Not a one, no, sir," Roy confirmed. "Course, those won't make no difference, being just pleasure craft. Where it'll hurt most is all them folks over to Sand Town that worked 'em."

320

"To hear tell along Shore Park, you'd think nobody's place got hurt but theirs." Perry grunted. "By damn, they're plumb lucky they didn't live yonder in Sand Town. What them poor souls is going to do is beyond me." After a bit he asked, "How's Chace Creighton doing? You hear today?"

"Miss Laurie's been to see him. Says he won't be up and around for quite a spell." Roy sat down on the tongue of the heavy wagon and rested one foot on the whiffletree. "Concussion. Doc Eichner says there ain't nothing to be done for it. Just rest and quiet."

Hiram Perry snorted. "It'd be a pure wonder if old Mrs. Creighton leaves him be in quiet! Why, Elmer Hobart and Hoyt Larcher said they come mighty close to having to use their side arms when they went to take a look at the old logging bridge. Seems the old woman and Arch was dead set nobody was going through their property. She'd had a fit when she found out what Chace went and done without asking leave of her and Arch. No, I reckon she'll not leave him be!"

"They both got a lot to answer for." Roy did not need to elaborate. Everyone knew of Arch's refusal to send crews and wagons to the rescue of Sand Town. Most were agreed the threats against him were justified.

"I hear tell the sheriff down to Los Olivos caught that fella who killed young Duncan Creighton on New Year's Eve." Hiram Perry buttoned his coat against the damp night air and turned his collar up to warm the back of his neck. "Ed Sickles says Mrs. Creighton ain't give him a day's peace since it happened."

"Seems like she's gonna have to wait a spell for his hanging." Roy chuckled at the thought.

"You're right about that—can't hang a man twice!" Perry joined Roy's laughter.

"What'd he done? Mrs. Hinshaw says she heard he'd killed some woman down to Hemet. That so?" Roy asked.

"Ed says this fella got mixed up in some land swindle down there, couple years ago it was, and had a falling out with his partners. Beat up the woman till she died and he took off. Law's been dogging him ever since.''

The old crewman smoked in silence for a minute before Roy said, ''That gives Riverside County first call on hanging him, don't it?''

''Won't suit old Mrs. Creighton,'' Perry said, ''But that's the law, her wants notwithstanding.'' Again the old men chuckled.

From out of the darkness just south of the intersection, too far away to see more than an outline under the street lamp, came the sound of a horse and jangle of spurs. The night was still and the chink, chink of metal rowels was clearly audible from where the men sat talking. They looked up, but light from the lanterns between them and the road prevented seeing beyond the barricade. They remained silent, listening.

''Must be that young fella Ed Sickles put out to patrol along Shore Park Drive,'' Hiram Perry guessed.

''Nope. Can't be.'' Roy gestured with his pipe to the east. ''Whoever it is, he's turning east on Main.'' He stood up and listened a moment more, then turned toward the bridge. ''I'll mosey down and see how the boys is doing. Ed Sickles still down there?''

''Yeah, he come just after sundown. Ain't gone back yet.'' The old man did not move from the sawbuck, but sat smoking in the dark.

''I'll be back directly, Hiram.'' Roy walked along the graveled road, breathing deeply the moist night air. Usually he relished his jaunts along West Main to the livery stables. He felt guilty tonight about enjoying his walk when he thought of the homeless, afflicted people who had fled along the road in the opposite direction. Somewhere in the forest to the south an owl hooted as it flitted from branch to branch. An answering series of hunting-hoots issued from deep within the pines of Beach Park. Roy was astonished the creatures would choose to hunt so near the activity by the creek. He smiled to himself. It was comforting to hear the bird's cries; it meant that part of life continued its normal course.

As he came to the canyon, Roy was amazed by the

322

frantic pace of reconstruction. The railroad had loaned the city its best engineers and mechanics, of course with an eye to the fine publicity such a move would make in the newspapers. Creighton Development had been shamed into donating the services of its crews, while volunteers from both Forest Shores and San Esteban brought tools and equipment and camped at the site. Tents had been pitched on one side of the roadbed, with wagons lined up on the other, and horses pastured north of the road in Beach Park.

"Evening, gents." Roy nodded to the men lounging about the cook tent and strode on toward the bridge. The creek in the canyon below roared in undiminished furor. Rain had ceased on the mountains inland, but it would be many hours before the run-off lessened. Evidence of the sea's destructive force was obvious even with only the light of lanterns and campfires. Trees lay in a grotesque, jumbled crosshatching, their roots thrust skyward. Shattered branches, parts of houses, and torn chaparral littered the sides of the canyon.

"That you, Roy?" Hoyt Larcher emerged from behind his delivery wagon and came into the light of the cook fire. His white butcher's apron was soiled and his stocky frame slouched from too many hours of boning and cutting. Wimbish walked back to the wagon.

"I see you're still at it, Hoyt," Roy said.

"Yep! They're one hungry bunch, I tell you!" He wiped his hands on a dirty towel which hung from a hook in the meat compartment, then sat on the step of the cab. "I'm driving back to town in a minute. Can I give you a lift?"

"No thanks. I was just going to see Ed Sickles about what the city aims to do about burying Kevin Purdy. Mrs. Hinshaw wants to see he's buried proper. Course, there ain't no Catholic cemetery here, so it'll have to be over to San Esteban." It saddened him to talk of the funeral of a friend. He was a simple man, and death, while accepted in all its guises, was a deep sorrow to him. He leaned against the wagon and smoked in silence.

323

"Say, what's all that ruckus?" Larcher looked in the direction of town. "Sounds like a woman." Both men started up, trying to see beyond the campfire and lanterns.

"Miss Laurie!" Roy ran toward the shouts. "It's Miss Laurie!"

Men poured out of the sleeping tents and from around the fires. A woman, running disheveled and wild-eyed, flung herself into Wimbish's arms.

"Roy! I've got to get Ed Sickles! Where is he?" She clutched a white paper in her hand and held it for him to see as if he should recognize what it was. "He. . .he. . .brought this for her to sign! He tried to force her to sign it!"

Hoyt Larcher called to one of the men nearer the bridge, "Get Ed over here quick!"

"Who? Who you talking about?" Roy's eyes narrowed with suspicion, jaws bulging as he clenched his teeth.

"What's he trying to do?" Larcher asked.

"This. . .this. . ." She waved the paper, incapable of explaining. She could hardly get her breath. "You've got to stop him! He can't do this! He's crazy!"

"Where is he?" Roy's voice was gutteral with anger.

"He came by a few minutes ago. Pansy pretended she had to get her glasses to read it. I was hiding in the kitchen. She gave it to me and said to run for Ed Sickles. She said he'd know what to do!" The words came spilling out in one breathless rush.

From the road directly east came quickening hoofbeats of a horse urged to full gallop. The chink and jangle of silver rowels could be heard as horse and rider neared.

"He's come after me! My God! He's come after me!" Before the men could stop her, Laurie ran west along the cleared path of the road. Her shawl slipped from her shoulders as she ran and her skirts whipped against her legs, slowing her. The horse sped closer, its hoofs thundering down the narrow road.

Across the bridge Laurie could see Ed Sickles as he passed the brilliant acetylene lamps where the engineers were working. He looked up as he heard the horse and shouts of the men.

Roy Wimbish lunged at the horse as it passed. He grabbed at the bridle. A whip slashed at his face and he groaned with pain as he fell.

Laurie stumbled on the rough planking, her heel catching in a crevice. She fell in the middle of the bridge, her hand still clutching the white paper. Spurs dug into the horse's sensitive flanks; the whip lashed mercilessly. The horse's hoofs pounded onto the fragile bridge. Unable to wrench her foot free, Laurie screamed.

It was in that instant that the great gray thoroughbred rose on her hind legs, shrilling her anger and fright. For only that bare instant the rider remained in the high-cantled saddle, his face, waxen with sudden fear, illuminated by the glaring work lamps.

In that instant he was alive. In the next, he was dead.

Hoyt Larcher held the bridle and caressed the sweating neck of the magnificent gray mare. Still wild-eyed with fear, she whinnied and jerked at the reins.

"Why'd the damn fool try to take that horse across?" Hiram Perry shook his head as he looked over the rope railing. "Lord knows I tried to stop him. Yelled my head off, but he wasn't going to stop. Kept whipping that horse like the devil himself was after him! Never seen anything like it!"

There was no sign of Archibald Creighton in the torrent below the bridge.

Roy Wimbish knelt beside the girl, his face bleeding where the braided whip had cut across it. A red welt was already swelling above his eye and across the bridge of his nose. Ed Sickles unlaced Laurie's shoe and worked her foot free.

"Is she all right?" Roy wiped the blood from his face on his sleeve.

"Fainted. It's just as well. Let's get her away from here before she comes to." Sickles took the document from her hand.

"What is it?" Roy asked.

"Something about establishing a conservatorship to handle Pansy Hinshaw's property and affairs."

"It ain't signed yet, is it?"

"No." Ed Sickles glanced down at the raging water below them. There was no way in which the man could have survived the fall. "Guess it doesn't have to be signed now." He thrust the paper inside his coat. "Hoyt, you said you were on your way back to town?"

"Sure, Ed. Put her in the back. Wagon's empty—floor's clean. Just throw my coat down for her. It's hanging in the back." The butcher handed the gray mare's bridle to Hiram Perry. "Roy, you'd best come along, too. I'll drive you over to Doc Eichner."

"Don't you let nobody but Bert Hutchins take that horse," Roy said. "Old Mrs. Creighton will likely try to have it killed. I won't stand for it. That's Chace's mare, and I aim to see it stays his. You understand me, Hiram?" Roy took the towel the butcher handed him and wiped the blood from his face and beard.

The old watchman nodded and stroked the horse's white-blazed forehead. "You can just bet I do, Roy! Look, I'm due to go off now anyhow, so why don't I just take her along with me? Send one of the boys to fetch Bert and we can decide what to do with her." He turned to Sickles and asked, "That all right with the law, Ed? I don't want to do nothing contrary to the law, but I sure don't want nothing to happen to Linette here."

"Sure. Go ahead. And don't tell anybody, not even me, where she is or who's got her. That way I don't have to lie about it, do I?" The policeman lifted Laurie and carried her to the delivery wagon. Hiram Perry led the horse into the darkness beyond the bridge.

By now the crew had gathered on the east side of the creek. One of the men stopped Sickles and drew him aside.

"You got one girl there?" he asked.

"Yes—Laurie Mathews. Lives just down the road at the old Hinshaw place. Why?"

"You seen two of 'em out there on that bridge, too?"

"Two?" Sickles did not understand.

"You know damn well what I mean, Chief! We all seen it!"

"I know what you thought you saw." The policeman attempted to sound unconcerned.

"Don't play games with words, Ed!" The man was visibly agitated.

"I've got one girl here. That answers your question," Sickles rationalized.

"You put it that way, and I'd say 'yes,' but you seen the other one! Look at this girl—she's got on a dark skirt—can't tell what color for sure in this light, but it's dark. That other one had on a light colored dress with some fancy stripes up and down it, jagged-like. Gold or yellow it looked! Nothing like what this girl's got on!"

"Some trick of the light. That's all it was," Sickles protested.

"No, sir! That don't wash! Whoever it was, she spooked that horse bad enough to pitch Arch Creighton right over the edge!" He folded his arms and assumed a defiant stance before the chief of police. "She just stood there, calm as could be, and that horse threw a fit!"

"Light does funny things out here. A sudden puff of fog—the lamps—odd effects. Besides, that bridge would spook most horses anyhow. You know that." Sickles did not want the episode to impede progress of the repairs.

"And I know damned well what we seen out there!" He was stubbornly adamant.

Sickles clapped him on the shoulder and laughed. "Well, we all thought we saw something, but we couldn't have, now could we?" He turned to Hoyt Larcher and said, "If you're all set, let's go."

Roy climbed into the seat beside Larcher, holding a

towel to his face, while Sickles crawled into the meat compartment with the unconscious Laurie. The older man gingerly touched the welt over his eye. His sight was unimpaired. He had seen the horse rear and paw at thin air. He had seen Archibald grab for the saddle horn before he was catapulted from the mare's back as she contorted in pain and fright. The silver rowels had flashed in the acetylene glare and were gone.

And he had seen her, too—the second woman on the bridge.

Chapter 16

Mayor Fulbright cleared his throat elaborately for attention. The occasion was not suitable for his gavel. He held one fat finger on hastily-drawn plans which still insisted on curling into a loose roll.

"Gentlemen, I don't believe we have any dissident opinions for once. I move the planning commission adopt the plans immediately and begin necessary legal steps this afternoon." Fulbright's face, normally red, was fiery in the warm committee room. He mopped his forehead and allowed the papers to curl. "All in favor, so state."

A series of 'ayes' circuited the table.

"Motion carried unanimously." He beamed at the easy success. "Fine! Now let's get on with it!" Resuming his seat at the head of the long table, he turned to Chace Creighton. "How long do you think it will take to get this La Gaviota tract in shape?"

"We've already begun logging and clearing. I'd say by the end of this week the surveyors can finish their work, providing the weather holds. With no delays, I think by mid-summer we can have the people moved in and settled."

"Now you've assured us there will be no question as to title on this piece of land. We're taking your word, Chace. It would be a terrible hardship if there'd be a cloud on that title." Knut Jepsen tilted his chair back and teetered against the oak wainscoting behind him.

"Preliminary search finds nothing, but your mother could give the city a lot of trouble if she wants to," Hoyt Larcher said.

"I give you my word, those two bills of sale are legitimate and binding. I bought the north tract from Duncan and Arch two years ago. They liked their gambling too well—you all know that—and needed cash. They couldn't very well go to Father or Mother, not after they'd been warned repeatedly, so they came to me. I bought their thirds free and clear, leaving me sole owner." He was not embarrassed by the revelation, for he had his own reputation and could not alter those of his dead brothers.

"Your proposal's certainly fair to the city. We'd all have to be fools not to take advantage of it, but do you mind telling us, for the record, too, how you came to this decision?" The mayor had to have something ready to quote when he would be questioned by doubting constituents.

"For the record? Yes, I can see why you'd want to know." Chace had to laugh. He knew Fulbright was a man to have all pertinent facts handy. "The people of Sand Town need a place to relocate. My men need building jobs. My company is in the building business.

"As I said in my formal presentation, the north tract is far more suitable as a residential district than Sand Town beach. It won't take much of an extension to run water and gas out there. Phone lines are already installed along Main and Shell Road. If those folks have steady work and decent homes, they can afford utilities, so electricity's sure to follow soon. Might as well run it out there now and wire the houses as they're built.

"That project will demonstrate what this town can do—what our own people can do. If we can show we care about what happens to our own citizens—if we can show sound, logical planning, not just haphazard mushrooming of makeshift shanty-towns, we can publicize Forest Shores, even all of California, in a positive way.

"The disaster will be remembered, but so will be what followed. That's the important thing. In no way could anyone regard the flood as beneficial, but we must use it for whatever good can come of it."

330

The men were silent, each remembering the solemn procession which escorted Kevin Purdy to San Esteban Cemetery and the gentle mourning of Henry Chew and his motherless son. Old Emilio Fabiano, who lived on Fish Row and packed fish for a living, had never been found. The mayor's own home at the foot of Ilex Street was severely damaged and his sloop demolished, but it was an inconvenience, not the heartbreak of the dwellers of Sand Town.

Atop City Hall the town clock struck twelve noon. There would be plenty of time to get the plans officially implemented before day was done. The aldermen filed from the meeting room, convinced that for once they had rendered a decision on an important matter, one that would improve the lot of their stricken neighbors and benefit the entire community. Chace Creighton walked across the square with Knut Jepsen.

"Come on in and I'll treat you to lunch." Knut was proud of his new fountain and the food it served. "Irma made baked beans and ham for today's special." They waited for a buckboard to pass, then crossed to the pharmacy.

"I'd take you up on that, but I left my buggy in front of Laurie's shop. I'm driving her out to look over the tract this afternoon and I promised her and Pansy Hinshaw I'd have lunch with them. Thanks anyway." Chace tipped his hat as several ladies entered the store. He extended his hand to the druggist. "And thanks for backing me, Knut."

They clasped hands as if brothers in conspiracy. "Just remember, if Hank Fulbright doesn't run for re-election next term, you've got another job if you want it."

"I'll remember that if I go broke on the north tract!"

Since there were no east-west alleys in the downtown district, Chace had to walk to Glasgow Avenue, then up Birch Street to the Ribands and Roses. Noon sunshine warmed the bright side of the street, but where shadow crept into doorways there was a crispness

331

in the air that urged one to move quickly. There had been no rain since the big storm and already dust was annoying fastidious housekeepers. In the weeks following the catastrophe, brilliant clear weather had set in, with balmy days and still, frosty nights. The air, no longer burdened with the stench of rotting seaweed, once more became fragrant with pine.

Inside the Ribands and Roses, Etta Korby lowered the green blinds which shaded the window display and hooked them into their grooves below the glass. She smiled as she saw Chace crossing the street from Glasgow Avenue.

"Here he comes, Laurie, right on the dot." She opened the door for him, setting the harness bells affixed to it jangling. "You're very punctual, Chace."

"Hello, Etta." He took off his hat as he entered and caught her staring at the back of his head. He squinted into the triple mirror at the hat counter so he could view it himself. "Looks pretty moth-eaten, doesn't it?" He fingered the shaved spot and grinned. "Got a transformation you can sell me?"

"Might be able to fix you up with a nice pompadour. You could wear it backwards." Etta was dwarfed by the man as she came to stand at his elbow. "But you know how Laurie feels about such things—I wouldn't wear one if I were you." She studied his head seriously, then said, "Maybe a size fifteen gentleman's hat would do it—one you could pull down over your ears. . ."

"Got one in stock?"

"Look, we've got enough trouble with *women's* hats, let alone men's!" She saw him eyeing a large bouquet of hot-house chrysanthemums and yellow roses which was displayed at the far end of the counter. "Aren't they beautiful? They came this morning."

At his raised eyebrows and questioning glance, she continued, "Don't worry! They're from Mr. and Mrs. Aaron Meister, the wholesaler in San Francisco. Laurie sent him a draft for our account in full last week; he sent these and a handwritten note from his wife wishing us

332

ack. Thoughtful, eh?"

"Yes, indeed." He took the note Etta handed him
and read it slowly. The writing was difficult to decipher
with its awkwardly formed letters, obviously not native
to the writer. "Business has been that good?"

"Heavens, yes! I think a lot of ladies had to come
to the shop just to see what Laurie looks like. You know
how things get spread around by word of mouth.
Everyone in town knew about her riding up to get you
the day of the storm, and how she and Olive stayed
down there in Sand Town. Well, they wanted to see
her."

She added with a broad smile, "And they spend a
lot of money." The seamstress followed his glance and
said, "I'll go see what's keeping Laurie. Excuse
me. . ." She went to the back of the shop and hurried
the girl. Laurie tied the wide ribbons of her new hat
beneath her chin and checked the effect in the mirror.

"Does it look all right?" She smoothed her tight
bodice and rearranged her short, braid-trimmed gold
jacket.

"You look beautiful. Now go out there and show
him." Etta pushed the girl out the workroom door and
down the hall. Chace turned and looked at her, his eyes
softening as they met hers. The deep-teal and turquoise
hat framed her face, enhancing her pale skin.

"Goodbye, you two! Have a lovely afternoon."
Etta watched a bit enviously as Chace bent to kiss
Laurie before ushering her out into the noon sunshine.
Across the street Emmet Lauder, tape measure about
his neck and needles in his vest, looked up from his
tailoring and waved as the young couple climbed into
the open phaeton and headed toward Main.

As Etta turned to unpack a new shipment of
summer-weight corsets her eyes were drawn to the
street. A black carriage, its storm curtains snapped in
place effectively concealing the driver within, slowly
crossed Glasgow Avenue and continued down Birch,
keeping well behind Chace's phaeton. It was not too
unusual for a closed carriage to be seen on the streets of

333

Forest Shores, but Etta could not help noticing as it passed that its dash held an expensive cast-brass whip socket and ivory handled whip.

Luncheon was served in the bay window, with Hallie Mae attired in a new black sateen dress, white ruffled pinafore and lace-adorned cap. Pansy had patiently instructed the girl on proper table setting and arrangement of the heavy silverware. The starched linen tablecloth was embroidered with pale blue forget-me-nots to match the delicate Staffordshire porcelain. Roy had contributed a bouquet of yellow calendulas and fragrant cinerarias in hues of blue and purple which Pansy arranged in her finest crystal bowl.

"I should really resent you young men." Pansy poured coffee from the tall silver pot.

"How is that?" Chace held his cup for her to refill.

"You're taking away two of my ladies, and almost at the same time. Ed and Olive have decided on the first week of July. He doesn't want to wait till then, but Olive insists she needs extra time to get everything ready."

"I heard they bought the MacLeod place on Edinburgh Avenue. That's one your husband built, isn't it?" Chace asked.

"Yes, back in '72, I believe it was. The MacLeods had just come over from Scotland that spring. It's been such a happy house, too." She explained to Laurie, "They raised their five children there—red-headed, every one of them, like their father. There was always something going on at their house. The Chautauqua group met there until the hall was built, and the Hook and Needle Club. Then Mrs. MacLeod started the Saturday Music School, too." The elderly woman smiled as she recalled earlier days.

"Why did they sell?" Laurie could not imagine selling a home where one had been so content.

"My goodness, it's much too big for them now! All the children are married and gone, and besides, she's teaching music full time since the school's expanded.

And Mr. MacLeod took on the new agency for those automobiles—Columbias, they're called.''

"Automobiles? I shouldn't think there'd be much of a market for them here.'' Laurie was not impressed with motorcars, not when exquisite horses were available.

"It's a sound business to get into. One of these days we'll see twice as many automobiles as buggies and wagons.'' Chace had seen both the electric and gasoline Columbias in MacLeod's showrooms and had been intrigued with their ingenious mechanical design. "Soon we'll have good enough roads along the coast here to accomodate them.''

"I do hope they're just a fad that will pass. Imagine all those horrid noisy things racing about the streets!'' Pansy rang a tiny crystal bell to summon Hallie Mae. "You may serve dessert now, so these young things can get on their way,'' she said.

"Yes, ma'am,'' the girl said as she came into the room. She turned to Laurie and handed her a small teak and ebony trinket box. "Roy asked me to give this to you. He says the glue's dry and set now. Can't even see where it was mended.'' It was the Christmas gift Chace had given Laurie. Pansy Hinshaw supressed a smile as she watched Laurie's face; she had known there would be a proper time to return it to Laurie, but it took Roy Wimbish to recognize the moment.

"Thank you, Hallie Mae,'' Laurie said in surprise. She exchanged looks with Pansy, who nodded her head just enough to let her know it would remain their secret that it had been retrieved from the trash. Pansy beamed as the girl examined the delicately wrought container. "Oh yes, he did a beautiful job on it!'' Her delight was apparent. "I must thank him, too.''

Pansy, to avoid further explanation, spoke up, "Chace, Thea Harris tells me you're going to speak to the owner of the Daily Dispatch over in San Esteban. . .something about Lucia Orozco getting her job back as manager again.''

"Yes, I'm going over there on business—some of

Arch's business, really. Seems Sherman Talley, the owner, had helped Ralph Donner in the Aguilar Valley development. When Arch went in as partner, Talley felt obliged to do Arch a favor, so he did, and let Miss Orozco go for some darned fool reason or other. I aim to get that straightened out right away."

"I must say the paper isn't what it used to be. Why, do you know they even dropped the ladies' page entirely?" Pansy was full of indignation. "You can just tell that Mr. Talley for me that the sooner he gets Lucia back, the better his paper will be."

Chace laughed at her anger. "I'll do that, Mrs. Hinshaw, but I don't think it will take much persuasion, from what I hear."

"Good! That makes me feel much better." Pansy settled back in her chair and watched as the young maid cleared the table, each move slow and deliberate as she removed the china and silver, the few remaining household items of real value which Pansy kept for guests, and treasured from sentiment. "That's fine, Hallie Mae; that was just right." The girl beamed at her praise. She was grateful to be learning under such gentle tutelage. Living in the Hinshaw home was far preferable to a canvas tent on the side of the Calabasas Hills.

Dessert, an ornate molded orange bavarian and sesame seed wafers, finished the meal. Pansy was elated as Chace devoured the rich gelatine just as he had when a small child. This afternoon she was sure she would need no sauterne to see her through the day. The glow of Chace and Laurie's happiness warmed her more than any wine. After they had gone, she remained at the window with her cut-glass bowl of flowers and porcelain demi-tasse of cold coffee, daydreaming of her own youth when she and Adam had planned their future together.

When Hallie Mae found her dozing, she tiptoed from the room and cleaned up the white-tiled kitchen. In her young wisdom she cranked up the cooler cage and placed a fresh bottle of sauterne behind the pail of milk.

Chace turned left where Beach Park Lane met West Main Avenue. Debris still littered the roadway and ugly smears of raw earth scarred the landscape farther down toward the creek.

"We'll put the Lane through the south side. That will be the through street. The others will be at right angles to it." Chace halted the little sorrel mare as a team of mules pulled out from the forested area with a load of firewood split from unusable splintered limbs. "This tract is high enough to be out of any flood danger. Even the bore didn't reach up here."

The new road was rough and full of holes which needed constant filling. On each side, timber had been felled to make way for housing. Heavy draft animals dragged stripped logs from the site to the lumber mill at the end of Shell Road. Dozens of men were busy with the project, and the entire area was loud with the sound of saw and ax.

The light buggy bumped over the rutted road as Chace showed Laurie their progress. She admired the way he spoke with his crews and the easy camaraderie between them. A spirit of optimism was evident in their speech and the way they eagerly cleared land and laid out rudimentary streets. Already the section had a look of potential homesites instead of dense wilderness.

Laurie recognized the faces of many workers as men from Sand Town. Their greetings were warm with friendliness born of their shared experience.

"I think half the men here are in love with you, Laurie!" Chace had not failed to notice their expressions as the girl acknowledged them. "I should be jealous."

"Are you? You shouldn't be." Her jet eyes told him it was so. "You'll never have reason to be, darling." Her hand was light on his arm. Chace let Tilda find her own way up the narrow path while he took the girl in his arms and kissed her.

"Why do we have to wait?" Her nearness brought the desire to possess her, a desire that was impossible to

337

subdue. "We could go over to San Esteban. . ."

"No, we can't begin that way. And you know why, Chace." She glanced south to where the Creighton mansion crowned a foothill that overlooked the tract. "We must give her time to accept our marriage—she's your mother. She'll be the grandmother of our children. She's suffered a terrible loss—Duncan, your father, and Archibald. You admit that she somehow blames me for those tragedies. I don't want to start out with hatred between her and us. We must give her more time."

He turned the horse and started along an older trail which skirted the base of the rise. Meadowland spread in an undulating ribbon parallel to the road, then diverse chaparral began once more.

"Where are we going?" She could see they were leaving the tract acres and heading into the sun. "We're going south, aren't we?" She was content to let him take her anywhere so long as she could be beside him. She shifted her parasol to shade her face.

"This is an old logging road that leads down to Mariposa Beach. I've had the men repair the bridge over La Gaviota Creek and fix the road bed. When the tract is finished this will be the easiest way to Mariposa Beach. The planning commission took a look at engineers' reports on extending Main that far, but it's too costly to go over those hills. They figure as I do that this is the best way. I plan to deed right of way to the city, then eventually we can incorporate the beach area into the city, just like Sand Town."

"You're really enthusiastic about the development of Forest Shores, aren't you?" Laurie asked.

"Not only Forest Shores, but all California—the entire West Coast," Chace replied. "This is where the population will come, and we must prepare for it."

"Has your mother said anything more about your plans for the hospital and sanatorium?" Laurie was worried. Sybil Creighton might still try to ruin his projects.

"Not a word since Arch died." He frowned as he said it. "Everything seems to be going smoothly.

338

Sacramento's moving right ahead, and over in San Esteban there's been no hitch in the allocations." He was obviously puzzled. "Maybe with all that's happened in the past few months. . ." He reached over and took her hand in his.

"No, darling, it *won't* be all right. I know that's what you wanted to say, but you know it would be a useless hope." She turned to him, wondering how she could tell him why Sybil Creighton did not want her as a daughter-in-law. She opened her lips to speak, but could phrase no words to explain. It would sound too fantastic, too ludicrous, even to Chace who loved her. He would think her mad.

Ahead of them a herd of deer broke from brush and dashed across the grassland toward the creek bluff. La Gaviota no longer roared, but tumbled placidly full along its watercourse. Does and fawns sped down the steep banks while several bucks stood sentry at the head of the twisting trail.

"They're so lovely! Oh, look at the little ones!" She was delighted with the sight and leaned forward in her excitement. "It's such a pity we frightened them." She tilted her parasol again as the buggy began to descend toward the beach. The road had been shored up, ruts graded and smoothed. There were few signs of it having been used. Hoof marks pocked the dust and hardened mud, but most were deer.

Below spread forest and salt marshes, clusters of rustic cabins and barns of weathered, silver-gray logs and siding. Wisps of smoke drifted through the pines to show where dwellings were hidden at the edge of the trees.

As they dropped to a ledge above a wide stretch of the Mariposa River, Laurie was suddenly seized by a sense of dread and foreboding. Sunlight was dazzling, air pure and clear; nowhere from horizon to horizon was there a cloud to mar the expanse of deep blue sky. No fog bank hid the distant purple arc of low mountains on the opposite side of Gutierrez Bay. Yet in the splendor of that magnificent coastline Laurie felt something ominous, dangerous. She shuddered.

"Cold, sweetheart?" Chace reached behind the seat and drew out a plaid woolen lap rug and placed it about her. "Better?"

"Yes, thank you," she said. She tucked the robe close, but the chill remained. As the little mare led the carriage around an outcropping of bald granite, Laurie caught her breath.

In her mind she could once again see the sketches from Mellona's trunk—river, dunes, chaparral-dotted bank, even the rocks were duplicates of those in the drawings. She grasped the parasol handle until her hand grew pained. As if in some awful dream from which she could not waken, she was drawn relentlessly downward, along the level, sandy river bank.

"The water came right up through here." Chace pointed to a rim of debris which had been pushed high up the steep bluffs which constituted the river's original banks. "Couldn't do much damage here. Not like at Sand Town. There's just flat, open beachland along this stretch. You can see where the river used to be. It's cut across this way several hundred yards, made an entirely new channel."

The Mariposa River, like a fickle woman, had changed its course, abandoning its old haunts and exploring new territory. It snaked through shifting sand dunes and gaunt heaps of eroded rock. Chace urged Tilda down a slight incline and onto the beach.

Sand was firm and hard beneath the horse's small hoofs. She fairly danced with delight on the pleasant footing, her head high and nostrils dilated to take in the air that smelled of both open sea and land. Water had sliced sharp ridges on the banks, as if it had been a knife making clean cuts and shaving away the sand to redeposit it far upstream. Gulls and waterfowl flapped away at their advance, then settled back to feeding and gabbling.

To the left ahead of them rose one singularly shaped dune surmounted by a gnarled, twisted tree trunk of enormous size. Toppled decades before, it had the gray-white patina of long exposure to salt air and sun.

Laurie felt as if she were going to faint. The feeling of abject horror gripped her, blanching her face and stifling her breath. She wanted to leap from the buggy and run to the spot, to dig with her hands in the warm sand beneath those grotesque roots. Instead, she clung to the arm rest and closed her eyes, praying that Chace would not notice. She turned her head from him and repositioned her ruffled parasol.

"I must remember the way here," she told herself. "I have to memorize each sign that will help me find the tree again." She forced herself to open her eyes and focus on every shrub, every rock, every dune along the way.

Even as the horse turned the next bend and began the climb toward the cluster of cabins at the beach colony, she knew she must return.

Sunday dawned warm and bright. By church time the temperature had risen to almost seventy. When the carillon atop the new Presbyterian church began *"Now Come Ye Faithful to the Fold"* at the end of the services, the thermometer nailed to the front of Sewel's Hardware and Ranch Supply registered seventy-four degrees. Instead of strolling directly home to dinners of pot-roast and browned potatoes, many families stopped by the White Front Cafe opposite City Hall for ice cream cones and a walk along the beach.

"We always have a heat spell this time of year. Never seen it fail." Roy Wimbish opened the north windows for Pansy Hinshaw and put a rubber wedge under the front door to keep it ajar. "That'll give you some cross ventilation. I put beeswax on them windows so Hallie Mae can get 'em up and down easier. Don't you try to fool around with 'em. Let her do it." Roy found he needed to bully Pansy a bit or she would tax her strength doing what might more easily be done by someone else.

"Yes, Roy, I'll have her lower them for me." She

knew that was what he wanted her to say. While the warmth felt good to her, she found the slight draft through the house refreshing. "That does help a lot with the door open."

She took off her Sunday bonnet and velvet cloak and placed them on the hall tree inside the front door. Olive had promised to go with her to an organ concert at the Baptist church at three o'clock. At the sound of footsteps coming downstairs she retreated to the parlor, unwilling for her tenants to think she was overly interested in their coming and going.

"Roy, do you think Bert Hutchins would rent me one of his Walkers this afternoon?" Laurie Mathews was attired in full skirt of black woolen canvascloth and a gold, high-necked linen blouse caught at the throat with a small brooch of golden topaz. Over her arm she carried a light-weight black shawl, a wrap appropriate for the unseasonable day. "Would he let me have Dora or Sally if I asked him?"

"I'll sure be glad to go along and find out. I reckon he'd do it for you anyhow, but I'll just make sure." He turned to Pansy in the front parlor. "If there's nothing else, Mrs. Hinshaw. . ."

"No, Roy, you run along with Laurie," the old woman answered.

"How are you, Mrs. Hinshaw?" Laurie stuck her head around the door and smiled. "It's such a lovely day I thought I'd go riding."

"I thought Chace was taking you to dinner." It was almost a question from Pansy.

"He is, but that's not for hours yet. I don't want to waste such a wonderful, warm afternoon by sitting in my room. Just wait till I write my friends in Chicago! A heat spell at this time of year!" Laurie tried to sound plausible in her reason for such an excursion.

"That's a lovely idea. Have a good time, dear," Pansy said. "If you see Mrs. Purdy, be sure to give her my best regards and tell her Hallie Mae's doing just fine. And tell her she's welcome to come see her any time she wants to. I'm afraid she feels it improper for

342

her to stop by."

"I'll tell her. I'll make it a special point to go see her." Laurie waited while Roy changed his shoes in the summer kitchen, then joined him as he crossed the lawn.

"You intending to ride all alone, Miss Laurie?" Roy sounded worried.

"Of course!" the girl replied. "You've said yourself Bert's Tennessee Walkers know every trail around here. If I get turned around, I'll just give the horse her head and let her take me back to the stables." Laurie corrected herself. "To what will be the stables when they get them finished. . ."

"Yeah, they're coming along pretty good now," Roy said. "Bert was hard put to it when it come to getting enough money to rebuild, but he's got friends all around. Guess they figure he's good for the loans." Roy took a dark blue handkerchief from his hip pocket and wiped his forehead and the leather band inside his hat. "Mighty warm day!"

He said nothing more about her riding alone, not even when Bert Hutchins helped the girl into the saddle, but his face furrowed with concern as the large horse struck her customary easy gait and disappeared into the brush.

Blooming amid grass which lined the trail, cream-cups poked yellow petals above the green. Orange poppies brightened unlikely places, their gaudy flowers proof of their tenacity as they clung precariously from steep cliffsides. Yellow tree lupine and red figwort already scented the air with blooms, while on the lower slopes checker-bloom dotted the soft green with its red and pink. Coaxed from hives by the early inflorescence, bees were busy, their hum everywhere along the trail.

To Laurie it seemed a nightmare. To be going on such a mission on a day bright with sun and gay with wildflowers seemed bizarre. After paying a quick visit to Bridget Purdy and her children in their flapping canvas tent, she took the ridge trail leading south. At the summit another trail joined at an angle and led almost due west down the opposite slope to Mariposa Beach. There she paused and listened. She was beset with the uneasy feeling that she was being followed.

As she came out of dense pine into broken scrub which spread down to the dunes, she could distinguish yet another trail which skirted behind the Mariposa Beach colony and led south to the river bank. Although on the cove side of the summit she had heard both horses and riders, on this side there seemed to be no one on the trails, either afoot or riding. It must have been her imagination, she thought.

Lizards stimulated to action by the warmth scuttled across the path and rustled into the weeds or sunned themselves on rocks, their drab coloration effectively disguising them until they moved. Black and orange monarch butterflies flitted from blossom to blossom like fragile, animated flowers. From the summit trail Laurie could see not even a wisp of smoke betraying the presence of humankind along the beach or river bank below.

Laurie let the horse amble at its own speed down toward the river, only nudging it to continue along the chosen path where others intersected. It was an easy, comfortable ride, and since she did not want to go to the colony itself, there was no difficult, steep descent until she reached the bluffs directly above the river. She had no trouble recognizing the exact spot where Chace had brought her in the carriage earlier. The tall granite thumb that protruded like part of a hand above horizonatal finger-like slabs, a series of ancient tree stumps and smoothly worn limbs bleached like so many gigantic bones, all pointed the way to 'La Barranca.'

Suddenly she was aware of a chill due not to the beach temperature, but to the same sense of foreboding and dread she had experienced in the buggy with Chace. She pulled the reins and halted the horse without a spoken word to break the silence. Sand whispered down the lee sides of dunes, and dried weeds rattled their dead stalks as if in warning.

Only isolated patches of beach grass gave the desolate spot any hint of life. Trees, rocks, even the moving sand seemed to belong to some dead and distant time.

Dora nickered, shook her head, and thrashed her tail impatiently at stinging flies that rose from damp smudges in the sand. Laurie urged the horse on a few more yards. At the sight of the grotesque ruined tree trunk she caught her breath.

Dismounting quickly, she tied the reins to one of the whitened roots which stretched heavenward as if in supplication. From below, the gaunt trunk stood like an eerie monument against the deep blue sky.

She listened. There was no sound but distant gull cries and the soft breeze sighing among the dead remnants of tree and weed. Cold dread gripped her, but she knew she must stay. From her skirt pocket she took the small oval spectacles and held them in her hand.

"You're here, Mellona," Laurie said. "I know you're here. I can feel you near!" It was the exact spot in the last drawing. She knew if anyone were near they would think her insane to speak aloud to no one.

She fitted the dainty gold bows over her ears and settled the lenses to her eyes. Slowly she walked to a slight rise and began turning about. Everything was out of focus. Dunes, distant forest, the summit high above the beach, the pile of rock at the mouth of the river where it joined the sea—all were indistinct fuzzy shapes and outlines.

"Help me, Mellona!" Laurie thought for a moment she heard a noise in the dried grass on the bank above, but when it did not repeat itself, she put it down to dread expectancy.

As she turned once more, she gasped. The spot immediately below the blasted stump came into clear focus. Even though within the sheltered spot the sun beat down with desert-like intensity, Laurie shivered. Roots so contorted and intertwined as to look like something from a lunatic fantasy still fastened the tree in place, but it was obvious the flood had shifted it considerably. The girl approached the spot, inching nearer step by step, following the clarity shown through the spectacles.

She circled to the left where the water had cut a sharp smooth edge into the bank. With a cry she pulled off the glasses and thrust them back into her pocket. As her hands tore at the warm sand she knew what would be there. Even as she touched it, she smothered a scream.

Smooth and white, bleached by three decades, the skull tumbled down the sand to rest at her feet. Laurie backed away, wanting to run, unable to make her body obey. Horror swept through her as the tide had swept through the riverbed. Covering her eyes with her hands, she swayed, wanting to faint and yet knowing she dare not. The feeling of danger increased, closing about her like an icy hand.

Summoning all her courage, she turned to the bank once more, scraping away more sand to expose several small, smooth white bones. She tore at the matted root of a bindweed which had prevented the water from completely washing away the grave. As she pulled at the roots, a glittering object separated from the sand and slid down the embankment.

Laurie stooped to pick it up. Gold wings flashed in the sun, gemstones, dulled by repeated immersions in sand and water, still glowed tawny amber. She rubbed the sand and root fibers off on her skirt and inspected the necklace. It seemed so familiar.

"The earring!" She looked closely at the delicate design. "It matches the earring!"

Dora pawed the sand and jerked at the reins, nickering. The horse pricked her ears toward the girl and with her eyes followed a shadow on the bank above.

"We'll go now, Dora." Laurie glanced at the exposed bones, tears welling in her eyes. "We've found what we came for."

In that split second in which she turned to leave, the tree trunk tottered and crashed to the sand below the bank. Laurie threw herself aside and ran as instinct whipped her to action. She heard the pounding of feet in the sand behind her and the snapping of dried twigs and

346

grass as she ran into the scrub.

Wildly, blindly, she dashed up the slope. Only when she paused to ease her bursting lungs did she realize her mistake. She was not running toward the cabins, but north and away from them! There were no dwellings in that direction, only the steep bluff which dropped precipitously to the shore below. She had trapped herself!

She listened intently, not daring to breathe. In the brush fifty yards away someone moved furtively. She must work her way south and try to reach the horse, or at least the beach where she could run freely along the firm sand. It was imperative she get to the cabins.

Cautiously she pulled her skirts tightly to her and sidled between tall clumps of lupine, ducking low as she crossed a break in their height. She trod the gravelly ground carefully, placing her feet so there would be no telltale noise. Behind her she could hear her pursuer smashing through the brush on the slope. If only she could gain the path along the bluff before her ruse was discovered!

Ahead to the right she could see the dropoff where the narrow road made its way to the beach via a series of switchbacks which had been put in repair and shored up by the Creighton crews. Laurie crouched low and ran as best she could, dropping to the ground at each small noise, waiting to hear if she were followed.

She waited. Not a sound of pursuit. The girl lifted her skirts and petticoats and ran, flying over the rough ground, her feet crunching on the rocky surface. Behind her, she could hear her pursuer in the brush making no attempt at stealth. Down the road she sprinted.

Emerging from the rocks at the cliff, but remaining in deep shadow, a figure moved to the edge of the pathway. Blinded by the brilliant sunlight, the girl could not identify who it was, but ran almost unseeing toward the shadow.

"Help me! Please help me!" she called as she neared. "Back there. . .back there. . ." She turned as she slowed and pointed up the slope.

To her horror she saw the great Tennessee Walke[r] cross from the scrub to the road, its reins dragging as i[t] wandered noisily through the brush after her.

Instantly she realized she had fled into the ver[y] arms of her pursuer. As her momentum carried he[r] within reaching distance, she saw two arms go up. Eve[n] in the dense shadow she could see the jagged boulder a[s] it poised over her head.

There was no time to scream. No time to think. She threw herself to one side and fell headlong down th[e] steep road.

The explosion she heard—had she just imagined it[?] She crawled to her feet, steadying herself on the grass[-] grown cliffside. Her hands were scraped and bleeding but she was too numb to feel them. There were sound[s] around her as she staggered down the road. Somehow she must reach the safety of the beach.

"Darling!" The voice was familiar, but echoe[d] strangely in her mind. She stumbled on down the road. "Laurie! Stop!" The voice commanded. She halted and waited, stunned and confused. Footsteps ran down the path toward her. Suddenly she was swept off her fee[t] and held close in strong arms.

"Thank God you're all right!" Lips warm and sweet pressed hers. The head that bent to hers blocked sight of Chace's rifle propped against the rock wall and the man who lay sprawled in the road. A red spot grew larger on the fallen man's plaid shirt.

"Chace! Oh, Chace!" She buried her face in his shoulder. "It was horrible!"

"I know, sweetheart; I know." He carried her around the rocks and lowered her into a sandy spot.

"Is she all right?" Roy Wimbish, his deer rifle still in his hands, stood anxiously beside the girl.

"Yes, she's shaken up, but she'll be fine." Chace pulled a handkerchief from his trouser pocket and tore it in half, then wrapped her hands as best he could. "That'll have to do till we can get you over to Morgan's place."

"I don't understand. Where did you come from?"

She looked at the two in bewilderment.

"We followed you. We knew you eventually would do something to make him come after you. Only we weren't sure who it was." Chace pushed back the black hair that fell across her forehead and tilted her chin with his finger. "We never thought it would come to this, believe me." He kissed her again, softly, gently. "Roy and Pansy love you, too, darling. They told me all about your mysterious Mellona Jolais. They've been terribly frightened for you all this time." Chace saw the look on her face. "But it's all over now."

They looked up as a horse and rider approached from the beach. Ed Sickles swung down from the saddle, paused to look at the man in the road, then came to the others.

"Guess I got here too late. Took longer by this route than we figured. You all right, Miss Mathews?"

"Yes, I guess so. But I don't understand any of this." She leaned against Chace, content to let him hold her. "Who. . .who. . .was it?"

Ed Sickles looked astonished. "You didn't know?"

"No!"

"It was Bert Hutchins!"

Chapter 17

Morgan Griffith poured brandy into the delicate Florentine glass goblet and handed it to Laurie. "I insist, gentlemen, this young lady stay here the night. There are several nice girls who can come stay with her so her honor will in no way be compromised." He bowed stiffly toward Chace. "She's in no condition to either ride back or go by buggy."

"Might be a good idea at that, Miss Laurie." Roy Wimbish accepted a shot glass of rye whiskey and without waiting for the others, downed it at a gulp.

"I think you should, Laurie." Chace cradled his rifle, ejected the spent cartridge and replaced the live shells in a leather bandolier. The girl winced as she saw the heavy rifles. Chace caught her look. "I'm sorry. That was completely thoughtless of me." He carried the rifles into the hall and left them by the front door.

"If you're sure it won't be too much trouble, I'd like to stay. I'm still shaking," Laurie said.

"It's all set, then." Griffith's dark face broke into a smile. "I shall be delighted to have you." He sat down opposite the girl, his back against a brilliant green cushion the color of the Florentine glass.

"I'm so confused—you must tell me how this all came about. Why did Bert Hutchins want to harm me?" Laurie asked. "He's always been so kind and considerate before. Why should he want to kill me?"

"You'd discovered where Mellona's body had been hidden all these years," Griffith replied. "He didn't want anyone to find it—ever. The grave had been exposed by flood water, but the chances of anybody finding it were slim. He undoubtedly heard the story about the other woman on the bridge and by some warped logic considered you a danger to him." Griffith rose to refill the men's glasses and brought the crystal decanter with him. It was an event that required more than one drink.

"What story?" Laurie asked.

"The night of Archibald's. . .accident," Griffith answered.

"I still don't know what you're talking about," the girl persisted.

Ed Sickles shifted uncomfortably on the long sofa, his legs stretched before him on the brightly-colored Navajo blanket-rug. He could not admit what he had seen with his own eyes, but could not avoid the tale forever.

"Everybody out there that night seen her, Miss Laurie. I don't understand why you didn't, too," Roy ventured.

"She fainted dead away, that's why," Ed Sickles reminded Roy.

"But what should I have seen?" Laurie was growing impatient.

"When Arch come onto the bridge after you, Linette didn't throw him just for meanness, though God knows she had reason enough to, what with him using his spurs and whip." Unconsciously Roy fingered the tender spot on the bridge of his nose where the whip had struck him. He held his glass for Griffith to refill. "Just a tot, thanks," he said.

To Laurie he continued, "We all seen her. You'd caught your foot and fell right in the middle of the bridge. Old Arch, he come roaring along and there she stood, between you and the horse! Standing just as calm like she was daring him to come closer. Linette must

351

have seen her, too, 'cause she reared up and sunfished like an unbroke colt.'' He drained his whiskey and put the glass on the rough redwood table beside him.

"Who? Saw who?" Laurie asked again.

"Why, Mellona Jolais, of course!" Roy leaned his elbows on his knees and clasped his gnarled fists. Sickles frowned and shook his head. "Now Ed, you seen her yourself! I know damn well you did. I seen your face!" Roy said.

"If I admitted that. . ." the chief of police began.

"You'd lose credibility with some people who don't hold with such things!" Griffith interjected. Seeing ghosts might be amusing conversation in the parlor, but for the chief of police to indulge in such talk would be disastrous to his reputation as a logical, hard-headed lawman. The Welshman was aware of Sickles reasoning.

"What I saw was some trick of the light. The acetylene lamps shining on moving fog. . ." Sickles tried to rationalize.

"Weren't no such thing and you damn well know it!" Roy insisted.

"Ghosts? I don't believe in 'em!" The policeman laughed.

Laurie got up and walked to the wide window at the end of the room. Deer were feeding placidly at the extremity of the cleared space beyond the house. A doe glanced up nervously, then lowered her head to the thick grass. The men watched Laurie as she placed the Florentine goblet on the sill and stood gazing out the window.

"What's wrong, darling?" Chace came over to her and took her hand in his.

"I've seen her." Laurie turned to confront the men.

"Who? The woman?" Chace asked.

"Yes." She addressed Ed Sickles, "You may not wish to admit seeing her, just as Roy says, but I've seen her many times. I thought at first I was becoming psychotic and I told myself the same thing you

352

have—that it was only a trick of the light." She shook her head. "It wasn't, I assure you. It was Madame Jolais!"

The girl went to the sofa and sat beside Sickles, her jet eyes daring him to contradict her. "Mellona Jolais led me to the beach today. She wanted me to find her grave. I promised her I would. Roy knows what I'm talking about, don't you Roy?"

"Yes ma'am, Miss Laurie. I do." Roy passed a rough hand over his face.

"You see, Mr. Sickles, I look enough like Mellona Jolais to cause Chace's father to have a stroke. I was sure Zedekiah Creighton had been her lover—that would have accounted for the terrible shock when he saw me the first time at the Lodge. Pansy and Roy saw it right away, just as Mr. Creighton did. I can't say for certain, but I believe Mrs. Creighton did, too. I think that's why she disapproves of me, although I'm only surmising.

"When I was on the train coming here from San Esteban I saw Mellona in the train window. Then I saw her in the wardrobe mirror in my room, the very room she lived in over thirty years ago! These. . .these. . ." She took the spectacles from her pocket and showed them to him. "I won't expect you to believe me. I wouldn't believe it if someone told it to me. I've seen her eyes in these glasses—her eyes looking back at mine!"

The man took the glasses from her outstretched hand and peered through them as if he expected to see what she had seen.

"No, you won't see her. Until you told me just now about the woman on the bridge, I thought I was the only one who could see her. I'm glad I'm not. At first I thought I was losing my mind; you see, I'd lost my fiance in the war, and I'd been in poor health. Then I learned what had happened to Mellona." She pleaded with her eyes and Roy took up the narrative.

"Somebody killed Mellona and hid her body. We

all figured the Creightons hushed it up." He looked apologetically at Chace, who waved his hand in a gesture to continue. "I always thought Sybil got dressed up like Mellona and hired that old Italian to row her out to the ship, then went on to San Francisco and disappeared. I guess I was wrong about that."

The handyman shook his head in disbelief and went on, "I never for a minute thought Bert was the one we was looking for! He'd been off buying horses and didn't get invited to the beach party. Mellona didn't know he was back from Santa Barbara—that's where he'd been. We found out the next day. . .why, he even helped us hunt for her. . .And he was my best friend all these years. . ." He could not go on.

"No one could prove anything, so by and by it was forgotten." Morgan Griffith resumed the narrative and poured himself another shot of whiskey, but held his glass in his hand, untasted. "Forgotten by everyone—but us." His face was set rigidly as he said, "I always felt Mellona's lover was Zedekiah. They were very discreet about it. She was pregnant, but that's all I knew for sure. She was happy about the baby. It didn't matter to her if she were married to the man or not. Just having a child by him, something conceived in love and to be cherished for a lifetime—that was enough for her.

"You'll pardon my speaking so frankly about your parents, Chace, but we're getting at the truth after all these years, so it must be said. Sybil Creighton was so furiously jealous of Zedekiah it was her all-consuming passion. She was sadly lacking in passion as it pertained to her marriage bed, however, and allowed her husband his conjugal rights as seldom as possible. This was common gossip. The Irish girls who worked in the house delighted in revealing such things—probably their way of getting even with Sybil for her abominable treatment of them. And too, they didn't mind accomodating Zedekiah.

"Mellona was not the sort a man would have to force if she were in love with him. If Zedekiah were her lover, he must have found a great deal of happiness in her arms." Griffith drank his whiskey, but held his small glass in his long thin fingers, rolling it about to catch and refract the light that poured through the west window from a lowering sun.

"The day Mellona disappeared, she had dressed up in her best gown, a spectacular creation of gold silk with chevrons of dark velvet about the skirt. She'd had it made in Paris just before we made the move here. She looked lovely in it. Mellona said she was receiving a visitor and wanted to look her finest. It was not a morning dress, but that was of little import to her. She was so beautiful it made no difference. I had the idea she was going to tell her lover about the child, but neither of us referred to it directly.

"He didn't come at the appointed time and she was terribly upset. When the carrier rode out with our mail, Mellona was careful to keep aside a letter with no return address showing on the envelope. I could see she knew who it was from—probably recognized the handwriting. When she had a moment alone she tore it open and read it, then dropped it into the fireplace. She seemed disturbed—paced about in a black mood for a bit, then went to her lodge and worked on an illustration series she was doing. I thought her behavior strange, but she was an emotional girl and I was accustomed to her ways.

"She'd had a letter from a gallery that morning, too. It said we were to have a group showing in a very prestigious gallery a friend of hers owned. After a while she rejoined the rest of us and quickly organized a beach party for later in the day to celebrate the good news. She dispatched some riders to town to invite people from there and to bring back whatever extra we needed. It was to be a fish fry with plenty of wine and beer.

"She changed to a simple cotton frock and canvas

beach shoes. As always, she wore that rather fantast
bee jewelry. I remember she'd misplaced one of her ea
rings—had us looking everywhere for it. Late in th
afternoon she told us she was going up to her place fo
some champagne she'd been saving. We offered to g
for her or to help bring it down, but she insisted on g
ing alone. I felt then Mellona was meeting someon
else—not the one she'd originally expected. She nev
came back. Whoever it was, she carried their secret t
her grave."

Roy Wimbish nodded his head. "That's just how
was."

"Well, we know now she went to meet Bert, don
we?"

"But why? She had no reason to meet hi
secretly."

"Unless he was her lover." Sickles could not co
ceive of the beautiful Madame Jolais taking the stock
horse trader as her lover, no matter how much more a
tractive he would have been thirty years before.

"No, that's not likely. He wasn't the sort of ma
she was drawn to at all." Morgan Griffith could n
agree that was the case either.

"But perhaps he was drawn to her," Laurie sug
gested.

"Yes, that must have been it." Roy still sounde
doubtful. "But if that's so, why'd Archibald try to sto
Miss Laurie from digging into the newspaper accoun
over to San Esteban? And he got Lucia Orozco fired o
her job, too, just for helping Laurie."

Ed Sickles held up his hand for their attention. "H
just didn't want to stir up trouble for Forest Shore
Arch came to me about it and I told him there wa
nothing the law could do to stop her. I advised him t
forget it, but he was bound he was going to stop an
scandal. I warned him to be careful or he might ru
afoul of me if he tried anything out of line. Remembe
Chace was doing his utmost to get state and county fu
ding for improvements over here. And, too, Arch ha

s own irons in the fire. He undoubtedly didn't want
me old scandal raked up to cause a lot of bad talk at a
ucial point in negotiations."

It sounded immanently reasonable, the way the
lice chief recounted the explanation.

"But why did Bert Hutchins want to kill
ellona?" Laurie wanted all the pieces to fit perfectly.

"Bert wasn't no different from the rest of us, Miss
aurie," Roy said. "I guess we was all in love with
ellona Jolais. You have no idea how beautiful she
as. Even the women folks liked her, so you know she
as pretty special. Maybe she got mad when he told her
: cared about her. Maybe he went too far, although
at wouldn'ta been like Bert at all. Not then—not
er." He shook his head as he continued, "I can't
lieve it was old Bert!"

Roy looked away from them, his eyes too full of
in to meet their glances. "It wasn't like him at all,"
said. "He never hurt a living creature so far as ever I
ew. Took in every stray dog and cat that came along.
hy, we was like brothers, the two of us, all these
ars!" He was overcome with grief that the rye
iskey had helped to surface.

"The three of us, Roy," Morgan Griffith added.
t really doesn't make much sense, does it?"

Sybil Creighton took the reins from Eusebio and
iled at the girl beside her. The little sorrel mare broke
o an easy trot and headed down the white gravel
ive, her hoofs lifting and falling in precise cadence as
she delighted in her outing. Laurie smoothed her gold
wn and adjusted her parasol to keep the early after-
on sun from her face. Sybil's smart black French
lking suit was in sharp contrast to the girl's bright
k. A black band was tacked to the sleeve of the dark
it, a symbol of the woman's mourning. Catalina
llareal smiled and nodded at her husband as the two
men took the south drive and disappeared around the
rn.

"It's time we got to know one another, Lauri
What's past can't be helped, but we can determine ho
the future shall be. I'm happy you could come and ha
lunch with me today so we may get acquainted." Th
older woman handled the light buggy as if she had do
so habitually. "Chace was so pleased. He'd complete
given up on me."

"I'm sure that's not so, Mrs. Creighton." Laur
was glad she had agreed to the luncheon although sh
had been reluctant to believe Sybil Creighton cou
change her mind so quickly. Perhaps it was Sybil
realization that she was alone except for Chace th
caused her to make the attempt.

"We were never as close as I should have like
Chace was always a strong-willed child, frequently
odds with both his father and me. But he has turned o
to be a fine man. I like to flatter myself that I am at lea
partly responsible for that." Her smile was st
beautiful, for neither smiling nor frowning had left the
marks upon her porcelain-like face, and her eyes r
mained a clear pale blue, sparkling with an intensity
one much younger.

Laurie felt tongue-tied with the aristocrat
woman, unsure of what she was expected to say. If sh
spoke only truth, she would offend; if she lied, sh
would sound much as Mrs. Arvidson and her sort
sycophant. "I've no idea what the south tract loo
like," she said. "Is it much like the north one, all fore
and low hills?"

"Oh no, very different. La Gaviota Creek cu
through it and several dry canyons run east and west.
suppose they drain into the creek during the rai
season, but most of the year they're bone dry. Why
the world Chace would want to build his own home o
in such a desolate spot is beyond me. It's true the road
already cleared through that far, but it is so remo
from everything." Sybil Creighton glanced at the gi
"But you young people won't mind being by yourselve
will you?"

"No, I'm sure we'll enjoy the isolation and quiet," Laurie laughed. "Chace says he intends to hire the Deleddas. If so, we'll have plenty of company out here."

The woman's soft chuckle was pleasant, but restrained. "Yes, I dare say they will fill up the corners. How is that youngest child of theirs?"

"Joey?"

"Yes, I'm sure that's the name Chace mentioned," Sybil said.

"He had to be taken to the sanatorium at Santa Eugenia. He's very bad, but the sisters say he may be young enough to recover." Laurie was saddened to think about Joey Deledda. "If Chace hadn't found him. . ."

"Perhaps it would have been kinder that way than dying slowly in a strange hospital, away from his own family."

"Yes, perhaps so." Laurie could not agree with the woman, but would make no issue of it.

"This is the beginning of the south tract, here where the surveyors' markers are." Sybil Creighton pointed with her gloved hand to the slivers of wood tied with bits of orange calico that demarcated the northern boundary of the section. "Just beyond there is the site Chace has selected. Shall we drive over?" She had already expertly turned the horse into the newly-graded road, and the carriage now bumped over the raw earth.

Hedge nettles were thick in the broken meadowland and as the buggy's wheels crushed the plants a strong minty scent rose from the fuzzy leaves. Countless bees hovered over the lavender-sprinkled field, constantly buzzing from bloom to bloom in their ceaseless quest for nectar. The bees darted out of the horse's path and hummed annoyance at being disturbed.

"Chace wanted to surprise you and bring you here first himself," Sybil said. "But this will give you a chance to decide for yourself whether you agree with his choice or not. I shouldn't think he'd object to my bringing you here."

The road crossed the field, then began to descend sharply. The graded path stopped at the end of the cleared area, and only a rutted, weed-grown trail hugged the steep hillside. No wheels had been over the road since the grass had sprung fresh and green after the rains. The slope which dropped away at an alarming angle from the cut was littered with shattered sandstone and rubble from the road-building process.

"Surely Chace doesn't mean to build down here!" Laurie exclaimed. The canyon below was filled with scrub oak and sycamore, but the open spaces were bald and rock-strewn. There was no level site anywhere to be seen.

"We've taken a wrong turn!" Laurie cringed as the wheels of the buggy turned dangerously close to the outer edge of the trail and sent gravel cascading down the sheer canyon wall. "We must have made a mistake!"

In that instant of terror she glanced quickly at the woman. In Sybil Creighton's hand was a delicate, ivory handled whip, its silver ferrules sparkling as she lashed madly at the mare. Laurie pulled aside a woolen lap robe which Eusebio had draped over the dash. She gasped as she recognized the ornate brass whip socket. Too late she realized who had been the driver of the mysterious carriage—who it was who had attempted to run her down.

"I've made no mistake, young woman!" Sybil Creighton's voice was low. "*You* are the one who has made the mistake!" There was menace in her tone. "Did you dare think I'd allow my son to marry you? You. . .you. . .who took my husband away from me!" Her strange laugh was almost inaudible.

"Mrs. Creighton, I didn't even know your husband!" Laurie clung to the arm rest as the light carriage lurched over a rock in the roadway.

"I stopped you then and I shall stop you now!" The woman slapped the sorrel's rump with the flexible, ivory-handled whip and stared straight ahead. "Zedekiah had to help me get rid of your body, you know. Such a delicious way to punish him, don't you think?"

"Mrs. Creighton, that was over thirty years ago! I'm Laurie Mathews!" The girl watched in horror as the horse picked up speed going down the sharp grade. She let go her parasol and grasped the seat.

"You're being absurd, Madame Jolais!" Taking the reins in one hand, Sybil reached into the pocket of her suit and took from it a small pearl-handled revolver. In her hand it looked too dainty to be lethal, but the barrel pointing at the girl demonstrated Sybil's intent. "And this time Bert Hutchins won't be around spying on us. Last time he suspected what I was going to do and tried to stop me, but he was too late!" Her laughter ran an arpeggio up to an hysterical high note. "I'd already shot you! And with the same little gun Zedekiah gave me for my own protection!"

"But I am not Mellona Jolais! I'm Laurie Mathews!" Laurie looked over the edge of the precipice to the bottom of the canyon. If she tried to jump from the carriage she had nowhere to go but straight down. Should she attempt to crawl over the back, Sybil was sure to shoot.

"Zedekiah could neither say nor do anything, because he would have been blamed. It was, after all, his gun—a very unusual caliber. And Bert can't help you this time either! Such a nasty thing he did, making us pay for his silence! If his letter had been used against us. . ." She laughed softly, the sound smothering in her throat.

"Please, Mrs. Creighton! Look at me! *I am not Mellona Jolais!*" The desperate girl moved to face the woman, but the revolver was close to her ribs. Realization that Sybil, not Bert Hutchins, had murdered Mellona made Laurie fully aware of her own peril. The woman was mad, time telescoped in her mind, identities confused. Nowhere in sight was house, cabin, or barn.

No human sounds could be heard, only the horses' hoofs and carriage wheels on the narrow roadway.

"This is a dangerous road. There used to be a silver mine a few miles farther on, but no one ever goes there anymore. Such a dangerous road." Sybil smiled, the pupils of her eyes mere pinpoints in pale blue ice as she turned to the girl. "Chace has often warned me not to drive down here. I shall tell him you fell out of the carriage when the horse acted up in a narrow spot. I shall see to it, of course, that the horse is destroyed for her impetinence."

The woman seemed to be watching the road ahead for something. They rounded a sharp turn. "Ah, there it is!" A few hundred yards away the path constricted to only the bare width of the carriage. A slide had erased the outer edge of the road. Facing northwest, the spot was still in shade, but even from a distance Laurie saw the danger. One shove, one unguarded movement, and she could be hurtled over the edge to the rocks far below.

Along the trail was a dense growth of hedge nettles, their spikes of rosy lavender alive with bees. How odd, it seemed to Laurie, that the bees, the only creatures to be seen, kept to their task while she drew closer and closer to her death. Sybil brushed at her face as one of the bees hovered near. In that instant Laurie lunged at the woman.

Reins forgotten, Sybil tried to pull the revolver into position to fire, but the girl twisted away from her. Sybil, with a terrible burst of strength, overpowered Laurie and pushed her sideways on the seat, forcing her closer to the edge. She braced herself on the dash and thrust her weight against the girl. Laurie felt her leg slip from the buggy; her foot dangled over the chasm. If her skirt caught in the wheel. . .!

With tremendous effort, she pulled herself back into the buggy only to face the revolver. As the woman's finger began to squeeze the trigger, Laurie slashed at her arm. The gun flew from her grasp and dropped to the floor. Laurie kicked backwards at it, feeling it slither across the boards. With a metallic clatter it dropped out of the buggy and caromed down the rock face into the cut. One shot rang out as the hammer fell into place, setting up echoes which made a miniature war with the rocks.

Sybil clutched at the girl's throat and managed to push her far out of the seat. For a moment she hung suspended over the canyon; only her hold on the woman's clothing preventing her from plunging to her death. Laurie groped for the arm rest and clung to it with one hand and tried to fend the woman from her. Her throat felt afire. She could not breathe as the gloved hands tightened.

With a horrible scream Sybil Creighton suddenly released the girl. She stood up in the carriage, her hands thrashing wildly at her face. Her screams echoed along the canyon walls and repeated her agony over and over. Her face and neck were crawling with insects, their loud angry buzz filling the air. They flew about the buggy, swarming up from the fragrant hedge nettles that had grown across the road.

The woman fell back into the seat, writhing in pain, her cries becoming weaker as the horse neared the narrow passage. Laurie picked up the reins and drew them in tightly. The mare halted thirty yards from the hazardous section.

Laurie sat very still, her heart hammering until she thought it would burst. Her breath raked her bruised throat. All around her the insects danced in fury. She could only watch as the woman ceased breathing, her pale blue eyes staring, bulging from her blotched face. There was no need to feel for a pulse in the elegantly gloved wrist.

Doctor Eichner closed the bedroom door and held up his hand to stop Chace. "You don't want to go in yet. Let Catalina take care of her first." He pulled up a straight-backed chair and sat down. "There are some people who are sensitive to insect stings. Sometimes just one bite is sufficient to kill them. With multiple stings like that. . .Funny, she never mentioned sensitivity to me in all the years I've treated her. But perhaps she didn't know about it herself.''

He hesitated before continuing. ''I'm sorry, Chace.'' He could say that much in truth. He was sorry for Chace, but only for Chace, not Sybil. ''I'll make all the necessary arrangements, if you like.''

''No thanks, Harry. I'll take care of everything.'' Chace paced the thick maroon and blue carpet in his mother's sitting room. Late afternoon sunlight made brilliant patches on the rug and sparkled the crystal drops of the chandelier and lamps. It was a beautiful room in every detail, with delicate Meissen-ware figurines and candlesticks, draperies of clear blue, and hand-loomed lace curtains. And yet there was a coldness in its very perfection. It was as though the room were created to exclude emotion.

''How that girl managed to get the buggy turned around on that road and get back here all by herself, I'll never know.'' Ed Sickles was uncomfortable on the small damask-covered chair. ''And it's a damn miracle she wasn't stung. I've heard of beekeepers who never get stung, but I never knew of it first hand.''

''Thank God she wasn't pitched right over the edge. What in the name of heaven made them drive down there?'' Doctor Eichner asked.

''Mother was going to show her the south tract where I plan on building our new home. Laurie said Mother took a wrong turn somewhere along the road and first thing they knew, they were on the old mining road. They had no place to turn around in, so they had to keep going.'' Chace ran his fingers through his unruly dark hair as he tried to reason it out. ''If only I'd known what Mother intended doing!''

''But you didn't, so don't blame yourself,'' Eichner said.

''Look, if you don't need me here, Ed, I'd like to

go to Laurie," Chace said. "With everything she's been through in the past few months. . "

"Sure, Chace. I'm finished here. I'll wait till tomorrow to talk with her. She ought to be over most of the shock by then." The policeman could only shake his head. "Terrible thing for her to see! You might just mention to her about my coming. Purely routine, but I don't want to upset her any more than she already is. It's better coming from you." Sickles rose to leave.

"One good thing came from their meeting today: your mother made it up with the girl. Your mind can at least be easy on that now. Catalina and Eusebio said they were getting along famously. Laurie seemed real tickled to take the ride out to the south tract with her. You know there was no bad feeling left, and that's something."

Pansy Hinshaw tucked the afghan about the girl's shoulders and drew the drapes against the sun. Roy stood, hat in hand, in the doorway to the front parlor. He had not changed from his heavy outdoor boots, but Pansy said nothing.

"Can I do anything, Miss Laurie?" He seemed pitifully eager.

"No, thank you, Roy." Laurie shook her head. "Only please stay a while. I don't want to be alone. Please, both of you sit with me until Olive and Thea get back home. I just couldn't stand to be by myself yet." Her face was as pale as a cameo in onyx with her black hair loosened and falling about her neck.

"Yes, ma'am. I'd be glad to." He looked at Pansy, who nodded and motioned to a chair beside the girl. He placed his hat on his knees as he sat awkwardly perched on the prim parlor chair. He peered at the girl's eyes, but he could say nothing, finding no words. Pansy wandered about the room as if searching for answers to their unasked questions.

Hallie Mae brought in a tea tray and placed it on the marble-topped table by the bay window. "Will there be anything else?'' She pulled up a small serving table before Laurie and arranged napkin, cup, and saucer on it.

"No, you run along and make sure the lamps upstairs are trimmed and filled. It'll be getting dark soon." Pansy stirred the pot and held the shallow silver strainer over the cup as she poured strong black tea. She waited until she heard the maid's feet on the stairs.

"It didn't happen the way you told Ed Sickles, did it?'' Pansy asked.

"How did you know?" Laurie's hand was surprisingly steady as she accepted the cup and held it.

"Child, I know Sybil Creighton! I've observed her handiwork over thirty years. I wanted to warn you against her offer of friendship, but it wasn't my place to do so. And there was always a remote chance she might be sincere when she said she wanted you to be friends." Pansy took a low chair across from the girl and sat down. "I wasn't afraid for you to just have luncheon with her, and visit the house. Catalina would be there every minute. She's devoted to Chace and would keep an eye on you. Had I known you would go for a ride with Sybil driving. . ." She shook her head sadly as if she blamed herself.

"I thought it odd," Laurie agreed. "But I had to go. Just as you say, there was a chance she meant what she said. I had to go for Chace's sake, didn't I?" She seemed to want someone to tell her she had done the right thing in meeting with Sybil Creighton.

"Of course you did," Pansy assured her. "How could you have known?"

Outside, a dray wagon rumbled east toward town and the horsecar rattled to a stop at Shore Park, then turned north on its circuit. From a distance came the shouting of children and barking of dogs. Ordinary early evening noises that contrasted with the day's occurrence served to emphasize the quiet within the old Hinshaw place.

"Do you want to tell us?" Pansy sensed Laurie's

need to talk. "It needn't go beyond this room. Roy and I are used to keeping our secrets, aren't we, Roy?"

"Yes, ma'am. We kept our secret for over thirty years." He tugged at his beard and shifted on the uncomfortable chair. "I still can't believe Bert Hutchins. . ."

"But he didn't! That's what is so awful!" Laurie exclaimed.

"I don't understand." Pansy looked puzzled.

"I didn't either, but it must be true." Laurie's hair, disheveled in her fight with Sybil, fell around her face and curled about her shoulders. With one finger she pushed it back behind her ears. She looked from one to the other, trying to gauge their belief. "Sybil Creighton killed Mellona! She admitted doing it!" Even as she said it, she found it hard to believe. "Then to get even with Zedekiah, she made him help bury the body. Bert Hutchins must have seen them, for he blackmailed them all these years!"

Pansy and Roy could only stare in unfeigned surprise.

"Zedekiah had given Sybil the gun she used on Mellona," Laurie continued. "Evidently she could prove it was his, because she used it as a guarantee against his exposing her as the killer. They, in turn, couldn't expose Bert Hutchins because he had left some sort of letter." Laurie did not notice the glance the two exchanged between them.

"It was horrid! She was completely insane! She thought I was Mellona and she had a gun!"

"Surely she didn't mean to shoot you! That would have been too hard to explain away." Pansy was shocked.

"No, she was going to force me out of the buggy on that road to the mine."

"The old silver mine?" Roy asked.

"Yes, that's the one."

"Why, it's a couple hundred feet straight down!" Roy was angry. He, too, had known Sybil Creighton.

"Course that's what she'd do. Wouldn't be her fault if you took a spill down that canyon!" He clenched his fists as he thought of the woman's viciousness.

"But the bees, Laurie. What about them?" Pansy asked.

"There were these plants growing thick all along the road. They were covered with bees. I guess the horse and wheels stirred them up as we drove through them. All of a sudden when she had me half out of the buggy, right over the drop-off, they swarmed all over her." Laurie shuddered at the remembrance of Sybil's grotesquely swollen face.

"And they never touched you!" Pansy sat back in the chair and folded her hands in her lap, a faint smile playing at the corners of her mouth.

"No! They flew all around me, but never so much as lighted on me!" Laurie sipped the hot tea, her jet black eyes lowered, her glance away from her friends.

Roy shuffled his feet and rubbed his face with the back of his hand. Finally he said, "You seen her again, didn't you? She was out there on that road, wasn't she?"

They knew. How they knew, the girl could not imagine, but they did know.

"Yes. Mellona was there." Laurie put the cup into the saucer and sat back in the sofa. She was amazed that she was so calm. "She was standing beside the road, in the shadow. She was so beautiful. At first I thought I was as mad as Sybil—that my imagination was conjuring her image to offset my fright." She looked from one to the other and found belief in their faces. "I didn't imagine her—she was there." Laurie closed her eyes, trying to visualize the scene. "And the bees were all around her. All I could see was Mellona and her gold gown and gold tiara—and the cloud of bees.

"I was frantic! I didn't know what to do! I've never driven a horse in my life. I had no idea how to get back from that awful road.

"Then suddenly I knew I had to drive on, that I'd

find a spot down the road where I could turn the carriage around. I'd never been on the road before, but I knew the spot would be there.

"When I came back to where I'd seen her, there were only the bees. Mellona was gone. It wasn't my imagination. It couldn't have been!" Her eyes pleaded for belief.

"No, child, you didn't imagine it. Never think that!" Pansy reached across the table and patted the girl's hand. "You really did see her. I think you were meant to come here and find where she was buried, and to learn what really happened to her." She settled back into her chair once more, smiling. "Roy's going to bring you a letter he's been keeping for all these many years. You can decide what you want to do with it."

The man nodded and without a word left the room. Pansy poured more tea for the girl and they waited in silence until Roy returned, bearing in his hand a battered envelope, its corners soiled and worn. He handed it to Laurie.

"Bert give me that to keep in case something should happen to him. I was supposed to read it and do whatever seemed right. Now I'm giving it to you." He resumed his seat opposite her. "If folks is happy thinking Sybil Creighton meant to accept you as her daughter-in-law. . .well, maybe we ought to just leave it at that."

"He's right, Laurie," Pansy said. "My Adam must have guessed what really happened when he saw those pictures Mellona drew. And he wanted to protect Zedekiah—that has to be why he put the trunk in the attic. He must have known Zedekiah was innocent, but would be blamed if Sybil spoke up. No wonder he wept when Adam was killed in that accident. . ." She could not go on for a moment.

"Chace won't never get over having to shoot Bert, either," Roy said. "Not that he had much choice when Bert was about to do you in, Miss Laurie. As we rode back to town that night, Chace says to me how bad he felt. . .after all, Bert Hutchins pulled Chace off that roof down in the cove and saved his life. You're going to have to help Chace get over killing Bert.'' Roy was saddened to think that such a turn of events had occurred.

"These have been terrible days, I know, especially for you and Chace," Pansy said. She touched the envelope in Laurie's hand and continued, "Roy's right—it can't hurt Bert Hutchins to be blamed for what went on thirty years ago, but it could hurt Chace if the truth came out now. We three know the truth—all of it—and Mellona's buried properly with a marker in the cemetery. That should be enough, shouldn't it?''

Laurie turned the envelope over in her hands, feeling its tattered corners with her long, slim fingers. It was not an easy decision to make and she had made so many wrong ones already in her young life. To reveal what had actually happened would be some sort of vengeance on her part, perhaps satisfying in itself, but the vengeance would include Chace. He had been so relieved when his mother suggested that she and Laurie should meet and get acquainted. To him, the truth would be devastating.

From south on Shore Park Drive came the sound of a buggy. It slowed and turned into Main, then stopped before the Hinshaw place. Pansy went to the bay window and drew back the drape and curtain. It was still dusk outside, with a golden sunset gilding the Calabasas Hills. A tall figure swung down out of the light phaeton, tied the horse to the iron ring in the hitching post by the curb. The old woman smiled as she recognized the unruly thatch of dark hair and square, outthrust wide chin. She turned from the window, letting the curtain drop back into place.

"It's Chace." She stood behind Laurie, her hands placed on the girl's shoulders. Roy started to leave, his eyes on Laurie's face. They were awaiting her decision.

Slowly she removed the brightly colored afghan from her shoulders and walked to the fireplace. From the brass holder on the mantel Laurie took a match, struck it, and touched it to the envelope. Roy and Pansy nodded, their old faces smiling approval. Laurie held the burning letter by one corner, letting the flame consume the contents, until at last she dropped it into the grate.

"Roy, as soon as you can, will you take the trunk out of the attic and burn everything?" Pansy hurried to the front door as Chace started up the walk.

"Yes, ma'am. I'll start right now." He turned to go, but Laurie stopped him at the door to the dining room. She put her hand on his arm and kissed him gently. She needed no words; her gratitude was in her dark eyes. He touched her pale, golden face with his rough hands. "I'll take the fancy ball gown, too, if you like, Miss Laurie."

"Yes, thank you," Laurie said. "You're a fine man, Roy Wimbish."

"Maybe not as fine as you think—I should tell you I went to see Zedekiah the night he died. When I saw them pictures Mellona made, I knew he'd been the one she was in love with. I thought he'd killed her, maybe because of Sybil. I went there to kill him. . .I took my deer rifle. Nobody knowed I sneaked into his room from the upstairs porch when the nurse went downstairs." He hesitated as if he found it difficult to finish his confession. "Only I couldn't do it. *She* was there. . ."

"Mellona?"

"Yes, ma'am. She stood there as if she was trying to tell me she still loved him and for me not to do this terrible thing. And when I saw him, well, he looked scared almost to death. . .he'd seen her there, too. I just couldn't do it." He did not look ashamed, but held his head proudly.

"I understand, Roy," Laurie said gently.

He nodded and left as Pansy welcomed young Creighton.

"Chace!" Laurie ran to the embrace of his arms, to

371

his kisses hard and sweet upon her mouth. His hands pressed her close to him, his fingers tangling in her jet hair. They did not know when Pansy drew the portieres and tiptoed into the dining room.

"Are you all right, sweetheart?" Chace could feel her body trembling.

She lifted her face to his. "I am, darling, now that you're here."

In the grate the charred letter collapsed into ashes. One last wisp of smoke wavered briefly and was gone.

Unnoticed in the old mirror above the fireplace was the luminous shimmer of a golden gown. For a moment the image lingered, then it, too, was gone.

UNDER CRIMSON SAILS

Lynna Lawton

Beautiful, spirited Janielle Patterson had heard of the reckless way pirate Ryan Deverel treated his women. He seduced them with the same abandon with which he plundered ships. To the handsome pirate, women were prizes to be won, used, and tossed away.

Ryan intrigued and repelled Janielle—and when they finally met, she was shocked to discover that her own nature was as passionate as the pirate's!

But while he was driven by desire, she was driven by a fierce hatred. Yet she knew neither of them would rest until she had surrendered to him fully.

LEISURE BOOKS   2002-5/$3.5

BE SWEPT AWAY
ON A TIDE OF PASSION
BY LEISURE'S THRILLING
HISTORICAL ROMANCES!

STORMY SURRENDER

Robin Lee Hatcher

WAR AND LOVE

At sixteen, lovely Taylor Bellman finds her gentle and elegant world crumbling around her with the death of her father. Forced by her half brother to marry a man over forty years her senior in order to keep their beloved home, Spring Haven, in the Bellman family, Taylor's platonic marriage becomes a source of strength and contentment to both herself and her husband. But Civil War threatens her peace—and a gallant Yankee visitor awakens her sleeping heart to the thrill of illicit love.

Though their passion cannot be denied, Brent and Taylor know they must part. So begins a saga of war and tragedy, and of burning love that will never die, no matter what obstacles fate has placed between them.

LEISURE BOOKS

PRICE: $3.75/$4.25 CAN
0-8439-2073-4

FOR THE FINEST
IN CONTEMPORARY
WOMEN'S FICTION,
FOLLOW LEISURE'S LEAD

2143-9	**AMERICAN BEAUTY** Maggi Brocher	$3.50 US, $3.95 Can.
2155-2	**TOMORROW AND FOREVER** Francesca Macklem	$2.75
2167-6	**BED OF ROSES** Rochelle Larkin	$3.25
2188-9	**DUET** Wendy Susans	$3.75 US, $4.50 Can.
2196-X	**THE LOVE ARENA** Pat Gaston	$3.75 US, $4.50 Can.
2207-9	**PARTINGS** Maggi Brocher	$3.50 US, $4.25 Can.
2217-6	**THE GLITTER GAME** Kaye Hill	$3.75 US, $4.50 Can.
2227-3	**THE HEART FORGIVES** Barbara Riley	$3.75 US, $4.50 Can.
2230-3	**A PROMISE BROKEN** Jennifer Peters	$3.25
2249-4	**THE LOVING SEASON** Rebecca Burton	$3.50
2250-8	**FRAGMENTS** Lou Graham	$3.25
2257-5	**TO LOVE A STRANGER** Jean Howell	$3.75 US, $4.50 Can.

Make the Most of Your Leisure Time with
LEISURE BOOKS

Please send me the following titles:

Quantity	Book Number	Price
_____	_____	_____
_____	_____	_____
_____	_____	_____
_____	_____	_____
_____	_____	_____

If out of stock on any of the above titles, please send me the alternate title(s) listed below:

_____	_____	_____
_____	_____	_____
_____	_____	_____
_____	_____	_____

Postage & Handling _____

Total Enclosed $_____

☐ Please send me a free catalog.

NAME _____
(please print)

ADDRESS _____

CITY _____ STATE _____ ZIP _____

Please include $1.00 shipping and handling for the first book ordered and 25¢ for each book thereafter in the same order. All orders are shipped within approximately 4 weeks via postal service book rate. PAYMENT MUST ACCOMPANY ALL ORDERS.*

*Canadian orders must be paid in US dollars payable through a New York banking facility.

Mail coupon to: **Dorchester Publishing Co., Inc.
6 East 39 Street, Suite 900
New York, NY 10016
Att: ORDER DEPT.**